# Finvarra's Circus

## Monica Sanz

**FINVARRA'S CIRCUS**
Copyright © 2011 by Monica Sanz
Cover Design by Lisa Rhodes
All cover art copyright © 2016
All Rights Reserved

First Publication: JUNE 2016

# TABLE OF CONTENTS

# ACKNOWLEDGMENTS

This book has been a journey that I never could have taken alone. It's full of moments, both big and small that I've shared with so many people who I now want to thank.

First and foremost, to God through whom all things are possible. Todo Cristo.

To Cliff, Aidan, Abby, and Aurora. I can write of love and happiness wholeheartedly because of you. You all are my magic and life, and I will love you forever.

To my family for being so incredibly supportive and understanding. I was blessed with all of you, and I'll never forget that. Los amo tanto.

To Alice. I don't even know where to start, seriously. I still remember the first conversation we had about this book where I thought it was a crazy idea, but you insisted I write it. Thank you for that and for your constant support! I'm so lucky to have you in my corner, and I'm not sharing you :) I love you, girl!

To Anna. How many times did we go over this book? Ha! Thank you for always being there and for helping me find my voice and not change it. I appreciate that more than you know.

To Lisa Rhodes. Thank you for being so selfless and generous, and I hope it comes back to you tenfold. You created an image that captured the soul of this story long before we met, and I think it was fate.

To Leah, Rebecca, and Erin. This writing journey is 10 times more fun and less lonely with you girls in it. I love you girls!

To Wattpad for creating an environment where I felt safe and comfortable enough to chase my dreams.

And last but surely not least, to every single reader who voted and commented and messaged and emailed. THANK YOU for your support. I love you all to Forever and back.

"LET NOT YOUR HEARTS BE TROUBLED,
AND DO NOT BE AFRAID."

JOHN 14:27

Finvarra's Circus

# Chapter One
## Impossible Magic

LEANNA WESTON looked at the newspaper on her lap and cursed her broken heart. Gracing the headlines in bold text were the words of her lifelong dream, a dream her damaged heart made impossible.

"Finvarra's Circus, coming to Winter Abbey," she whispered, trailing a finger along the vine-like symbols bordering the header. A sad smile curled her lips as her hand danced over the printed images of tents, clowns, and lions. Each gentle stroke unfurled memories of her mother's stories, tales of dancers performing fluidly atop white unicorns, of fire breathers riding chariots pulled by centaurs while battling each other's fire dragons.

"Don't even think of it, child," her nurse, Edith said, pouring Leanna a glass of water. She set it at the night table and took the paper from Leanna's lap. "You're much too weak for a journey to Grover's Field, much less in this cold."

Leanna ignored this. Though the newspaper was gone from her hands, she held fast to her memories and to the crystal necklace that dangled around her neck. "If opening night is in three days and their show so grand, they should be here by now." No tent peaks marked the landscape in the distance, but she sighed wistfully at the thought of them there. "I do wonder how long they'll stay. Maybe if I get better before then—"

"Even if your heart were healed, it's dangerous all the same, and your father will forbid it," Edith replied from the wardrobe. "You've heard the tales, those poor girls always found near the fairgrounds, heartless and deformed. I was told the last girl had the loveliest eyes and she was found with them gouged out." She shivered, her cheeks matching the red gown she pulled out and held before her. "Finvarra is a fiend."

"Oh, come now. Do you think there would be a circus if that were true?

Besides, there have been numerous investigations, and no evidence has ever been found of his involvement."

"I don't know how he does it," Edith said, inspecting the muslin gown as if the secrets of Finvarra's crimes were hidden within the fabric. "But I remember your mother's stories. His beauty is unparalleled. Surely he drinks their beauty to maintain his, and he takes their hearts because he doesn't have one himself."

"I remember her stories, too, and I don't see how someone who brings such magic to life can be guilty of those crimes." Leanna turned her gaze away and settled back against the pillows, the way she used to do when listening to her mother's magical tales of Finvarra's Circus.

"Maybe a rival circus wants to ruin him or…" She trailed off, her eyes caught by the stack of books at her night table: stories of magic and hope, and nothing like her reality of loneliness and sick hearts.

"Or what if that girl was his lover?" She twirled the cool stone between her fingers. "She was forbidden to be with him, and so he weaved a spell to make everyone think she was dead so they could finally be together."

"Nonsense," Edith scolded her, brushing strands of her silvery hair from her forehead. She always got so flustered when Leanna spoke of such improprieties. She closed the wardrobe doors and gathered the breakfast tray, sure to take the newspaper with her. "This isn't one of your books, Leanna. That man is dangerous and I'm glad you won't be going anywhere near him."

Leanna curled her knees to her chest, looked to the distance where the tents would soon stand, and considered the rumors. What if Finvarra was the monster he was believed to be? Her soul stirred with conviction. "He isn't dangerous." Her grip on the crystal tightened. "I know he isn't."

"Yes, well, I know something too," Edith said and opened the door. "There is no way your father will let you go, so you're best off ridding it from your mind." With her usual smile, she walked out and closed the door behind her, leaving Leanna to her world of ghostly tents, heartless ringmasters, and memories of her mother's stories that blurred the world around her.

She had been ten, and after a week of snow, it had seemed as if the sky had fallen and pillowy clouds covered the ground. No one had been by the house to call, and no calls were paid. It was an utterly depressing situation for three girls—well, two girls, seeing as Leanna was content losing herself in a book rather than in stuffy drawing rooms overhearing gossip of a world she wouldn't ever be a part of, not as the youngest of three sisters. Unless, of course, she married into a better situation.

On this day, their mother gathered them around the fire.

"Did I ever tell you of the most magical circus in the world?" she began, as she often did. The sisters welcomed the reprieve from boredom and gathered around Mrs. Weston, inhaling her warm, sweet scent of jasmines and honeysuckle. As always, Mrs. Weston held Leanna closest to her heart, as if her own heartbeats would make up for the lack of Leanna's.

Her tale of Finvarra's Circus quickly flowed from her lips, bewitching them into this labyrinth of tents where a pixie like girl danced in the air, a strong man lifted an elephant over his head, and a contortionist folded and twisted into herself while balancing on the handle of a sword.

Yet, not even the magic from their mother's words nor the promise of vanquished boredom could keep the sisters from wandering off. Soon only Leanna was left, enchanted by the world her mother's words painted of Finvarra's Circus.

After her tale was told and the other girls gone, Mrs. Weston sat Leanna down on the divan by the arched windows and walked to her writing desk where she retrieved a small box. Leanna watched curiously as her mother opened it with longing and slipped out a small ticket.

Mrs. Weston gazed down at the yellowed ticket, then up at Leanna with a smile touched only by memory. "I want you to have this," she said quietly, joining Leanna by the window. "It is my ticket from so long ago. But this isn't just any ticket. It was given to me by Finvarra himself."

Leanna's breath caught. "You met Finvarra!"

She nodded. "I returned something that belonged to him—a curious box that was taken from his tent by a strange silver bird. It was the most peculiar thing. I can't ever forget. But I rescued it for him, and he told me that by returning it, I'd saved his life. He gave me this very ticket and told me that I was always welcomed to his circus. Then he opened the box and gave me this," she said, and paused. Her mother unclasped a crystal pendant from around her neck and looped it around Leanna's.

"He told me that just as I'd brought him back his life, maybe one day I could also bring him his Leanan Sidhe, his muse. He gave me this necklace and told me to keep it on always and bring it back when I've found her. I like to think it's brought me luck and kept me safe, and I want you to have it."

Leanna's eyes widened. She touched the crystal. It was cold and smooth.

"You're giving it to me?" she asked, confused, as she couldn't recall a moment she'd ever seen her mother without it. "Not to Lydia? She's the eldest. Or perhaps you should keep it. He gave it to you, and if it's meant to keep you safe—"

Leanna's hands had been taken from her then, cradled delicately in her mother's. "Your father, your sisters, and you are all the magic I could ever want or need in my life. I won't always be with you, and when that time comes, I want you to remember my tale." She'd pressed the ticket gently into Leanna's palm. "What makes life worth living is to believe in the magic all around us. If the day ever comes where you can't find any magic in this world, you take this ticket to Finvarra. There you will find all the magic you need to go on. It's more than just a circus, Leanna. It's magical, truly magical."

Leanna tore aside her blankets. Rushing to her writing desk, she retrieved the old yellow ticket from her keepsake box and ran from her room as fast as her legs would take her. She wasn't used to running and, after a few seconds, the exertion left her feeling as if a tightrope was wound firmly around her chest. Her run withered to a clumsy sort of shamble where she tipped forward onto her next step. But against this discomfort, she hurried to her father still. He had to let her go. In a time when she couldn't trust her heart to keep her alive, she needed something to believe in. Something as impossible as magic.

Leanna burst into her father's study and paused. Sunlight filtered through the stained glass windows, bathing the room in a kaleidoscope of colors. The magical hue, however, did nothing to beautify her father's vexed expression. Ticket in her hands, she forgot her intentions when he rose from his desk, his knuckles pressed into the mahogany wood.

"What on earth do you think you're doing out of bed?"

He began to say more, but broke off when Leanna jerked back against the door. Possessed by a hollow cough, she felt as if the room sought to steal the air from her lungs, but her chest constricted in refusal. At her side in an instant, her father ushered her to the high-back chair before his desk. She sat and caught her breath while he huffed on about dismissing Edith for not carefully watching her.

"Edith doesn't know I'm out of bed," she said through more stable breaths. "I ran here because—"

"Good heavens, you've been running? After Dr. Luther's diagnosis?" Her father's pale pallor darkened to a deep burgundy that hinted at purple. Leanna thought he very well might have burst, if humans ever exploded.

15

"I know, but I had to come and see you. Finvarra's Circus is coming to Winter Abbey and I must go."

He hauled in a breath with which to speak, but saw the ticket in her hands, and deflated with a long breath. "Why did your mother have to fill your head with those foolish tales?"

"They're not tales, Papa. If you had stayed to listen to her, you would've seen the way her eyes lit up when she spoke of it. She believed in the circus's magic, and so do I. That's why she gave me this ticket."

Squeezing his blue eyes shut, he groaned. "You were just told you'd never dance again. You were in a bad way and in desperate need of something to take your mind off your condition. That's why she gave you that blasted ticket, so you would have something else to think about."

"No," Leanna breathed, her hand enfolding her crystal pendant.

"But you're not a child anymore, Leanna." He walked back around his desk and sat. "You are eighteen and old enough to understand that there are no unicorns or elves, and there is no such thing as magic. They're illusions, mere tricks done with proper lighting and fancy movements, all to trick naïve minds. Nothing more. You're sick, and no magic can fix that."

"But it's just a circus, father, please." Her voice broke.

Her father's steely gaze softened and he lowered his eyes. Leanna tried not to hope, but her pulse quickened in wait.

He looked back to her and sighed, a soft breath that crushed her.

"I'm sorry, but Dr. Luther ordered that you stay off your feet and that's what I intend to see done."

Numb, Leanna rose and walked to the door. She opened it and stopped. "Why do you care so badly that I live," she said, turning, "if while alive, I am already dead?"

Her father's squared shoulders lowered, his anger taken by a pain and guilt she hadn't seen since her mother's death. Walking to her, he pulled her into an embrace. Leanna stiffened in his hold, the affection unlike him.

"I am so very sorry, Leanna," he spoke over her head. "But we are all dealt our lots in life and must deal with them the best we can. You will live your life. One day, sooner than you think, a man will ask for your hand and you will be delighted to become his wife—"

Leanna recoiled from his embrace, each word a knife being thrust at the bulls-eye of her pain. "Truly? You think this is the best time to mock me? No man will ever want the sickly sister. I've never been courted or asked to dance for fear I'll fall dead in their arms. They're frightened of me. How can you not see that?"

"I see a lot of things you wish not to see. There is a real world outside of your books and your daydreams. One that is full of its own magic, magic you won't ever find in some blasted circus. You only need to lift your eyes from your pity to see it."

Leanna looked away, hot tears prickling behind her eyes.

Mr. Weston tilted her head back to him. "And you were your mother's favorite, you know this. I promised her I'd keep you safe. How could I ever forgive myself if anything happened to you?"

Leanna cringed, the words a blow that crushed what was left of her heart. She deserved to go. He was being wholly unfair. Her father's frown killed these coming words on her lips. Leanna drew in a slow breath and nodded as the world turned to speckles of light and shadow behind her unshed tears.

"That's my girl. Now let me ring for Edith, she will take you back to your room." He kissed her head lightly, and with a satisfied pat on her shoulder, he abandoned her by the open door. "And enough talk about this ridiculous circus. Once you're all better, you will see grander ones. Dr. Luther says some great advancements are being made. We must be patient and hope that maybe one of them will… fix you."

He forced a smile that failed to hide the same hopelessness she felt. It was his smile, the unwillingness to accept her reality, that hurt Leanna more than his refusal. He wouldn't ever let her live her life as long as she was sick, and the sharp pain in her chest told her that those advancements wouldn't come soon enough. Not for her.

That night, when only the low howls of the wind hushed through the trees, Leanna pushed away her blankets and climbed from her bed. Her heart in her throat, she padded lightly to her wardrobe and dressed quickly. Edith never bothered to check on her in the middle of the night, and so Leanna was confident, as she slipped on her black cloak, that her indiscretion would never be discovered.

Opening her door with a frightful ease, she peered out into the hall. Her father's thunderous snores resounded, but all else was quiet. She slipped out from her room, crept downstairs, and into the kitchen. She pulled the door open. A frigid gust pushed her back as if to keep her from going, but with her free hand tight around her pendant, Leanna stepped outside and pulled the door closed behind her.

Darkness swallowed the forest, cut by streams of moonlight breaking through skeletal branches. Leanna considered the blackness, gazed up to her window, and paused.

Fear, now a small voice in her mind, whispered that she shouldn't go. What if she were to fall ill, alone, in the middle of the woods? What on earth would she do? It was foolish. Yet, steeling her spine, she hauled in a deep breath, adjusted her hood, and darted into the black. There was no way she would miss the circus, and she would go back every night until she saw it, even if she lost her heart in the process— to the cold, or to Finvarra.

# CHAPTER TWO
## THE RAVEN & HIS DOVE

THE WAY THROUGH Abbey Forrest was long, and the night cold.
Creatures of the night rustled in the thickets, and branches cast shadows on
the ground that looked to be dusted with powdered sugar, or so thought a
famished Leanna. But she heard little through her chattering teeth and
grumbling stomach. She saw even less, her eyes fixed on the black and red
round-top tent of Finvarra's Circus.

Leanna ducked behind a brush. A dense fog skirted the fairgrounds,
luminous under the lights of the circus. But—

"How peculiar," she whispered. There was no gate. She inched her head
over the bush and breathed freer when she saw no guard either. Only a line of
spikes capped with crystals fenced the field. They were a curious adornment,
those white rocks fastened with thick rope on each wooden spear. There were
dozens of them, circling the outer edge of the circus.

Leanna inched a little closer. Perhaps they were enchanted in some way
to keep trespassers out? She gulped. What if they were all-seeing eyes looked
after by witches or Finvarra himself? Her bitter half held fast to this fear and
also offered, *what if they are cursed and they turn you into a frog? Or worse, a
beetle?*

Leanna wrinkled her nose. That would be unfortunate.

But remembering the necklace around her neck, the ticket in her pocket,
and the desires of her heart, she knotted her hands and moved closer to the
stakes.

"Now, you may be magical, or maybe I'm saying this to appease my own
conscience, but I am no trespasser. I have a ticket from Finvarra himself, and
this necklace." Leanna drew the ticket from her pocket and held it up to the
nearest crystal at eye level. She then shifted her shawl aside and angled herself
toward the patches of moonlight so the all-seeing crystals could have a clear

view of the necklace.

"Ringmaster Finvarra told my mother to bring it back when she found his Leanan Sidhe, but my Mama passed away and never found her. It would be awfully wrong to keep Mr. Finvarra waiting, so I'm going to pass through now. Please don't turn me into a beetle."

When the crystals didn't answer, nor light up in any manner, she hitched up her muslin skirt, crouched low, and shuffled past the stakes.

A gust of wind howled, and for a moment the crystals flashed white. Leanna flinched and dashed into the shadow of an unhitched wagon. Heart pounding, she pressed against the wood. She searched her arms and legs and found that she was still human enough, when coolness pricked her palm. She opened her hand to find the ticket was gone. Only droplets of icy water seeped through her fingers. Brows furrowed, Leanna searched all around her. She hadn't dropped her ticket. But if so, where could it have gone?

Cognizant of time and place, she wiped her hand on her cloak and abandoned the mystery. If anyone saw the crystals flash, it was only a matter of time before they found her hiding there.

She peeked out from the wagon and surveyed the fairgrounds spread before her. Her brow gathered. For a circus having just arrived, there was a strange sort of exactness to everything, as though it never moved. The erected Big Top dominated the right side of the field. To the left was a white pavilion, smaller than the Big Top, but larger than the numerous white tents sandwiched between the two at center field. Pathways cut between the labyrinth of tents, and tall pole torches lined the lanes.

She had read of this area countless times: the Backyard, where props and animals were kept, and performers readied for their acts. But she cared little for props and animals. She would see those later. Focused on the Big Top, she adjusted her hood and darted out toward it, the lazy tune of a calliope beckoning her near.

The Big Top towered over Leanna. She strained her neck to take in every black and red stripe that shot upwards into the dark.

"I have dreamt of you all my life, and here you are." A smile tipped her lips, and she pressed her hand against the rough canvas, as if to feel its heartbeat through the currents of music. "Finally."

Leanna eyed the parting in the canvas curtain, but that was much too risky. There was no way she could just stroll inside. She would have to find another way.

The curtain flap blew open.

Leanna dove headfirst behind a sign propped against the tent and crouched down onto the cold grass by a stack of wooden crates. She curled into herself and held her breath as the sound of male voices cut through the hazy music. Their words went unheard; a bright light beam whisked across the inside of the tent. A small ray seeped from beneath the sidewall and stretched past her hands like golden fingers reaching to lead her inside. Leanna smiled. This was her way in.

When the male voices faded, she darted a glance around. The coast clear, she lifted the bottom of the canvas, thanked the heavens she was so small, and slipped inside. She added an extra prayer of thanks in finding herself underneath the gallery seats. Whether or not there was magic, it was good to have a little luck on her side.

Muddied and sore, Leanna dragged herself forward under the bleachers. She skittered into the shadows and peeked in between the rows. It was here that the world vanished around her. No, it became another world altogether.

Under the hypnotic melody of the cimbalom and the whines of the violin, a red-haired man arched back while swallowing a fiery torch. He withdrew it extinguished and snapped forward, a roaring flame bursting from his mouth. Leanna's own mouth parted when, with dramatic motions of his arms, he shaped the flames like clay into none else than a dragon. He released its fiery tail and clapped once. The flaming reptile whisked off to the steady beat of the drums that rumbled the ground beneath her. It whirled around the tent once, twice, and on the third, exploded into a rain of glitter and confetti.

Leanna clapped a hand against her mouth, stifling a squeal. This was more than she ever imagined! She fought the urge to reach out and touch the confetti that glittered on the seat level with her eyes, but failed and swiped a fleck from the seat. Holding the crimson paper in front of her eyes, a smile spread on her lips.

"Is that magic enough for you?" she whispered to the memory of her father.

The fire blower bowed and jumped down from his platform, joining a group of performers that sat on the ring's edge. Confetti continued to fall as the drumming slowed to the steady beat of a calm heart.

*And now Ladies and Gentlemen, we bring you a tale of love..."*

Leanna gasped. Ringmaster Finvarra! The confetti slipped from her fingers at the soft baritone that echoed all around her. The words were said softly, yet seemed to come from below and above, everywhere at once. She jerked forward, but couldn't see where the voice came from.

*"A tale that will challenge you to shed a love that is false for a love that is real. I present to you, The Raven and his Dove."*

The crowd of performers looked up all at once. Spellbound, Leanna tottered closer to the bleachers and followed their gazes to a blond girl standing on a platform above. In a black feathery dress that glittered, she was like a black star against the red stripes of the canvas. At once, the girl flipped onto an almost invisible string, and Leanna bit back a scream. The girl landed effortlessly with a pirouette. Then another flip, and again. Pirouette. Flip. Land. Twirl. Back flip, land—

Her foot slipped. The cable jolted. The drums thundered. The crowd didn't react, but Leanna dug her nails into the seat. The girl's hands shot to her sides for balance, and by and by the rope steadied. Here, she extended an arm longingly to the other side of the tent. Like puppets stringed to her hands, the crowd followed her reach to a parallel rope on the opposite side of the tent.

A man in black leapt onto the rope with a flip. He danced the Raven girl's exact routine, more brusque, but just as beautiful. Reaching center rope, his gaze fell upon the Raven girl.

She danced for him then, yet, in all her beauty, he turned away and continued with his dance toward the opposite platform. The Raven girl stopped. For a moment, she didn't move and only hugged herself. Leanna's heart stirred, feeling the rejection as if it were her own.

Slowly, the Raven girl unlaced her arms from around her body. Hundreds of small lights flew from her dress as if she were exhaling her soul of fireflies. They flickered and streaked the air around her like shooting stars as she danced again. The more she moved on the thin wire, the more incandescent the fireflies grew until the entire tent basked in their glow. And with every wave of her arms, wisps of black smoke emanated from her dress until it was no longer black, but luminous white feathers.

The Raven man stopped and turned to her. Seeing her as her true self, a glittering white dove, he extended a hand to her. She too reached for him, but in all her excitement, the rope wobbled. She shot her hands out to her sides again, but this time they flailed, grasping for air and fireflies. Without a harness, she fell back into the open.

Leanna crawled out from her hiding spot, fists balled at her mouth as the Dove descended, her white gown fluttering like the wings of a bird. There was no net to catch her, only confetti, glitter and sawdust blanketed the cold, hard

22

ground. But they couldn't just let her fall!

The Raven swooped in, and Leanna's breath cut short. With luminous black wings arching from his back, he caught the Dove midair and held her against him. They whirled faster and faster until smoky wings sprouted from her back. Entwined, they floated the rest of the way down. Their tipped toes touched the ground, and snow began to fall from above them.

One collective gasp resounded from the crowd of performers, and the music warped to a stop. The troupe jumped to their feet, wide eyes and shocked expressions shared by all.

"*The Raven and his Dove,*" Finvarra said, his voice now touched by sadness that swelled in Leanna's throat. The gathered performers encircled the Raven and Dove and lifted their hands to the snow with the awe of never having seen it before. But their sorrow too was unmistakable.

Leanna winced, two hands clamped down on her shoulders. From behind her, a burly man with a hard-set face gripped each of her arms.

"*Bring her to me.*" Finvarra's demand cut through the tent. The troupe's gazes finally snapped to Leanna, but hers swept past them to the tent door, to the tall figure veiled by the shadows there. He spun on his heels and strode through the curtains, his cape billowing in slow waves behind him.

The strongman's grasp tightened on her arms, and he moved her forward. But neither fear, nor the promise of Finvarra could ever take away what she'd just experienced, and she shed her tears openly because her mother had been right.

It had been truly magical.

# CHAPTER THREE

## ILLUSIONS & SNOW

LEANNA KICKED THE DAMP earth beneath her feet, sure her numbed toes were nearly purple, if not already black. It was one of many discomforts, but she thought it best to take everything in stride. Fear and hysteria never did anyone any good, or so her mother always said. So she did not plead as the burly man bound her hands. She cringed but did not resist as he pulled her out of the Big Top and through the labyrinth of tents. She asked no questions when he thrust her down onto a cushioned bench outside a large, white tent with a raspy, "Sit here."

Under normal circumstances, she wouldn't have been frightened of a man in a sequined vest and silvery balloon pants. Reality now far from the bounds of ordinary, this bald man with a painted smile was utterly terrifying, and so Leanna sat. The strongman walked to the fold at the curtained opening. Wordless, he turned out to the night and manned the door.

Leanna bit her lip. Was Finvarra making arrangements as to how to dispose of her body, of her heart? Worry bubbled in her throat. Did she really want to know?

The strongman inclined his head.

Trailing his gaze, Leanna found the Raven and the Dove approached. Still in their performance attire, one in black and the other in white, they wore matching expressions of melancholy. They stopped before the strongman and his mood, too, dimmed as he put a hand on the Dove's shoulder. It was a quiet affection, but the finality it held reverberated deep in Leanna's chest.

The strongman lowered his hand and stepped aside. The Dove's shoulders dropped with a cloudy exhale and she entered the tent, followed closely by the Raven.

A flame was ignited within. Three shadows bloomed against the thin canvas, with two huddled closest to the opening. The third and tallest of the silhouettes walked the length of the tent, its lean outline stretching away from them.

"Say something, Finvarra, please," the Dove said. "I know it is sudden, and the last thing I want is to hurt you, but you saw the snow. My performance has appeased the Elders. They have forgiven me. After so many years, how can I possibly shun their mercy and reject their invitation to return home?"

Silence trailed her words.

"You're my brother and I love you more than I can stand," she went on, "but with every girl that is slain, I can only watch you fall deeper into this darkness you've surrendered to. It pains me not to be able to help you."

Leanna stopped the agitated twisting of her fingers. After all the years she defended Finvarra's name and scorned the vicious rumors, it couldn't be that they were true. He couldn't have killed those girls. She gripped her skirts tightly and listened.

"With every performance, I fear Machina more. She is relentless and I am tired. Tired of running. Tired of feeling scared for you. For the circus."

Grim quiet settled over them. Only the winds cried lowly, as if lamenting all the pain in her words.

"Please, dear brother." Her shadow floated forward and paused before his. "I can't say no. Jin gave up his life in Forever to share in my punishment. I just want to go home." There was a small sound—a sob, as she began to weep.

"There is nothing more to be said then, is there?" Finvarra said, and the winds howled.

There, in the patchy shadows, Leanna tilted her head to hear more of his voice, a low, elegant sound that echoed in her ears in a dizzying manner. If the silvery strands of moonlight that night were the strings of a harp, Leanna was certain Finvarra's voice would be their harmony.

"If you wish to leave this circus and follow the snows to Forever, the choice is yours. Nothing I say will stop you."

"You can tell us to stay," said the Raven. His outline drew closer to Finvarra. "You know it is your sovereign right to demand we go on performing until you are forgiven. But I speak now, not as a subordinate, but as your friend. Though Ellie is your sister by blood, I like to think that over the years we have all grown into something of a family, and families stay together."

There was a pause where Jin moved back by Ellie's side. "If you need Ellie and I to stay, we will stay. All of us are willing to remain by your side, performing until the skies part and your snow, too, falls. Tell us now what you desire and it will be so, Ringmaster."

Finvarra's silhouette lowered and disappeared behind the outline of a chair. He chuckled darkly and Leanna shivered, no longer able to distinguish his sound from that of the winds that whipped around her.

In her unease, she clutched the crystal necklace.

At once, reality swayed in her mind like a dream, only it was no dream, nor was it reality. Stuck in this in-between, her spirit felt locked inside a house of mirrors that pulsed around her like a heartbeat, despair, centuries-old agony, and guilt reflected back at her from every turn.

"I envy your devotion," he said, and the crystal grew colder in Leanna's hand. "You were all punished because of my foolishness, bound to the rings because of my vanity, yet you stand by me still." He trailed off with a derisive chuckle. "Sadly, I think I'm just as selfish now as I was the day I was banished. Unlike you, if the Elders granted me my forgiveness, I would leave this place behind without a thought for anyone else."

"You don't mean that," Ellie moaned.

"Then maybe you know me better than I know myself, dear sister. But does it matter whether I mean it or not? The Elders will never forgive me. Many snows will come and go, but never mine. Even in this realm so far away from home, the Elders mock me. They find pleasure in continuously conspiring against me, digging pits for the purpose of watching me fall."

"You mustn't think that way," Ellie cried. "If you give up hope now, all else is lost."

Finvarra laughed, a dark amusement that flashed as explosions of colors before Leanna's eyes. A distant part in her mind whispered that she was going mad. Somewhere in the psychedelic swirls of color, she wondered if this were true. The thoughts, however, were frail, and with each current of his laugh, the crystal grew colder in her hands and her grasp on reality weakened.

"Hope?" he asked and the temperature plummeted. A thin sheet of ice spread above the ground thick with half-withered dandelions. Leanna cowered into her cloak and lifted her feet, lest the ice creep its vines up her legs and freeze her all the same.

"I'm afraid I lost hope a long time ago in one of the many trenches the Elders clawed out for me. Don't you see that you stand in one with me at this very moment? Or shall I explain how hopeless it all is? In the past month, another crystal has turned black. Inara clings to what life she has, and all I can do is watch it happen, watch this circus vanish from around me. But even then, I always thought I would have you. Now they want to take you away from me."

Spellbound, Leanna closed her eyes and surrendered consciousness to his voice, brittle and grieving.

"In a world now blinded by science, I need true spectacular magic to turn skeptics into believers. You are that, Ellie. You are my main act— inimitable. I need you. And now you're asking to leave."

Silence swelled again. Ellie and Jin's shadows merged as they embraced in wait for Finvarra's answer.

"Yet, if I demand you stay, then I am the selfish monster the Elders believe me to be. Selfish and heartless, a madman with innocent blood on his hands." Finvarra rose, his outline visible now. "And you two will be forced to remain bound to this circus. You will realize that my snow will never fall, and you will grow to hate me for keeping you from Forever. Your scorn will only send me into a deeper pit of despair for I will know that I have failed you, again. "

Leanna shook her head, tears welling in her closed eyes. Sweat beaded at her pores, her heart physically straining with these foreign emotions. Finvarra's despair clutched her soul, only she couldn't release the crystal; her soul conscious that Finvarra would be lost in this hall of mirrors if she did.

Finvarra walked to the conjoined shadows of Ellie and Jin. He exhaled and the ice beneath Leanna's feet melted to pools that glistened under the half-moon. All the flowers lay black now, dead.

"May the Elders have their laugh," he said, defeated. "May this circus fail a million shooting stars over, but never your scorn, Ellie. Never. If going home is what you wish, then may the snows carry you safely into Forever."

Pain tore Leanna in half, to where she could no longer breathe. The strongman glanced side-eyed, but never spoke a word. Leanna surfaced for only a moment between labored gasps, enough time to release the necklace. When it fell back onto her chest, the house of mirrors in her mind shattered and her hands shot to her ears at the sound that spliced her eardrums.

Quiet words were spoken inside, and embraces exchanged in the shadows. After some time, a hand parted the curtains. Ellie walked out first and Jin followed close behind her, their hands entwined. She stopped short and pressed her free hand against her chest as violent sobs wracked her small frame. Coming around her, Jin tilted her downcast face to meet his. No words were exchanged between them, but his stare was so clear that Leanna heard the words of his heart clearly within hers.

*"Do not be frightened, my Dove. I am your Raven, and I will protect you."*

He extended a hand out between them and nodded encouragingly. Ellie still cried, but slid her dainty hand into his. He twirled her into his arms and together, they vanished into the shadows between the tents. The distinct sound of flapping wings resounded and then all was quiet.

Leanna sat in the cold for a long time after, unaware that any time had passed at all. She stared unseeing to the dark where Ellie and Jin had vanished. The world had righted itself now, reverting back to cold air and a star speckled sky. But something had shifted. Hazy recollections gathered in her mind, talk of realms and snows, of Elders and Machina.

Yet, she could not place these thoughts. It was as if she had dreamt it all. Maybe she *was* going mad.

"The Ringmaster will see you now." The strongman held the curtain open with one hand and motioned for Leanna to enter with the other. Leanna stood, but fear rattled down her spine and fixed her to the damp ground. Against her best wishes to seem unafraid, she trembled violently. She couldn't lose her heart. Sure it was broken and she could not trust it, but for better or worse, it was hers and she was quite fond of the years it had given her.

When she failed to move, the strongman placed a firm hand at her lower back and guided her forward into the tent.

# CHAPTER FOUR
## CAGES & HEARTBEATS

SHEER SILK CURTAINS gave way to a large space, much bigger than what it appeared to be from outside. Awed, Leanna took a hesitant step when a tap beneath her feet rooted her. Hardwood floors stretched under her. Brow furrowed, she lifted her eyes and looked about the room. There were countless shelves lined with books, and a yellowed map of the entire circus hung at the wall behind a sprawling mahogany desk. The crystals from outside were demarcated on the map, strange marks written around them. Spells, Leanna figured, scared at what those spells might be and whether one had been set upon her when she crossed the crystals.

"You're the trespasser."

Leanna spun to the voice, and her breaths arrested at once. Finvarra stood by the fireplace, one hand on the mantle, the other at his waist. Blond hair veiled his downcast profile as he stared to the flames. Each strand sparkled enough to make even the brightest star wither in envy, or so thought Leanna, who against good manners stared at him until the strongman gave her a nudge.

"Th-there seems to be a misunderstanding, sir," she said, stumbling forward. "I am no trespasser."

Finvarra lifted his head a touch, the corner of his thin lips curled. "Ah, so your little feet wandered here all on their own, did they?" he replied before looking at her.

Then he turned.

Pale blue eyes met hers, cold and emotionless. They gave way to a sculpted nose and thin lips that twisted upwards into a scornful grin. While the room was bathed in the fire's crimson hue, Finvarra's pale skin radiated a soft silvery glow as if reflecting the light of the moon.

Leanna digested his comment and searched for an answer to his question, but found she could only stare and grow colder. Though her lips failed to produce words, her mind reeled with thoughts at how it could be that her mother met Finvarra—this very man before her—when he could be no older than thirty. But soon, in holding his gaze, Leanna's thoughts muddled and drifted off into the same pit of confusion she experienced when sitting outside.

Finvarra abandoned the fireplace and crossed the room to the large desk. Sitting, he was quiet a moment, the silence only interrupted by the taps of the clock on the mantle.

Tap.

Tap.

"What I dislike more than a trespasser is a liar," he said. "So I will ask you—and choose your words wisely—how did you know we were here? How did you get in?" He leaned forward. "Do I once again have a traitor in my midst?"

"I am no liar, sir. What I meant was that I trespassed, yes, and for that I am sorry. But please understand that I wouldn't have been allowed to come had I not come tonight, and so I… I ran away and snuck in through the southern part of the field."

Finvarra sat back gradually, watching her through narrowed eyes. He reached for a silver goblet in front of him and brought it to his lips. Here he stared at her over the rim for a long moment before taking a drink. "You snuck in? Walked right through and into the tents?"

She nodded. "Through the wagons in the southern part—"

He slammed down the chalice and silenced her. Droplets of wine spilled onto his long fingers that he tightened around the stem. "I heard you the first time you lied. I'd advise you against doing so again. Now, I will ask you once more. How did you get in?"

"I told you, I snuck in," she said, clenching her muddied skirt. "It's not like there is a gate protecting the grounds."

"There are many things protecting these grounds, things your simple mind could never understand. Yet, here you are…" He whipped out a handkerchief and wiped the wine from his hand, finger by finger. "I'm curious as to how you managed to cross through our safeguards without knowing what they are. Only those with a ticket may enter, and we have not sold any as of yet." He settled back into his chair, brow arched and lips tightened. "What I detest more than a liar and a trespasser, is a coward. Unfortunately for you, you are all of those things."

The insult went unnoticed by Leanna, who let out a little gasp. "I have a ticket!"

Finvarra extended a pale hand.

"Well, I did, but it... it dissolved when I came through the crystals..." She trailed off, realizing how terrible it all sounded, and worse, made her look.

"How convenient." Finvarra curled his waiting fingers to a fist. "You're testing my patience, liar."

Leanna bristled and made to argue, when a glint at Finvarra's shirt caught her eyes. A crystal pendant just like hers hung on a thin silver chain just outside of his shirt, casting faint rainbows on the white fabric.

"I should have known." Finvarra chuckled and twirled the crystal between long fingers. "Have you come for this, spy? Was it the Elders? Did they send you?"

Leanna's eyes widened. "What? Who—no, I—"

His face hardened. "Machina, then?"

"No! No one sent me. I came here on my own foolish accord! And why would I want your necklace when I have one of my own?" She jerked the necklace from inside of her dress.

Finvarra shot to his feet, his tiny pupils widened to open cores of black. Leanna lowered her hand from the crystal. Perhaps her choice to expose it hadn't been so wise...

The fire snapped and Finvarra was in front of her. Leanna gasped and jerked back, but the strongman gripped her arms and held her firm as Finvarra wrapped his hand around the crystal and stared at the rock for long minutes. In his contemplation, his stare darkened to a look Leanna knew well— the same guilt in her father's stare every time he looked at her.

"This was not given to you, which makes you a thief as well." He snatched the necklace free and said through clenched teeth, "I despise those most of all."

With the whirl of a wrist, Finvarra turned back to his desk as the strongman picked Leanna up with little effort.

"But I didn't steal it!" She pulled herself forward while the strongman yanked her toward the curtained door. Finvarra only stared at the crystal now cradled in his hands.

"Please! My mother gave me the necklace—"

The second layer of curtains brushed past.

"You told her to bring back your Leanan Sidhe!"

The cold air of the night slammed into her when—

31

"Tomas, wait."

In a sick waltz, Tomas whirled to Finvarra, Leanna still in his grasp like a rag doll.

Silent, Finvarra gestured for Tomas to sit her down before his desk. Obeying, Tomas deposited her at the winged chair and resumed his position behind her.

From across his desk, Finvarra poured Leanna a glass of water and slid it toward her. His eyes remained fixed on her crystal that now lay flat on his desk, a spectrum of colors gathered beneath it like a downed rainbow.

"What is your name?" he asked.

"Leanna Weston, sir," she replied, struggling to hold the cup steady in her hands.

"*Leanna...*" His soft baritone travelled about the room, though he'd said it a little above a whisper. For a moment, Leanna wondered if he had spoken it directly into her mind.

"So tell me, Miss Weston, am I to think you brave or a fool? Did your mother not tell you the fearsome tales surrounding my name the day she cursed you with this necklace and the ticket?"

"I know of your reputation, sir, and I am not scared."

The left side of his lips curved, his eyes very blue. "Indeed? And what reputation is this that precedes me in this realm? It seems every one has its tales."

*Realm?* Leanna wondered as Finvarra leaned forward onto his desk, pale hands clasped loosely on top. She said slowly, "It is said that as payment for bringing your circus to a particular town, you steal away the most beautiful girl and..."

"And?" he encouraged her. The gilded hue of the candelabras reflected dangerously in his eyes.

"And you take from her whatever you find most beautiful, while also taking her heart because you are heartless."

Finvarra rose from his seat and jaw tight, he unfastened the golden spade buttons of his waistcoat. Unsmiling, he opened a drawer and retrieved a dagger.

Leanna's breath hitched. She bolted to her feet to flee, but Tomas caught her. His fingers dug into her arms and she winced as he yanked her back against his chest. She shrunk into the brick wall that was Tomas, eyes shut against an approaching Finvarra.

When he stopped just before her, she lifted bound hands over her heart.

One tug and her hands were free. Leanna opened her eyes to the rope sliding from her wrists like dead serpents.

Finvarra set the dagger down at the desk behind him and unclasped the buttons on his shirt until porcelain flesh peeked through the parting in the fabric. Leanna averted her gaze, all words lodged in her throat. Never had she had a man so close, so exposed.

He took her hand in his and lowered it to his chest. She struggled, but trailed off when the constant beat of a heart pulsed beneath her palm flush against his skin.

"You see, my dear girl," he murmured. "Against popular belief, I have a heart, as much as a curse as it may be."

His frigid fingers curled further into her wrist and he jerked her closer. He glanced at her trembling fingers. "Not scared?"

"No," she said, breathless. "Your hands are cold."

Their stares held for a moment where Leanna wondered if he remembered she still touched him.

Finvarra's chest rose and fell with a long exhale. "Foolish girl." He released her hand and the moment shattered. Twisting on his heels, he stalked back to his seat and paused, his gaze caught on the crystal at his desk. "Heart or not, Miss Weston, why did you come if you knew of these tales?"

Leanna retracted her hand, not having noticed it still remained extended. "I've heard of your circus my entire life, from my mother. She said that if the day ever came where I couldn't find any magic in the world, I should come to your circus." She shrugged sadly. "Here I am."

"Why didn't you wait to come with her?"

"Because she is dead, sir."

He flicked his gaze to her with a look so direct, she took a moment under his stare.

"My doctor said she suffered from a bad heart, too, but it went undiagnosed for so long. Mine was discovered sooner since I dance—well, danced. She passed away shortly after I was diagnosed. It happened quickly. She didn't suffer."

Finvarra gripped his own pendant. "A dancer with a damaged heart..."

He chuckled then, but there was no humor in it. Something unsettled him, of that Leanna was sure. She replayed her previous words in her mind. There were none that should have caused him distress. Yet minutes later, the only sound between them was the crackling flames, the taps of the clock, and their breathing.

Finally, he let out a rueful breath. "Then we will heed your mother's words. You will stay with us."

"Stay? What do you mean *stay?*"

"You didn't think I could let you leave here, did you? I still don't know whether or not I can trust you. It would be safer to end it all now to be honest."

"You... really mean to take my heart?"

He chuckled. "Surely, you can't expect me to let you walk out of here after all you have seen and heard."

She clasped a hand protectively over her heart. The other she reached over his desk. "I don't dare trust what I have seen or heard. The elixirs I am given cause me to hallucinate sometimes. I have seen frightful things in my dreams, terrible things I would never share with anyone. Please believe me. I won't tell anyone what I have seen. They will much faster send me to an asylum before believing me."

"Then those are rotten people and you shouldn't want to be with them anyway," he said plainly, and rose.

All the frustrations of her life roiled to an uncontrollable fury within Leanna and she burst from her seat. "You are the most insufferable, impossible, infuriating man I've ever had the misfortune of meeting! You want my beauty? Then I'm sorry to disappoint you, but there isn't much. You want my heart? Take it, set it on fire, eat it. Do with it what you like. Who cares anymore? You'll be the foolish one to want it as it's already broken beyond repair—"

Leanna cut off abruptly, winded. The room pirouetted around her, a swirl of crimson hues and shadows. She stumbled back.

"Sit down, Miss Weston," Finvarra ordered.

Leanna gripped the edge of Finvarra's desk. "No—"

Tomas gripped Leanna's shoulders and shoved her down into her seat.

Finvarra said after a careful moment, "I don't want your beauty, wherever it is. I'm a busy man with a circus to run. I can't be bothered to find it under all of this." He waved his hand over her scraggly appearance. "As for hearts, I'm not in need of one. Not your heart anyway."

"No one ever is," Leanna replied, in barely a whisper, his words hurting her more than she liked.

"Since your heart is worthless to me, there must be something else you can do. Now, this is not an offer I would make anyone, but, you did bring back my necklace, and seeing that my troupe has thinned as of late, I have need of you."

Finvarra paced around in a perfect circle, each loop of his journey tying knots around Leanna's chest. What would he have her do? Clean the animal cages, perhaps? Clean the tents? Whatever it was, anything was better than losing her heart, surely. Maybe he would have her sell tickets at the box office—

He stopped. "It is settled. Miss Weston, you are our new tightrope walker."

Leanna's eyes widened. Even Tomas's hold on her wavered from behind.

Finvarra remained unruffled and spoke to himself in murmurs, tapping his chin and plotting as if he were the only one in the room. "I doubt she will be ready in two days, but I'm sure Kioyo can train her."

"What? No, you can't do this. I tell you I'm sick and your first thought is to have me walk across a tightrope? You're mad!" She steeled her spine and crossed her arms. "I refuse to be your tightrope walker. It's beyond all bounds, and I simply won't do it."

He hummed, and sitting, he slid a ledger before him where he began to write. "You've left nothing for us to discuss then." After another minute, he had yet to say another word.

"That's it, then?" Leanna swallowed. "I don't have to be your tightrope walker?"

He chuckled over his books. "Despite my reputation, Miss Weston, above all things, I am a gentleman. If a lady refuses to do something, who am I to force her?"

She let out a slow sigh. "Thank you—"

"But I still can't let you leave. Tomas, could you escort Miss Weston to the cages?"

"Cages?" she asked archly. Tomas clamped his hands down on her arms. Leanna pulled forward, kicked to be freed, but Tomas's hold only tightened as he dragged her to the door.

"Yes, I'm certain the lion will enjoy your company, however brief it may be," Finvarra called out from behind them.

Leanna dug her heels into the earth, but she was quite small and so Tomas plucked her from the ground with little trouble. She screamed, but he didn't stop and no one came to her aid, their silhouettes frozen within the white tents.

A dense fog skirted the menagerie tent, the white sidewalls like an extension of the mist. A sign with the words *Hungry Lion, Keep Out* hung by a wire on a rusted stake stabbed into the entrance pillar of the tent. Leanna had only a moment to read the carved words before being pulled through the curtain flaps.

Though her heart pounded a maddening rhythm, her screams died. Her fight, too, dwindled at the sight of the beautiful beast asleep inside of a gold and red wagon. She'd read about lions before, but never would have imagined them to be so large, so gorgeous. Its caramel mane kissed by reddish strands glowed under the faint gaslight and infused the terrifying creature with a dreamlike quality.

A large paw slipped from in between the bars, and Leanna pressed back against Tomas, reminded of the nightmare she was set to endure at the mercy of that lion.

"I'll do it," she said in heated whispers. The second the words left her mouth, Leanna regretted them. However, faced with the possibility of two rows of sharpened teeth, she pled with much more vigor. "Tell Finvarra I will be his tightrope walker!"

Tomas stopped. A tense quiet settled above them. In the void, the scent of vanilla and hyacinth filled the air. A frigid gust whipped past, and the curtain flaps lifted with a sharp rustle.

Finvarra entered, his wintry eyes fixed solely on Leanna as he walked around the cage slowly and watched her from in between its gold bars. He trailed a hand behind him, one ringed finger colliding against each passed bar. "Do the winds deceive my ears, or have you chosen to accept my offer?"

Leanna glanced at the lion, then pinned him with a glare of a thousand daggers. "I hardly consider it a choice."

He rounded the cage and stopped before her. "We are all given a choice, and I have given you yours: the cages or the circus."

"Why not just let me go?" she countered. "You can have any girl. Droves of them, more beautiful and talented than I, would be here in a day's time if they knew you needed a new tightrope walker."

Tomas released a cloudy breath, clearly agreeing.

"I don't want other girls or their beauty. It was you who brought back the necklace, and it is you who needs to stay."

All the blood drained from Leanna's face as the events of the night pieced together into a devastating reality. "You think I'm her, your Leanan Sidhe…"

Finvarra stared, eyes sparkling like the watchful stars above.

"You do!" An arched cry mixed with a humorless laugh exploded from her mouth. "Surely you can't. I'm no muse. I'm nothing but a girl!"

"Whatever you are, Miss Weston, I need you. But maybe, just maybe, we can free each other." He extended his hand toward her and cut off her attempts at speech. "Do we have a deal?"

Leanna glanced down at his hand and twined her fingers.

"The cages then." He spun to leave.

"Wait, I said I would do it. I will be your tightrope walker, but I have a condition."

Finvarra stopped. "You trespass onto my circus," he said, turning, "and are proposing a condition?"

"Indeed I am." She held her chin a touch higher. What did it matter anyway? She was set to die, a rather gruesome death if Finvarra had a say in it.

Finvarra leaned back onto the gilded bars of the cage, a dangerous amusement in those very blue eyes. "And this condition…"

"I must be allowed to go back home to say my goodbyes. I couldn't bear leaving my Papa to fret over my life without as much as a word." After their argument that morning, he would never forgive himself upon finding her missing. Sure he'd cared more about establishing her two sisters, but Leanna was sure he loved her in his own way.

A line creased Finvarra's brow. He pushed off the cage, stepped closer, and poked a cold finger into her cheek. Despite her desire to flinch, Leanna willed herself to freeze. What on earth was he about?

He retracted his hand and his frown deepened. "Are you sure you're not a troll? They're the type to make strange bargains like the one you've just made me, and, well, I utterly despise trolls."

"Nasty little lot they are," Tomas muttered from behind.

Leanna opened her mouth. She closed it. *A troll?*

Finvarra sighed. "I suppose I will have to wait until morning to see whether you are or not. Until then, if you're still alive by the end of rehearsals tonight, I will consider letting you go home." He extended his hand.

Leanna bit her lip and surveyed his hand. "How am I to know I can trust you?"

His face turned very serious. "You shouldn't. Now your word, Miss Weston?"

Boring her eyes into his, Leanna shoved her hand into his. Finvarra's fingers coiled around hers and the corners of his lips curled like the wrought bars of the lion's cage.

Before she could wonder what she'd just agreed to or what on earth Finvarra found so amusing about their agreement, he pulled her closer and spun her under his arm in one fluid move. He pressed her back against his chest, their flushed bodies facing the cage.

"You have given me your word." He said nothing more. There was no need. Proof of what would happen if she went back on her word slept in front of her behind golden bars.

Finvarra held Leanna there an added moment, quiet, his fingers gripping her upper arms tightly… gently… until releasing her. Leanna's mind urged her to move away. Before she could heed its guidance, a sparkle caught her eye.

Slowly, Finvarra lowered her crystal necklace before her until it rested just beneath her collarbone. The necklace secure, his hands fell away. Just as his hands had kept her captive, it was his voice against her ear that now imprisoned her.

"Welcome to Finvarra's Circus," he murmured, his breath warm against her skin.

A breeze blew, and she felt him no more.

Leanna spun wildly, insults on the ready, but no words came. Tomas was there, but Finvarra was gone.

# CHAPTER FIVE

## FALLING STAR

KIOYO LEANED BACK against the tall ladder leading to the platform and tightrope above. His lean arms were crossed over his chest, and on his face a scowl. In the time she had sat there, Leanna had been careful not to stare for too long, but it was hard. Whereas Finvarra's beauty had been ethereal, Kioyo was handsome in a feral sort of way. Olive skinned, his ears pointed slightly and his nose was very pronounced. But his wolfish beauty could not hide the frown that marked his mouth since Tomas had dropped her off.

He let out a harsh breath and, as if accepting that she wasn't just going to disappear, he pushed himself upright. "Let it be said, I don't know who you are, where you came from, or what you did to convince the Ringmaster to let you stay, but your charms won't work here. If he's back to his old ways, so be it. My job is to prepare you to walk that rope. Your job is to walk it. If we can see eye to eye on that, there's no reason this can't work. Now, let us begin." He stepped aside and motioned to the ladder. "You go first, I'll be right behind you."

Leanna blinked. "You want *me* to go up *there*?"

"The Ringmaster said I'm to train you. Well..." He motioned to the ladder.

"But I've never been anywhere so high, and what if—what if I fall?"

"Impossible," he said, confident. Leanna simply stared. Kioyo slumped against the ladder, his arms crossed over his chest once more. "Do you want to go home or not?"

"Yes, but—"

He pointed upwards.

Following his gesture to the thin rope above, Leanna cowered back a little more. "How do I know you don't mean to throw me over?"

His frame bounced with a chuckle that kissed his golden skin with a brighter glow. "If the Ringmaster wanted you dead, you would be dead. There are other ways that are faster and less messy. So no, I don't mean to throw you off the platform."

Leanna gulped. Finvarra probably had murder down to an art. But she shook her head and banished the thoughts away. Fear and hysteria never did anyone any good, indeed. She would not fear them. They were probably just trying to scare her. All she had to do was climb. She could do it. Besides, it was either the rope or the lion.

She moved closer to the ladder. She set one foot onto the first wooden bar, and then another, until the rhythm of her steps brought her onto the small platform leagues in the sky. She crawled onto the stand and cowered into the corner.

The lights from below did not reach up toward her nightmarish heaven. Only the glow of the lamp beside her offered any consolation as did the small glow of the mirroring lamp on the opposite platform. The light however was faint, and the wire seemed to vanish in the distance, swallowed by darkness.

With what little she knew of Finvarra, Leanna thought it to be all an illusion. There was probably no rope. He had said *if* she made it through rehearsals alive. Her heart beat a little faster and she scurried closer to the pillar. If only she had held out and refused Finvarra a little longer. If only she had fought Tomas a little harder. If only she had listened to her father....

Kioyo climbed up after her. He stood on the edge, nearest the rope. "Good. Now, we begin."

"But you said I had to climb the ladder. You never said anything about walking across the rope."

"Anyone can climb a ladder, but this rope is where the magic happens." He stepped back onto it. Leanna gasped, and instinctively reached for him, but he eased back out of reach.

"All you need to do is walk across. Arms out, back straight, and walk, and then you will be allowed to say your goodbyes." He extended his arms out at his side and steeled his spine. Nodding once to stress his point, he took one step back and then another, his body swaying the further he moved back on the rope.

Leanna's hold eased on the pillar. In spite of the danger she found herself in, she could not deny ever having seen anything as striking as Kioyo on the rope. Surrounded by the glow of the fireflies, he was radiant.

Lowering his arms, he walked back to the platform. "Now you, just like that, to the other side. It's only a rope on which to walk on like you would walk on the ground below. I will be right here behind you." He knelt and extended a hand to her, his eyes more golden than she remembered. "Trust me."

Leanna's fingers tingled, as though knowing she could. She stared to the rope behind him and her hold tightened on the pillar. "I want to believe you, but this is all happening so fast. I shouldn't be up here. I'm not fit to do this."

Kioyo scoffed and dropped his hand. "And you believe in magic?"

"Yes, I believe in magic. I believe in card tricks and rabbits being pulled from top hats. I also believe in falling to my death!"

"For the love of Forever, you will not fall!"

His passionate conviction struck Leanna oddly to where she was tempted to believe him. Maybe she wouldn't fall. She looked down over the platform and curled closer to the pillar. "Can I at least wear a harness?"

"Ellie never wore a harness."

"Of course she didn't. She could fly! What of me? In case you haven't noticed, I have no wings sprouting out from my spine."

He started to speak, but Leanna said, "Look, I do believe in magic, with all of my heart. But what if I should fall? You have no wings... unless you do. It may help my fear a little if you were to tell me what you are. You know, for my sanity's sake. Or perhaps if we start a little closer to the ground?"

"Excuses," Kioyo muttered. His midnight eyes narrowed and lightened to a golden brown, much like a feline's eyes. "And when you're done with them, we will proceed."

He came at her in one lithe move. Before Leanna could process his words, the change in his appearance, or scream, she was cradled in his arms. A cool breeze rustled her dress and hair as the ground below dashed by in smears of light and shadow.

The opposite platform blocked her view again.

"When you're ready to get over this fear, cross over to the other side." He deposited her on the platform and spun on his heels. Frantic, Leanna reached for his arm—that was much hairier now—but it slipped through her fingers. She watched wide-eyed as he walked across the tightrope and climbed down the only ladder.

Only the fireflies remained, dashing across the open darkness.

Fear a poison, Leanna crumbled to her knees and flattened herself against the platform. Grasping the edge tightly, she screamed continuously, desperately for help.

At her frantic sound, the fireflies flew up to the crossbars. They extinguished one by one, and no one came.

The night wore on, growing colder. Leanna lay still, her cries of help long faded to silence once it became clear no help would come. Time, too, fell to a void. Finvarra must have cursed the night with his timelessness, she thought fleetingly, as the night felt endless.

Morbid thoughts drifted within her mind, that of her lifeless body tossed amongst the brambles and downed leaves of Abbey Forrest. Her brown hair, matted and knotted, would shield her vacant expression and pale face. No doubt Finvarra would take nothing of her body seeing as he didn't find her particularly beautiful and didn't want her heart. No, he wouldn't be blamed. They would say she was foolish for having wandered so far from home, knowing that her heart would fail. Her poor, poor heart...

Leanna pushed up onto her elbows and sat up. She could wait. Come morning light, Edith would discover her missing and the Constable would come for her. But, she slipped her dangling feet onto the platform. With every minute, it only got colder. She would die before anyone came. If this was to be her death, she would not die a coward.

Rising, she fixed her eyes on the small glimmer of the mirroring lamp on the opposite platform. Perched on the edge, she sucked in a breath to steady her shaking and slid one bare foot forward. Cautiously, she felt for the rope. It wobbled, but much less than she imagined. Maybe Kioyo was right. Maybe she could do this.

She curled her toes around the thick rope. Extending her arms at her sides, she steeled her back the way Kioyo had instructed her and slid her hind foot onto the cord. Breathless, she slipped the front foot forward along the rope.

Steady.

One step.

One... more.

She blinked.

Instead of ridding her eyes of tears, the action wiped the fogginess of her mind, and she sucked in a breath realizing that she stood on a rope about to walk across! Fear buckled her knees and the rope jerked beneath her. Leanna screamed, twisting her toes around the rope. She waved her hands at her sides, grasped at the open spaces for balance, but there was only air and it slipped through her fingers.

Wind rushed past her ears and her dress billowed as she fell. Above her, the fireflies kindled, but didn't move. And so she closed her eyes and fell, until she fell no more.

# CHAPTER SIX
## TRY & SAY GOODBYE

LEANNA'S EYES SNAPPED OPEN. A suspended moment passed, and then awareness swooped in like a bird. She no longer fell. It took her mind an added second to realize this, that she was not dead and could in fact fully feel her body, however numb it proved to be.

The saw-dusted ground was still a distance away, where Ellie stood, a wide smile on her lips. Leanna gasped and turned to the black vest she clutched. A smile curved the Raven's full lips. He chuckled and waved luminous black wings once, twice, the tips of each feather slicing the darkness with a streak of light.

The cool breeze of their ascent nipped at Leanna, and she curled closer to the bare chest of this man-bird who nestled her as his young. When his feet tapped on the wooden platform, Leanna held on still. What if it was all a dream? What if she were to open her eyes and find that she still fell? She shuddered, and against all proprieties dug her nails deeper into the soft leather.

He knelt down and released her gently onto the stand. "You're alright," he said over her head.

A small gust whispered past and a hand brushed Leanna's hair from her cheek. She unearthed her head from the crook of Jin's neck to Ellie who knelt beside them. Ellie offered her hand for Leanna's taking and, smiling, nodded once. Leanna swallowed and hesitantly took hold.

"That a girl," Ellie whispered and rose evenly with Leanna. For this Leanna was grateful, as her heart was no longer the only untrustworthy part of her being. Her legs wobbled uncontrollably.

She tried to clear the fog of her mind, to at least find the words to say thank you, but all the stresses of the night rushed to the forefront and only tears unfolded. She apologized for her crying.

Ellie pressed a cold palm to her cheek. "You, my dear, did a brave thing and have nothing to apologize for, much less cry about."

"I hardly call falling while screaming like a baby, brave." She lowered her head away from Ellie's touch.

"Well, you were quite the shooting star." Ellie giggled, her curls bobbing with each hobble. "But you have a brave heart and are meant for this. I can feel it. I daresay any other girl would have frozen to death before braving the rope."

"A brave heart?" Leanna shook her head. "This heart you speak of has failed me countless times before, has kept me a prisoner in my own home, a blemish to my family. It's not brave. It's damaged, and this is all a mistake. I shouldn't be here."

Ellie tilted her head, her blond brows knit together. She moved before Leanna and lifted her shoulders. She lowered them with an exhale and white wings bloomed from her back like wisps of smoke, folding and unfolding into one another.

She said, "My wings are just that: wings. They can't fly on their own. I must believe in them, that they can move me. Only then can I fly. If I don't think they can carry me, then I, too, will fall. Your heart didn't fail you earlier, did it? Rather, it gave you the strength to cross. And though you fell, you were caught." She pressed a hand gently on Leanna's chest. "Trust in it. All else will fall into place."

Ellie stepped aside. She walked around Leanna while Jin circled in opposite rotation.

Watching Ellie vanish and Jin appear, Leanna wondered if this was all a dream. After all, she had just fallen from grave heights only to be caught by a man with wings. Reality, however, reasserted itself when Ellie's hands came onto Leanna's waist.

Before them, Jin mocked a bow. "My lady, may I have this dance?"

Ellie giggled, and cupping Leanna's elbows, she lifted them parallel to the ground. "Keep your hands out at your sides like so. You will tip less." She pressed Leanna's stomach in and tilted her chin up. "Always remember: arms out, chin up, and back straight. Then you step out. Jin is there to lead you. I will hold you from behind."

Obediently, Leanna kept her arms out to her sides though they shook horribly. Fear-numbed, she barely felt Ellie's hands, only the grit of the rope beneath her feet when she slid her foot forward. Feeling the cool cord, Leanna froze and clenched her fingers to a taut fist.

"Fear and magic cannot coexist," Ellie whispered in her ear. She pried her hands open gently. "Surround yourself with the memories of the things you love most. When you walk this rope, walk toward those memories. Fear can't take that away from you."

Blindly, Jin stepped back.

Frightened, Leanna followed.

They continued their promenade until they stood suspended in the middle of the rope.

Ellie drew close behind her. "Tell me, did you love dancing?"

With her arms out at her sides, Leanna barely nodded, afraid any action would cause the rope to wobble. "It was my life."

"And that is your magic," Ellie whispered. At this, hundreds of fireflies ignited above. They detached from the canvas and descended around them like shooting stars. Leanna gasped. There was no doubt in her mind that this wasn't a dream. Never could she imagine something so beautiful.

Following their trails of light all around, she caught sight of Kioyo on the opposite platform, a quizzical smile on his face. Before her, Jin wore the same mien. At the platform behind him, Ellie floated down beside Kioyo.

But if Ellie was there, who was holding her from behind?

Leanna stiffened.

The rope jerked.

"Focus!" Ellie rallied. "Arms at your side. Remember, the memories. Walk toward them!"

Leanna waved her arms and bent her knees. Her heart slammed against her ribs, but she steeled her spine as Jin helped her find her center. By and by, she stabilized the rope beneath her until she stood perfectly still.

Her pulse in her ears, she closed her eyes and centered herself in Ellie's words. When she opened them, Jin stood before her. But she no longer saw him, only the pearly image of her mother there behind Kioyo and Ellie. Her mother loved to see her dance, and the same devotion marked her face that shone under the light of the fireflies.

Chin up, back straight, and the fireflies all around her, Leanna took one step toward Jin and another, the desire to make her mother proud an invisible string reeling her closer.

Another step and one more—

The ground beneath her solidified and she stumbled onto the wooden platform. Trembling hands flew to her mouth. She had done it. She had walked the rope and still lived!

Ellie and Jin congratulated her, but Leanna saw none of this, just her mother's ghost that smiled and vanished into specks of floating light.

"Very impressive," Kioyo said, stealing her attention. "I imagined you would do it, eventually."

Leanna flushed, arms crossed tightly over her chest. "And leaving me on a platform was your vote of confidence?"

He shrugged and leaned back against the wooden pillar. "I could have told you a million times over that you were safe, but you never would've believed me. I take that back. I told you a million times over that you were safe and you didn't believe a whit."

Her frown deepened. "So you tricked me."

"You can say that, yes. But I am a clown. It's my job to fool you." He grinned and tipped his hat. "Welcome to Finvarra's Circus."

Leanna dug her toes into the damp earth, comforted by cold blades of grass that tickled underfoot. The scent of decayed leaves and moisture filled her nose as she hauled in a lengthy breath and let her head fall back. Though hours of endless walking back and forth across the rope had passed, night still ruled the skies. Leanna wondered if days, in fact, had passed, only they had been so engrossed in dancing that she had missed daylight altogether.

Persuaded by Ellie, they now sat in the cookhouse, which to Leanna's surprise was not a house at all, rather another tent. More surprising still, no one was cooking, much less eating. Performers and help hands congregated around long tables, some on seats while others favored the wooden tabletops. Regardless of their manners—or lack thereof—they were all so elegant, each one possessing a sliver of Finvarra's timelessness and glow.

None of the other troupe members had spoken to her, but there had been plenty of murmurs in passing. *Back to the same*, some said. Others talked of *traitors* and *Machina*, but Leanna forced herself to ignore this. The world now a different place, she sat unfazed by the tail of a small fire dragon cradling her cup of tea. Bertrand, the fire breather, placed a baby dragon in the middle of each table, the fiery reptiles providing light and warmth for those around it.

She stroked the leathery skin, awed by the darker flames beneath each rustled scale. "This all seems like a dream. I believed there was magic, but never this."

"It's one thing to say you believe in magic. It's another to truly believe." Ellie smiled down at Leanna from the tabletop where she sat with her legs gathered beneath her. Her feathery skirt made it seem as if she sat on a cloud.

Leanna shrugged. "Still, had Finvarra not threatened to feed me to the lion, I never would have experienced any of this or met all of you, and never would I have imagined walking across that rope." She chuckled. "I'm almost tempted to forgive him."

Ellie's eyes widened. "He threatened to feed you to Kia?"

"Is that how he got you to stay, he threatened you with the lion?" Kioyo asked. He and Jin exploded into a fit of laughter. "No wonder you were so scared!"

"I hardly find that comical," Leanna muttered from beside him, twirling one of the baby dragon's fiery whiskers around her finger.

"We're not laughing at you, Miss Weston," Jin clarified. "But have you ever seen Kia?"

"Kia?"

"The lion," Ellie said, slapping Kioyo's arm in feigned reprimand. "You have no need to fear him. He is our guard. He watches over the cages, though we haven't needed them for quite some time. As fearsome as Kia may seem, he only fancies berries, grass, and perhaps a bit of ale on his down days. After learning Jin and I were leaving, he drank himself to sleep. Had Finvarra put you in his cage, the most Kia would have done was cuddle. That is if he even realized you were there."

Leanna's small hands gathered into tight fists.

Instead of sympathy, the men laughed harder.

She huffed. "How you've survived working for someone so cold and heartless simply evades me."

All laughter withered into an awkward silence. Everyone around her looked to the ground as if suddenly it were the greatest of fascinations.

Ellie slid from the tabletop and sat beside her. "My brother may seem a little rough and…"

"Arrogant," said Jin.

"Pompous," chimed Kioyo, with a grin.

"As if you lot are any better," Ellie said, playfully narrowing her eyes at them. She placed a hand above Leanna's. "He may appear to be all of these things, but he isn't. Circumstance has hardened his heart, but he does indeed have one." She squeezed Leanna's hand. "Whatever you have heard of him, please don't believe it, even if Finvarra himself claims it to be so. Remember, here of all places, not all things are as they appear, and I've never seen that apply to someone more than it does to my brother."

"Circumstance? Do you mean Machina?" Taking in the wary expressions around her, she added, "I don't mean to pry, but I've heard the name quite a few times since I arrived and it's never good."

"It has everything to do with her," Ellie said finally, deadened. She shivered and goose bumps covered her arms. Jin reached for her hands and gripped it reassuringly. Still, Ellie's pale pallor flushed over red, and her eyes gleamed with unshed tears. "Machina is a toxic error my brother drags through life, a never ending punishment that shadows his every step. He should have never entertained her, but Finvarra was blinded. She was beautiful, and he was a fool. But it is her evil that knows no bounds. She is the heartless one. That is why I beg you to abandon all you've heard. It pains me that those girls were victims in a vendetta they never should've been a part of. But while Finvarra's carelessness and conceit share in the blame, he is not the monster."

Leanna swallowed and rubbed her arms, Ellie's goose bumps suddenly contagious. "So the tales are true? Girls have indeed been killed?"

Ellie nodded, her watery gaze distant.

"But has he told anyone that she is the one committing this violence? Surely the constable can help."

"If only it were so easy," Jin said, a sad smile at his lips. "I'm sure you know we are not of your kind. Neither is Machina, not anymore. The evil that fills her is never-ending and abides by no rules, except for that of the stones, of course. Their white magic keeps her out and us... in."

Though the rumors had made their rounds about Winter Abbey and all the surrounding lands, Leanna had held out a sliver of hope that they were just that: rumors. She had always known it wasn't Finvarra that killed those girls, but this was worse than she could have ever imagined. In spite of her previous anger, a slight amount of sympathy stole into her heart for Finvarra, for all of them.

She hugged herself against the chill touching her bones. "So Machina is out there, watching?"

Ellie deflated with a sigh. "Oh dear me, as always, I have said too much. You've just rid yourself of fear. The last I want is for it to come back with a vengeance with talk of Machina. Machina was a mistake. She is a trouble that I hope you never have to deal with. But you mustn't worry about her. You are safe here." She smiled, but the joy never reached her eyes. "For now, just

49

remember that beneath Finvarra's cold exterior, there is indeed a heart, a very big one."

Remembering the feel of his pulse beneath her hand, Leanna's fingers tingled and pink mottled her face. "I know."

Ellie smiled broadly, and Leanna lowered her face embarrassed at how transparent she truly was.

"But where will you be going now that you are leaving? You mentioned Forever, but where is it? I've never heard of it, just as I never thought a girl could fly." Leanna paused. "You said you are not of my kind, but… what kind *are* you?"

A stiff silence waved in like an uninvited guest, extinguishing all conversations in the tent. Every eye focused behind Leanna.

Cut off by the stark quiet, she turned.

Finvarra stood at the entryway donning a black frockcoat paired with form fitting hose and black boots. Only the strands of his golden hair distinguished him from the darkness of the night. A black cravat adorned his black shirt and vest. Tall and dark, he was a sight that called to every eye in the room. Surely it also beckoned every heart to abandon propriety and fall at his feet—or so thought Leanna who felt her own heart falter in rhythm, and cursed its fickle nature. She struggled to hold fast to her anger, but even with her blood turning to fire at the sight of him, she was unable to deny it: Finvarra was beautiful.

His eyes, shadowed by the brim of his top hat, sparkled like two stars as they scanned the room and fell upon her. Under his stare, she swallowed. Her desire to look away was there, but she could only meet his gaze moment for moment, accepting that he didn't need to take anyone's heart. Surely women gave their hearts to him willingly.

Thinking this didn't make her feel the least bit better. Worse was realizing that beautiful girls were not the only ones who had given him their hearts. Somehow, whether by trick or of her own volition, the moon herself had lost her heart to him. He glowed with her pull alone, as if having devoured her.

And Leanna, furious as she was, was but a wave.

So as Finvarra approached, she rose to meet him.

He stopped a breath away and slid off his top hat, assessing her coolly. "You're not dead."

Leanna held her chin a touch higher. "No, I'm not, and that's after I walked across the rope numerous times."

Finvarra cocked an eyebrow. "Did you now?"

Leanna nodded her reply. She would have laughed in his face, but surely that wasn't the conduct of a proper young lady. However, he did think her a troll, and so she allowed herself a smirk.

Finvarra reciprocated. "You survived the rope today, but, my dear troll of a child, walking and dancing are as polar as night and day. Walking is courtship, whereas dancing..." He leaned in close to her ear. "Dancing is passion. It requires more energy, devotion, and fire than a mere stroll ever could. It is a flame I have yet to see in you."

He shifted back, and Leanna felt less steady than she did when standing upon the tightrope. A deep flush roared up her body, making strange knots of her stomach in the process. Noting his indecorous nearness and all the eyes watching, she cleared her throat and smoothed down her dress futilely.

"We shall see then," she said, unable to frame any other words.

Finvarra hummed and moved to walk past her, but she gripped his arm and stayed his retreat. "Wait, we had an agreement. You said I could go home if I made it through rehearsals."

He glanced to her hand upon him, but she didn't release him lest he vanish into the winds again.

"She did do marvelously," Ellie said from behind.

"And I can escort her," Kioyo offered. "The bonfire hasn't been lit so the chances of Machina knowing we're here—"

Finvarra cut Kioyo a glare, and Kioyo silenced instantly.

"You've enchanted my sister, amongst others," he murmured, lowering thick lashes to the small dragon bundled around her teacup. He stroked the reptile's lengthened neck. Between them, the small dragon abandoned the table and floated above the room like a flamed kite. "Witches are not as bad as trolls, but they cannot be trusted."

Leanna's hand fell from his arm. "Whatever I am, witch or troll, spy or a bloody magician, I must go home before anyone discovers me gone." She sighed, frustrated. "We had a deal."

Finvarra watched the small dragon wrap its body around the torch and vanish into the flames from whence it came. "Very well, I am a man of my word. You will go home and you have until mid-day to say goodbye. Under no circumstance are you to tell anyone of what has transpired here today or of where you will be. You tell them whatever is needed to free you, but if you utter a single word to anyone about our agreement," he lowered his voice for her ears only, "the crystal will warn me, to where then I will—"

51

"Save your threats. I've given my word and I intend to keep it. I will return." Truth be told, she couldn't bear the thought of never returning.

Finvarra opened his mouth—

"Finvarra," Ellie breathed beside him, touching his arm.

Finvarra followed her gaze to the horizon, and a quiet agony flashed over his stare. On Leanna's chest, the crystal grew cold and a swift sadness swelled in her throat. This had happened before, only now she had a sense that this vast sadness was, somehow, not hers.

And as brother and sister reached for one another's hands and snow began to fall once more, Leanna also understood it was time for them to say goodbye.

A solemn caravan of performers followed Finvarra out of the tent and gathered outside of the Big Top under the flurries of snow that brushed across the meadow. Light advanced across the field, the first ray of sun breaking through the skeletal branches of the trees. In the midst of the fog, the world of tents before them vanished slowly. In its place, a snowy meadow appeared that glittered like a field of diamonds.

Leanna blinked, sure her mind played tricks on her. Or rather it was all a waking dream, one of fairy tales unfolding before her eyes.

In the distance of this ice-covered forest, the towers of a glacial palace reached toward the sky. They stood luridly white amidst thin silver clouds. Soft blue light spilled out from within. The pale hue illuminated the frozen countryside and softened the stark edges of the surrounding mountains.

A hand flew to Ellie's chest and wide-eyed she turned to Finvarra. Pain flicked across his eyes, but vanished just as quickly. In its place, he offered her a small smile.

Leanna remained beside Finvarra as Ellie and Jin made their way around the half circle embracing their friends one final time. After years of solitude, the thought of saying goodbye to this friend she had made in one impossibly long night tore open loneliness within Leanna, much worse than a million broken hearts. When her time came and they stood before her, she lowered her eyes to her twined fingers, unsure of what to do with the raw ache.

Jin reached out and cradled her hand in his. He pressed a luminous black feather into her palm and closed her fingers around it. "No fear."

Squeezing her hand, he stepped aside for Ellie. Leanna clenched the feather tightly, and strained against her coming tears.

Ellie tipped Leanna's face to meet hers. She smiled though the whites of her eyes glistened. "You can do this, just remember to believe. There is a reason you have come on the same night as my forgiveness." She put a hand over Leanna's heart. "You were made for this."

"It's a coincidence, nothing more." Her voice broke, faded to a whisper.

"You say coincidence. I like to call it Fate. Now come." She brought Leanna into her arms.

After an eternal second gone too fast, Ellie stepped back. "I believe in you, darling, darling girl." With the smile, she broke away and approached the last in line: her brother.

Standing a breath apart from him, Ellie stared up at Finvarra. She tried a smile, but it faltered to quavering lips. The same hesitation played on Finvarra's face, and they stared at one another until with a half-smile, he took in a slow, shuddering breath and held out his hand to his sister.

From down the line, a pudgy man with peppered hair stepped forward and began playing a slow tune on a violin. Ellie brushed into Finvarra's arms. She pressed her cheek on his wide lapels and took his offered hand. Love trumping all proper structure, Finvarra rested his head in her bundle of wispy blond curls.

Quietly, they took off into a waltz. The mist wrapped its wispy fingers around them while they danced, swirling perfect circles in the snow. Ellie's tears turned into giggles as without form, Finvarra spun them gracefully in and out of the shadows, through the grey traces of night and into the pale pinks of the coming morning. Her smoky wings grew resplendent as she clung lovingly to her brother, until their waltz deteriorated to entwined figures laughing merrily as if all were as it should be.

But it wasn't, and not even Finvarra's timelessness could detain the light reaching over the horizon. Ellie crumbled into his chest and they drifted to a stop as the violin whined one last time.

Finvarra moved away first. Just out of her reach, he took another second to stare at her and then he bowed. Flushed, Ellie barely curtsied. Pain found Leanna once more when in tenderness unlike him, Finvarra reached out and tapped Ellie's nose.

"I know," Ellie whispered, her cheeks wet with tears. She turned away and met Jin at the icy fringes of Forever. Translucent, they offered one last glance at the troupe and turned to the distant mountains. Hand in hand, one step after another, they walked into the pearly field until fading alongside the mirage that died to the morning light.

Soon, only tents and snow remained.

And darkness.

A familiar gloom settled in Leanna's heart, like the days that depression engulfed her to where she could barely walk. She had never known what it was, but the same debilitating sorrow buckled her knees under her. Instinctively, she reached for Finvarra's arm.

At once, a vision came upon her and she was caught in it. She stood alone on the jagged rocks of a shore. Screams resounded in the wind gusts that whipped around her. Lightning flashed above, revealing images of deadened eyes, lifeless bodies, and blood—so much blood.

A moan overpowered their sound. Leanna turned to the angry black waters, and her breath caught. Finvarra struggled in their midst. Watching Ellie walk away left him bereft, drowning and unknowing how to swim. He tried to stay afloat, but the towers in the distance instigated the waves, and he choked on the salty waters, close to surrender.

"Finvarra!" she called to him.

The vision vanished as quickly as it came, abandoning her to Finvarra's widened stare. But Leanna could think of it no more. Caught in his maelstrom of agony, her hand slipped from his arm and she crumbled unconscious to the ground.

# Chapter Seven
## A Metal Contraption

FIRE HISSED AND POPPED a song between the flames and thick logs. In the corner of the Weston House morning room, Leanna tightened her shawl about her shoulders and kept away to where this firelight could not reach her. Enrapt by flares upon flares of thought, she stared as if transfixed by the flames. But she didn't see her favorite sight of crimson curls and orange vines pirouetting to nothingness in the shadow of the flue. Though she was present in body—a weary, sore body—her mind wandered far, walking the thin line of tightropes and goodbyes, that of a snowy Forever and the tempest of a man's mind. That of leaving her home forever, the only home she'd ever known.

The room blurred to a speckled mess behind her tears. She twisted the cool crystal between her fingers, comforted that at least Finvarra had been honest enough—truthful enough for a manipulative, arrogant, boorish man with manners to be desired. Still, murderer or madman, he had kept his word. Somehow she had woken that morning in her own four-poster bed, her tattered garments returned to their perfected state.

And now—she looked to the clock on the mantle as it struck half past eleven and sighed—it was a time to say goodbye to her family.

"Do you mean to sulk all day?"

Her older sister's arched tone righted the world around Leanna.

"You've been sighing all morning and all throughout breakfast," Sarah went on. "If it weren't for Dr. Luther's call this morning, I'd have Edith take you to your room since our company is such a bore." She scoffed and strode to the window. With a grunt and a tug, she snapped the thick velvet curtains open. Leanna jerked back and shielded her eyes from the light that burst through the arched windows, filling the room in gold.

Sarah dusted her hands proudly. Resting them on her corseted waist, she stood back to admire her rather miniscule work. "There. We don't want Dr. Luther to think we live in a mausoleum, as deathly as some may seem." With her nose high in the air, she strode toward the console table between the two windows and turned her attention to an arrangement of peonies and white roses.

"I do wish you'd do without that sour expression," Lydia started in her usual bored drawl, appearing beside Leanna. Actually, her eldest sister might have been there the entire time, but Leanna was much too tired to notice. Her body ached to where it seemed her soul was burdened with its skin and bones, and she dragged as such, as if wanting to leave it behind. And her mind, well, she wondered if it'd ever left the fairgrounds at all.

"I just don't see why Dr. Luther is coming when he was just here yesterday," she said. "And why must we all be here if he's only come to see Papa? And where is Papa? I told him at breakfast that I had something important I wished to discuss with him, with all of you in fact, and I haven't much time."

Lydia dismissed this with a feeble wave of her hand. "Dr. Luther called on all of us in fact, and we must all be present."

Leanna groaned. Though only three minutes had passed, it was three minutes closer to noon. "But I—Ouch!" She pressed a hand to her cheek. Lydia had pinched it and she made to pinch it again. Leanna slapped the dainty hand away.

"Sit still." Lydia batted away Leanna's hands as if a pesky fly. "I'm doing it to help you. You're so pale."

"It's called illness," she said, evading her sister's pincer-like fingers.

Lydia ignored this, her attack insistent. "And these dark circles under your eyes are ghastly."

"Ghastly?" Sarah snorted from over the vase of flowers. "Ghostly, more like it."

Leanna was left without air. Sarah's insult was not surprising, but that morning it hurt. In her moment of distraction, Lydia broke through Leanna's failed defenses and pinched her cheek. The deep ache from Sarah's insult diluted the prickle and Leanna didn't even flinch.

"Some color on your cheeks will do you good," Lydia said with one final nip. She then took to the silk ribbons on the sleeves of Leanna's gray muslin gown. "And why on earth did you wear this dreary thing? I'd told Edith to set out the yellow one."

Lydia yanked two tassels together into a tight knot. "You've so much to learn. Pink reflects innocence and youthfulness. Yellow, health and joy. You wear gray and all one can think of is a miserable, dejected spinster." Her fiery blue eyes widened a fraction more. "And you didn't even wear the pearls I left on your dresser?"

Leanna blinked. The natural action seemed to clear the fog of her thoughts, and her mind woke from its slumber of Big Tops and snowy fields. It became conscious of the world around her, one where two sisters who always avoided her now kept her company willingly. More, they beautified her and the room around her.

"Is there some occasion I've forgotten?"

"Of course not. Why?" Lydia perfected the knot on her sleeve, moved to the one by her other shoulder, and never once met Leanna's eyes.

"Well, you've never let me wear your jewels before, much less your pearls." She turned to Sarah who hummed a sweet tune to the flowers beside the bookcase. "And you, Sarah, why are you suddenly so concerned with the state of the drawing room? You hate flowers."

Sarah shoved the stem of a single white rose into the vase and pinned Leanna with a dry, thorny gaze. "Here we are, slaving in trying to do something nice for you, yet all you do is badger us and give us a hard time." Sarah stalked to the vase on the side table of the divan. There she abused a few more flowers while muttering bitter nothings under her breath.

"Oh, do stop being so dramatic, Sarah." Lydia stood up and tucked a strand of hair behind Leanna's ear in delicateness unlike her.

Leanna met her sister's stare in a way she never had. There was joy in Lydia's eyes. Leanna forced herself to believe it was because after many years, they were all spending time together. She smiled at her eldest sister.

As if snapping from a dream, Lydia cleared her throat. "And you, stop asking so many questions. It's not very becoming."

Muffled voices came from outside the drawing room. Lydia silenced and tilted her head toward the invading noise. Sarah paused in her flower arrangement and turned to Lydia. Immeasurable secrets saturated their shared look, and Leanna swore they smiled at each other.

Footsteps echoed down the hall, drawing closer. A strange, steady rasp accompanied the steps, that of something being dragged or rolled. Lydia yanked Leanna's arm and dragged her to the settee in the sitting area at the center of the room. She resumed her seat beside her. Sarah rushed to the winged back chair opposite them just as the scraping stopped and the door opened.

Mr. Weston walked into the room. The handsome gray haired man, whose love of chocolate cake in the morning was prominently displayed by his rounded belly, smiled and Leanna's chest ached. In spite of all their disagreements, now conscious of how much she'd miss him left her without air.

He stepped aside and allowed for Dr. Luther to enter the morning room. Leanna found her breath readily. Dr. Luther's dreary black coat was replaced with a brown, tweed walking suit that hinted toward caramel in the sunlight. This was surprising; Leanna knew very well the cost of such a suit, especially on a young doctor's wages. It must have cost him a small fortune. Also perplexing was the distinct absence of his Gladstone bag, which, were it not for him setting it down at every appointment, she would have thought it attached to his hand.

But it was the furtive look shared between her father and doctor that stoked her suspicions. She studied the two men earnestly. There was a touch of something in her father's eyes, something bright and hopeful. Something she couldn't quite put her finger on.

Dr. Luther inclined his head and smiled at each of the Weston sisters. He held Leanna's stare for a slight longer. His normally clear gray eyes were darkened with an emotion. Worry? Fear? Leanna forced a hello, hoping to decipher this foreign look of him.

"Dr. Luther, how lovely of you to call on us this morning," Lydia said. "Forgive us, it appears you're outnumbered."

He smiled. "No apologies needed. My father was supposed to join us, but was forced to cancel, sadly."

Mr. Weston motioned a hand, welcoming the doctor to sit at the settee opposite Leanna's. "Yes, yes, how is Constable Luther fairing? He must be quite nervous about this preposterous circus making home in Winter Abbey." At the bar, he poured two glasses of sherry. Leanna's brows knitted. Her father only drank sherry when he was in high spirits. He hadn't drunk sherry in years.

Dr. Luther sat on the edge of the settee, stiffly. "Not nervous, no, but concerned about the welfare of the young women in Winter Abbey. This circus does not travel without its share of scandal, but Father won't tolerate that here. If anything at all happens, he will make sure they never operate in another town again. He'll be watching them very closely once they arrive."

Leanna blinked. "Once they arrive?"

"Yes, they have postponed the show, but I suspect they will be arriving soon. The advance men have already passed through and put up new posters for the show. Everyone is in quite a tizzy over their new tight rope act, some sort of '*magnificent faerie goddess.*'" He waved a hand dismissively. "Regardless of their lure, they will be closely watched."

Leanna paled. Surely it couldn't have been referring to her. She was no faerie goddess, and definitely not magnificent.

Mr. Weston handed Dr. Luther his tumbler and raised his glass. "Tell Constable Luther he has my full support. At least I will have some comfort knowing Leanna won't be anywhere near there."

"Oh Papa, don't be ridiculous," Sarah said, giggling. "Leanna would be the safest of us all. Finvarra would never want *her* heart."

Lydia shot Sarah a look. "I'm confident there is a man out there who will want Leanna's heart just as it is." She placed a hand over Leanna's and squeezed it gently. "And speaking of magic and hearts, to what do we owe the honor of your call, Dr. Luther?"

Leanna noted the time. She had to get rid of this man and say her goodbyes. "Yes, what is the nature of your call?" she said quickly. "If you're here for my sake, I can assure you, I've never felt better. Forgive Papa, he tends to worry prematurely. I hope we didn't ruin your plans for the day, but the day is young!" She rose. "I'm sure if you leave now, you can salvage the rest of your morning. Shall I fetch your coat?"

Dr. Luther chuckled. "You've such a kind heart, but not to worry. Nothing is as important as my best patient."

*Best patient?* Leanna's smile wilted under his direct gaze. She sat, not liking it at all.

He swallowed visibly and set down his tumbler. "Actually, I had planned to return tomorrow, but I couldn't force myself to wait. You see, I can't say my visit here is entirely business." He tugged a pale yellow handkerchief from his pocket and dabbed at his brow.

"Is that so?" Mr. Weston said. He patted the man's shoulder gruffly with a knowing grin that inundated his cheeks in red.

Dr. Luther excused himself and stepped into the hall. The strange scraping sound started again and when he reappeared, he rolled a wheelchair before him.

As if synced with the rolling wheels, everyone turned their heads to Leanna who paled in the same slow speed.

"Isn't it marvelous?" Sarah clapped her hands. "Isn't it amazing?"

Leanna's chest cracked with every clap, but she couldn't tear her sights from the chair of plush blue velvet and two large wooden spoke wheels on either side. It couldn't be that the wheelchair was meant for her…

Dr. Luther stopped before her and Leanna froze.

"Your father disclosed to me your concern at not being able to enjoy the simple things in life. I suggested that perhaps this would solve that little problem." Dr. Luther came around the chair and knelt before her. "This chair will let you travel further than you ever imagined without exerting yourself. We won't let your heart imprison you anymore."

Around her, everyone congratulated Dr. Luther for his gift of freedom, but it all fell to indistinct chatter in Leanna's ears, her gaze caught on the metal contraption. Cold, she said nothing.

Dr. Luther chuckled and slid onto the divan beside her at Lydia's urging. "It's a bathchair. It's much more comfortable than it looks. I can assure you that once you sit on it, you'll never want to stand."

"Yes, do sit on it," Sarah nudged with another clap.

Leanna winced. Their scheme now tangible, she dug her nails into the settee edge until the pain numbed her fingers. Sadly, it did nothing for the hurt in her heart.

"I know what it is," she said. "What I wish to know is why it's here? Last I checked it was my heart that was the problem, never my legs. Or are you wrong about that as well? Recent developments have led me to believe that my heart is not as damaged as you claim it to be."

Sarah gasped. "Oh doctor, do forgive her. She's been acting a little strange…well, stranger than usual."

"Leanna, we spoke of this." Her father moved closer to the chair. "I told you there was indeed a world outside of your books and of this ridiculous circus. Here is true magic, real innovation!" He tapped the chair as if testing its sturdiness. "Even when you're not feeling your best, Edith can take you into the gardens instead of you fading away in your room. We thought if you felt free and not so confined by your condition, you would be open to accept other proposals."

At these words, Dr. Luther took her hand in his. "Proposals I do hope you consider."

Leanna cried out, the truth of it all squeezing the air from her lungs. *Proposals?* They didn't just want to force her into this chair—they wanted to force her to marry this man! They wanted to get rid of her.

Lydia's smile withered and breathed life into her suspicions with a look that warned. *Don't ruin this,* it told her. *We can finally be free of you.* It could have also been Leanna's bitter half misinterpreting things, but then and there, she couldn't differentiate family from traitor.

She clutched the necklace tightly to the point she thought it'd pulverize in her damp palms. If they only knew of how she had walked on air the night before, they wouldn't relegate her to this chair. If they'd only seen how brave she'd been.

One by one she met their eyes squarely, seeking refuge in one of their stares. One of them had to know the feelings of her heart. Did not some link of sheer blood create this bond? She couldn't marry this man!

First she met Lydia's stare, and then Sarah's, and finally her father's. The glimmer of hope in their eyes made the room grow smaller and colder around her.

She stumbled forward. "I need air…"

Sarah rose and dragged Dr. Luther to his feet. "Yes, air! What a fabulous idea. Why not take her into the gardens? The trees are always beautiful this time of season, all the reds and gold and—"

"Don't," Leanna said, a firm hand between them. She rolled the dreaded chair away from her with a grunt and managed the short distance to the doorway. Grasping the wooden frame as her only lifeline from the floor, she turned and for an irrational moment, she laughed.

"You wish to bind me to this chair and to this marriage, and call it freedom?" she struggled to say in between gurgles. "How dare you?"

Dr. Luther met her by the door. "Forgive me, I didn't mean to upset you, but after your father disclosed how alone you felt, I knew I should have made my feelings known."

She scoffed and turned her head away, wordless. Her father had not only betrayed her trust, but her confidence as well.

"I know it comes as a surprise, but I believe my position not only assures you are in the best care, but it also means that I truly understand how you feel. You are not alone." He shifted closer, much too close for her liking.

She moved back, but he caught her hand, gently yet firm. "I know your loneliness as if it were my own. I see it in patients every day, yet I've never felt any of their woes as closely as I feel yours."

Leanna snatched her hand away. "Don't do this, Dr. Luther. Please don't say any more, for I can't marry you." She turned to face her family. "For reasons I can't tell any of you, I found my freedom last night. I have the chance at a new life in a place where my illness no longer plagues me, where magic is real."

Lydia rose to her feet, fists gathered at her sides. "Don't be a fool, Leanna! There is no such thing as magic. This dream world you speak of isn't real." She walked alongside Dr. Luther and put a hand on his shoulder. "This is real life. Dr. Luther is a real man with real possibilities. Let him care for you. Listen to us. We know what's best for you, and he is it."

"But if you knew of the things I can do, of the things I've done. Of how I walked across—"

In her bosom, the crystal flashed cold and stayed her tongue.

"Oh, damn you," she said to the memory of Finvarra and his threat. "Damn you!"

"Leanna!" Mr. Weston started, but she stormed from the room, leaving them to stare at a closed door and an empty chair.

In her chamber, she dismissed Edith in a hurry and threw open the windows, needing air, more air than she could get in the confines of the four walled prison that was her room.

How could they do this to her? How could strangers such as Jin and Ellie have believed she could cross a rope high in the air, yet her own family didn't trust her to live her life with her feet planted firmly on the ground?

Leanna collapsed onto the bench before her window and rested her head against the frame. And now there was no way out. There was no way she could leave after that outburst, after all she had said. She didn't have to hear them to know that downstairs they were plotting as to who would come up to her room and convince her of their plan. If she dared run, her father would ride his horse to the ground to find her, and then force her into marriage or an asylum. Besides, she never could run very fast. But she couldn't marry Dr. Luther. She just couldn't.

The bells in the distance tolled the hour.

Noon.

"What am I going to do?" she whispered to the trees.

A strong gust rustled the leaves and the treetops waved in her direction.

"You're going to come along," a voice whispered in the passing draft. "Or lose your heart to me," it spoke then from behind her.

She didn't need to turn to know who it was. That scent, that voice, could only belong to one man. But she did turn and the sight made her heart want to break free from her chest. There in the middle of her room stood Finvarra in the same garments from that dawn. The sadness from earlier in the morning cradled his eyes, made his skin paler, more ethereal.

Leanna cupped her mouth and stared as if watching the coming of an angel—an utterly deplorable, ill-mannered beast of a fallen angel. But coming undone, she tore from the window and ran to him. Gathered against his chest, she closed her eyes and inhaled his scent of vanilla and hyacinths.

Finvarra stiffened, growing colder and harder than the icy towers of Forever. He held his hands tightly at his back, as if tied there against his will. But whether he pushed her away, mocked her tears, or took her heart that instant, for those few moments Leanna dug her fingers deeper and felt him there—real, cold, and unmoving.

And she wept. Hopeless, she had felt herself fall into the pits of a forced marriage, into the seat of a metallic prison. But Finvarra was there, and he was no dream.

# CHAPTER EIGHT

## TOMB OF DREAMS

THE ENSUING SILENCE was deafening. Save for the muffled rhythm of Finvarra's heartbeats, the world fell quiet around Leanna, as if stunned by her illicit embrace. The world wasn't the only one frozen at her actions, however. Though Finvarra's pulse beat evenly beneath his damp shirt, his chest failed to rise and fall with the regular tempo of life.

She lifted her head from his chest. His face turned down in equal measure. Blond strands tumbled over his shoulders and veiled their stares behind curtains of golden hair at either side.

"I wish you hadn't done that," he murmured. There was no anger in his stare, rather sorrow as he cradled her shoulders and eased her away.

A swell of heat and shame flooded Leanna's cheeks. "Yes, of course. I—I don't know what came over me..."

Her voice faltered. Her steps did not. She shifted back and a little more until knocking against her vanity table. If only she could have kept going and vanished right through the wall.

Finvarra turned to the window and trailed the outline of the landscape. "It has been done and can't be undone. We can only hope that age has long blinded the trees."

Leanna followed his gaze, his cryptic words hinting at one thing, *Machina*. She shivered and hoped the trees were in fact blind. "Forgive me. I..." She sighed. "It's been a very trying morning."

"Trying for us both, but it must never happen again, for your sake more than mine." He met her stare finally and inclined his head, an understanding gesture that told her they would speak of her embrace no more. She drew a breath and nodded.

The matter now closed, Finvarra severed their stare and spun in place.

"Where are your things? We leave at once."

Remembering the troubles from that morning, Leanna deflated. "I can't leave. My father won't let me go that easily."

Finvarra was quiet for a thoughtful moment. He clasped his hands at his back and walked around her bed quietly. At the vase on the night table, he admired the snow white lilies, caressing a finger down the stem. He eased the flowers aside and peered within the porcelain vase.

"The last I heard, it was your heart that was the problem, not your legs. Unless you lied, of which you told me you were not a liar." He let the lilies tilt back to their belonging stance and regarded her. "But then, it is like a liar to lie."

"I am no liar, but—"

"Then there should be no problem. You've your own legs to walk with and a mind to lead you. Whether you let your father or any man control it for you is another matter."

Leanna clenched her hands into tight fists. "No one controls my mind, or my legs. But that means nothing now. My father knows my greatest dream was to see your circus. For me to vanish so close to when you're set to arrive—I may as well leave a note telling him where I will be. However you've managed to keep the circus hidden will mean little once I go missing. When your precious circus appears to the world, they will come down on you like vultures. Wings and feathers, fire dragons and icy towers, this magical universe you live in does not extend to me. There are actions and consequences in my world that can't be fixed by flying off into the wind—oh—"

She cringed with a moan and curled forward, taking in a few deep breaths against the tight pain roped around her chest. "Magnificent, you say? Your job is to sell illusions, Mr. Finvarra, not to believe them."

Finvarra stared at her as if waiting for her to catch her breath and her wits. He walked to the window then, and when Leanna was certain he was about to snap his cape and disappear into the wind again, he shut the curtains in one even stroke.

"Then only one thing can be done," he murmured. Pale hands trailed down the length of the velvet hangings until falling back at his sides.

Leanna gulped. There was but one prospect, and the realization trickled cold down her spine and to her fingertips.

He set off around the room as if caged—which he was, by whatever thoughts possessed his mind. He searched in corners, drawers and closets, but shook his head to himself and muttered more words. Leanna trailed his weaved path along her room, not daring a breath. He was probably looking for something with which to cut her heart from her chest.

Perhaps not finding anything sharp enough, Finvarra tilted one polished shoe outward, the soles spotless. It was as if his feet never touched the ground.

He lowered it and held a hand to her. "I need your boots."

"M-m-my boots?"

He dropped his hand with a pat and moved toward her.

Leanna stepped aside and away. "Why do you need my boot?" Surely he didn't mean to beat her heart out of her. "Wouldn't it be easier if you used something sharper than my boots? Oh!" She fell back onto the chair by her reading table. Cornered. Caught.

Mid-step, Finvarra stopped. "Good God, I don't want your blasted heart. I need the dirt from your boots. A very small amount will suffice. I would get them myself, but I imagine my touching your foot would be utterly improper, and would make me an insufferable, impossible, infuriating man. Did I get them all?"

Leanna frowned. "Are you mocking me?"

"Miss Weston, please. Mercy, I say. Your boots?"

She skewered him with a glare. He didn't deny it. He was mocking her. He thought her bound by society, incapable of tolerating a simple touch. Leanna sat up on the winged chair and lifted her skirt, enough to expose one booted foot. Lips tight and brow arched, she slid it toward him and met his mockery measure for measure. Where this boldness came from, she didn't know. But the surprise that flashed across his face was pleasing.

Finvarra strode forward and loosened the tie of his cloak. The knots he undid magically retied in Leanna's stomach—or so she thought, feeling her stomach twist with each flutter of his fingers.

He shrugged once and the black fabric eased down his arms with a hush. He tossed it coolly onto the chair opposite her. As it floated down, he crouched at her feet. Finvarra set her terse leg down on his knee and eased the black laces from each hole. She fisted her skirts tighter, simultaneously wondering and cursing the fickle nature of her heart that now pounded unfailing as if normal. Maddened at her body's reaction to his feather light touch, she turned her face away.

"This is difficult for me as well," he said. His eyes remained hooded beneath thick lashes as he spoke into the open air between them. "But we can be of great use to one another if we could simply try to get along. My behavior yesterday was untoward, but for the sake of my troupe, I have to be. I can't apologize for that, but I will do my part to make our arrangement as painless as possible. We may have our differences, but I do not wish for us to fight at every turn." His fingers stilled on the laces, and he lifted his eyes. "Nor do I wish for you to fear me."

For that instant, his mask of indifference and arrogance fell away, and left but a man appealing to a kindred spirit. Feeling her heart in her throat, Leanna swallowed. *I don't,* she wanted to say. She didn't—she did—oh she didn't know. All she knew was that not knowing how to feel was the worst feeling of all.

Reason warned her that he had fooled her before. *He's a liar,* it told her. *A beautiful, murderous liar...*

Her heart, however, made her hands relax from around the fabric of her skirt. "I'm not frightened. I've never been frightened of you."

Finvarra held her stare at this, and nodding, set her foot down and worked through her other boot. Straightening, he moved to the bedside, raised the black shoes over the bed, and tapped them together, side by side. With each tap, small bits of dried earth chipped away from her soles and heel, and crumbled onto Leanna's white sheets. He reached for the vase at her bedside. Holding the lilies in place, he drained the water onto her boots and washed off the remaining dirt onto the bed. He set the vase and shoes aside, then plucked a strand of his hair and dropped the luminous tress over the murky water. As it floated down, he pinned back his draping sleeves.

The thread of hair now lying across the muddy puddle, he pressed his hand onto it. For a moment, nothing happened. Leanna frowned. How on earth was smeared mud supposed to free her?

In the void, Finvarra's eyes grew distant as if he chased a lost memory through the course of his veins. He whispered words that swirled from his mouth as curls of white, incandescent smoke. It was then Leanna realized how cold the room had grown.

Finvarra retracted his hand and stepped back. At once, vapors wafted from the bed and a foul stench filled the room. Leanna couldn't be bothered to cover her nose. Especially not when with each second, the smeared mud grew to a small mound that unfolded and doubled, until only a long, solid matter lay in the middle of the bed. Within seconds, the shape of a human surfaced...of a girl. Leanna clapped a hand over her mouth. It was a replica of her!

Strands of silvery thread sprouted from the muddy figure. The silken buds intertwined creating spider webs of ice across the lifeless corpse. Color sparked through these veins, the way a slow flame burns at the frayed edges of a canvas. It shaded the hair, the face, the neck, and the shoulders with color until he held up a hand abruptly.

"What happened? Did something go wrong?" Leanna asked readily. Strange or not, that was the most magical thing she had ever seen.

Finvarra walked to the foot of the bed and raised the quilt to the mannequin's bare shoulders. Stepping back, he whirled his wrist. Magic resumed.

When color crept down the doppelganger's shoulders and lower, Leanna blushed, understanding the need for a quilt. After a moment, fabric flowered along the pale skin. Soon Leanna's exact dress covered the mannequin's naked body and the ribbons Lydia had perfectly tied burned into existence.

Finvarra stepped back and appraised his work.

A spellbound Leanna abandoned her chair and neared him, doing the same. "How did you—where did you—what *are* you?" she breathed.

"I'm a cursed man with dirty hands and nothing more," he said, stained hands up before him in disgust. Leanna tilted her chin toward the basin, where he proceeded to wash his hands.

Tearing her gaze from his somber figure, she sat on the edge of the bed, transfixed by every feature that though her own, seemed so foreign. She trailed a finger along the pointed nose, the sunken, freckled cheeks. Dark circles cradled her eyes and a sad, belonging expression marked her mouth as if she never smiled. Limp brown strands framed her face, making her seem paler, deathlike. Leanna's amazement wilted. Had her loneliness and illness really overcome her so?

She lowered her eyes and ran her gaze along this tomb of everything she was. Sad, miserable, lifeless...

It hit her then.

"I can't do this. There must be another way." She retracted her hand to her crystal. "After our argument, Papa will think I died of sorrow and will only blame himself. He was wrong in forcing me to marry, but he wasn't ever a bad father. He doesn't deserve this."

"I figured as much," Finvarra murmured. He stared at the lifeless figure while drying his hands. Contemplation drew a deep line on his brow. "There is another way," he revealed quietly. "I can make it so she lives."

Hope soared within Leanna. Surely that was the way!

"But," he said, clipping her wings, "it doesn't mean you can return. If I give her life, you will still lose everything. We must leave this place at once and never come back."

A shiver scurried to her limbs at his grave tone. "Because of Machina?"

Finvarra set down the towel and walked to the bed, opposite her. "Machina is bound to come, eventually." He brushed a strand of hair away from the doppelganger's cheek. His finger lingered a moment, then he dropped his hand back at his side. "I can never give her what she wants. But if I grant you this freedom you desire, there will be no doubt that she will appear sooner rather than later. She will smell my magic like the beast she is and will come for blood."

"But my family, will they be in danger? Will she hurt them?"

He looked her straight in the eyes and shook his head. "They mean nothing to me, thus they are safe."

Warmth bloomed in her cheeks. They meant nothing to him, but she did, even if only his tightrope walker. "Then I need you to do this. I need you to give her life."

He sighed weightily, a deep frown at his mouth. "Very well. Once I give her life, she will always be tethered to you, and as long as you live, so will she." He walked around the bed toward her. Leanna shot to her feet, but did not flee. She said she wouldn't fear him and heaven help her she wouldn't.

Cold hands cradled her shoulders and she blinked. Surely he didn't mean... mean to kiss her?

He held her close, his hands an impossible mixture of gentle and firm. "To give her life, I will need some of yours. Breathe," he whispered onto her lips.

Distracted by the intoxicating paradox of his touch, of danger and security, impropriety and belonging, coldness and heat, she couldn't.

The look in his eyes changed and his hands fell away from her shoulders. He took a step back, and with it, his mask of coldness reemerged. But as Leanna had seen it fall once before, she saw the cracks now in his perfect façade of indifference. And in those crevices, his disappointment. *You do fear me,* it said. *In spite of all you say, you fear me and what I may do.*

He made to move away.

She grabbed his hand and stayed him. Closing the space between them, she lifted her face to his. An exhale stole from her mouth: her apology.

Finvarra tilted his head closer, drinking in the white cloud in one slow inhale. Leanna shivered, swayed against him as he drank of her breath and her life, feeling the exchange pull at her soul. Taken by the sweet scent of vanilla on his skin, by the feel of his hand at her shoulders holding her steady, she closed her eyes and let him drink freely.

He released her so suddenly, Leanna stumbled back. Breathless, she pressed back against the wall as he moved to her bedside, her breath caged in his mouth as if his own. Sitting on the edge of the bed, he cupped the doppelganger's chin and whispered words against its lips from behind his veil of hair.

At his words, the figurine's back rounded up with a sharp gasp.

Leanna too gasped.

Finvarra shifted back and pressed a hand gently on her stomach, easing her arched body down onto the mattress. Her eyes remained closed, but her chest now waved with the unbroken rhythm of life. Quiet, Finvarra pulled the blanket up further and watched her sleep a moment.

The minute over, he rose, moved across the room, and recovered his cloak from the reading table chair. He whirled it about him and secured it quickly. "We must leave, now."

There was urgency in his words, and after such a display of magic, Leanna knew Machina would be coming with a vengeance. She rushed to her window and lifted the window seat, where she had hidden her carpetbag. Snapping it open, she thanked the heavens she had at least been wise enough to pack it before Edith came in that morning.

She dashed to her vanity and grabbed her hairbrush and her curling papers. She spun to Finvarra, but her eyes were taken by the girl now sleeping in her bed, in her room, in the only home she'd ever known.

Her throat swelled. Suddenly she felt more alone than ever. "I suppose in the end, I had to lose my life to get my freedom."

"I warned you," Finvarra said.

"I know," was all she could say, because he had.

She turned to the window, where Finvarra stood with a hand extended toward her: the culmination of his promise. Perhaps it was the hand of a demon bathed in silver. Or that of a cursed angel draped in darkness. But there in the shadows, she saw it clearly for what it was: the hand of freedom.

Mastering her sorrow, she met him by the window and slid her hand into his. He drew her close to his side, where a breath was all that kept them apart.

Finvarra parted the curtains, just barely. Outside, the day had grown bright with early afternoon and the gold and amber treetops swayed in the breeze. He let out a slow breath that ruffled against her hair in a like manner and where once he'd drawn her hands down, he now led them to his chest.

"Whatever you do, never let me go," he warned, his arm tight around her waist.

His words died to a blur of black fabric when he whisked his cape around them to the sound of crashing lightning. Enveloped in a violent wind and the scent of vanilla, Leanna felt the ground vanish beneath them.

She never let him go.

# CHAPTER NINE

## HOME

WARMTH MET LEANNA'S SKIN once more. A retreating breeze dragged away the remnants of her scream as her gown danced around her legs in a few rustled sways. The smell of sawdust and paraffin met her nose and patches of faint conversation her ears, but no howling winds were heard.

They'd arrived at the circus.

Home.

She peeled back slowly and blinked the world into focus. Finvarra's chest met her first, the crystal necklace casting a faint rainbow against his shirt. Lifting her lashes, she met the blue eyes of her captor, a small dip in his brow.

"You sure you've no relation to the Banshees?" he said.

She pressed fingers to her lips cognizant of how loud she'd screamed, and no doubt in his ear. "Sorry," she started through her fingers. The curtain rustled sharply and stayed the rest of her words.

"Ringmaster."

Leanna turned to the agitated gruff voice—to Tomas's immense frame blocking the afternoon light that streamed in from outside. He crossed the second layer of curtains and stopped. Dusky brown eyes fixed on Leanna first, flicked to Finvarra, and then lowered to his hands around her waist. He took a futile step behind the sheer curtains. "Forgive me for interrupting."

Suddenly mindful of Finvarra's arm around her, Leanna shifted away, forcing Finvarra's arm from her waist.

"You've interrupted nothing," Finvarra said. He set Leanna's carpetbag down on the chair before his desk and whirled a hand for Tomas to come. The muscled man entered. The burgundy of his ornate vest complemented the reddish undertones of his onyx skin, a direct contrast to Finvarra's snowy complexion. His bald head was smooth and in no way matched his ruggedness.

"I suppose introductions are in order," Finvarra said. "Miss Weston, this is my trusted valet, Tomas."

"A pleasure." Tomas inclined his head as if the prior day had never happened, regardless of the bruise on her arm that belied this belief. Leanna mirrored his greeting and turned her head away, rubbing the concealed bruise. Though his greeting lacked the petulance from the prior night, it didn't excuse him in any way.

Finvarra walked around his desk. "Now then, Tomas, you look concerned." He smiled and small crinkles marked the sides of his eyes. "Did the stars fall from the sky while I was away?"

Tomas swallowed visibly. "I'm afraid not, Ringmaster. We could only be so lucky."

Finvarra laughed, a rich velvety sound, but in noting the concern on Tomas's face, his laugh withered to a grin that disappeared altogether. He reached his chair and cradled the rounded knobs at the wings. "Do I want to know?"

A cool shiver waved through Leanna's body at Tomas's nervousness. For someone that big and intimidating to be so hesitant was disconcerting. "P-perhaps I should go—"

"No," Tomas said at once. "That wouldn't be wise. It would be safer for you to remain here."

In a habit birthed over a lifetime, Leanna clasped her crystal pendant and turned a worried gaze to Finvarra. *Not Machina,* she feared. *Not so soon.*

"Machina cannot cross the crystals," he replied as if having read her mind.

Leanna's eyes widened at this connection, but Finvarra severed their stare. "What's happened?"

"Inara's horn…" Tomas lowered his head. "It has fallen off."

Finvarra leaned forward onto his desk and dug his knuckles into the dark wood, as if wishing to unearth the right words to say. Dread pooled around Leanna's knees and she lowered down into the cushioned chair opposite her travelling purse. She watched Finvarra, trailing the changes on his face—from worry, to anger, to disbelief.

"First my sister, and now this..." He chuckled then, an inhuman laugh that wavered on the thin line between sanity and madness, amusement and anger, surrender and defeat.

"Finvarra!" someone growled from outside. Finvarra's laugh came to a sharp halt. The sidewalls muffled the brusque voice, but its anger was clear.

Tomas came forward. "What would you like me to tell him, Ringmaster?"

Finvarra rose slowly and untied his cloak. He slid it off and draped it behind his chair, gripping the knobs again, his knuckles white. "I must speak to him myself."

Tomas moved closer to the desk. "Do you think that's wise? Krinard will not listen to reason."

"I don't know," Finvarra said. "But I made him a promise. Inara's horn falling is my promise failing. Whether or not he listens, something must be said, and it must come from me."

"Finvarra!"

He lowered his head and let out a breath. At the hearth, the fire wilted with a hiss. In this new muted light from outside, the Finvarra from the prior night re-emerged, not a crack in his façade. His biting stare sent a shiver curling down Leanna's spine. But it was not one of fear. She pitied him greatly.

He set his shoulders back and moved from his desk. Long strides drew him past Leanna as if she didn't exist. With one hand, Tomas brushed aside the sheer curtains and held them open for Finvarra to cross. Finvarra stopped just outside the parted curtains.

"Perhaps it's best you remain in here while I handle this," he murmured the suggestion that was no suggestion at all.

Leanna forced a nod.

Adjusting his black waistcoat, he walked through the curtains. Tomas followed and closed the curtain behind him, taking away the afternoon light.

Leanna rushed from her chair and inched close to the door, just outside of the ray of sunlight. She held her breath and listened.

"What is the meaning of this, Krinard? You're calling me out as if for a duel," he said darkly with an even duskier chuckle. "Why? You've lost to me since we were children. What's changed?"

"A lot has changed, except for you," Krinard said. "But I'm done trying with you. Where is the girl? I hope you were wise enough to kill her before I'm forced to."

Leanna sucked in a breath. Surely he didn't mean that.

"Miss Weston is inside and in my care," Finvarra replied coolly.

"Just as Inara is in mine! It is my duty to protect her from everything and everyone, including you. If I must lay my life down to do so, I will, but you will not drag us further into hell with you, Finvarra. I won't let you."

"Let?" Finvarra laughed—the devil's laugh. "Had I not known you for so long, and did I not know why you're so angry, I might not be so merciful."

A hollow step resounded, bringing Krinard's shadow closer to Finvarra. "Give me the girl or your mercy will be put to the test."

Finvarra took a mirroring step forward.

"Please stop!" Leanna gathered her skirt and rushed through the curtains before another thought.

Murmurs sparked from the gathered troupe at the sight of her. She recognized some faces from the night before. She may have remembered more, had she not then looked at Krinard. First she met black eyes beneath a prominent brow. The rest of him followed suit, tall and fierce. He stood proud, shoulders back and his bare, sculpted chest puffed forward. His black mane kissed his tapered waist, billowing against his olive skin. In dropping her gaze lower, Leanna fought to feign indifference, but could not for the life of her look away from the muscular body of a stallion that graced Krinard's lower half.

But regaining her composure, she said, "Please don't quarrel for my sake. You asked for me and I'm here, ready to answer any of your questions, just as I'm prepared to prove to you that I am not the enemy."

A scathing smile twisted the centaur's mouth. "Don't be fooled, my brothers and sisters," he addressed the troupe over his shoulder. "She comes into the circus and Inara's horn falls. See her for who she is, the enemy masked as a sickly coward. The death of us all!"

The painful pricks of cold at Leanna's skin vanished under the heat rushing through her body. Finvarra didn't look at her, but from the corner of her eye, she noticed his jaw clench. He had told her to stay inside. Krinard's hatred and the hesitation in the rest of the troupe gathered behind him made Leanna half wish she would've listened.

"Now you're quiet." Krinard took one step toward her. "It makes no difference. You don't need to say a word. Your scent tells me everything I need to know. I can smell the black magic on you."

A collective gasp resounded from the troupe.

"That's enough," Finvarra said, a pale hand at Krinard's chest. "You are right, but also wrong. The magic you smell is not Miss Weston's." He lowered his hand and his voice. "It is mine."

Krinard's eyes widened. "You used black magic? You fool! You will lead Machina straight to us!"

"What type of magic I used is of little consequence. Machina is bound to come, you all know this," he replied to Krinard and all the onlookers. "What matters is that Miss Weston is here now."

"Little consequence? You've risked all of our lives for her when she was the cause of this!" Krinard moved so fast, Leanna had hardly any time to process what happened until a thud resounded at her feet. She didn't dare look down. She had an idea of what was thrown at her feet. As Finvarra bent down to retrieve it, all the pieces came together in her mind. If the centaurs from her mother's stories were true, then so were the unicorns.

Finvarra straightened, a long twisted spear in his hands—the snow white horn of a unicorn. He trailed his fingers along the grooves, his frown deepened.

Krinard stomped closer to him. "This world has devoured her magic. We have mere weeks until the crystals fail us and she dies. You promised me this would never happen. You promised me!"

"And I am a man of my word!" Finvarra roared, his composure faltering. Leanna recoiled and the congregation too flinched. His eyes remained downcast, fixed on the horn. He bristled then, as if having heard some distant sound. He lifted his head and the lines of his mouth bowed.

Leanna followed his gaze to where the troupe parted and three centaurs approached. They all shared Krinard's dark features and olive complexion, but whereas Krinard was angry, the rest were deeply saddened.

The source of their melancholy trot behind them: a cloaked horse. A pale white snout peeked out from underneath the black hood, veiled partly by blond strands waving in the breeze.

As they approached, everyone lowered their heads. Leanna thought to do the same, but was unable to look away from the hooded mare that halted just behind Krinard. It whiffed a soft neigh against his back that tousled strands of ebony hair over his shoulders. Krinard moved aside, albeit jadedly, his eyes trained on Finvarra.

The majestic horse strode forward. Finvarra raised a hand to her mane and brushed it away from her eyes, that one act holding more emotion than an apology ever could. A hollow depression marked the center of her forehead.

Inara turned pale gray eyes to Leanna. Grief swam in their depths, a sense of hopelessness, fatigue, heartache, and surrender.

A hand touched Leanna's elbow, Kioyo suddenly beside her. "Come," he said lowly. His warm hands cradled her shoulders and encouraged her away as Inara and Krinard entered Finvarra's tent. Leanna let him, glad to be taken from such a scene. Still, she couldn't help but glance over her shoulder to Finvarra who stood outside the tent, as fallen as the horn cradled before him.

# CHAPTER TEN

## DEGREES OF YEARNING

THE FLAGS ON THE PEAK of the Big Top rustled violently in a new, aggravated wind. Sea mist clung to the outer, overgrown fields of the fairgrounds as if trapping them all in this dream of tents and magic. The crystal stakes were now shadows in the fog, their peaks coalesced with the mist. Leanna's heart sank. With Inara's horn fallen, soon their power would be gone and the circus would be left to the mercy of the greatest of unknowns: Machina.

She forced her thoughts away from such glumness and lifted her gaze to Kioyo. His midnight eyes were focused straight ahead on the black and red tent, as if hypnotized by the swirling sensation they fashioned under the afternoon light. Though he could be no older than Lydia's twenty-one years, the stress upon his brow aged him. And while not in his clown attire, dressed simply in shirt, brown breeches, and an open coat, no paint on earth could ever hide the traces of worry dulling his face.

"What happened to Inara?" she asked. "Why did her horn fall?"

Kioyo shrugged, his frown deepening. "She's been ill for some time, however much Krinard wishes to blame you for it. Some say it's the stress of moving the circus from realm to realm and protecting us against Machina. But we have been away from Forever for many years now, and she has never been like this. It just... happened. Every tonic and elixir Minerva has tried has failed to work. There's nothing else we can do."

His frame deflated with a sigh as they passed the stables. "There's supposed to be no death within the crystals, but with her horn fallen, I'm afraid that is no longer the case."

Leanna took in a quiet breath, thinking she ought to say something, perhaps thank him for drawing her away. She did neither, and spoke not a word of what had transpired. There was no need. It echoed in the silence between them.

Once inside the Big Top, the stillness was dispelled. The violin player from the previous night sat in a small stool at the furthest ring, playing a slow tune. Leanna remembered the melody. It was a slower variation of what played during Ellie and Jin's performance.

The man's brows gathered while playing this somber tune, as if searching for something lost deep in memory. Beside him, a dark haired girl stretched back into herself, creating a perfect loop while balancing on a pole. Effortlessly, she knotted and re-knotted into herself, unable to free her body from this self-made prison. Leanna refused to breathe, scared that the slightest take of air would send the pole wobbling and the girl would fall.

"That is Yelena, our contortionist. And playing the violin is Vicente, our bandleader."

Leanna braved a breath. "It is all so beautiful."

His mouth finally curved into a small smile. "Come." He led them to the nearest ring. "You will see the rest of the performances soon enough. For now, there is practice to be had."

"I wonder," she said, "Why do you all practice if you already know the routine?"

"What else is there to do? We can't leave the protection of the crystals. Well, we can, but who would be foolish enough to do it? This circus is all we have." He patted her hand twice, though she wondered if it was more to soothe his own heart.

He released her arm and walked to the gallery seats, where he fetched a bundle of clothing. "And now, for rehearsals—"

"Wait, wait! You cannot begin, not yet."

Bertrand, the fire breather, strode toward them. He was a jovial man with an upward swept coiffe, sculpted like a stagnant flame. The red tresses remained unmoving in his dramatic approach, and Leanna wondered how much pomade went into the style and then worried as pomade was highly flammable.

He came to a sharp stop before them and held out his hand to her. When she slid her hand into his, he bent over it.

"What now, Bertrand?" Kioyo groaned. "I have work to do."

Straightening, Bertrand scoffed. "Why, I haven't told our dearest fairy girl that I am here for whenever she needs me." With a great exhale, he bowed. "At your service, my dearest Leanan."

Kioyo rolled his eyes. "Let's not frighten the girl."

Leanna smiled. "Nonsense. I'm glad you're here, regardless of, well, of what has happened."

"What happened to Inara is a tragedy, of course. But Krinard is—how do you say it?" Bertrand mused, turning green eyes upward. "Ah, right. He is a lunatic." His thick accent stressed the c, sounding more like a spark of fire. "You are her, I know it, here to inspire hope in this circus. Why else would you have come when we are so close to death?"

The mood between them instantly darkened, but Bertrand warmed the air just as quickly.

"But enough of this gloom," he boomed, and with even more whirling of the hands in extravagant gestures, added, "Now it's time for you to dance. And as you do, I can send beautiful sparks into the sky, making you appear as the angel you are, my divine Sidhe."

At this, a burst of fire shot from his hands and dashed into the distance above. They exploded into crimson streams that by and by dissolved into nothingness.

"How did you… how is it that you all do these wondrous things?" Leanna marveled, forcing her eyes from the remnants of colored fire that evaporated above her. "Those flames came from your hand?"

Bertrand held his hands at his sides and wriggled his fingers. "Where else, my dear? Just as Ellie and Jin had wings, I make fire. I can wield it into anything I like. Hence, the dragons."

"Incredible," she breathed. "And you, Kioyo?"

Kioyo fumbled with the white fabric in his hold. "Unfortunately, my ability is not as mesmerizing as either Ellie and Jin's, or Bertrand's."

"So says the clown that abandoned me on a platform leagues in the air?"

A sad smile tipped his lips. He shrugged. "Perhaps I'll show you some other time, once I have redeemed myself with honorable qualities. But don't expect anything as great as wings or fantastic as fire."

Leanna tilted her head a little. "Well, I'm certain I will find it beautiful and breathtaking."

Kioyo's face reddened and he walked away toward Bertrand at the gallery seats. "Now for that practice," he said, clearing his throat. "Here."

He tossed the bundle he held at her. She caught it blindly, her face suddenly buried behind layers of fabric upon fabric. Peeling them apart, she unearthed a short muslin gown, long hose, and slippers.

"Those were supposed to have been for Ellie," he said when she held up the slippers before her eyes. "You two are about the same size, so they should

80

do."

She clutched the clothing to her chest. "How could I ever thank you? I left in such a hurry, and I'm so unprepared."

"Don't thank me. Thank our seamstress, Minerva—well, don't thank her yet." He paused. "Perhaps you shouldn't thank her at all."

Leanna shot him a curious look. He rubbed the back of his neck and rocked back on his heels with a sheepish shrug. "You see, she doesn't know I've taken these yet."

"I couldn't!" She held the garments out to him. "You must take them back. There is no way I could wear these. After this morning, everyone hates me, and now they'll think me a thief."

"Relax." He eased her hands back toward her. "Minerva wasn't there. She won't be awake until later on this evening, at least until the sun goes down. She has, well..." He trailed off, struggling to frame the right words. "She has an extreme light sensitivity of sorts."

Bertrand snorted. "Yes, the deadly sort of sensitivity. The type that will make you burst into..." He snapped his fingers and sparked an orb of fire in his palm.

Kioyo rolled his eyes and slapped the fiery sphere to the ground. It rolled and extinguished with a hiss. "Never mind him. Minerva won't mind. I will take full responsibility."

Leanna toured her gaze between them, confused. "Well, when she wakes, I would very much like to thank her and apologize, if you don't mind taking me to her."

"Yes, yes, there will be time for apologies, but we must begin, so if you would please go and change," Kioyo said, encouraging her to the back door of the Big Top.

She walked away and didn't quarrel with him any more as she knew she would meet no harm with the likes of Kioyo and Bertrand... or at least she hoped not.

Through the curtain folds at the rear side of the Big Top, Leanna encountered a narrower room connected to the Big Top—the dressing tent. Long tables and mirrors lined the walls, and on the opposite side costumes hung in rows. She would have liked to walk around and trail her hands along the feathers and sequins, even along the chairs, if only to feel the lingering anticipation from past performances. She closed her eyes, imagining how alive she would feel opening day. The mere thought sent her stomach into a series of somersaults. But there would be plenty of times for dreams. She found a secluded area between two racks of costumes and changed as quickly as she was able to with trembling fingers and the cold.

Once dressed, she gathered her things and intended for the door when sight of her reflection gave her pause. She approached the large mirror, transfixed by the stranger staring back at her with bright brown eyes full of hope. Her skin, though still pale, was now more like the delicate petals of a white rose rather than the ashen white of a sickly girl. It was as if the circus infused her with its magic, healing her.

She touched the lace that adorned her bodice and ran her hand lightly along the scooped neckline. Though just for practice, never had she looked so beautiful. She twirled once—twice, giggling at the feel of the light muslin floating in the air. Coming full round, she tucked her necklace between her skin and the soft fabric, gathered up her belongings and rushed back into the Big Top.

At her appearance, Bertrand clapped louder than was necessary. Kioyo's brows rose slightly, his dark eyes unable to hide his approval. A small smile toyed at his mouth. Leanna's face grew hot, but she didn't lower it. Mirroring his grin, she set her previous attire down on the gallery seats and met him at the ring.

"So, Finvarra tells me you're a dancer. What dance experience have you got?" He climbed onto the wooden edge of the ring.

"I danced ballet since I was a little girl. I haven't danced in quite some time, so I fear I may not be very good."

He hummed. "We need to make you better than good."

"You mean magnificent?" she taunted him and herself.

"You've seen the posters, then?" He wrinkled his nose. "We can worry about those later. First we stretch, and then I'll show you the routine as it should be performed."

Stretching, to Leanna's dismay, was as painful as it was hard. It'd been so very long since she'd stretched and pushed her body to such length. Practice from the prior night had taken its toll and she was reminded of it with a pang when she attempted to bend. Touching her toes brought with it a few snaps, reaching to her sides a few cracks. And after a few more pops from numerous bones and joints, she pressed her heels together, mustering up as many memories of lessons, and as much courage as she could manage. She could do this. She had to.

As she lamented her aches, Kioyo explained, "Each show has a theme.

Finvarra likes for each piece to tell a part in the story as a whole. Thus your act must follow within the main story, illustrating your own personal experience with the theme."

"What is the theme for this performance?" she asked.

"Degrees of Yearning. In my act, I make spectators laugh through my desire to learn to ride a unicycle. Bertrand longs to rid the world of darkness. And look there." He pointed to Yelena and Vicente. "Yelena wishes for freedom, but everything she does only enslaves her more. The image of her haunts Vicente's memory as he has loved her all his life and only wishes to help her. Thus they are trapped in this desire, in yearning."

She tore her eyes away from the paradox of beauty and sadness. "And my act?"

"You, my dear, will perform one of Ellie's old performances. We have no time to come up with a new routine and it fits with the theme of yearning, so we will use it. You must call to mind whatever memories you have of an unrequited love and dance such as this…" He twirled once. En pointe he swayed through a series of movements so fluid, he looked to be coming out from within his skin.

The actions evoked sentiments of pain, of ache, of longing, akin to Vicente's song. Leanna forced herself from the awe of watching him dance to pay attention to the actual movements. They were simple enough, a sway here, and twirl there. Simple, yes, but it was more. There was a plea to his every move, to the way he held his hand out to this invisible ghost he desired. Lost in this world of furtive love, his brows furrowed in agony as his fingers extended to the reaches before him, to no one at all who was everything to him in that instant. Leanna found her heart putting words to his florid dance, one of waiting eternities for love, only to have it there, just out of reach.

After various displays, Kioyo bowed and jumped down from the edge and into the ring. He faced her and with an incline of the head, he stepped back.

Leanna moved forward. She rubbed her fingers on her gown, hauling in deep breaths to tame the twisting in her stomach. If only she could have attempted it without everyone around.

She pressed her heels together, but her hips felt tight and the stance awkward. She disregarded this, loosened her hands and extended them at her sides—but no, that was wrong. She lowered them. Looping them before her, Leanna arched her back and put her feet together. Yes, that was right. She took a breath, and… did nothing. She dissolved.

Trying again, she regained her posture, tipped her chin up, and set off on her memory of the routine. She stumbled through the many steps, clumsily bumping into Kioyo at every turn. Arabesques withered into tipping forward, pirouettes led to Kioyo getting hit. Badly she tried to lose herself in the moans of the violin, to somehow liquefy her movements the way Kioyo had done. But her heart pounded its own song, the familiar, erratic tune of fear. Fear of it failing her, fear of her failing everyone.

And so where she was to look as if a blooming flower in a spring sun, she appeared more to wilt under a harsh winter's snow. Where she was to soar like a bird, hesitation clipped her wings and she crashed miserably. Instead of feeling her soul yearn to come out of her body, as Kioyo had done, she felt caged behind the bars of her ribs and those of her dread. Something as natural as breathing became as unnatural as a mechanical heart.

When she managed to reach the end of the routine—what she could remember of it, anyway—she turned to Kioyo and Bertrand.

For a moment, they just sat there, stunned.

Leanna twisted her fingers together at her core. She walked to the ring edge and sat down on the wooden rim. "It's a disaster, I know."

"Not a disaster, no. Well, not exactly." Kioyo leaned forward, a line at his brow. "What are you thinking about while dancing?"

"Getting the routine right, I guess."

"And therein lays your problem. It is about feeling. All the training in the world cannot teach you to feel." He stood, walked to her, and extended a hand. When she slid her hand into his, he tugged her to her feet. "Ellie's routines are not so much about structure and exactness. It is freer flowing. It is your soul pouring out of you through your movements."

With his words, he waved a hand above him and traced a line in the air. On the way down, his fingers trickled like raindrops. He whirled behind Leanna and cradled her elbow, encouraging her arm into the air in a like manner. "Show me how your spirit yearns, how it wants to leave this body only to meet the soul of her love. Think of that one person you love and wish for your own, only they don't know you exist. Better yet, think of your first kiss, of the moment just before, as their lips lingered but a breath away from yours. Only imagine them backing away, taking with them the kiss that should have been."

Leanna's cheeks tingled pink and she lowered her head. "I… I've never desired anyone," she confessed a little under a whisper, wondering whether she should disclose that she'd never had her first kiss either.

"Then it's a good thing you're in the circus, where illusions are our way of life," he said. He encouraged her downcast face upwards with a finger, where he gave her a sly smile. "We will fake it as best we can."

"And what if we can't?" she asked.

Bertrand's face lit up like the very fires he possessed. "Then we will need lots of fireworks."

Rehearsals blurred the hours into a smear of dizzying pirouettes, failed arabesques, and painful echappes. The moon was but a little less than a half in the sky when she finally mastered the routine as best she could. However, the stagnant crease on Kioyo's brow made it clear she still fell short of expectations. After expressing hunger—perhaps a mere guise for frustration—he now led them down the outer path toward the cookhouse until he brought them to a stop before a tent.

"And this one is yours," he said.

Embossed butterflies marked the white canvas. Their wings glittered in the red hue of the torchlight and appeared to flutter as if trapped within. Leanna pressed a hand to the canvas, half expecting to break through the magic that kept them imprisoned and free them all. She parted the curtain of beaded stars and sheer hangings, and swept inside.

White fabric draped the walls and stringed butterflies dangled overhead, their white wings fluttering in a non-existent breeze. Leanna crossed the wooden floors of this magical tent and made it as far as the plush white bed. Just like Finvarra's tent, bookshelves lined the walls. She smiled, seeing some of her favorite books there.

She walked back to Kioyo who remained outside. "Is it really mine?"

"It was Ellie's. The Ringmaster thought you would like it best since you two took to each other so quickly."

Leanna looked toward his white tent in the distance where Tomas manned the door. Though the pavilion was illuminated inside, Leanna knew that no fire or light could soothe Finvarra as he mourned his sister and Inara's horn.

"I wonder how he is," she thought aloud.

"I'm sure he'll be fine," Kioyo said. "He must. Sadly, the show must go on."

"Yes, I suppose it must," she said and bid him goodnight. Kioyo inclined his head and left, assuring her that if there was something not to her liking in the tent, they could speak to Finvarra come morning. But there would be no need, Leanna thought as she watched him leave. The one thing she would change was something that could only be fixed with Ellie's return.

# CHAPTER ELEVEN
## LAMENTATIONS

THAT NIGHT SHE DREAMT of blood and fog. It was the same dream she'd had for years, the vision that began guised as sounds in the dark. Squeaks and moans of hinges in need of oil were trailed by sharp taps and rasps… and whispers. Leanna's mind's eyes narrowed, seeking out the sound. Fog pooled and pulsed around her like the smog encircling the circus, only this mist was thick and black. It beckoned her closer, and she moved toward it. There was something on the other side. Something she needed to know. Instincts told her not to go, but she reached out and touched it.

The urge to run seized her joints, but vines of darkness whipped around her limbs. The touch was human-like, though the blackness had no form. Leanna screamed, but other voices echoed in the fog, feminine, urgent, and scared. The sound overpowered her, their shrilling cries bounced off one another. *Help!* some screamed, *save me* cried others, all underscored by one moaning lament: *Finvarra*.

Leanna struggled, needing to run from the horrible sounds. She froze; something skittered beyond the black. A gashing slice resounded, and the desperate screams united into one loud, resonant *no*. The vines around Leanna's wrist loosened. Blood spilled over the darkness and she knew those girls found death.

Leanna woke to muted light streaming through the skylight. For a minute, she stared at the stringed butterflies, not knowing where she was. It was hard to believe that she was even alive. She had dreamt of Machina. Now that she knew her name, Leanna knew she had dreamt of Machina for years.

"Oh!" A pitched cry came from somewhere in the room.

Leanna turned her head, but groaned; her neck stiff as though she'd spent the entire night shaking her head from side to side—which, she imagined, may have been the case.

Yelena stood across the room. "Forgive me," she said, shyly with a quick curtsy. She clutched a blanket tight to her chest. "I was on my way to practice when I heard you scream. I came in and found you shivering and thought to fetch you another blanket. What awful things you must have been dreaming. You were terrified. I thought to stay here until you woke, in case you were scared. I probably shouldn't have..."

Cheeks reddened, Yelena lifted a hand and adjusted a coral like comb that swept her hair on one side, away from her face. Even in the early hour, her skin glowed and her emerald eyes were bright. Leanna wasn't sure she could say the same for herself, not if she looked the way she felt.

"Thank you. That was very sweet of you."

Yelena smiled. "Of course. Not all of us are as angry as Krinard, you know? But vile as he may be sometimes, it must be hard, unable to do anything to keep the one you love from dying. But don't blame yourself. The Ringmaster told us he asked you to stay and it's hard to resist the Ringmaster's charm. Faerie glamour is supreme, especially the Ringmasters, especially for a human."

Leanna's heart pounded. Finvarra, *a faerie?* She flipped through the many pages of books in her mind, recalling every fact she knew of the mythical creatures that though appearing human were, in fact, magical beings. There had been tales of their exceeding beauty, of their control over the elements, of their glamour. Other stories spoke of them appearing and disappearing at will, of their mischievousness.

"Then you are a faerie, too?" Leanna asked.

"A Merrow," she corrected her, kindly. "The last addition to Finvarra's Circus, well, now there's you, of course. A great honor, you know? Not everyone is asked to perform for this circus. Your family must be proud."

The words stung. Leanna gazed down, hating how viciously her heart ached for people who conspired against her, how her eyes watered for people who would never miss her. She would not cry. Not for them. What for?

With Inara's gloom mounted on her own, and the memories of those innocent girls, a tear escaped her anyway.

"I didn't mean to upset you. I heard you left your home quite suddenly so I imagined this to be the case. But you got to say goodbye, yes?"

Leanna batted the tear away. "I suppose, just not under the best of circumstances."

"It seems they never are. When I left my home, I thought it was for a day. That was ages ago." Pacing away, she stroked the braid that hung over her shoulder, her gaze more distant with each stroke. "We Merrows are given a cap in our youth that allows us to visit the surface. It is a gift from our distant cousins, the Sirens. I lost mine. My mother always said I was too careless with it. She was right." She swept a teary gaze to Leanna. "Sometimes I feel that, no matter what I do, I will never get it back. I would do anything to go home."

Leanna watched her, Yelena's lamentations stoking at Leanna's own. She frowned. Even if not under the best circumstances, she should have been grateful to have said goodbye, but it was impossible, the memory of their betrayal feeling to map her veins with pain.

Later that morning, she danced without rest. Nice as he was, Kioyo was ruthless when it came to training her. If Leanna didn't know any better, she would have thought *again* was the only word he knew. At times it was as though he was the one with something to prove, but she couldn't be sure. He never revealed anything of his life, or who—or what—he was. Come to think of it, Leanna thought as she followed him up the ladder, she didn't know anything about him at all. They reached the small platform, and she forgot about this.

They'd been rehearsing on the thin ring's edge, getting her comfortable with the routine and limited surface. Bruises lined her body, and try as she might, Leanna could never get the sawdust out of her hair. But, now on the platform, she wished she would have asked for one more go at the routine on the ring's edge.

Lightheaded, she shot a hand beside her and grasped the banister tightly. The platform, it seemed so much higher from the ground than days before.

Unaware of her turmoil, Kioyo walked out onto the rope. Dizzy, Leanna leaned back against the handrail, a clammy hand pressed to her forehead.

Kioyo turned with a heavy sigh. "This is—"

He was beside her in a flash, warm hands cradling her shoulders. "What's the matter? Is it your heart? Are you in pain? Should I get the Ringmaster?"

She shook her head no and clutched Kioyo's shirt, focused on his hands on her shoulders, on her hands upon him. He was unmoving. Stable. He was there.

"I'm sorry. It appears I underestimated my fear. Being up here again, it's..." She let a long, hollow breath speak for her.

Kioyo's hands dropped from her shoulders. "This is exactly the same as below, just the wire is a bit thinner than the ring's edge. That's all."

"And much higher," Leanna murmured.

With a heavy *are we going to do this again* sigh, Kioyo took a step back and folded his arms over his chest.

"Before you threaten to leave me up here by myself again, may I just say now that I do believe in magic," Leanna said readily. "I do, but the last time, I had Jin and Ellie to catch me. What if—just what if I should fall? Not that I don't trust you, but it seems you have no wings..."

"No, I don't have wings. But should you fall and I am unable to reach you in time," he pointed upwards with a grin, "They will."

Leanna followed the gesture. There was nothing there but darkness and the fireflies that drifted along the tent peek. They floated aimlessly, marking the expanse with glittering streaks of gold. Others framed the pillars and crossbars like stringed lights. There were hundreds, if not thousands, but surely Kioyo didn't mean them.

Answering her unasked question, Kioyo lifted an open hand into the air and whistled a strange, high pitch whirr. Within moments, one of the fireflies, a shade brighter than the others, detached from the crossbars of the tent. It floated down, creating loops of iridescent light that sprinkled away like the sparks of Bertrand's fireworks. The small orb landed in Kioyo's waiting hand.

The display of lights was lovely, but Leanna frowned. "And how exactly is a bug supposed to keep me from falling?"

The small firefly rushed her, streaking the air around her with wild flashes of light. Leanna yelped and crouched down, clutching onto the pillar while swatting away at the bothersome insect.

After torturous seconds at the tiny hands of the nipping light, a laughing

Kioyo reached out and cupped the firefly in his hand. "There, there, Luna. Settle down. She doesn't know any better."

Brushing madly at her hair, Leanna grunted. "I could have fallen!"

"Then you shouldn't call them bugs, or insects for that matter, unless, of course, you want to upset them." Kioyo smiled down into his cupped hands. "I think you owe Luna an apology."

Leanna crossed her arms over her chest and scoffed. She'd nearly been sent off the edge of the platform and *she* had to apologize? "Well, what exactly am I apologizing to?"

Kioyo held his hands toward her and unfurled his fingers. In the crevice of his joined palms was, "A pixie. They are the harness should something ever go wrong."

The orb of light was the size of a nail, but at the bright core was the faint outline of a person—a very small person with wings akin to sheer, iridescent leaves. Though its light appeared yellow, at center it flicked through a kaleidoscope of colors. It was difficult to make out her face, but not the unmistakable glare.

"Oh, my…" Leanna drew closer to Kioyo's outstretched hands. "I am so sorry, little pixie. I didn't know, but I do now. Indeed, you are no bug, or insect, and I won't ever make the mistake again." Leanna opened a hand and held it out before her.

The pixie whirred and floated into her palm. Leanna giggled at the prickle of its wings against her palm, still unable to believe her eyes. There was a real pixie in her hands!

"It appears you've been forgiven. Now that introductions have been sorted, we dance. Go on, Luna. Assemble the others."

Nearing his face to the pixie, Kioyo blew a sharp breath and knocked Luna from Leanna's hands. With a high pitch squeak that tickled Leanna's eardrums, Luna zipped toward a laughing Kioyo who shielded himself from the buzzing attacks. After a few playful nips, Luna dashed away in glittering circles to her counterparts above.

The army of pixies detached from the pillars and abandoned the tent peak, their sound that of faint sleigh bells. Some hovered a slight above the rope, others just below. The rest scattered about like stars in a night sky.

"We will start with a simple stroll across. Follow my lead, okay?" Kioyo stepped backwards onto the rope. "Keep your back arched and stomach in. But most of all, remember—"

"No fear." Hauling in a deep breath, she slipped her hand into Kioyo's and her foot onto the rope.

Kioyo's hand was warm, very warm, especially compared to Finvarra's. Under the gilded shade of the pixies, she parceled him, partly out of curiosity and part to busy her mind from the thin wire beneath her feet, from the distance between her body and the ground.

Instead she mused on what creature lay just beneath Kioyo's honeyed skin and chocolate brown eyes. Something exotic and beautiful, certainly. She took in his arms, lean and sculpted. *And strong...*

"A wolf—no, no—a lion?"

Kioyo stepped back. "Pardon me?"

"You're a lion. You're warm, and fast, and strong. You have great sense of balance, and you're quite graceful. I say you're a lion."

Kioyo shifted back, the corners of his lips curled upward. "Flattered as I am that you think so highly of me, there is only one lion in this circus, and that is Kia."

Leanna frowned. "A hint, then?"

His smile faded. "What I am, I don't deserve to be. I'm not ready to have you think badly of me."

The weight of his regret clenched Leanna's heart. She squeezed his hands. "Never mind I asked, okay?" She took a hesitant step forward. "I would be happy to know anything about you like... dancing. Tell me instead how you ended up as part of this circus and how you learned all of Ellie's routines."

"Well, this wasn't always a circus—not an actual circus, at least." Kioyo paused, taking inventory of her posture. He lifted her arm a little higher, level with her shoulders and tipped her chin up a touch. Pleased, he continued his story and walk. "In Forever, every solstice is a time of celebration. There are festivals all throughout the land in the days leading up to it, but the greatest celebration is on the night of the solstice, within the ice palace."

"You mean the one from the night Ellie and Jin were forgiven?"

He smiled and nodded. "It was all I heard of while growing up, tales of performers travelling from all over Forever and its neighboring lands just to perform for the king under the ever falling snows and light of the pixies. Only the best of the best were given audience. If you were good enough, you were welcomed to stay and perform on behalf of the kingdom the night of the solstice. All palaces had similar celebrations and troupes, but no one topped Forever's, and well—"

Leanna stumbled forward. Feeling solid ground beneath her, she let out a breath, not having realized they'd reached the opposite platform. The pixies whisked off with a pitched whirr and repositioned themselves. Kioyo too turned, and they set off on their promenade of the rope once more.

Finding her steps with more ease, Leanna listened as Kioyo went on. "I didn't stand a chance. Dancing wasn't allowed in my village, just fighting and politics and war. Everyone who had come to audition trained their entire lives under the greatest instructors, with musical arrangements composed just for them. I practiced secretly in an icy cave with only the droplets of melting icicles as song. But I loved dancing. It had always been the only way I could let go of all the frustrations I built up from my people, of the disappointment I was to them."

Kioyo's eyes unclouded and he cleared his throat. "You're stiff. Feel the rope. It is an extension of you. This bond must be solidified."

Leanna sensed him trying to brush the memories back under this wall of indifference he'd erected over so many years. Understanding his pain, she let him. "How do I solidify this bond?"

"With a dance, of course." He nodded once and took one step forward, one step back. "One, two, three. One, two, three..."

Light pressure came along her spine, the pixies lined up behind her. She smiled and followed Kioyo's impromptu dance.

"I auditioned with a piece I choreographed and gave it my all, but I was still rejected," Kioyo continued. "I gave up everything to go. My family, my home, and I failed like everyone told me I would. But then, just as I turned to leave thinking I'd never dance on that icy floor again, a snow angel floated down before me."

"Ellie," Leanna whispered.

Under the pixies glow, Kioyo's eyes glinted the way a rippling pond reflects the light of the moon. "She put a hand on my shoulder and told me that just as my dream was dancing in Forever, her dream had been to dance as beautifully as I just had. Though she and Jin were already an act, I was offered to join the troupe and choreograph some routines for them. Eventually, a clown was needed and I took on the role."

Stepping back onto the platform they'd then reached, Kioyo saw Leanna off and smiled. It never reached his eyes. "That is my story, dear girl. I got to dance for Finvarra's troupe, and Ellie got to dance as beautifully as she'd always wished. We made each other's dreams come true and, well, here I am." The last of his words faded to a broken whisper.

He leaned back onto the veranda and was silent a moment. "It hurts not having her around," he said as sullen as the shadows they stood in. "I miss her, and Jin. And as much as I don't like to think of it, I miss my home, whatever is left of it."

Leanna came up alongside him. Never did she wish to be a muse as much as she did there. She thought to tell him that he would see them again, or that it would all get better. Yet, remembering the times it was said to her, she kept quiet. Nothing she could say would alleviate his pain, but she could stand with him so he would not be so alone in his sadness.

Their rehearsals over, they walked down one of the many paths toward the cookhouse. With the show a little over a week away, Leanna hoped rehearsals had gone somewhat better. Whereas the previous day, Kioyo's face had all but told her her attempts were less than acceptable, this night, she did not know what to think. He had carried his somber mood since earlier in the day, and not even Luna's taunts dispelled this. Curling into her cloak, Leanna merely walked beside him, and hoped that if she was supposed to be this muse of inspiration, she could perhaps bring him some joy, even if only a little.

She stopped abruptly, halting Kioyo's steps as well. A hooded white horse crossed the field a distance away, alone. She bit her lip. Perhaps if she went to her, to introduce herself, and apologize—

"Don't even think about it," Kioyo muttered from beside her. "Krinard will never allow you to talk to her. Look." He jutted his head toward the cookhouse. "He's watching her like a hawk until she enters the tent."

"I need to do this." She watched Inara until she vanished into the dark tent, determined. "You're right, he watched her go in, but he has looked away." And he had, now deep in discussion with Bertrand. "This is my chance. I will say what I need to say and be gone before he realizes I've been there. I only want to see how she is, and introduce myself, and let her know that I mean no harm."

Before Kioyo could disagree, she drew closer. "Please, Kioyo, I'm not asking for your permission, just your support. I would feel safer with you by my side, but you can turn away and pretend you never saw me enter. I won't hold it against you in any way."

A deep crease marked his brow, and his stare flitted across the field. "But Krinard…"

"Inara is ill and alone. I know all too well how she feels. It hurts, and I can't just leave her there to suffer this alone as I did. Sometimes a smile would have brightened my day, would have made my illness more bearable. Please. Even if she runs me out, at least I will have tried."

There was a pause where Kioyo looked to the tent, to the cookhouse, to the tent, then back to Leanna.

He groaned and dragged a hand through his hair. "You must be the Leanan Sidhe driving me to this madness. Come on, then."

Leanna allowed herself the sigh she'd gathered in her chest in wait for his reply. As he laid down their plan, she listened intently and trembled, but from cold or nerves, she wasn't sure.

Kioyo held a finger over his lips. On prompt, they took off between the tents. Their hands bridged them together as they found their way under the cover of night. Leanna's heart slammed wildly against her ribs like death knocking at her soul's door, yet she had never felt more alive than she did there, with the cold, damp grass bleeding through her slippers, with Kioyo's warm hand never letting her go as they dashed across the grassy field toward risks unknown.

With the invisible fingers of the wind pushing them toward their destination, they ducked outside the ring of lamplights and passersby, and reached Inara's tent undetected. Another count and Kioyo steered them inside.

The world fell away for Leanna, bowing out to the sight of Inara lying alone in the only stream of light coming in from outside. On her side, Inara's whitish mane spread on the grass in rippled rows that glistened like spider silk in the faint light. Around her, buds of snowdrop flowers sprouted from the earth with each of her inhales and died with each exhale.

*"You're not supposed to be here."*

Leanna's brows gathered. Inara hadn't made a sound, and yet the soft, feminine voice echoed in her head as though a thought.

She neared her. "Did you just speak?"

Inara lifted her head and focused snowy eyes on her. *"As my guardian and mate, Krinard can hear me. Finvarra as well, but it is his sovereign right. I suppose some abilities are extended to you by the crystal you wear."*

Leanna drew the white rock from inside of her dress.

*"Just as beautiful as I remember it. I am glad to have seen it again before I…"* Her eyes dimmed, and sighing, she lowered her head to the blanket of dead flowers. *"Before I join the stars again."*

Kioyo hissed and rolled his arms for Leanna to hurry.

*"But that is not the reason you are here..."*

Leanna forced her mind to the task at hand. "I know I should not be here," she said, "but I've come to introduce myself, and to let you know that despite what Krinard thinks, I am not the enemy. If I caused your horn to fall or made you sick in any way, I'm sorry. I know what it feels like to be ill and alone, and I would never wish that on anyone else."

Inara stared in silence for a moment. *"I do not blame you, Leanan. It is not your fault my horn has fallen."* She lowered her head. *"Or that Krinard is too afraid and stubborn to accept the truth."*

"Truth?" Leanna whispered.

*"Fear drives out all magic."* A shimmering tear trickled from Inara's eyes like the dying remnants of a shooting star. *"I fear every day."*

"Fear what? Machina?"

*"Krinard and Finvarra,"* she said, weak and solemn. *"I fear what this circus is doing to them, what they do to each other, to themselves. We were like family before all of this—circuses and statuses and Machina, but now Krinard blames Finvarra, just as Finvarra blames himself. He has given up. They are losing themselves to this blackness and I do not know how to keep them from it. My wisdom has failed me and I fear I will lose them to their hate and desperation, long before ever losing them to Machina."*

She let out a weary breath. *"And I am losing myself. I used to love to simply ride, but this grief consumes me and I can't bear to move. I am tired, Leanan. So very tired. Caught in between these crystals, all I can do is wait for death at the hands of sorrow or at the rusted hands of Machina."*

Leanna opened her mouth, but emotions gathered in her throat and consumed her words.

"I smell Krinard. He's coming," Kioyo hissed behind her, angling his body to peer outside of the curtains. "We need to go!"

*"Go,"* Inara said. *"And thank you for coming, Leanan. I am glad to have seen the crystal again."* She bowed her head onto Leanna's lap and shed one more tear. *"Hopefully your arrival will make Krinard see beyond his anger and hope once more."*

Leanna gathered up her skirt and tucking the necklace back within her dress, scurried to Kioyo at the door. She turned back to the dying unicorn that lowered her head onto the damp ground, defeated. Her heart strummed. Too many times she had laid the same, cried the same...

Conviction swelled. She tore away from Kioyo's hand and fell back down beside Inara. "You must make do with what you have," she spoke hurriedly. "Forget about all else and ride because you can't imagine not doing so. Not for Krinard. Not for Finvarra—"

"Leanna!" Kioyo whispered.

"Ride because you yearn for freedom, because if you don't feel the breeze at your hair, because if you don't feel the blood bursting through your veins, because if you don't go faster with each step, you will go mad."

"Leanna!"

"Even if you falter and fall, ride again because it is what you truly love, what you are meant to do. Ride because if you don't, you will surely die."

Kissing Inara's whitish mane, Leanna pushed back to standing and ran to Kioyo's outstretched hand.

Together they slipped out into the shadows of the night.

# Chapter Twelve
## Asleep & Awakened

A PLATE OF HEARTY SOUP sat untouched for a long while before Leanna. As if a looking glass, all she saw in between the chunks of potatoes and meat, crimson broth and curls of smoke that soon vanished, were Inara's eyes, and the pale mare lying in the dark, surrounded by her fellow horsemen and her fear. No longer able to stand the quiet haunting, Leanna fashioned a pretext of being tired—which wasn't entirely a lie—and excused herself from supper. She had to speak to Finvarra of his war with Krinard, of Inara and her fear. She had to see him.

And so she stood now in the shadows, a distance away from Finvarra's illuminated tent, her eyes focused on the doorway blocked by Tomas. Conviction moved her forward toward the tent, determined. One step, and then another. Her heart pounded fiercely the closer she drew, drumming the beat of her approach. She was going to see Finvarra. She hadn't seen him all day, but she was going to see him now—

She stopped abruptly, a little breathless all of a sudden. There was no pain, no. Only a strange airiness that suddenly possessed her heart and made it flutter a little lighter, a little faster…

Her brows furrowed at this new sensation. It was almost as if she were nervous, she mused, taking inventory of her feelings. Maybe she was nervous, anticipating even. Perhaps she *wanted* to see him—

*Nonsense*, Leanna reprimanded her thoughts with a shake of her head. She wasn't accustomed to all being demanded of it. She'd exerted herself more that day than she had in years. She was … adjusting, Leanna told her meddlesome conscience. That was all. Setting her jaw, she started again toward the tent.

She paused. After what transpired with Krinard, no doubt Finvarra was somewhat annoyed with her. He'd only be more bothered knowing she'd meddled in his private affairs—*again.*

Yes, Leanna decided, and turned away from his tent. Maybe it was best she leave and come back later. But Inara...

"Miss Weston." Tomas's gruff voice rumbled behind her and halted her steps. Leanna whirled to see he held the curtain open. "The Ringmaster wishes to see you."

Leanna dithered, but closing the space between them, she passed Tomas and strode through the curtain.

The light of a blazing fire cast dancing shadows along the room. Finvarra sat before this flame, though Leanna could not see his face. With the back of the chair toward her, only his arm was visible on the arm rest, and in his hand, a snifter of brandy. One leg was crossed over the other, the golden hue of the fire reflected on his polished black boots. An air of calm radiated from his quiet frame like a fog, and in its midst, Leanna forgot what she had gone there to say. Truth be told, she could have curled up at the chair beside him and gone straight to sleep.

Against this effect of him, she clung to the image of Inara and her pain, and cleared her throat. "You wished to see me?"

Finvarra sighed slowly, and before him the fire grew agitated. The shadows hovering high in the ceiling waved in a like manner. "I believe we said we would free one another," he said finally, his tone calm, the vocal manifestation of the serene air in the room. "I've upheld my end of our bargain, have I not?"

Leanna nodded as if he could see her. She paced forward a few steps, enough to bring her through the sheer curtains, but did not near him. "You have."

Finvarra turned his face, though it remained veiled by the chair. "Then, Miss Weston, give me a taste of what is due me, of what awaits me when you fulfill your part of the agreement."

Leanna moistened her lips, her throat dry. "How do you suppose I do that, sir?"

A dark chuckle resounded, a drawled sound. "Surely not by speaking to me from across the room," he said, and before she could answer, Finvarra transferred the goblet into the unseen hand and gestured to the chair beside him. "Sit with me..."

One moment, she stood by the sheer drapes. The next she neared his beckoning hand though she didn't remember her mind ever making the choice to move. But something did, and now tentative steps drew her closer until she reached the chair opposite his and sat down.

In the stillness, Leanna braved a glance and took in the man beside her. His black attire had been replaced by tanned breeches and a white shirt carelessly open at the collar. Blond strands were tied back, leaving his face unobstructed for Leanna's consideration. And she considered him, watching him as he watched the flames.

"I am here," she said, "Though I hardly see how my sitting with you could possibly free you as you have me."

"Freedom from the clutches of my thoughts is taste of plenty." It was then Finvarra who considered her. Trapped in his stare, it felt like roses bloomed in her face, the deep red pricking her cheeks from the inside. Leanna looked away. Still, she felt his gaze linger, travelling along her in quiet scrutiny, first at her coat, then the muslin gown and hose from practice, to the slippers.

Leanna bit her lip, hoping he didn't ask.

"You've been by to see Minerva, I see."

"Not yet. Kioyo was kind enough to get me some things for rehearsal," she said, sure to omit his thievery, "but I haven't been to see her yet."

Finvarra hummed, a low, guttural rumble within his chest. "But you have been paying calls to others."

"I beg your pardon?"

Blue eyes flicked to her hands folded at her lap, and his brow arched pointedly. When Leanna trailed his stare, all blood drained from her face. Slowly she lifted her hands before her eyes, awed. They sparkled as if doused in a pool of dissolved stars. "What on earth?"

"Unicorn tears." He took a sip of his brandy and said nothing more.

Leanna set her hands on her lap gradually, her face warm. "Fine, yes, I visited Inara. She was sad, and I felt it wrong to leave her there to suffer this alone and fearful." Haunted by Inara's confession, she deflated. "And I think it sad that no one felt the need to be with her, to reassure her when she needs it most." She looked at Finvarra and her heart strummed, hurt and angered, just as she'd felt after each prognosis she was given, and then left in her room to grieve them alone. "No one."

Finvarra swirled the amber liquor in his cup. "I have comforted her," he said, too casually for Leanna's liking. "But fear in Machina is not something I can alleviate—"

"She fears for you," Leanna clipped. At her sound, Finvarra paused. "She fears for you and Krinard, and it's this fear that has robbed her of her magic and of her horn."

He slid a frigid stare to her, watching her closely. "And she told you this?"

Leanna nodded. The volatile mood in the room wavered between wrath and gloom. Not until Finvarra nodded to himself, did she dare another word. "This war between you and Krinard is draining her, and she's scared that she will lose you both to this hatred you each harbor, before she ever loses you to Machina. She cares for him and for you, deeply. Losing you will be her undoing."

Finvarra's frame hitched with a bitter chuckle. "Her fear for me is futile, and I hope you told her this in the midst of your meddling."

"Why would I ever tell her such a thing?"

"Because you of all people know I've long drowned."

Leanna blinked, her mind awash with memories of nights before, of blood stained skies and tumultuous oceans. She clasped the crystal pendant and broke away from his stare.

Finvarra let out a heavy breath and set down his cup. "I said I would try my best to make this arrangement as painless as possible. I expected the same from you."

"I don't think I've done otherwise. I visited—"

"You visited Inara, which will bring nothing but trouble, same as the trouble from this afternoon." Finvarra shook his head and turned back to the fire. "I had asked you to stay inside."

The quiet reprimand settled in the pit of her stomach and her anger flared. "You did, but it was all a misunderstanding and I refuse to let anyone quarrel for my sake. Above all, Krinard was—*is* your friend, and he was angry and bereft. Yes, his behavior may have been violent and untoward, but sympathy leads me to let go of my own anger and pardon his offense. And Inara would not be in this situation if others were to cast aside their pride and do the same."

He turned to her at this, wintry eyes freezing the words on her lips. After a long pause, he exhaled and looked away. "He frightens you," he said, abandoning his previous reproach.

"A little," Leanna confessed just over a whisper, surrendering her own upset.

His jaw clenched ever so slightly. "Krinard may have been angry, but he's no fool. He would never touch you. You're safe here, you know this."

Again, he turned to her, and in this nocturnal privacy, her breaths arrested at once. She found no strength to nod while staring into those eyes that undid every lock of strength and bolt of pride. It seeped past all the layers of indifference she'd erected over many years of solitude, and appealed to her soul. The soul that had in fact been deathly terrified of Krinard. The soul that had not known it was safe. The soul that now did.

A furious heat stole through Leanna's body, and against this new warmth of protection, the crystal grew cold against her skin. Shaken at feeling him so present within her soul, to the point she was certain words were no longer needed for them to communicate, Leanna severed their stare. "What will happen to Inara?" she asked, a little breathless.

Finvarra took a sip, watching her over the rim. He swallowed slowly. "It depends."

"Depends on?"

He settled back, and his head lolled back to the play of lights and shadows above. "On when my Leanan Sidhe arises."

It took Leanna a moment to digest this, but as it went down, awareness burned bitter and cold. "So then you don't...you don't think that I am her?"

Finvarra didn't answer. Standing, he walked away from her. An unnaturally long draft swept around the room, coolly, and like his hope in her, the fire at the hearth dwindled to a faint flame that abandoned them in more darkness than light.

"There are legends about her, about my Leanan Sidhe," he started, focused on the shadows of this new darkness. "Stories about her beauty, dark and otherworldly. Tales about her inspiration that burns like fire. And about her gifts, one in particular I desire." He stared before him, unblinking, as if seeing her there.

"I've thought of her, constantly. Every day she trespasses onto my thoughts and daydreams, to where now I know her, how she smells, how she feels, how she tastes. Then one night, she didn't trespass onto my dreams. She trespassed onto my circus." He turned his head to Leanna. "But where tales say she is a beauty, fierce and unearthly, she has come to me bathed in mortal flesh, the mere, delicate beginnings of a woman. Inexperienced and insecure, and unable to bear the direct gaze of a man. Where I imagined her as fire, steady and burning, she stands here with me now, a weary spirit with a broken heart. She is not the gilded angel of my dreams, not even a shadow." He shook his head slowly. "I have made many mistakes in my life, Miss Weston, and they only fray at my conviction. They tempt me to doubt that you are her. You can't be her."

Leanna bristled, disappointment crashing into depths she never knew existed. She had known that it was all an error all along. She was no muse, and how could she inspire a circus that hated her? But to hear it from his mouth...

The room grew smaller around her, colder, and she could no longer bear being there.

Finvarra opened his mouth to speak—

"Please," she held up a hand, "say no more. I don't fault you. With Inara's horn falling, I'm sure you aren't the only one disillusioned." She shrugged weakly. "Maybe hope and desperation led us to... to believe things that aren't so." She laughed a little then, a bit too cheery. "Come to think of it, it was all a little ridiculous, but thankfully we have come to our senses now. Yes...I should go."

She turned away from him before he could see the tears in her eyes. Oh, she had been a fool to think she was special. An absolute fool to let herself get carried away by his preposterous notion.

"But then I look at her hands..." he said.

Wish as she did against it, her steps halted. She should have walked out, and every fiber of her mind begged her to do this. But footfalls resounded quietly behind her, and she could think no more.

He stopped just behind her, and taking her hand into his, he raised it before her like a gift, cradled tenderly in his own. "But then I look at her hands, so small and fragile, unblemished. It is then I understand that legends and stories are meant for children. As a man, I realize that though being everything I never imagined her to be, she has come exactly as she is supposed to—a reminder of everything I ever did, of everything I am ashamed of. Of all the innocence I've robbed and lives I've ruined. *I* know this, only now it is she who does not know who she is."

Leanna twisted to him. His eyes seized hers, and he didn't release her. Rather, he curled his hand gently, folding hers into the protection of his long, cold fingers. "She knows not of this soul she carries within her because it has been silenced and has fallen asleep under proprieties and woes, broken hearts and loneliness. But she is in there, within this body, and only when she is awakened will she bring me the inspiration I seek.

"So do I doubt you?" He shook his head, just barely. "No, Miss Weston, I don't doubt you. You may not be what I dreamt, but whether human or troll, banshee or witch, you are my punishment and my forgiveness. You are my Leanan Sidhe, and I could never deny you."

The riddle of his words left her with so many questions, but rapt in his stare, by his touch, she was frozen. Lured by the slight scent of vanilla and maleness on his skin, she was intoxicated. With their respective crystals glistening between them, intentions fell into a house of mirrors, and she could not decide whether to move away or closer.

And then there was the new and strange twisting in the darkest depths of her stomach as if a butterfly were caged—no, not a butterfly, but a bird. This caged fowl burned and fluttered madly within her. And in the closing space between them, Finvarra's warm breath stole its way into her parted lips and fueled the bird's flame. It rattled with more vigor, struggled to be freed, yearned to soar and spread those wings as if to fan the flames of sun itself.

But, imprisoned behind bars of proprieties, and stifled under the ignorance of an inexperienced girl, Leanna's heart pounded sharply, jolted with awareness. Realizing where she was, seconds away from his lips, she sucked in a quiet gasp and shattered the spell between them.

Finvarra let out a slow breath, the corners of his lips bowed. He didn't move away, didn't say a word. He only held her and looked at her as the confirmation of his words echoed all around them. Lowering his lashes, he lifted her palm between them and pressed a soft kiss upon it.

"Goodnight, Miss Weston," he whispered and lowered their entwined hands. He gazed down at her palm a moment before releasing her, and stepped back.

Frozen, Leanna didn't move away. Not at first. She could only stand there as the firebird within her crested to a painful flame, then dissolved into nauseating ashes. Confused, ashamed… terrified, she turned away, parted the curtains and swept uneasily into the night.

She moved blindly past Tomas toward anywhere. Anywhere that would give her freedom from this sudden confusion. Anywhere that would keep her from going against manners by walking back into that tent to discover more of this firebird within her. Anywhere away from Finvarra, the only person who'd ever ignited it within her.

She may have floated or walked. Leanna reached her room and sat on her bed, unsure. She sat for a long time, until only faint warmth lingered in the air, the flames now but embers glowing in the fireplace. She ought to have lit the firebox. She knew how. But there were things she didn't know, and those were more troublesome than the cold.

Leanna opened her palm at her lap and shook her head. He'd kissed her hand. And she'd left.

She curled her fingers into a loose fist and sighed. She had indeed left. She had done the logical thing. The appropriate thing. The thing those older and more seasoned than her had taught her as being proper.

But if so, she wondered, what of this deep loneliness? What of this hollow emptiness that though at a time was her daily companion, now felt like the most unnatural of sensations?

*Yes, what of that?* Her heart mused. *What of that?*

Leanna remained transfixed by her thoughts, until the room fell into complete and utter black. Still, she found no comfort in the dark. She could only stare down at her hand glisten with the faint hue of unicorn tears, yearning for a kiss that should have been.

# Chapter Thirteen
## A Gift of Song & Truth

SOMEWHERE BETWEEN A SETTING MOON and a looming sun, Leanna burrowed into her cloak, her sights and steps directed toward the Big Top. The gentle giant stood tall, the bluish gray of the coming day softening its edges, making it appear more like a dream.

Inside, the band tuned their instruments, readying, but the rings were empty. More troublesome, Kioyo wasn't there. Leanna turned out to the fairgrounds, to the tents in the distance. One of the tents had to be Kioyo's, but which?

"Excuse me, Miss," came a voice from behind. Leanna whirled to Vicente waving her over with a thick hand. He met her at the foot of the stage and bowed, brushing back peppered strands that fell over his brown eyes.

"I don't think we've had the honor of introducing ourselves," he said, and presented himself and his five-member band. They looked to be gypsy and this warmed Leanna's heart. A gypsy caravan had once travelled through the outskirts of Winter Abbey, and with her father away, Mrs. Weston had taken the three sisters to see them in the outer fields where they were camping. Of all things, Leanna remembered their music the most.

Introductions complete, Vincente said, "We apologize for not doing so earlier, but we were worried Krinard may have been right. But it was wrong of us to exclude you, and we are sorry."

"It's been forgotten," she assured him. "I understand your worries and can assure you I mean this circus no harm."

"We know, little Sidhe, and as such, I would very much like for you to hear this." He walked back to his small stool and retrieved a polished violin. "You see, I saw your difficulties yesterday and know what the problem is."

Leanna cringed with a wry chuckle. "That I'm a lousy dancer?"

He smiled. "No, little one. The problem is that the song from yesterday

106

was not written for you, and thus you could not connect." He put a hand to his heart, bow in hand. "When I compose a song for a performer and their act, I must see them and feel their spirit." He pressed his lips together as if searching for the right words. "That song you performed to yesterday was Ellie's, born of her pain and her frustrations, out of her dreams and her love. But when I saw you on the rope yesterday, it was as if a flame had been lit. I saw you. I saw your spirit." Brown eyes gleamed with keen joy. "I saw your song."

"Oh, my..." Appreciation left her winded. "I—I'm very grateful, and honored, but the routine I'm performing isn't mine. It was Ellie's old act. You don't have to trouble yourself to compose a song for me."

His brows gathered and his eyes grew distant with understanding. "Then you have two problems, my dear. Perhaps you not only had the wrong song, but also the wrong dance." He nodded to himself. "Yes, yes, that is it. Listen to the song and let your heart decide what is right."

She opened her mouth, but closed it. How could she refuse him when he had worked so hard on her song? Surely her mother had taught her better than that.

Vicente lifted a hand. In queuing the band, he closed his eyes. On the count of three, the trickling keys of the piano resounded. The violin eased in slowly, underscored by the fullness of the cello. The remaining instruments joined, and a minuet ensued. Gentle and haunting, each note dragged out in pained moans that blurred the edges of Leanna's sight. Fogginess rolled into her mind on the repetitions of c-notes, possessing her joints as if intoxicated by the intervals. She closed her eyes to hear—to feel more of this ethereal song.

It was there in the dark that images of ghostlike movements whispered through her mind, a gorgeous routine she had never seen, much less performed. Still, she could see herself in the wisps of silvery smoke, dancing as Vicente's melody played on.

Lost to this ghost of her mind, she stretched her hands to either side and swayed in short waves that rolled from fingertips to shoulders to hips. Whereas previously emotions streamed from her eyes as tears, in a way that had not happened in many years, they now poured from her body in a routine that came to her as naturally as breathing.

The violin whined, and she arched east toward beliefs and dreams. The cello replied, and wants and regrets dragged her west. Curving back, she found the memories of her family. Straightening slowly, she met the mirage of a Ringmaster's kiss. She withered into a pirouette that sent this world whirling around her until all her thoughts became one—one cage, imprisoning her as she turned and turned and turned. Desperate for release, she pushed out her hands to the phantom bars around her and retracted them in quick movements as if touching the walls of this cage burned her fingers.

The keys stroked at largo and she stopped, then stretching her arms at her sides, wishing to extend the pain and confusion of her life to the farthest reaches of the earth. And though she fluttered like a bird en pointe, weighed down by the burdens of her heart, her feet never left the ground. Gathering her hands at her broken heart, she bent forward, withering... fading.... dying.... having never found flight.

Her hands fell back at her sides, and incomplete, her dance came to an end. The ghostly images bowed into the dark recesses of her mind, and the song faded to silence.

Opening her eyes, the world gradually gained color and shape. First into focus was Vicente, a smile on his lips.

"Has your heart decided, dear girl?" he asked lowly, as if scared that any louder would cause her to dissolve.

Unable to find words, she nodded as a tear wet her lashes.

Vicente's worry dissipated to a contagious laugh shared by the entire band. He clapped a hand on his thigh with a loud pat. "Perfect! Then it is to be your song. It shall be called the Leanan's Minuet. A gift, from us to you."

"Thank you," she breathed, unable to form a coherent thought or frame a proper sentence. "It was magical, and the dance—oh, it was..."

"Not our routine."

Leanna spun to Kioyo who stood a measure away, arms crossed over his chest. Emotions played at his face, and unsure whether he was angry or annoyed, Leanna's heart sunk.

She neared him a little. "I know I should have been rehearsing Ellie's old routine, but..." She cupped her mouth, a light laugh breaking through her fingers. He must have thought her crazy, but she didn't care. "I couldn't help it. It just came and possessed me, and it was—it was..."

"Beautiful," he said, his expression finally settled on awe. Relieved, Leanna mirrored his smile that widened with each step toward her. "It was yearning. Painful and beautiful and inspired..." He trailed off and stopped, a strange awareness settling over his eyes. "It was inspired."

"What is it, Kioyo?"

"Nothing." Clearing his throat, he jerked his head toward the ladder while starting toward it. "We have practice."

Leanna fell into step beside him and took his arm. "If it's nothing, then why do you look so concerned? I thought you'd be happy."

"I am, I…." He sighed, cradling the back of his neck. "Look, I don't know what changed since the last practice, but your dance just now was nothing like what I saw from you before. It's none of my business, and you have proven that you are smart and brave, and you never need explain anything to me, but some of the troupe mentioned seeing you at the Ringmaster's tent, and that you were flustered, and—"

Leanna gasped. "Surely you're not implying that I—that Finvarra and I—that we—oh, nothing happened, and for you to say that, you have no right!"

"Forgive me, Leanna, please." He neared her, deflated, and cradled her shoulders. "That was wrong of me and I didn't mean to upset you. Just, something within you has changed, and the way you danced proves that. But as beautiful as it was, and as strong as you have proven yourself to be, you must be careful."

He let out a harsh breath and dropped his hands from her shoulders. "Over the years, I have seen girls, so many girls of exceeding beauty and strength fall under his spell." Sitting, he leaned forward onto his elbows and shook his head. "I stayed quiet then. We all did, but I don't want the same fate for you."

Leanna sat beside him, silent. *So many other girls…*

Of course a man like Finvarra would have droves of willing women, beautiful women fawning over him, wanting him. She knew this. But the thought was vexing.

"I don't mean to upset you more, but I'd like to consider you a friend, and as your friend I tell you this. The Ringmaster is a good boss, but if he believes in or wants something, he will do anything to get it." He took in the Big Top with palpable shame and guilt. "Something as big as this circus, to something as small as…" He trailed off, musing for an example.

But Leanna knew of one. Something as big as a declaration, to something as small as a kiss. She gnawed at her lower lip. A kiss Finvarra had almost given her. Not because she was special, no. After all, there had been other girls… *so many other girls*. His intended kiss was only to prove his point that she was asleep, and that she needed to awaken in order to give him what he wanted: freedom. Leanna's stomach soured. Once again, she'd been fooled by him.

"I would hate to see you become just one of so many other conquests. Stories are told about him for a reason, and whether or not you are his Leanan Sidhe, take care. Sadly, a broken heart can still be broken."

Kioyo stood and faced her, serious. "It's also why I will insist on one thing. The name of the song must be changed. Regardless of what the Ringmaster thinks, and regardless of what myth he thinks is housed within you, it is you that will be dancing. It is your passion alone that will carry you across that rope. The song is not for the Leanan Sidhe, but for you." He extended a hand to her. "You will be magnificent."

Leanna stared at the open hand for a long moment. Through the shame and disappointment in Finvarra and in herself, she realized that Kioyo did not believe she was the Leanan Sidhe. But he believed in her, and that was the greatest gift of all.

She slid her hand into his, and standing, she gave it a gentle squeeze. "Thank you."

Kioyo nodded and averted his face to the ladder, but not before Leanna saw crimson creep beneath his golden complexion. "Very well then." He cleared his throat and brought her hand to his arm. "We'll have to work harder today seeing as we have few days for you to dominate the routine and rope. You may even think me cruel and evil," he teased, managing to look a tad bit evil, which made her smile.

Tension waved through him, and his smile fell. He tilted his ear to the air, his gaze narrowed and alert.

One moment, they stood side by side. The next, Leanna was enveloped in his arms being twirled away from a furious galloping that overtook the sound waves around them.

Vicente's music came to a chaotic end. Kioyo released her and whirled her behind him fluidly, his body hot to the touch. Still, Leanna stayed close, her heart beating wildly at his back.

"Where is she?" Krinard galloped around them, eyes wide and fists clenched at his sides.

Kioyo didn't waver. He shifted from one foot to another in crossed motions, weightless, while guarding Leanna, who mirrored his steps behind him. "Where is who?" His voice was huskier and full, closer to a purr.

"Inara is gone! She is nowhere within the crystals. Her snows didn't come, so she was taken. You did it, snake! I smelled you all over our tent. Inara denied it, but I know you were there. Where did you take her?"

Leanna searched her mind for an answer, but *Inara* and *gone* were the

110

only words she could process. She shut her eyes against the memory of her words. She had told Inara to ride, in spite of them all. Oh, but she never imagined she would run away—literally!

Krinard reared and stomped the ground with his front hooves. "Move aside, clown, and make yourself useful. Run and tell Finvarra that either she tells me where Inara is or I won't be the only one losing a mate."

"Why not tell me yourself?"

Leanna stiffened at the voice, at the sight of Finvarra approaching, flanked by Tomas and Bertrand, and the three centaurs behind him.

Through the distance, Leanna caught Finvarra's eye, his stare saying *I told you so.* Indeed. He'd told her visiting Inara would only bring trouble, and it had.

Krinard's nostrils flared as if the invading scent of vanilla sickened him. "So now you show your face," he hissed. "Where were you when Inara was taken?"

Finvarra's lips drew to a tight line. Leanna moistened her lips at the sight, recalling how warm his eyes had been when staring into hers, intentions of a kiss from those lips warming the air between them.

Now, there was just ice and indifference.

"Tomas tracked hoofmarks leading out past the tent, beyond the crystals," Finvarra revealed. "They were Inara's tracks alone, and so I have no reason to believe she was taken. Rather, she has gone willingly."

"Rubbish! She would never leave the safety of the crystals, knowing of the dangers. It was her doing!" Krinard stabbed a finger toward Leanna. "First she drove away Inara's magic and now she has driven her away to her death. Even you can't be so blind as to not see this. You said she was to be *your* freedom, yet she schemes to be the death of us all!"

Leanna fought to stay quiet, but not when confusion from the prior night, and Kioyo's words hurt her soul. When dancing from the previous practice hurt her body. When Krinard's accusations hurt most of all, as only the truth could.

Exasperated, she stepped out from behind Kioyo.

"You say fear drives out magic, but what of pride? You did this." She speared a finger toward him. Hers did not tremble. "You and your boorish conceit led her away. And her magic? You are guilty of that as well. Your anger for Finvarra is stifling it, dousing it, and that is why she fled. Yes, I went to see her." She turned the finger to her own heart. "I comforted her; I let her pour out her soul to me with no judgment or fear. A fear she feels because of you. And yes, perhaps I could have chosen my words more wisely, but it changes nothing."

Kioyo put a hand on her arm, but she snatched her arm away. "She was tired and couldn't bear to stand, much less ride. These crystals imprisoned her, while your anger poisoned her. So I told her to ride for herself in spite of you." She stared fiercely at Finvarra. "In spite of you both."

Krinard's jaw clenched, as did his fists, but it was he who averted his gaze first. He turned and trotted away, but stopped beside Finvarra, shoulder to shoulder. "I am going to find her, and you better hope I do for the sake of your precious muse." He made to leave.

A pale hand on his shoulder halted his retreat. "You're not going out there."

Krinard turned a dark glare down to Finvarra's hand and swiveled out of Finvarra's hold, his body stiff with violence. "And who's going to stop me?"

Frantic glances were cast around the group, knowing this could end very badly. Finvarra bristled, but said nothing. After a moment, he lowered his eyes.

Krinard shook his head and neared him. "It's too late to pretend you care. The only true illusion in this circus is you having a heart."

Leanna's chest ached at Krinard's words, but it was the wavering look in his eyes that hurt her soul. Saying those words to Finvarra hurt him. After all the years of anger, here at the bitter end of their friendship, he clearly still felt for his friend. No wonder Inara's horn had fallen, Leanna lamented. Seeing them quarrel this way, seeing their friendship overcome by mistakes and pain was unbearable, even for an onlooker. Had she a horn, she was certain it would have dissolved.

Krinard jerked his head for the horsemen to join him and turned away. A grim quiet settled over the group. Tomas and Bertrand lowered their eyes while Kioyo shook his head, watching the three horsemen break from Finvarra's side. It was a mistake, and Leanna half expected the gentle cries of a violin to accompany the death of a friendship, and soon the death of them all.

Finvarra curled his fingers into fists at his side, intent marking a line on his brow. He wanted to say something, and Leanna wished he would, but she bit her lip to keep her mouth shut. She would not meddle.

The centaurs met Krinard, and Finvarra's knuckles grew paler. They all turned toward the tent door, and Finvarra's lips parted. Only a cloudy breath whirled at his mouth. He shut his lips against it and turned away in the opposite direction.

Krinard walked east, Finvarra west, and Leanna stood at center. But things couldn't stay this way. Finvarra had to speak his mind and Krinard had to listen. But she said she wouldn't meddle. She simply couldn't meddle—

"Bertrand." She rushed to him before she realized she was speaking. "Stall Krinard. Make something up about Inara's tracks, or about anything!"

"Ah, smart girl! Don't worry your pretty head, my dear. I am on it." With a wink, he ran off, calling after Krinard.

Leanna dashed after Finvarra and caught his arm. He whirled to her, but before he could speak, she said, "Whatever you meant to say, say it before it is too late."

Finvarra glanced over her shoulder, his gaze locked on Bertrand delaying Krinard. His lips pursed. "Don't you think your meddling has caused me enough problems, Miss Weston?"

"I meddle, but at least it's because I care. I can't stand by and say nothing when I know you're making a mistake. This circus is all I have now. It's my home, beside all of them. Beside you. I must meddle."

Blue eyes pierced her, pale under the soft glow of the fireflies. He took in her words and looked back to Krinard. "It will make no difference. He refuses to listen to reason." The muscles of his jaw clenched. "If he decides to leave, let him. I'm heartless, remember? If he wishes to lose his life to his stubborn pride then so be it."

He turned to leave, but she moved before him. "Not until you've said all that needs to be said. If you fail to tell him this now, he may die and never hear it. Whatever your mistakes of the past are, don't let this be one of them." She paused, her cheeks growing warm. "And no, I don't remember you being heartless. All I remember was my hand upon your heart, and your heartbeat beneath my fingers."

She turned a quick glance to Bertrand. Krinard was walking away from him, and in meeting her eyes, Bertrand shrugged. He'd done all he could, and now Krinard was closer to the curtain.

Desperate, she placed an open palm over Finvarra's chest. He stiffened as if branded by her touch. His eyes shot to her in shock, but Leanna gave him no time to deny her. There was no time. "I still feel it. Regardless of what anyone says or believes, it is no illusion." She nodded encouragingly and let her hand slip away. "Please, whatever you need to say, say it for Inara."

After an eternal second, Finvarra slid his gaze to Krinard who lifted a hand to part the dressing tent curtains.

"Krinard, I'm sorry," he said, his gruff voice echoing in the tent.

Tomas and Bertrand looked to one another, Bertrand's amber brow arched. Kioyo stood beside them, eyes wide and unblinking. Leanna knew then, Finvarra had never apologized before. Not to Krinard. Not to anyone, for anything.

Krinard dropped his hand from the curtain and turned slowly. Finvarra closed the distance between them as everyone, from the horsemen to the musicians, watched on in awe. Leanna gave him his space, and followed him until reaching Kioyo.

"Our feud led Inara away," Finvarra said. "And our anger robbed her of her magic. I accept my blame. For that, and for everything, I am sorry. In spite of all that's happened between us, I will never forgive myself if I let you go alone." He held out his hand. "Let us find her, together."

Leanna froze, his words a stone in her stomach. *Together?*

Doubt still marred Krinard, but with a single nod, he wrapped a strong hand around Finvarra's wrist, just as Finvarra did to him. Tomas and Bertrand neared them, joining the gathered horsemen that looked on with stone faces, but a glimmer in their eyes. Leanna trailed behind with Kioyo and joined the semi-circle, part of her glad of their reformed friendship. The other half mourned, wondering what on earth had she done?

Releasing one another, Krinard and Finvarra turned to the waiting group. Leanna's throat swelled at the sight. No doubt Inara's horn would have grown had she seen the two men she loved most cast aside their differences for her sake.

Finvarra took a gold timepiece from his pocket. He frowned. "We haven't much night left, but it will have to be enough for now." He returned the watch to his pocket. "We should be able to search uninterrupted until daylight. The bonfire has not been lit, and so I'm confident Machina doesn't know we're here yet. Inara wouldn't have left had she sensed any danger."

"Tomas, you can track her," Krinard said.

"But I must stay here. I am the only one that can hold off Machina if Inara is…" Tomas paused, swallowing. "If the crystals fail."

"But without you, we have no idea which way she went," Krinard rallied. Everyone began speaking at once.

Kioyo stepped out from beside Leanna. "What of me, Ringmaster? I can track her."

All chatter ceased at the sound of his voice.

A strangled sound exploded from Krinard's mouth. "What for? No one needs a coward who will leave us to die at the first sign of danger."

"Krinard." Finvarra held up a hand as if to detain the hurtful words, but it was too late. Kioyo's eyes dimmed, his body tense with offense.

Finvarra lowered his hand. "I need you to stay here, Kioyo."

"But I'm the fastest, my senses impeccable." He glanced at Krinard. "Especially next to a horse's. You need me."

"I do need you, which is why you must stay. Inara or not, Miss Weston must be ready opening day. I also need someone I can trust to guard her. Tomas has enough to worry about, and he can't keep an eye on her as well."

Leanna crossed her arms over her chest, mulish. "I'm not a child, and do not need to be *watched*."

"You also said that this would be painless." Finvarra turned an even stare to her.

She opened her mouth to protest, but at that, she shut it and shifted back beside an equally dejected Kioyo.

Finvarra began assigning roles at once. Tomas was in charge of the circus operations until his return, and Bertrand was to send his dragons to patrol the grounds.

"Everyone must be on alert," he said. "If Inara is harmed and the crystals fail, we may not know until it is too late. Gather what you need. We leave at once." He nodded once, and the crowd took their cue. The horsemen galloped off, as did Bertrand and Tomas leave.

Finvarra watched them go, then turned to Kioyo. "This is not about your past mistakes, we've all made them. But I trust you and need you here. Guard her with your life."

"Yes, Ringmaster," Kioyo murmured. He focused on the doorway all the others had just vanished through. All others, but not him. Shaking his head, he walked away and sat on the edge of the nearest ring, crestfallen.

"He'll keep you safe," Finvarra said from behind Leanna. "That is if you manage to stop meddling and stay out of trouble."

Leanna's pulse quickened. The last she needed now was his reproach, especially after Krinard's. She slid him an incredulous look, expecting to find scold. When blue eyes fell upon her, all expectations shattered. A faint smile touched the corner of his lips, and in his stare, gratitude.

"Though," he said low and soft, "I suppose some good has come of your meddling this time."

Leanna's cheeks flushed at the taunt in his eyes and at the warm appreciation beneath it all. It made his eyes a little lighter, a little more welcoming. And when he looked at her like that, the world around them disappeared.

If only it wasn't so easy to get lost in his gaze, Leanna would have appreciated his effort at thanking her. If letting them drag her away wasn't so tempting, she might have said *you're welcome*. But with Kioyo's words playing at the edge of her conscience, Leanna stepped back. "You should go. Inara or not, the circus must open, right?"

Finvarra's jaw tightened, and whatever gratitude existed vanished in an instant, behind his perfect mask of indifference.

Not waiting for his reply, she turned and walked to Kioyo's side. She wouldn't fall under Finvarra's spell. She couldn't. Not again.

*He's dangerous,* her mind whispered.

*He is,* her heart agreed, *but his eyes…*

The eyes were the window to the soul, her mother always said. In Finvarra's, she had seen his unspoken appreciation. Leanna slowed to a stop. Could she believe him, just this once?

She turned to gauge his sincerity.

All she found was Finvarra's lean outline vanish through the curtains.

He never looked back.

# CHAPTER FOURTEEN
## ICE KISS

NIGHT WAS RETREATING, but darkness and speckled lights still ruled the skies. Bertrand leaned into a fire cupped in his hands, his mouth illuminated by the bluish light. Whispering quiet words that spiraled from his mouth as white vapor, he thrust the flame into the air. A hiss and a flourish swivel, and the curl of fire speared upward, growing redder, until coalescing with the fiery dragon that flew in a continuous loop around the fairgrounds. It watched from overhead, casting a red glow on the mist encircling the circus. From below, Kia padded in the opposite direction, his mane glowing like a halo under the light of fire dragon.

Just as with Ellie and Jin's departure, the small troupe came together a distance from the crystals to bid good luck to their departing horsemen and ringmaster, though Finvarra had yet to appear. Murmurs blanketed the crowd in one steady hum of dread, and worry found a home in Leanna's heart.

"I wish they would hurry on and go, instead of throwing it in all of our faces," Kioyo muttered under his breath from beside her. "I could have found Inara by now, in all the time they've wasted parading around, basking in everyone's adoration. And where is the Ringmaster?" He scoffed. "Probably deciding which coat looks best in case there's a woman in need of saving."

The words were irksome, but Leanna smiled, reigning in her discomfort. She looped her arm around his and with her free hand, smoothed his arm in soft strokes.

"If it helps any, remember that I am supposed to be magnificent, and for that, I need you." She straightened, held her chin high, and forced a feigned firmness to her voice. "As this faerie goddess I'm supposed to be, I forbid you go. You must stay here with me and teach me, or else..." She bit her lip in thought. She'd never threatened anyone before, real or pretend. She hummed. This was harder than she thought. "Well, I have yet to think of punishments and such, but you can't go. There, it has been handled." She patted his arm, putting an end to the issue.

Kioyo cast her a sideways glance. Though he said nothing, a small smile trounced his frown, mirroring Leanna's. He brought his hand on top of hers and gave it a gentle squeeze.

"Besides, look at Krinard," she said, focused on the centaur who arranged various vials into a muddy colored saddlebag. "He hardly seems happy about going. None of them do."

"I may risk my neck for disagreeing with the magnificent, royal, faerie goddess," Kioyo said through his smile, "but sadly, you're mistaken, Your Highness. That sour expression you see there is Krinard's every day look. It's actually not so bad today."

A giggle burst from Leanna's mouth and she turned her face into Kioyo's shoulder to stifle it. Kioyo's frame hobbled a bit with laughter, and in such glumness, his sound and scent dispelled the darkness a little.

The assembled crowd parted, and their laughs withered. First came rhythmic, hollow thuds on the turf. Finvarra appeared then, leading a black stallion by the bridle. Dressed in a silver sprigged waistcoat beneath a red overcoat, and black breeches, he was regal. He held his chin in a belonging highness; his top hat could have very well been a crown.

He caught her stare in the distance, blue eyes still marred by disappointment. Locked in each other's gazes, neither said a word, neither one made a gesture. His gaze dipped to her hand covered by Kioyo's, and for the briefest moment, he paused. Part of her urged her to take back her hand… the hand he had kissed. Her other half, paralyzed under his expressionless scrutiny, didn't know what to do.

The minute over, he mounted the fine black stallion that was as kingly and intimidating as his master. With a firm nod to the horsemen, he signaled their departure without saying goodbye.

Wind shuffled through the trees. In the spaces between the gusts, Leanna heard it: the taps and rasps of her dreams. She looked up to the trees that towered over the mist, into the dark hollows and shadows between them. Though sure the noise was only the crackle of branches and the rustle of the dead leaves upon them, she still couldn't help but wonder. Was Machina in there, somewhere? Would the trees tell her of Finvarra's departure? Of Inara's disappearance? Trembling now, she held fast to Jin's words. *No fear.*

Yet, when the departing men turned to the stakes, an ominous shiver trailed down her spine. So much was at risk of being lost, much sooner than they foresaw, so soon after much of it had been gained, and it was all her fault.

Trapped in this coffin of silence, each hollow hoof beat nailed this blame deeper, drew Finvarra closer to the crystals and away from her. Perhaps for the night. Perhaps, forever.

A breeze moaned, and fear propelled her feet forward. The mist curled toward Finvarra, and the name burst from her mouth. "Finvarra!"

He came to a sharp stop, but didn't turn. From paces behind, Krinard held up a fist to his horsemen and they too stopped. Ignoring his stare and the subsequent mutterings from the crowd, Leanna walked the distance toward Finvarra and stopped beside the black horse.

"Before you go," she started, the cold nipping her lungs with every inhale. While she took a moment to catch her breath, muffled thuds clapped as Finvarra turned round, stern blue eyes first, followed by the slow turn of his body and horse. Leanna was grateful for this slight movement, as the horse and its rider now blocked her from the gathered troupe behind him.

"Finvarra, light approaches. We must go." Hooves resounded as Krinard trod forward behind Finvarra. "I will ride out first and check the grounds, then signal you all when it's safe."

Krinard's black gaze lingered on Leanna for an added moment before he trampled off. With each gallop, he gained speed and then vanished past the crystals with a hiss. The fog curled and swallowed the impression left by his departure. Soon it was as if he never existed. Leanna lowered her eyes away toward Finvarra's black stallion, wishing to pretend it'd never happened either. However much he hated her, seeing him disappear into that unknown left her feeling a little hollow and guiltier. She lifted a hand toward the horse.

"I wouldn't do that if I were you," Finvarra said, tightening his hand around the reins. "Cróga doesn't like to be touched."

Leanna offered her palm to the horse still. Within seconds, Cróga rested his muzzle in her hand. Feeling the warmth tickle her fingers, she neared it and gently stroked its mane. It was a lovely horse, a dark beauty like its master.

Cróga nestled against her fingers, whiffling contently at her tender strokes.

Something in Finvarra's eyes softened at the quiet affection being exchanged for an instant before it froze over once more. He cleared his throat. "Is there something you wished to say or is my traitorous horse free to leave?"

Fear churned in Leanna's stomach. She gulped. *Don't go. It's*

119

*dangerous...* "Just that I hope you find Inara," she lied, guarding the truths of her heart.

"Are you sure?" He slid his gaze to her hand upon Cróga's mane. "Your hands, they tremble."

"Yes, well..." She fisted the midnight tresses gently. "It's dangerous out there, and I worry for Inara, and..." *for you.*

Faltering, Leanna shook her head and whispered endearments to the stallion to keep from looking up to its rider, who would undoubtedly see the whole truth in her eyes. He would know in an instant she was frightened for him, that any harm would befall him. Her mind tried to deny it, but regardless of Kioyo's words, in spite of so many other girls in his past and perhaps to come, her heart felt what it felt and she was helpless against it. *Foolish, foolish heart*, she cursed it, *you're nothing but a fool.*

Her breaths hitched quietly at the feel of Finvarra's cool fingers under her chin. He encouraged her head upward, where his fingers splayed and cupped her cheek. There was a unicorn to find, there was an enemy somewhere beyond the mist, and there had been so many other girls, but in that instant, with their mirroring crystals between them, time stilled. Shielded from the world by the black stallion and the fog, there was just Leanna and Finvarra, and a soughing breeze that carried what leaves remained on the skeletal branches between them. There was just his hand at her face, a thumb grazing the delicate skin while he searched for the truth in her eyes, in her soul.

"Is that all?" he murmured. *That is not all*, his eyes told her, begged of her.

Against the feel of his hand, she closed her eyes briefly before he could see just how much his touch moved her. *Curse this fear*, she thought. It changed everything. It made her care for him and be angry at him all at once. More, it made her want him back before he'd ever left.

She parted her lips to speak. Finvarra focused on her intently.

*I hate that I am scared for you. I hate that I feel this way.* "I..."

A pitched neigh resounded, and squawking ravens streaked the pale gray sky in black. Behind Finvarra, the horsemen nodded to one another. It was time.

"That was all," she said hastily. "I had nothing more to say." She released Cróga's midnight mane and stepped back away from him, away from Finvarra's touch. The spell now shattered, she clutched the crystal necklace to hide the tremble of her hands.

Finvarra lowered his lashes, tension marking the sides of his mouth. His brows dipped, troubled, but before she could see more, he put on his top hat. The leather harnesses crunched as he wound the reins tighter and trotted away to the horsemen waiting just inside of the crystal. The silence then was painful.

One by one, the three horsemen rode out. Finvarra was last to enter the mist, his outline now a shadow in the silvery white.

A sudden terror gripped Leanna. "I'm scared," she whispered, a secret between her and the air. Regardless of how many others there had been, of how many others he had loved, "I'm scared for you."

The tempo of Finvarra's retreat stopped. He turned, and though she could not see him clearly, she felt his gaze find her at once. She looked at him, too. At the whiteness behind him, at the grayish blackness above.

Her hand tightened around the crystal. "Be careful," her mind, heart, and voice whispered together, finally in agreement.

Finvarra's shoulders rose slightly with an inhale as if devouring her words that blew in on the wind. A moment later they lowered, and with it, the winds shifted. A cool draft curled the fog toward the circus, toward Leanna.

She closed her eyes as the breeze reached her, a cool, tentative caress that stirred her hair and skimmed her skin in phantom strokes scented of vanilla. The breeze retreated then, and in its last traces of life, brushed away from the back of her hand as an icy kiss. Leanna gasped at the sensation and opened her eyes. Frozen onto her skin was an intricate web of frost in the form of a feather. Though smaller than the one Jin gave her, the message was the same: No fear.

Closing her other hand around the frosted feather, Leanna brought them to her heart. As it melted and cold droplets seeped through her fingers, she lifted her eyes.

Finvarra was gone.

Rehearsals passed without any further interruption, yet with each finished cycle of her routine, Leanna grew more and more unsure as to whether no interruption was a good thing or not. In the end, she mused it was a good thing. The distraction made her movements freer as she did not worry so much as to what it looked like compared to whether Inara had been found or not, to whether Finvarra was safe or not. It was what she forced herself to believe. For the sake of her dancing and of her heart, she just had to.

While she danced to keep her mind from wandering, Kioyo spent a great portion of the time with his hands clasped behind his back, focused on the rope with a tense jaw. Leanna worried her dancing had yet to please him, and so with every finished turn she asked him how she had done.

His only reply each time was an absent, "Good, good. We'll try it one more time."

One more time carried them into late night, and Leanna knew he was worried as well.

# CHAPTER FIFTEEN
## LOSING THINGS

THOUGH THE SUN HAD RISEN and set, it felt like the clocks hadn't changed for hours. Time stretched indefinitely in this stilled universe of magic, dance, and longing. There was definitely something afoot with this timelessness, Leanna realized. She hadn't grown hungry or sleepy at all. But after a long day, such mechanics were not something her worried mind dared tackle.

Many acts had come and gone, but only she remained with Kioyo now, and the tired pixies that lined the rope emitting a faint light. Luna curled on Leanna's shoulder, flickering slowly through her colors. A whirring sigh squeaked in her ear.

"Go on, darling," Leanna whispered. "I daresay we're done for the night. And even if we're not, you most certainly are." Leanna gathered the small light in her palm and held her hand in the air to give Luna a head start. "Off you go now, little one."

Luna whirled into the air and joined the pixies on the crossbars of the tent. At once, her light extinguished.

"Goodnight," Leanna said.

Kioyo stopped his pacing, his brows snapped together as if roused from a deep thought. "Goodnight?" He glanced around. No longer seeing the pixies about, he lifted his eyes to the crossbars where they barely glowed. "Yes, yes, let them rest. You did well today. A bit distracted, but good."

"Me? Distracted?" Leanna scoffed. "You barely saw one full performance. I even did a somersault once and you missed it."

Kioyo folded his arms over his chest. "I did not miss it. It was quite brave, and I commend you."

Leanna plucked his upper arm. "I never did a somersault! See, you were distracted this whole time—still are."

"No, I am not."

Leanna pinned him with a look. Lips pursed, she trailed it down to his clasped hands, where his thumbs plucked restlessly at one another, no doubt keeping the beat of his thoughts. She lowered it further to his foot that tapped compulsively, as it had been for the entire rehearsal.

"Fine, yes. Maybe I am a little distracted, but leaving me behind was a mistake. I could have found her by now without the need to involve anyone else, without the need for the Ringmaster to set foot outside of these crystals." He shook his head and went straight to the ladder.

Down on the ground, he raked a hand through his hair and tugged at the nape. "Our luck being what it is, you arrive at last and that's the moment Machina finally gets her iron claws on him. But that can't be remedied now, can it?"

Leanna walked around him and sat at the gallery seats, defeated. "Sadly, I fear Finvarra may have been right. Had I not meddled, Inara never would've left. If I hadn't convinced Finvarra to go after Krinard, he would still be here. How can I fix this?"

"You don't." Kioyo straightened. "You keep rehearsing. The pixies know their job. They will keep you safe."

"Why would you not be here—?" Leanna gasped and bolted to her feet. "You mean to go out there after Inara don't you?" In his silence, Leanna clutched his shoulders and forced him to look at her. "Tell me you don't mean to go past the crystals alone."

He met her stare. Focused. Decided. "I have to do this. Inara is in danger, and so is the Ringmaster. I refuse to be a coward. Not anymore."

"You don't need to prove anything to them. Who cares what Krinard thinks?"

Kioyo cradled her elbows, gently, cutting her off. "I need to prove it to myself."

"But it's madness. Finvarra shouldn't have gone. He should have told me to mind my own business. Now Inara is gone, and Krinard and Finvarra, and now you're going, too." She released him and buried her face in her hands. "This is all a disaster."

His light laugh pierced the darkness behind her fingers. He held her forearms and pulled her gently into an embrace. "It isn't a disaster—actually it is," he chuckled. Leanna didn't share in his mirth. She closed her eyes against his shoulder, hauling in the deep scent of pine.

He sighed, the gentle breath rustling her hair. "But it's what's supposed to happen. I may not have believed it before, but I daresay you've inspired us all to be a little better. You even got the Ringmaster to apologize!" Kioyo pulled her away a bit, enough to look down at her. "We're all following our hearts because of you. Without even knowing it, you've given us a bit of that freedom we so desperately seek. That's nothing to be ashamed of."

"Nothing I say can make you stay, will it?" she asked, her voice small. Kioyo shook his head.

"Then, please, be careful. You have to come back. That's an order."

Kioyo laughed lightly. "I know, Your Highness, I know. I must return so you can be magnificent."

"No, you must return because I need my friend back."

Kioyo took her hands in his and gave them a gentle squeeze. "I promise to return, but I need to go now. My vision is better at night. Everything will be okay," he said, though Leanna felt it was more to himself than her.

She held on to his hand for an added moment before she nodded and let go. Whatever his reasons for undertaking this madness, she had to be strong for him. For all those outside of the crystals.

Kioyo put on his hat, and then helped Leanna with her cloak. Bringing the hood over her disheveled hair, he pinched her cheek. "I expect you to be magnificent when I return."

Leanna forced a small smile, but couldn't help but wonder if he would ever return at all.

They stood now side by side in the shadows beside the stables. Kia was due to pass at any moment while the two-headed fire dragon above would cross its path in the opposite direction. Bertrand filled the gap between the two. He circled the field and tossed flares into the air, feeding the dragon life against the cold. It was the dragon's front head that approached now.

Kioyo shifted them back further into the shadows. The fire dragon's front head came and went, but just as she had calculated, Bertrand was approaching.

"How are you going to get across? Bertrand will see you, or the dragon's rear head will," Leanna whispered into his ear. She pulled back, and in the faint crimson light of the dragon, she saw he grinned.

"I told you I was fast, but I can only evade one. I will need your help. You must distract Bertrand, only for a second so I can make it across. Can you do this for me?" The black of his eyes shone in the reddish hue of the fire like the surface of the ocean under a blood red moon. Just as intense, just as beautiful.

Leanna nodded.

"Ask him how to get to Minerva's tent. Knowing Bertrand, he'll have some nonsense to add which will be more time than I need."

Again, stricken by fear, Leanna found herself with no words. In her last shred of bravery, she released Kioyo's hand. She clutched hers to her chest, sheer will stifling the desire to take his hands and pull him back. Back toward the Big Top, back toward safety. She hadn't done it with Finvarra, but she could do it here, with Kioyo. She had failed with Inara, and abysmally with Finvarra. Was this her second chance to keep someone she cared about safe?

Kioyo slid back into the shadows and all intentions vanished. It wasn't her second chance to make things right. It was his. Did he not do this, she was certain the guilt of his past would magnify and slowly destroy him.

Kioyo took one step into the darkness. Leanna took one back into the light.

"Leanna? What are you doing out here?" Bertrand called from behind. As he approached her, Kioyo gave Leanna an encouraging nod and vanished into the black.

"It's dangerous for you to be here so close to the crystals. What if something happened to Inara and they fail?" He started to say more, but Leanna turned and he saw her teary stare. "Is something wrong? Are you hurt?"

She shook her head. "Not hurt, just a bit cold, and it makes my eyes water."

Bertrand arched an auburn brow incredulously. Leanna bit her lip. She was a lousy liar, but for Kioyo, she would try her hardest.

Lowering her head into her hands, she pretended to cry. "Kioyo was upset about being left behind and doesn't want to speak to anyone, so he went to his tent and left me alone," she sobbed. "But I need to get to Minerva's tent, and I got lost and had you not found me, I would've kept going in circles. And I'm freezing, and tired, and this is all my fault!"

Bertrand neared her and patted her shoulder. "Don't cry, little Sidhe. Kioyo is just a little hurt, but this isn't your fault. Look here, Minerva's tent is straight up this path, all the way past the Ringmaster's tent. It's the only black tent in the entire circus, and quite frightening. Take care not to nip your skin on any needles while there..."

As Bertrand went off in a tangent the way Kioyo told her he would, Leanna flitted a glance over his shoulder. His words fell to the attempts of a mime when a white blur whisked across the ground and disappeared into the mist. There was no doubt in her mind the white fog had been Kioyo, and now he, too, was gone.

Leanna pressed shaking fingers to her mouth. Though a victorious smile twisted her lips, genuine tears trailed down her cheeks. She had to do it, but she hated seeing him go. She hated the mist. She hated an enemy she didn't know. She hated feeling so helpless and guilty. And she hated losing things most of all.

Minerva's black tent was hitched in the shades furthest from the Big Top. Even with the dragon's flames, Leanna would have missed it had she not known where to look. Light and shadow conspired, and in the darkness, the surrounding shrubs and tent were one and the same.

A stake was stabbed into the ground at the entrance, curved to a loop at the tip. Dangling from the hoop was a silver bell. Leanna considered the bell. No light shone from within the tent. Was Minerva still asleep? Leanna rubbed her skirt between her fingers, which reminded her: Kioyo had stolen the garments she presently wore. What would she tell Minerva of that? More, would Minerva be cross? A chill washed down her spine and she stepped away from the bell. Bertrand had told her in so many ways what Minerva was. Maybe it was best she come back later, with Kioyo…

"Are you going to stand there all night or are you going to ring the bell?"

Leanna whirled to the feminine voice behind her, to the older woman standing a slight up the path. She wore a pleated red skirt, various shades of the color added in layers. A coined belt adorned her waist and dangled in her approach. "Oh, I intend to ring, but I—"

A gust of wind whipped Leanna's hair over her face to the sound of jingling coins. She brushed it away madly and spun to where the woman stood. She was gone.

"But you're afraid I'm a vampire?" the woman's voice whispered behind her.

Dread pooled at Leanna's joints. She turned slowly to the voice at the tent, to Minerva standing at the door.

A catlike smile spread on her ruby red lips. "Yes, I'm a vampire." She lifted the tent flap aside, her perfectly sculpted brow arched. "Now that that's been sorted, shall we?"

The first half hour was spent in polite silence as Minerva prepared tea. And staring. There was lots of staring. As politely as she could, Leanna stole glances from under lowered lashes to the woman who sat at a drafting table beside piles of fabric and streams of ribbon dangling from the desk.

Minerva was striking, in a cold way. Not timeless like Finvarra. Her skin was paler than his, or perhaps the same, but the contrast of her black hair and eyes, and blood red lips made it appear blancher. In all, she looked frozen... dead.

Leanna forced her eyes down to her reflection in her tea cup. She reached for it, grateful that it would force her trembling hands to ease for the sake of not spilling tea.

"You're late."

Leanna jumped at the sound. Tea waved from her cup and sloshed onto her saucer and the white lace tablecloth. She hurried to wipe up her mess. "I'm so sorry. I'm—"

"Frightened," Minerva injected from over her own tea. She took a sip. "Your fears are futile, and if we're to work together, they must cease." She set down her cup and rose, unsmiling. "Bertrand is an idiot. I've not desired human blood in over a century, if that will ease your fears some."

"I don't mean any offense. I'm not frightened, just..." She trailed off, wiping her spilled tea as best she could with her napkin. "I'm sorry if I—"

"Stop apologizing."

"Of course. I'm sor—"

Minerva brushed before her, a blur of dangling coins and red fabric. Leanna bolted to her feet, but Minerva's icy hands clasped her shoulders and stayed her. Leanna pressed her lips together and didn't dare move.

Minerva did move: closer. "I've not fed in more years than you've been alive. But though I may not drink blood, I can hear it, and it doesn't lie. Don't tell me you're not frightened when your blood boils with fear, pounding so hard, it threatens to leave me deaf." She moved closer still, the tip of her nose against Leanna's cheek. "If you're going to jump whenever I speak, the only blood you will shed will be from pins sticking you, and it will be your fault." Nearing Leanna's ear, she repeated, "This fear must cease."

With that, Minerva moved back, but didn't release Leanna. A heavy silence burned, where she scrutinized her, slowly. What she wanted, Leanna didn't know, but after several moments of being held like this and nothing happening, Leanna released the breath gathered in her chest, and then another.

Minerva hummed, satisfied, and released her. She moved back, walked to a circular platform, and motioned a hand for Leanna to join her.

Knees still a bit weak, Leanna willed her feet forward and stood on the platform. Minerva paced around the stand, her heels tapping a slow, steady beat on the floor. "Finvarra told me you were a small thing, but heavens, you're tiny."

She came full round, but she didn't stop. Rather, she walked past Leanna, her chiffon skirt swishing behind her as she went to her drafting table. She retrieved a cloth tape measure and shuffled through papers absently. "I tried to sketch some different designs based on what Finvarra has told me of you. He said you had lovely eyes, brown with specks of gold." She held up a sketch, but flicked it aside. Back at the platform, she lifted Leanna's head a touch toward the light and hummed. "But he never mentioned how pale you are. The gold gown won't do. I'm afraid none of them will. They will either wash you out or swallow you whole. What a shame. They would have been radiant."

They probably would have been, but Leanna couldn't bring herself to care about gowns, or paleness, or even vampires. She pressed a hand to her burning cheeks, caught by Minerva's words.

*He said you had lovely eyes...*

The simple thought made fire of her blood, her head a little light. Minerva turned slowly, a smirk on her cherry red lips. However, in her eyes, there was only pity.

"He's charming, but you should think no more of it."

"I don't know what you're talking about. I—"

"The blood never lies," Minerva warned under an arched brow. "He has woken something within you, but for your sake, think no more of it. Finvarra is trouble that can only be solved by Finvarra himself, however much he wishes for you to save him."

She abandoned Leanna to her confusion and walked to the sketches again. With a gnash of her teeth, she moved them aside, retrieved a pencil and notebook, and sat down. After a few low hums and taps of her pencil, she set off on a feverish sketch. Her speed and the shadows of the room made her hand appear like a haze of black smoke.

Within seconds, she set down her pencil. Lips pursed, she studied her sketch. "Yes, I think this will work. When I'm done with this new gown, you shall be a fairy goddess, indeed."

"New gown? No, no. Surely I can wear Ellie's costumes. It would be much easier to adjust them rather than to make them entirely new. I'm the third daughter. I'm used to hand me downs and quite frankly, don't mind."

Minerva scoffed, waving her hand airily. "Nonsense, child. I'm immortal and my pleasures are few. Give a woman something to live for, at least before the wrath of the Elders or of Machina takes that away."

Though the room was cold, it was hearing the name Machina that sprouted goose bumps along Leanna's skin. She rubbed her arms. "If you don't mind my asking..."

"You want to know about Machina," Minerva said, and flicked her eyes to Leanna with a knowing smile.

Leanna nodded. "I don't mean to pry, but it appears when I came here, I not only gained a new life, but a new enemy. Problem is, I don't know who she is."

Minerva let out a slow breath and shook her head. "You're just a child and look at this mess he's brought upon you." Tape measure around her neck, she came onto the platform behind Leanna.

"He isn't to blame. Well, not entirely. I was the one who snuck into his circus," Leanna started, but sucked in a breath when the tape measure came around her waist. Minerva's touch was cold, and she had to look down to believe it hadn't burned through her dress.

"I've heard," she murmured. After a series of measurements, she walked back to the table and scribbled notes on the previous sketch. "But why on earth would you come to this place? Your life couldn't have been so terrible that you would subject yourself to a cursed circus of all things."

Memories of forced marriages and metal contraptions came to mind, but Leanna ignored these. "A cursed circus? I thought they couldn't go home because of Machina."

Minerva tilted her head, her brows furrowed. "Look around you, child. Do you think Machina could keep this troupe away from Forever? Would keep them imprisoned behind these crystals? I daresay many would risk Machina's wrath if they could live beyond the crystals, but the curse doesn't allow for it. This world will drain them of their magic, and they will die." Minerva made a sound of pity. "They can't leave, unless they are forgiven."

"But Finvarra told Ellie that his snow will never fall. What does he wait for? If everyone else is forgiven, what will happen to him?"

Minerva only stared, the answer clear in her black stare.

"No," Leanna breathed.

"Oh, how your heart pounds at the truth." Minerva draped the tape measure over her chair and leaned back against the table. "Sadly, the curse is that Finvarra must give his heart away if he wishes for his troupe to be forgiven. But if the circus fails before everyone finds their forgiveness, then everyone in the circus dies. That is why the Ringmaster flees Machina, to keep them safe long enough for them to find their forgiveness. If she traps him, the circus will undoubtedly fold and those remaining here will perish."

"But...but that makes no sense," Leanna stammered, words failing her as she struggled to understand. "If Machina traps him and the circus fails, he will die too. She will accomplish nothing, and the one thing she wants most, she will never have."

Minerva gritted her teeth, waving a strip of sheer fabric in the air dismissively. "Machina will never let Finvarra die. She will stitch a mechanical heart into his chest so that he lives and belongs to her forever."

All air left Leanna at once. She'd overheard Ellie and Finvarra talk that fateful night, and they too spoke such things. But that was before. Before dances on tightropes and newly forged friendships. Before Kioyo. Before the confession and kiss of a Ringmaster.

Her nerves and senses muddled, she let out a humorless laugh. "This can't be," she said. "I have heard of—of strange things, read of even stranger, but mechanical hearts and iron monsters? That's preposterous."

"You must quit thinking of this in mortal terms!" Minerva turned to her, a hint of frustration in her voice and stare. "Look beyond the limitations of this world. Has this circus taught you nothing?"

"But I can't. Centaurs and unicorns I accept. Bird people, fiery dragons and pixies. Finvarra being a faerie is... shocking, yet I have come to terms with that as well. But what you are asking me to believe is that Machina will stitch a heart of metal into his chest to keep him alive while everyone else dies. Why?"

"Because she loves him too much," Minerva replied, her voice much softer. "What greater madness is there that would drive someone to such extremes as an unrequited love?"

An answer evaded Leanna. She had never known love, much less unrequited. But to be driven to such madness over an emotion? The thought was as foreign as love itself. She pressed a hand over her crystal and walked

131

blindly to her chair. Too many questions left her without a word, worry left her without a breath, while the truth left her with all the fear in the world.

Minerva exhaled and joined Leanna at the small table. "Bless your innocent heart. Perhaps once you know why Machina pines for Finvarra, and why in turn he will never give his heart away, you will better understand."

Leanna shivered. Around her, the night took on a different spirit. Cold clung about her like a fog, but she knew this was not the regular night cold rather that of looming Death. It had come for her many times before. But there, on the verge of all the answers she had always wanted, she had never felt so afraid.

# CHAPTER SIXTEEN
## STRAIGHT THROUGH THE HEART

MINERVA STARED DOWN at the knit tablecloth, her sculpted brows gathered in contemplation. "Finvarra loved women. Human women in particular. Perhaps it was curiosity over their emotions, their humanity?" Her gaze grew distant in thought.

A hum and a shrug brought her back to present. "When Finvarra saw a girl he desired, he persuaded her to steal away with him into Forever where they could dance the night away and love freely with little regard for anyone else. Many legends spread in the human realm of girls vanishing at night, but there was no proof. The women he took were always found in their beds the following morning with only hazy memories of an icy palace and the scent of vanilla on their skin."

Leanna rubbed her arms, remembering the scent all too well. Bitterness nudged her heart. A slight of jealousy answered back.

"One day, however, a girl did not return. Her name was Aithne, the most beautiful girl in all of Éire. Her husband was so proud of her that he held festivals to celebrate her beauty, day after day." Minerva leaned forward, smoothing the tablecloth in slow strokes. "His castle was filled with music and dancing, feasting and tributes, all in her honor. The praises were so many, the winds carried them through the veil of our world and into Forever, into Finvarra's ears. Intrigued, he went to her that night, while her husband slept. Like the other girls, she didn't deny him, and he whisked her away to Forever for what was supposed to be one night."

Leanna swallowed deeply, her cheeks hot and prickly. To hear of so many other girls burned with a fire she wished didn't exist.

"Many nights passed with Aithne at Finvarra's side. You must understand, Forever is no place for a human. It is timeless, pure and clean. This purity makes it so that there is no sickness, no storms, just pure magic."

Minerva's brows lowered, troubled. "Human hearts are dangerous, and their spirits corrupt and insatiable. In a land of such purity, they become addicted to this magic, to this freedom, much like an addiction to laudanum. They want to live in it, forever. Aithne was no exception. It happened that when Finvarra meant to take her back to her home, she begged him to let her stay." She shook her head. "He should have denied her, but she was beautiful and he was..."

"Blinded," Leanna said, remembering Ellie's haunting revelation. "And a fool."

"Blind and foolish, indeed, and sadly, for far too long. The more time Aithne remained in Forever, the uglier she became. Not in semblance," Minerva pressed a hand to her chest, "but in spirit. Rapt by her beauty, Finvarra failed to see that vanity had long corrupted her heart. Weakened by this conceit, her time in Forever made her heart grow black. He realized too late that she had to go home."

Minerva sighed as if weighed down by this heartbreaking tale. "They say he rode her out to the threshold where the human world meets Forever. She begged to stay with him, but no longer a fool for her tears or her beauty, he denied her. What he didn't know was that Aithne expected him to say no, prepared for it. When he bid his goodbye, she took out a concealed dagger from her sleeve and stabbed herself straight through the heart."

Leanna cupped her mouth and gasped through her fingers, feeling as if the world shifted beneath her. She shook her head, unsure whether to curse Finvarra's foolishness and pity Aithne, or—or what to do with this impossible situation.

"It was a tragedy," Minerva lamented. "But for human blood to be spilled on Faerie ground is an abomination. Faeries believe in life and nature. There is nothing natural in a suicide. The effects of it were felt all the way to the Otherworld, where the Elders of Forever spend their eternity."

Leanna swallowed through a thickened throat. Aithne loved him, and killed herself because of a broken heart. That hurt Leanna the most. "And I suppose that is why he was cursed?"

"In part. After Finvarra took her body back home, to be buried beside her ancestors, he was gone for some time. Many hoped that the tragedy had changed him, that he would have learned his lesson." Red lips bowed to a frown, telling Leanna he didn't. "When he returned, he continued finding other girls to entertain, making certain to never let them stay longer than a night. As always, they were found in their beds the next morning until they began disappearing, later discovered dead outside of the gates of Forever, robbed of their beauty and of their hearts."

"Machina," Leanna whispered.

Minerva refilled Leanna's tea, no doubt having heard the strain of her voice. "Somehow, Aithne was brought back, only what was once a girl returned a machine."

As much as she wished against it, a sickening pity lurched into Leanna's soul for the poor girl. How many tears did Aithne—Machina cry over her broken heart? Did she cry still? Was there any part of her that remembered being anything other than the monster she had become?

Minerva set down the porcelain pot and settled back. "No one knows how it happened, or who could have done such a thing. For many years they tried to defeat her, but her evil and obsession only grew."

Leanna pressed a hand against the concealed pendant. "I always had a sense that the rumors of Finvarra weren't true. That he wasn't responsible for those murdered girls, but I never imagined this." She pressed fingers to her lips and took a moment. "Never this."

"He may not have killed them directly, but Machina was always watching. He underestimated her jealousy and still took to his vice, saying that she would not control him, and that he would never bend to her will." Minerva made a face of disgust. "It was a terrible time. So many lives were lost to this sick game of power between them. The resulting bloodshed began to poison the veins of Forever until snow stopped falling and the ice began to melt. Though unprecedented, the Elders were forced to act or the murders would eventually be the end of Forever."

The winds outside howled a chorus of foreshadowing laments, and a cold tremor passed through Leanna like a ghost. A ghost, indeed, she believed. The ghost of her ignorance abandoning her.

"The Elders cursed Finvarra for his vanity and selfishness. For all the girls that lost their hearts to him, he was in turn given a heart and banished. Only when he gives away this heart will he be allowed to go back home."

Leanna paused the restless twine of her fingers. "But you said mortal hearts can't live in Forever. If he loves a woman and gives her his heart, how can they be together?"

"And there is the rub, my dear. They can't. Finvarra must part with his love, never to be with her again. As such, fear has made him more of a prisoner to these crystals than a curse ever could. He is afraid of finding this love, afraid of leaving her to the mercy of Machina who will kill her the same way she kills any woman he cares for. But, I suppose, it's in losing the woman he loves that he will understand the pain he caused those innocent girls."

With a shake of her head, Minerva rose. She slid her chair in and gripped the knobs tightly. "That, child, is the curse that bound Finvarra and his court to this circus, and left Forever without her King."

Leanna felt her world topple—no, it stopped. It most definitely stopped. "King?"

"Indeed." Minerva walked across the room. As she moved, the soft swish of her skirt sounded more like the *tsk, tsk* of pity Leanna often heard from her sisters when forced to miss the simple joys of life because of her illness.

"Though he has many names, he is, in fact, Finvarra, High King of the Faeries. The members of this circus were those of his court who were also punished for doing nothing to prevent him. Sovereign or not, they should have put their morality first and appealed to him to stop. But they turned a blind eye, content with their lives of dancing and relishing in the glory of Forever. Thus they too share in the punishment." She stopped at her desk, retrieved her tape measure again, and turned back to Leanna. "Their lives were a circus, and thus they were cursed to become one. As their king, Finvarra became their Ringmaster."

After Minerva's last word, Leanna said nothing for a long time. It was so much. It was all so much.

"Not what you expected, I know," Minerva murmured absently, draping red cloth over the shoulders of a mannequin.

"I… I don't know what to say." Leanna swallowed the rest of her words. Though a weight had been lifted in finally knowing who Finvarra was, who Machina was, the load in her heart and shoulders had never felt so heavy. "With so many answers, I feel more lost than ever. I don't know who to pity, who to hate… and all those innocent girls."

"Finvarra was a young king, and stupid. But this world has aged him, and he has learned. He hasn't catered to any girl, however beautiful to however frivolous, not for many years now. Machina, however, is relentless and will kill the most beautiful girl in the town as a guarantee Finvarra will never see her or desire her. No woman can be more beautiful than her."

Minerva paused. She wrinkled her nose at the red fabric and tossed it aside. Retrieving a black one in its stead, she said, "But now you have come, his long awaited Leanan Sidhe. He seems to think you will be the last of his trials and his circus will soon be free."

Leanna bit the inside of her lip to stay its tremble. "That is the worst part of all. What am I supposed to do?" Like a lost child, she gazed up to Minerva. "How can a muse fix this?"

"The Leanan Sidhe is not just a muse. Yes, she does inspire, but it comes at a price."

"What price?"

Minerva considered her for a moment, a war in those black eyes. Her lips pursed, she turned back to her mannequin.

"I deserve to know," Leanna demanded. "If I'm supposed to help somehow, I need to know what it is I am and what I'm supposed to do."

Minerva exhaled, but said nothing.

Possessed by her desire for truth, Leanna rose and walked around the mannequin. Minerva made to ignore her and insert another pin, but Leanna clutched her wrist. "Please."

Minerva's look of surprise changed to one of approval. "You have spine. You'll need it for what I'm about to tell you and for what's to come."

Leanna released her wrist. Whirling her hand in a slow circle, Minerva walked to her desk and set down the pin cushion. Their stares locked for long moments. Leanna nodded once, encouragingly, prepared—or at least she hoped so.

"When Finvarra was cursed, the Elders added a clause," she started. "Since they believe so much in the natural order of things, they said the troupe can be forgiven if Finvarra gives his heart away or if he dies of natural causes. At the time, this clause seemed unimportant since Faeries have exceedingly long lifetimes. A natural death won't come soon enough for Finvarra. Every day he's alive is another day Machina can trap him. He won't risk the lives of his troupe waiting to die. He needs death to come faster."

"And what does that have to do with me?" Leanna asked.

"Everything. Lovers of the Leanan Sidhe live highly inspired lives. Inspired, but brief lives. Any man she impassions is slowly driven to madness, as they desire more of her. This devotion not only eats away at their sanity, but also at their lives. As his Leanan Sidhe, you will inspire him to madness and death. That is why he has waited for you all of these years. You are his natural death, the only way he can guarantee that everyone in his troupe will be forgiven."

Leanna opened her mouth. She shut it. The world around her shattered and reshaped itself into a nauseating reality. "There is no way..."

She spun to Minerva, hot indignant tears clouding her eyes. "First, I am not his lover. All I am is a meddling fool. All I've brought upon this circus is trouble. I couldn't ever inspire him to the point he'd desire more of me, and much less to the point I'd drive him to—"

"To madness?" Minerva cut in gently. "If I'm not mistaken, he has used black magic to free you from your family, knowing Machina is always watching. He risked this entire circus by making you his main act. He crossed beyond the crystals where his enemy lies in wait, after you convinced him—a king—to allow you to go back home. He apologized to Krinard…" She leaned back against her desk, a brow arched. "How much more madness do you seek?"

It all made sense, but Leanna shook her head vehemently. "No, it doesn't matter. I'm not going to take his life. I've spent my entire life being told what to do, but I'm free here and it is my choice not to submit to this." Arms folded over her chest, she held herself still, mulish. "Someone else can do it, but I can't. I won't."

"No one else can. He can't kill himself. He can't be murdered. For the Leanan Sidhe to drive him to madness, to the point he dies, *that* is natural. This is why he needs you, Leanna. You are his natural death."

Leanna sat down on the platform. Though her chair was but a few steps across the room, the weight in her heart was heavy and her chair much too far for her watery knees. "So all I am to him, all I've ever been, is a loophole."

"You and I both know that isn't true. Your will is strong, but he's the faerie king. His glamour is as supreme as it is flawless. No mortal has ever resisted him, yet he didn't kiss you and let you go with your virtue intact."

Leanna winced, having forgotten all about the dreaded near kiss. "How did you—"

"Psh." Minerva waved her hand airily. "You're not the only one that frequents me needing answers. Did Finvarra not care for you in his own cold way, did he have no regard for your feelings, he would've kissed you that night. He never would have let you say goodbye to your family. Don't doubt his feelings. Yes, fear drives out magic, but fear can be dispelled and you can find magic again after it is gone. Doubt is much worse," she warned. She poked her chest with a firm finger. "It digs roots that remain forever and slowly suffocate love until the heart turns to ice. It is doubt that kills love, and there is no greater magic than love. Promise me you will remember this."

Hearing the words burned. "His feelings?" Leanna scoffed. "All I am to him is death in mortal form."

"Don't let your emotions rule you, child. You know there is more to you and Finvarra that exceeds that of his desire for death. You two have been bound long before you came into this circus."

Leanna knew this, but her heart ached with bitterness and she saw no reason past the irrefutable truths presented her.

Minerva gritted her teeth. "He should have told you."

"That's the thing. He did," she confessed in a quiet voice. "From the moment we met, he told me I would free him and I agreed." Frozen, she stared unseeingly at the groves on the wooden floor. "I agreed."

"But what is it that *you* will do? What do *you* believe? A muse inspires, but how you inspire is up to you. Will you inspire him to give you his heart, inspire him to give it to another? Inspire his troupe to rise up and come against Machina so that he can find love without fear? Inspire the death he desires so much? That is for you to decide. We are all given names, but in essence, they are just words. What legacy we make of it is up to us."

Leanna opened her mouth. She shut it. What could she possibly say that would make it any better? The facts were all there, had always been there, from the moment she first met him. Memories flitted through her mind of that first meeting. He'd looked at her so earnestly, confessing, *Whatever you are, Miss Weston, I need you. But maybe, just maybe, we can free each other.* And instead of asking the right question, anger and pride had led her to agree. Not finding any more words, Leanna kept to her silence.

The rest of the appointment passed with measurements taken and no words spoken. Minerva made no attempts at polite conversation, and for this Leanna was grateful.

The visit over, Leanna rose quietly, clutching her old rehearsal attire to her chest. Now clad in black muslin with a glittering trim and hose, she walked to the door. She may have murmured a thank you, a good night, or might not have said anything at all as she turned her back on Minerva and walked out into the night.

Zips of light streaked the sky, parallel to her dash across the field. Blinded by Minerva's painful revelations, she let her spirit guide her somewhere, anywhere—someplace, anyplace where she could forget the innocence and ignorance that haunted her all her life.

Patches of conversation, of carefree laughter, and the soft strum of a guitar eclipsed the crunch of her steps. Sitting at the center table of the cookhouse was Vicente with his guitar. Eyes closed, he plucked away a joyful song while around him, the performers congregated, some dancing, others singing wholly out of tune.

In the midst of such darkness, there in the cookhouse was some happiness. The sight wound itself around Leanna's heart, tightening with each ragged breath. She was their salvation. This joy didn't have to be temporary if she did what was expected of her. What Finvarra needed to free them all.

Tears in her eyes, she clutched her crystal and turned away.

The circus forgive her, but she couldn't.

# CHAPTER SEVENTEEN
## FALLING STARS

THE NIGHT WAS COLD, and it felt like icicles stabbed at her lungs with each breath. Leanna embraced this discomfort and staggered forward into the empty Big Top. She cast her cloak aside, fall where it may, and breathless, she bound up the ladder, needing the rope. Needing another type of fear that would suffocate the hellish ache in her chest. It threatened to devour her alive. She reached the platform on one breath and focused on the rope. Only the rope.

Luna floated down toward her. She whirred around Leanna, creating loops of light that glittered behind the tears Leanna forbade to fall. She would not cry.

Flying right and then left, Luna floated out over the platform. She returned to Leanna's side with a long whir that sounded very much like *yooo-yooo*, followed by a question-like squeak.

"Kioyo isn't here," Leanna replied and took a deep breath to steady her words. "But I'm sure he won't mind. All I want is to dance, please." Her voice broke. "I need to dance."

Luna squeaked and flew up to her counterparts. On her piped call, the pixies detached from the crossbars and whisked down, lining the rope like little specs of fire. In position, Luna flew down to Leanna with a confirming whirr.

Whereas once her pulse would have quickened, Leanna's heart slowed with pleading pangs for her to step out onto that rope and abandon all she'd learned on the platform, everything from curses to unrequited love to the damned duty of the Leanan Sidhe. Her body disagreed. Weary and shaking, it wanted to collapse onto the platform and mourn the waking nightmare it was being forced to endure, the guilt over lives that could be lost because of her.

She closed her eyes and made Vicente's tune a melody on her lips. Like a siren's song, her soul couldn't resist the lure. The unfinished dance appeared once again in the darkness of her closed eyes, and possessed by it, she picked up her dance where she had left it last, her soul dying within the gilded cage that was her life before the circus.

To the sighing whirr of the pixies, Leanna caressed the air with her arm in one vertical stroke, opening the door to this cage that had been unlocked by a cursed Ringmaster. Curling her hand back to her heart, she abandoned the cage the way she had abandoned her home, and stepped out onto the rope.

Her movements flourished again into a parallel imitation of her life. In the way she had trespassed onto the circus, she crouched low and straightened like a blooming flower. She reached longingly into the air, remembering her hand upon the Big Top for the first time. The pixies floated down around her in slow, swaying motions, reminiscent of Ellie and Jin's falling snow.

With an arabesque, she reached up to one of the withering lights. She caught it in her hands the way Jin had caught her, and blew it away like a phantom kiss. The rest of the pixies ignited brighter. So did the smoky memory of the one who sparked longing in her heart with a like kiss. The one whose life she was destined to take.

"Finvarra," she whispered to the opposite platform. Though it was empty, she imagined him there, waiting for her. To the memory of her palm against his heart, she extended a hand toward him. The other she reached back toward this fictional cage where her old life resided. En pointe, she moved further to the center of the rope, her body swaying backwards, forwards. Toward him and away...

Every extension whispered, *Come to me.*

Every withdrawal, *Stay away.*

Every reach, *I will be your lover.*

Every recoil, *but never your death.*

Like the flutters of a butterfly's wings, Leanna sprinkled her fingers, each one an isolated thought in her mind. What was right? What was wrong? Should she stay? Should she go? Wavering between this new life and her old existence, each sway thrust her deeper into confusion.

Torn in this world of longing and duty, she lifted her arms up to her sides where the pixies hovered around them and gave her wings of light. Reaching out to the smoky memory of Finvarra, she extended a glowing wing toward him. Maybe, just maybe, she could fly them both from curses and hearts. From society and fear...

Yet, recalling how she would indeed take him away from curses and hearts—from life itself, her tears smeared the rope. Gathering her hands back to her chest, her fingers brushed against the cool crystal. One angry tug and she tore it from around her neck. Undone, she clutched it tightly. Her mother had said it would keep her safe. Why didn't it protect her from this heartache?

Embraced by the pixies, Leanna closed her eyes and wept, and the dance faded, once again incomplete. Why did it have to be this way? She could have endured being his lover, whatever it entailed. With pleasure she would have inspired him with kisses of her own. This raging fire he'd awoken within her core wanted him, yearned for him. She sobbed into her hands, screamed the frustrations of her life into her fingers. If she was to drive him to madness, then why did it feel as if she was losing her mind?

In the darkness of her closed eyes, a melody resounded. Leanna lowered her hands and blinked her eyes open, the sound more beautiful than any she had ever heard. With the pixies tight along her, she turned.

Yelena knelt on the platform's edge, her eyes turned down toward the rope. She rocked back and forth, humming the solemn lullaby. Leanna swallowed, the beautiful intervals settling heavy in her chest as though the laments of the circus and of her life had been given voice.

"Yelena?"

Pitched whirrs squeaked, followed by a pinch at her arms. In front of her, the pixies streaked the air, their lights flashing frantically.

"What on earth has gotten into you?" Leanna scolded the pixies. "Stop it! I'm going to fall!"

Luna zipped to her, her light flickering between bright fuchsia and yellow. Fluttering a manic circle in the air, she whirred louder than normal. Around her, the pixies' discordant sound of pitched flutes hurt Leanna's ears and afflicted her balance.

Nips at Leanna's skin made her cringe and hiss, while Yelena rocked and hummed her song. The melody echoed unnaturally, as though her voice were that of legions.

The pixies that had embraced and comforted her as she cried now pressed against her. What she could imagine being their small fingers dug into her arms as though... as though clinging for life. Leanna's heart pounded.

"The song," she realized. "Yelena, stop it. You're hurting them!"

Emerald eyes cradled by black circles met hers, her skin pale. Leanna gasped at the look there, hopeless. Vacant. Dead. Yelena brushed aside her cloak and slid a dagger from her side. Rocking back and forth, she pressed it to the rope.

Leanna froze. "Dear God..."

Above her, pixies charged toward the opposite platform like a cloud of fire. Yelena opened her mouth, and her song left her lips as black smoke. Twines of fog enveloped the many pixies, and in this murky cloud, their light quickly waned.

"Luna," Leanna breathed, fear compromising her voice. "Get help!"

Luna whisked down instantly as the pixies plunged at Yelena in waves. They never reached her, their lights tangled in the curls of smoke and song.

"Yelena, please," Leanna begged. "Look at me, you don't have to do this, please."

Yelena cringed as though wanting to stop, but being unable to. "I have no choice," she moaned. While she spoke, the song continued around them with a life of its own.

The pixies that held Leanna steady formed a glittering wall of light before her and shielded her from the imminent fog with their small bodies. Yelena groaned, tightening her hand on the blade as she serrated faster.

"Go!" Leanna yelled to the pixies as she took a step back. Venomous smoke curled outward, killing all in its path. There were not enough pixies to catch her were she to fall, but they could save themselves! "It's me she wants! Go, please!"

Two more steps and Leanna's joints grew watery, her feet numb. Lightheaded, she struggled to stay upright. But as her shield of pixies grew thin, and the black mist enveloped her, pain settled in her chest and the scene froze in time.

In this world where pixies rained from the sky like stars burdened with too many wishes, Leanna met Yelena's gaze and knew she looked into Machina's essence: pits of desperation and pain, of black magic. Of surrendering to hopelessness when with one final slice, she cut the rope.

Leanna's world slowed and she, too, fell, dying amongst the pixies. As the fringes of her sight darkened and her heartbeats succumbed to the poison, the crystal in her hand grew blistering cold.

At once, she felt herself split in two. One part of her watched Yelena stand on the edge, open her arms, and tip into the open. The other part gazed down at a black stallion's mane—Croga's mane as he trod through a dark forest.

"Finvarra," she breathed with the last of her strength. Being both within his body and hers, she heard the winds echo her call in his ears.

The sound wound itself around his heart, and his head snapped up. "Leanna?"

Krinard drew up beside him. In a bond only years of friendship could forge, his stare darkened with understanding.

The winds blew then, and something else came. A strange scent of decay, death, and something colder... staler... metal.

Krinard drew his sword and met Finvarra's stare knowingly. "I will hold Machina back. Go!"

Finvarra snapped the reins in tune with the rumbling thunder. With a high-pitched neigh, Croga bolted forward like the subsequent lightning cutting through the clouds.

The sky opened and rain fell. So did the crystal from Leanna's hand. The last she heard before it slipped from her fingers was Krinard's roar to charge over the metallic shrieking of a beast.

The last she felt before her body met the earth was the rain whip Finvarra's skin as he rode for his life to reach her.

# Chapter Eighteen
## The Reason She Lives

THE HOLLOW PITTER-PATTER OF RAIN on the canvas drew Leanna from the blackness of sleep. Her lids fluttered open. Above, shadowy marionettes waved across the ceiling in the amber light. A few more blinks and their outline defined into the many butterfly wings of Ellie's tent. She let out a slow breath and settled back into the pillows, her body suddenly heavy and aware. Something had happened. Of that her throbbing mind was sure. Her limbs ached with this knowledge. But what?

She frowned. In searching her thoughts, there was only fog. She lolled her head sideways onto the pillow, toward the hearth across the room. Maybe the pure fire there would dispel this haziness in her mind.

The fog remained, but breathless, she clutched the blankets at the sight before the flames. Damp hair tied back in a loose pony tail, undone cravat and mud speckled boots, Finvarra was there.

Leanna pressed her lips together, tears pricking her eyes. The desire to run to him, to touch him... heavens, just to feel him safe beneath her hands was overwhelming. In all her anger, in all the horrible things she had learned of his past, it was the memory of him vanishing into the mist, the thought of never seeing him again that hollowed her soul.

Minerva sat opposite him, knitting at the winged back chair. Though the needles in her hand moved at a steady pace, her face was turned up toward Finvarra who focused on the fire, his mind distant with thought. "She will feel some lingering effects," she said to him. "But it's nothing a few hours of sleep can't fix."

His shoulders fell with a slow breath, as if not wanting to disturb the air with his exhale.

Minerva set down her needles. "Though her heart was weak, it has grown stronger. *She* has grown stronger. Her illness will not plague her here

146

behind the crystals," she said, her voice stern. "Don't fear for her. It will do us no good."

The muscles of his jaw tightened, but he kept quiet.

"Neither will this guilt you feel," Minerva said. "You can't blame yourself, not for this. Whatever madness possessed Yelena was not of your doing. Miss Weston still lives, and that is what you must focus on."

Finvarra looked to his hand where a crystal necklace dangled from his fingers. "But I brought this upon her."

As if hypnotized by this glinting pendulum, Leanna froze. Images of Yelena and her poisonous song tore through the fog in her mind, chased by memories of falling pixies and necklaces. Her heart pounded. Something had happened, indeed.

Minerva turned round at once. A smile curved her lips, though sadness haunted her once stoic black eyes. She set aside her knitting and rose.

The movement snatched Finvarra from his daze, and he turned. His gaze fixed on Leanna instantly, and around them, the world failed to turn. She didn't breathe. Neither did he. He only slid his eyes along her, slowly, as if wishing to ascertain her well-being with one look. Warmth swelled in Leanna's core, rising into her chest.

Minerva sat on the edge of the bed; the dip in the mattress nudged at Leanna's attention. "How are you feeling?" she spoke between their stares. She brushed an errant strand from Leanna's forehead. "Does anything hurt?"

Leanna shook her head. She regretted it instantly. The world waved before her eyes though, beneath her, it remained soft and still.

"My head," she said weakly. "But just a little."

"Good, good." Minerva swallowed. "What about your feet and arms? Can you feel them?"

Hesitantly, Leanna willed her fingers to flex. An answering crack from her joints resounded.

Nodding encouragingly, Minerva then focused black eyes on the two lumps of her feet under the blanket. Leanna extended one and then the other quickly wishing to dispel the fear. Minerva smiled at the moving mounds and settled back with a relieved sigh. At the fireplace, Finvarra's shoulders lowered with an exhale and he turned away, his reaction a secret between him and the fire.

"You had quite a fall," Minerva revealed, patting Leanna's hand. "Thankfully, Tomas arrived in time. Had he not remained behind, this would've all ended very badly." She stood and aided Leanna in sitting up.

A bell rung outside and Leanna grimaced. The echo resounded in her head; the bell could have been right behind her eyes.

"Come in," Finvarra said just above a whisper. He moved toward the tent door.

Minerva made to adjust Leanna's blanket higher, but when she touched her arm, Leanna hissed. Lifting the sleeves of her nightdress, she sucked in a breath. Small bruises marked her skin in tiny blotches of black and blue.

"The pixies," she breathed. "They held onto me, to protect me, but Yelena's song..." Cut off by flashes of the vicious attack, she stammered, "Are they alright? So many of them fell, and her song hurt them."

Tomas walked in, and she silenced, the answer to her question marked by the solemn look on his face. Still, she kept her eyes fixed on him, refusing to believe it. He would reveal something different from her fears. He just had to.

He met Leanna and Minerva's eyes respectfully, then turned to Finvarra. "Ringmaster," he murmured and nothing more. When Finvarra nodded for him to continue, Tomas shook his head and lowered tired brown eyes. "We saved some, but the others... "

"No," Leanna moaned. Though under the blankets, she shivered as the room grew colder with the familiar chill of death. At her side, Minerva swallowed deeply and lowered her face. She reached out for Leanna's hand and gave it a tight squeeze.

Finvarra shut his eyes a moment as though the pain of Tomas's words sought to map his veins. He turned back to the fire, his hands curled to fists at his sides. "Did you find anything?"

"No, Ringmaster. We've searched Yelena's tent and her things, but there were no signs of black magic. I asked around, but no one found her behavior alarming. Something else must have brought this on." Tomas's brows gathered, thoughtful lines marking his forehead. "To be honest, sir, I believe it to be something beyond the crystals."

"Do you really think it was Machina? Could the trees have told her we'd arrived?" Minerva poured Leanna a glass of water at the bedside. "They're the only ones that could have known we were here already. Perhaps Yelena went beyond the crystals and made her deal. It wouldn't be the first time."

Finvarra shook his head. "It's fall here. The trees have no reason to be angry with me. I didn't bring the cold." He sighed. "Your theory, however..." He squeezed the bridge of his nose and took a moment. "Another traitor in my midst."

Numb, Leanna lowered her gaze to the glass of water handed her. The surface rippled, her hands shaking at the painful truth. She caused this. Yelena must have been so desperate for freedom, perhaps angry at Leanna for having encouraged Finvarra to go beyond the crystals and endangering their forgiveness. Yes, once again she had meddled, and this time many had been killed.

Shutting her eyes, she clutched the glass tighter. If only the damned glass would shatter and dig shards into her hands, maybe then the pain of guilt wouldn't hurt so badly.

But the glass didn't break, and Leanna opened her eyes, left to absorb this truth in its entirety. She had caused this. How much more pain would she bring upon this circus?

"Keep looking," Finvarra said. "We can't afford another attack before we've even opened."

"Yes, Ringmaster." Tomas made instantly for the door. He stopped. "And what of Kioyo?

Leanna's head lifted at once, her pulse quick. "He hasn't returned?"

Finvarra's mouth drew to a grim line, and the temperature in the room dipped significantly. At the fireplace, the flames swayed with a snap. "Instruct the crystals to deny him entrance. He disobeyed my orders and is not to be allowed back in."

Leanna sucked in a sharp breath. "You can't leave him out there!"

Minerva put a hand at her shoulder. "That's not fair, Finvarra." She rubbed Leanna's back in cool, soothing strokes. "You're angry and will regret this."

He slid his gaze to Minerva, a stare of ice and chained fury. "If he wants to risk the lives of this troupe for his foolish pride, he can risk his life as well. A fair punishment."

"He is risking his life," Leanna cried, "by trying to find Inara."

"He left you," he rasped.

"So did you!" The sight of him glittered behind her angry tears. "So did you."

Finvarra stood deathly still, watching her. Though seeming impenetrable, those eyes grew bluer, colder. Dangerous. "Tomas, do as I said."

"No!" Leanna thrust aside the blankets and bolted to her feet before Minerva could stop her. In a speed birthed from desperation alone, she rushed to the door and blocked it. "Tomas, you will do no such thing."

149

Tomas froze at the door. He was so much bigger than her, and Leanna had little doubt he could puff a breath and blow her away. Those kind brown eyes, however, told her he never would.

Finvarra swept between them. "This does not concern you. Tomas will do as I say, and you will not meddle!"

"I will meddle when I choose," she said, equally harsh. "You are not my king!"

Finvarra's eyes flashed, shock and awareness warring there. The fire in the grate wavered, the room left to more darkness than light.

Minerva appeared at Leanna's side. She cradled her shoulders, coaxing her with quiet words to move away from the curtains and sit. Perhaps she should have. The winds that blew through the curtain were frigid and she shivered. But shrugging Minerva's hands away, she stepped closer to Finvarra and stared up at him, mindful of what he was. More, of who: the faerie king whose glamour could bring her to her knees.

Still, she steeled her spine and met his stare for each venomous measure. The look in his eyes told her she had crossed the line, but for Kioyo's sake, she had to.

"Leave us," he barked over her shoulder, his anger thinly veiled. He moved beside the door and faced Tomas. "When Kioyo arrives, take him to my tent and wait for me there."

Leanna exhaled slowly, the relief dizzying.

"Yes, Ringmaster." With a curt bow, Tomas exited the room.

Finvarra turned to Minerva who had yet to move. He arched a brow, to which she pursed her lips.

"Good God, Minerva," he said. "I don't mean hurt her, if that's what you're so concerned about."

"Oh, I'm not concerned," she said mildly, moving Leanna away from the gust of cool wind that filtered through the curtain. "I'm here because you never asked me to leave."

Frustration marked his eyes. "I said to leave us."

"And that, my dear, is an order, not a request." She gave him a firm look as she set Leanna on the edge of the bed. "But since there is much sewing to be done before sunlight, I will excuse myself."

Leanna toured her gaze between them. No subordinate ever spoke to a king that way, not that she had been in the company of many kings anyway. But Minerva was no subordinate, of this she was certain.

Before she could give it another thought, Minerva tipped her chin and bore a strong gaze down into hers. "You will feel a bit tired, so rest. Is that understood? And no more quarrelling." She brushed Leanna's hair over her shoulders. "It will give you wrinkles."

Leanna smiled, in part to keep her lips from trembling as Minerva's support sprouted tears in her eyes. Bringing her shawl over her hair, Minerva walked to the door. She passed Finvarra, shook her head and chuckled, and walked through the curtains.

Left alone, Leanna hugged herself. Though only she and Finvarra remained, the room felt crowded with lingering anger and mean-spirited words. She hugged herself tighter against the memory of them, having regretted the moment she had said them. But, the damage was done.

At the desk, Finvarra tapped a small butterfly pendulum gently. Utterly helpless, he stared down at the swaying motions. His normal glow dimmed, he looked exhausted and drained. Anger left Leanna feeling the same. But she folded her arms across her chest and set her jaw, needing to hold fast to her irritation. She would fold otherwise. For Kioyo's sake, she couldn't.

"We said we would try to get along," he said, his tone softer.

"We did, but I can't sit by and let you put this unjust blame on Kioyo."

"Unjust? I specifically asked him to guard you with his life. Instead, he left and you nearly lost yours. And *I* am unjust?" Finvarra scoffed, raking a hand through his hair. His ponytail dissolved into a disarray of blond strands that he fisted at his nape. Gripping the edge of the reading table, he hung his head. Blond strands veiled his face, but Leanna didn't need to see it to know of his anger. The air sweltered with it and she held her breath, half expecting him to clear the table in one angry swipe.

"This is madness," he muttered to himself. "Complete and utter madness."

"Then why do you blame him? Shouldn't you be blaming me?" Leanna shrugged weakly, a bitter smile at her lips. "Is that not the point of my existence in your eyes, to inspire you to madness and death?"

He lifted his head.

"Don't tell me it isn't," she said, heading off any words. "I know the truth now. That's the freedom you seek. That's all you've ever wanted of me." Her voice broke.

He straightened, but didn't turn to her, didn't say a word.

Leanna shook her head, his silence painful. "You know, I may make mistake after continuous mistake, but they're never out of ill will. But you…"

Against her wishes, a tear fell. She batted it away angrily, glad he didn't see its descent. "You're a bastard, and I never should've trusted you. You should've told me who you were, what you really wanted from me. This was supposed to be my home, and now I find that it's all a lie."

He spun to her. "I never once made myself out to be somebody other than what I am." His eyes blazed with a conviction that weighed on her chest. "Whether a commoner or a king, I am but a cursed man looking to free my troupe. I always told you you'd bring me my freedom, and in return I would give you yours. I never promised anything else."

The last of his words were spoken a little over a whisper, but tore through Leanna like a hurricane. Had he yelled them, perhaps their meaning might've been diluted in the screams. But he hadn't and she understood them for what they meant. She'd been a fool.

"All I want is freedom for my troupe, Miss Weston. Yours was a doppelganger, my troupe will find it in snow. I was not a good man, and will only find mine in death. It's something I have long accepted."

Leanna opened her mouth to speak, but… what on earth could she say?

"Understand me," he said, meeting her stare. The look in his eyes stole at her breath; a deeper well of regret and loneliness resonated there. Remembering their shared vision, she turned away finding it difficult to accept this defeat. *Understand him*? How could he ask her to understand his desire for death? Magic wouldn't be the same without him. Neither would the circus or Forever or her life.

"I won't do it. I'm not this muse you expect me to be. I'm sorry, but I can't be. All I want is for your circus to be free, but if the cost of such freedom is my taking your life, I can't."

He bristled, lips pressed together into a line, but he said nothing.

"Please, don't surrender to this hopelessness. You too can find your forgiveness, find a way to be free of this curse. What happened is in the past, and if you were to see beyond that, maybe you could find a way to care for another without fear, the way Ellie wished you to."

Finvarra straightened, but didn't turn to her, instead focused on the flames. His body grew rigid and his mind distant, as he seemed to wrestle with his thoughts.

"Please," she begged him. "Think of your sister, think of Forever. You need them and they need you. You may have made a mistake in keeping Aithne, but you loved her. You did not put that dagger in her hand; you did not thrust it into her heart and take her life. You are not the reason she died."

"But I am the reason she lives!" He turned to her, shame and agony and

152

pain all reflected in his frame. The whites of his eyes glinted in the firelight as he confessed, "I commissioned the heart that gives her life."

Leanna sat down slowly, the revelation stealing at her strength. She turned to the fire. The door was too far to leave, however badly she wanted to… or didn't want to. She just didn't know. She didn't know anything anymore.

There was much to be said, yet for a while, neither of them spoke. The void was filled with the pops and licks of the flames, with the wavering intensity of the rain upon the canvas and the low howls of the wind.

"At first, I didn't know what to do," Finvarra said. Quiet footsteps drew him closer, and he sat in the chair beside her. "When she drew the dagger, I stood there, frozen, unable to save her from herself. So many thoughts crossed through my mind in that sliver of a second as I watched her fall to the ground with that dagger through her heart. I thought of Ellie and how ashamed she would be. I thought of Jin, the only one to ever tell me how foolish and careless I was in my ways. I thought of my land, my people. I thought of Aithne, of who she was before me, of who she became because of me."

He held empty hands before him as though still able to see her there. "She clung to me as life left her, and I could do nothing to keep it, to keep her. It was my fault. You are right. I didn't put the dagger in her hand, but had it not been for me, she never would've had the need for it. But as I held her lifeless against me, her blood staining my robes and snow, I thought that if somehow I could fix it, if somehow I could fix her, then it would be like time had reversed, and though I could never have her again, at least she would live."

He lowered his hands and his voice. "I did the only thing I could. I rode out with her, to someone I never should have trusted, an old friend who was not a friend anymore. He tinkered with things that covered his land in ash and soot, but I knew what he was capable of. The abominations that had cost him his kingdom could save Aithne's life. I begged him to save her, whatever the means."

Finvarra shook his head, his eyes distant with memory. "He took her from me, and I knew I went against the natural order I swore to uphold, but I couldn't bear to let her die. And I didn't. When I took her back to her home, to her husband's side, she lived. My dear girl now kept alive by a mechanical heart."

*His dear girl…*

Numb, Leanna curled into herself. She never imagined him capable of such a love, but his tale proved otherwise and made her hate him, pity him, want to hold him all at once.

"It was supposed to have fixed things," he went on, "but something else found a place within her, and she became what she is now. It was too late that I realized I had made a deal, and I was betrayed."

Standing, he moved away from her. "The heart had been powered by an old evil that has sought to destroy my kind since before the Elders descended from the Otherworld. It took root in her obsession for me, and it will not rest until she has destroyed all I hold dear, everything and everyone, until there is only me left for her taking. So you see, Miss Weston. I was not a good man, and this circus is a punishment that I deserve."

Leanna kept to her silence. There were no words for the heartache.

He sat forward, the crystal pendant cupped in his hands. "A part of me thought you knew these things. Your mother gave you the crystal and there are stories about me, about the Leanan Sidhe. I saw the books all over your room. Surely you must have come across at least one tale."

Leanna considered this. Her thoughts fluttered like the butterfly wings above and she rose, unable to stand the nervous energy. "I looked in all the books I was allowed, the ones she brought me, but never found anything about you or about your Leanan Sidhe."

Following his train of thought, she grew cold. "She kept them from me," she realized. "I was always so sick; my mother was the one who brought me all my books. She must've kept from me any book where I'd learn of you or of your Leanan Sidhe. She said I was her inspiration. She must've believed she found your Leanan Sidhe in me." She walked away, working through her memories as the room grew smaller around her.

*If the day ever comes where you can't find magic in the world, you take this ticket and go to Finvarra's Circus. There you'll find all the magic you need.*

"She always spoke of the magic she saw here, magic capable of anything. I think she truly believed it could heal me." She turned a watery gaze to Finvarra. "I've defended your name my entire life, refusing every rumor and vicious story. She knew I wouldn't have come if I suspected for a moment that I was to cause your death."

Having found her answer, she stopped pacing. "She knew and never told me, and now I'm here." She faded into a terrible silence. She understood her mother's reasons, but the truth burned cold. She hugged herself, feeling alone most of all.

Lost in the agony of her realization, her breathing hitched when a blanket came upon her shoulders. Too hurt to turn away, too tired to care for proprieties, she stood there as Finvarra cradled her shoulders gently.

"You defended my name?" he asked.

She clutched the blanket closed before her and lifted her gaze to his over her shoulder. "Always."

Finvarra met her stare and his hands slipped from her upper arms. He walked away, to the curtained windows. "Ultimately it is me that Machina wants. You have your freedom."

"What are you saying?" Awareness trickled down her spine, cold and slow. It couldn't be that…he meant for her to leave.

"When I gave your mother the crystal, I sent her away, and told her it was imperative she never to return, unless she found my Leanan Sidhe. At the time, I believed the Leanan Sidhe was but a fantasy, something I dreamt of but that, like freedom, would never come. As such, I never imagined your mother would find her, and thus, she would never return."

He looked to her. "But then you came, sickly, unearthly, and strange. You snuck into my circus like a thief seeking to steal in the dark. Instead, standing before me, refusing a place at my circus while making demands, you stole my heart that for the first time failed to beat."

Leanna didn't refuse the tear that spilled onto her cheek. His words were magic of their own, that fixed her feet to the ground while somehow carried her mind into the clouds.

He neared her, and brows gathered, trailed a hand along her jaw. "That is why you must leave. I will draw Machina away from here, away from you. You can take your freedom and leave far from this place where you will be safe and will want for nothing. I will make sure of it."

Seeing him standing there awaiting her answer, Leanna was certain if she chose to leave, he wouldn't force her to stay. She'd never had a more aching thought.

"Even if I wanted to leave, I don't think I could," she said. Not wanting to see his reaction to her imminent confession, she turned and paced to the hearth. "I know there have been many other girls, and perhaps I am just another one who so happened to have a ticket and necklace. Pride tells me that is so, and it begs me to leave. I'm not a faerie goddess nor am I this otherworldly woman of legend." She chuckled sadly. "But then I think of how you've haunted me for most of my life..."

She tightened the blanket around her shoulders and closed her eyes, imagining his hands still there. "I belong here. A part of me has always known this, and I can't imagine it any other way." She opened her eyes. "I won't leave. I can't. I don't want to."

A soft breeze blew and he was behind her. Slowly, the crystal lowered before her, coming to a rest just beneath her collarbone. Feeling it cool against her skin and his gentle touch clasping it at her neck, a tear spilled from her eyes.

His hands came upon her then and smoothed down her arms. "You've haunted me as well," he said, his breath skimming her hair. "Your mother had the necklace for many years, yet, I never felt her. But you...I knew your spirit, long before I ever saw your face."

Leanna closed her eyes, his words reaching the deepest parts of her existence. They were the right words. But most of all, she stood there and surrendered to his arms, knowing that they were true. She knew his spirit, the same way he knew hers. She had suffered his terrible dreams with him, felt offense at the rumors of him, and shared the agony of living with a cursed fate. And that, above curses and broken hearts, had to stand for something.

The flames at the grate began to wither, casting intimate shadows around them. The rain intensified and washed out all other sound. With her eyes closed, Leanna's senses heightened to his hands journeying her arms, to the scent of rain, of vanilla, and him. A sigh stole from her, blissful. This was something else they could have: each other. No longer did they have to exist together in spirit, but now they could be together in body as well. How could she give this up without discovering all of it?

She clutched the blanket closed at her chest and turned to him. She knew Machina killed every woman he favored, but then and there, caged by his arms around her, by his hands that smoothed down her back in an unhurried stroke, she couldn't bring herself to care.

"There must be another way," she said. "I can't be the death of you."

"There is, but you know the risks of the alternative. I can't allow—won't allow it." Taking her hand, Finvarra turned her wrist over. He grazed his thumb along her pulse and pressed a kiss against it. The coolness of his lips sparked the dying embers of their previous night, and Leanna exhaled, forgetting the world, forgetting proprieties, forgetting all about the risks. There were just his lips at her skin and the inviting darkness.

Finvarra lowered her hand. His grip loosened, and the moment shattered... almost.

Tightening her hold on him, Leanna didn't allow him to go. This moment couldn't break. Yes, pixies had fallen, and there was Machina. There was evil and darkness enough to swallow them whole, but not there. Nothing could hurt them there.

Finvarra gazed down at her hand staying him then lifted his lashes, uncertain. The black of his eyes widened, and his fingers against her skin trembled lightly, barely enough to be felt. But she felt it—felt his need to hear her answer. Was she certain that she wanted him?

Tentatively leading his hand back around her waist, she stepped forward and nodded. His brows lowered as if her action wounded him, but the core of his eyes blazed and burned the world from around them.

And in this privacy, he kissed her.

# CHAPTER NINETEEN
## KISS OF DEATH

DEATH.

His lips met hers, and she thought of death. It'd come for her before, only to leave her weary and hopeless, though never lifeless. But at Finvarra's mouth, Leanna was certain she would die. Either her heart would fail because of his kiss or Machina would tear it from her chest for the same reason. But forsaking consequence, she parted her lips and accepted his kiss, welcoming sweet death, whatever its form.

His lips molded to hers, gently easing her from inexperience. Slowly, patiently, he showed her how to receive his affection and give it in return. Their rhythm a pulse, he pulled her closer as if wanting to absorb her into his being.

Leanna released the blanket to the floor and slid her arms around his neck, wanting the same... more. They tumbled back blindly, hands exploring, lips tasting until a bookcase supported the labors of their love. Their bodies shifted and aligned, twined, until no space remained between them. His crystal pressed against her skin and hers against his. At once, the stones grew blindingly cold, and Leanna felt him so present, she was certain she once again invaded his soul.

Falling.

Being within him felt like falling. Like a million rising suns and setting moons, she fell through darkness and light, through Finvarra's soul. In this never-ending universe of his spirit, each star was a memory of his life, free for her to explore. There were so many. She should have focused on these things and learned the truths of his life. Yet, being within him, tasting him, running her hands along him, she saw but one truth. He trusted her wholly with all the secrets of his soul—the ultimate vulnerability, the ultimate trust. Tears spilled from her eyes.

Heart to heart, she shed all fear and doubt, and opened her soul to him as well. The crystal's burn intensified, but weaving her hands in his silken hair, she kissed him with every truth she had. That she'd been dying before the circus. But beside his troupe, beside him, she lived. That she would be his lover, but never his death.

*I will take your heart,* she confessed into their bound souls. *But never your life.* In knowing his every fault and transgression, she would.

Sharp, concentrated pain twisted at her chest. She clutched tightly to Finvarra's shoulders and stiffened, eyes shut tight against the stabbing pain. The crystals burned as if wishing to tear her open and burn away her heart.

Finvarra's fingers dug into her back just as violently. He moaned into their kiss and surfaced with a gasp. Leanna's eyes snapped open, and she froze at the sight of him. Struggling for air, he stumbled back, clawing at his shirt. He fisted the fabric and ripped it open. A light shone brightly at his chest, pulsing like a heart.

"Finvarra!" she cried. Fear moved her forward and she reached out to him.

At once he opened his eyes, panic in his stare. He scrambled away from her and crashed back against the reading table, one hand clasped over his chest, the other clutched the table for support. He groaned again, and had his teeth not been clenched, Leanna knew he would've roared.

"What did you say?" he rasped. "What on earth did you say?"

She retracted her hand to her own chest and hissed. The crystal had blistered the skin above her heart, a large red mark coming out from under her nightgown.

Finvarra's vise-like grip tightened on the desk's edge, his knuckles white. By and by, the light between his fingers faded, and his labored breathing returned to normal.

"What just happened? Your heart was glowing, and the crystals—they burned us and we were within each other's souls," she stammered, stumbling on the thoughts that came faster than she could speak them. "What just happened?"

"A mistake!" Finvarra barked, bringing his fist down on the table. The butterfly pendulum on the desk crashed onto the floor and shattered, muting Leanna's gasp. She never imagined him capable of losing his cool, but wild and savage he gripped the table. "I'm a selfish bastard and I shouldn't have done it. And it can't ever happen again."

Leanna stepped away from him until by the bookshelf. Standing beside the books that had coaxed her broken heart for so many years, her heart broke a little more.

"A mistake, of course," she breathed. Once again, he'd travelled her soul, and she his, and it was all a mistake. A hollow ache invaded her chest. So many conflicting emotions warred within her, pain and pleasure, love and shame.

Realizing his choice of words, Finvarra deflated. "Leanna," he lamented, the fire in his eyes dimmed. He straightened and in one sweep was before her, cradling her arms. She stiffened, but feeling those hands upon her again, her will withered and she walked into his waiting arms.

"Forgive me," he whispered against her temple. "Your kiss was a gift I didn't deserve, and I'm a bastard for not putting your well-being before my desires. But there are things that can't be said. Things I simply can't give you."

He broke their hold, only to frame her face with his hands. Eyes black with chained desire, he slid a desperate gaze along her features. "Not because I don't want to, but because if I give you what you seek, what you deserve..." He ran his hands along her hair, his restraint palpable. "Damn it all, if I give you what has long belonged to you, I would never forgive myself."

His voice was stern, but the look in his eyes betrayed him. *If you ask for my heart, I will give it to you,* they told her. *Please don't ask for it.* He trailed a finger along her lips, a war of duty tangled with need. The air hummed with magic and passion waiting to explode. He brought her against his chest roughly, an embrace of apology. Of if not able to kiss her, to at least hold her.

Leanna closed her eyes against him, clutching at his back with just as much vigor. What she felt there was not a king, but a man that would never find forgiveness in white snow, only in Black Death. A death she would bring him.

"God, help me," she whispered.

The bell outside tolled once, echoing around them. They held each other tighter and ignored it, a silent agreement not to let reality in, not yet.

Mere seconds, and reality rung again.

Finvarra let out a slow breath, but didn't release her. Not at first. He held her firmly as he pressed devotional kisses at the bare skin of her shoulder, at her neck, her cheek, her temple—each one more painful than the last for Leanna. With one final kiss on her forehead, but never her lips, he slid his hands down her arms until entwining his fingers with hers.

Their eyes met with mirroring looks of sadness, of what could have been were they different people, in a different place with different hearts. If only it were so simple.

But it wasn't, and lowering his eyes, Finvarra stepped back. Their fingers were last to separate. It took sheer will for her to let him go.

"Come in," he said hoarsely. Raking a hand through his hair, he walked to the middle of the room.

The hush of the curtains resounded, and Tomas entered. "Ringmaster, Kioyo waits in your tent."

Leanna stiffened. "Is he alright? Is he hurt? Did he… did he find Inara…?" She trailed off, her joints suddenly weak. She blinked, and the room swayed before her. "Never mind, I'll go and see him myself," she said quickly, hoping Finvarra didn't notice how her words slurred or the sweat dewed on her skin.

"No, you need to rest." He turned to Tomas. "I will be there in a moment."

"I've been stuck in bed *resting* for most of my life. I'm coming with you." She wiped the sweat from her brow and spun to get her cloak when the world faded in and out of blackness. One moment she was making for her cloak, the next she was in Finvarra's arms, her head tucked in the crook of his neck. He held her against him, the soft thuds of his heart a gentle lullaby that soothed the burn rushing through her veins.

The walk to the bed felt eternal to her hazy mind, but entirely too short once he set her down. She protested this with a sleepy groan.

"Sleep," he said softly, his voice blended with the blackness that fringed her sight and beckoned her to sleep.

In her weariness, Leanna sought out his hand. Cold fingers tangled with hers, and she held them tightly. "Please don't punish Kioyo for this."

The muscles of his jaw clenched.

"Please, he only wanted to help."

Finvarra's cool fingers tightened around hers reassuringly. She attempted to return the gesture, but numb fingers made it impossible.

"Thank you…" The image of him grew hazy once more.

Finvarra bent over her and pressed a light kiss on her forehead, his lips lingering. Leanna closed her eyes and surrendered to sleep at the sound of him whispering,

"Sweet dreams, my love."

She had no nightmares that night.

# CHAPTER TWENTY
## FOR THE PIXIES

THE CIRCUS HUMMED with a strange energy that met Leanna when she stepped out of her tent and headed toward the Big Top two days later. Though a somber cloud cloaked the performers and help hands heading to and away from the massive tent, the air stirred with awareness.

One day until opening day. One more day until she appeared to the world, and perhaps to her sisters, as the magnificent Leanan Sidhe. This was enough to cause any stomach to tighten. But Leanna barely felt it, the butterflies fluttering within her much stronger.

Finvarra had kissed her. It had been heavenly, his every touch patient and every sigh heartfelt. She pressed fingers to her lips, a gradual smile curving there. He'd also come to see her while she'd slept. Of all of Minerva's help, Leanna was most grateful for her disclosing of Finvarra's frequent visits and furtive caresses as she slept.

Then there were the books he'd left at her bedside, next to a vase of snow white vanilla flowers. One on top of the other were *The History of Faeries* and *Pixies, Goblins, Elves, and Other Magical Beings*. The top book, however, *The Kings of Forever*, had been the greatest gift of all. A small sprig of vanilla peeked from in between the pages. When Leanna flipped to the page, she found it marked to *King Finvarra*.

Remembering that night, how he had opened himself to her like a book, heat bloomed in her core. Shyly, she darted her gaze around the field. Maybe she would see him? Her thoughts muddled when in reaching the Big Top, a familiar voice boomed from inside.

"One more time, Vicente," Kioyo called. "From the top!"

Within moments, a violin and a harp resounded. Leanna sucked in a gasp. Kioyo's performance! She dashed into the Big Top and froze beside the gallery seats, shielded by the shadows there.

Kioyo sat on the ring's edge, his painted eyes open wide as he gazed at a red unicycle in the middle of the center ring. He stood up and at once the music slowed. Flutes and xylophones were favored over drums and cymbals, and to accentuate emotion, the trickling notes of a piano like raindrops on the keys.

In equal fluttering steps, Kioyo abandoned his seat and stepped into the light, his gold vest adding a glow to his olive skin. He stared at the invisible audience with a wide painted smile, and raised his brows twice.

With beautiful fluid swirls en pointe, he whirled to the unicycle. Pressing a finger to his mouth as if wondering how on earth to ride the thing, he looked to the pixies above. His face brightened as an idea came upon him— one he demonstrated by digging into his pockets and throwing a handful of glitter into the air. He picked up the unicycle and attempted to jump on, but it rolled forward. He fell back into a tuck and tumble that sent sawdust and glitter into the air. Leanna giggled, but covered her mouth to stifle the sound.

Numerous times he tried to climb, only to fall into a cloud of sparkles. After trying once and again, he finally mounted the unicycle. It slipped, but he shot his arms at his side and maneuvered it back under him. He remained there for a moment and never fell. Covering his face, he hefted a theatrical sigh of relief that slumped his shoulders.

He lowered his hands and pedaled once... and again...and again, keeping his hands at his sides until he rolled around the ring, free and smiling. Leanna was moments away from clapping when his mouth looped into an O as he rode faster, unable to stop. He covered his eyes and hit the ring's edge. Thrust forward, he landed flat on his back. When he lowered his hands, his painted smile was a frown.

Kioyo stood up and moped away from the unicycle, fear having gotten the best of him. He needed no lover to yearn for, not when he had this metallic paramour that rode away from him the more he wanted it.

He stopped sharply and turned to the audience. *No*, his look said. *One more time...*

He tossed his hat and vest aside and walked to the unicycle, determined. Mounting it fluidly, he took off on a journey of the ring. Again, he began to go faster and faster. Where he previously covered his eyes, he held his arms open and let the breeze brush away his fear. Leanna clapped silently. He was doing it!

He danced and spun and twirled, balanced on the seat while in arabesque, the unicycle now lost to his movements, an extension of himself.

163

He was positively radiant.

By and by the music faded and he slowed until coming to a stop. All that remained was Kioyo, his unicycle, and the painted stars trailing from his eyes, mirroring Leanna's real tears of wonder.

Kioyo nodded once at Vicente and turned, wiping the sweat from his brow. He stopped mid-stroke, catching sight of Leanna.

No longer able to hide, Leanna abandoned her shadowy corner and approached him. Kioyo dismounted instantly and did the same, but in seeing her tears, his steps doubled in time and he reached her before another tear fell from her eyes.

"Did something happen?" he asked.

Leanna shook her head, hauling a deep breath through her nose. "I'm sorry, it's just I've always wanted to see this circus. My mother spoke of its beauty, and when I walked in you were performing..."

He chuckled. "Was it truly that bad that I've reduced you to tears?"

"It was everything I dreamed it to be, and I am so happy to see you."

"And I you," he said quietly. Holding her stare, a troubled look clouded his gaze and his smile fell. He raked a hand through his hair and turned away. Without another word, he walked to his belongings and began wiping away the face paint with a towel.

"What's the matter?" Leanna walked up beside him. "I really did think it was beautiful."

He lowered his hands. "It's not that. I...I didn't find Inara." Twisting the towel in his hands, he shook his head. "She's covered her tracks well. I suspect she's not only hiding from Machina, but from us as well, and I couldn't find her."

"Neither did Finvarra. And Krinard is still out there." Leanna uttered a quiet prayer for his safety. "There is still hope."

"That isn't it, Leanna. I failed. My reasons for going out there mean nothing now because I failed to find her... and I failed you."

Leanna opened her mouth to negate this, but brown eyes met hers and she swallowed her words. "Why are you so hard on yourself?"

Sitting, he leaned forward and shook his head. "My people were going to war," he started. "It was all they ever did, but this time it was different. A rival clan went against the code of our kind, and aligned with the trolls to take over our land. They promised the trolls the precious stones found in our mines in exchange for their help at driving my people out from our land. The trolls had more advanced weaponry. We knew the battle was lost before the first stone had been cast, but my father was the leader of our tribe. Regardless of whether we won or lost, he had to fight for our honor. He sent letters and messengers, asking me to be there when they rode out. But I…" He raked a hand roughly through his hair. "I didn't write back. I didn't join them."

"But you had a life in the circus." Leanna sat beside him. "You had to perform and had other responsibilities. Surely they couldn't have expected you to go."

"I didn't go, but not because of responsibilities and performances. I was scared. I hid behind the gates of Forever, too afraid to join my father. We were taught to honor our parents and our ancestors, and I should have faced him, should have at least been man enough to tell him face to face that I wasn't going to fight. But I was scared of his reaction, scared of dying. So I hid like a coward, and now they're all dead."

Kioyo stood up and walked a few feet away as if to create distance between him and his memories. "Of everything, the worst has been wondering what my father's last thoughts were. Did he die hurt and ashamed, thinking that his son abandoned him? That his son was a coward?"

He let his head fall back and stared at the remaining pixies. "I thought this was my chance. If I found Inara and endured Machina, I could finally prove to myself that I could be brave. Instead you almost lost your life, and I ended up proving to everyone that I'm a fool. I failed my people, I failed Inara, I failed the Ringmaster, and I failed you." The painted joy on his lips accentuated the shame in his eyes. "What I did was stupid. You were my responsibility and it was for me to protect you, but I didn't."

"Enough of that," Leanna cut him off. "I was a burden to my family for too many years. I refuse to be one here. I am under no one's responsibility, and it was wrong of Finvarra to make you my guard. No one knew Yelena was capable of what she did. She was angry and desperate…" Remembering her words, her tears, and the hopeless look in her eyes, Leanna's heart dampened in spite of her anger. "She just wanted to go home."

"Still, I should've been there." Kioyo made to say more, but she shook her head. Eyes fixed on his, she neared him and slipped the towel from his shoulder. She gave him a small smile, finally understanding the significance of his performance and of his pain. "You are brave. Not everyone would run out past those crystals, knowing of the dangers waiting. But you did." She brushed away his hair from his forehead and wiped the painted starry tears with gentle strokes. "This is not your fault."

Cradling her elbow, Kioyo stayed her hand. "Neither is it yours."

Her hands fell away from him at once. "I wish I believed that." She lifted her eyes to the remaining pixies, and her guilt deepened. "I look up there and still see the pixies falling. I still see Yelena there so hopeless, and I caused it. Had I not snuck in that night, Inara wouldn't be gone, Krinard wouldn't be out beyond the crystals, Yelena wouldn't be dead. I know it just happened, but I don't think the guilt will ever go away."

"Then we'll face it, together." He squeezed her shoulder reassuringly. "You have to get back on that rope, but you have nothing to be scared of. I'm here now, and we can do a simple routine, until you're ready. I'm sure the Ringmaster will understand."

"No. The pixies deserve more. They died for me, and I will not honor them with fear." Leanna slid off her cloak and set it at the nearest seat. The little glass beads on the skirt caught the light, and reflected small rainbows against the white fabric. "I have to get on that rope, regardless of how many times it is cut beneath me."

Kioyo tilted his head. "Something has changed. You've changed."

"Everything has," she admitted. "I finally realized that my link to this circus were not the hallucinations of a lonely, sickly girl. I have been a part of this circus, of all of you, long before I ever came here." She clutched the crystal tightly. "I know you warned me against it, but I know him, Kioyo. Call it magic or fate, but I know Finvarra. This circus means everything to him and he carries the desire to free you all within his soul. I want to help. I'm going to fight for him, for you, for this circus. It will start by climbing that ladder and dancing on that rope, for the pixies."

Kioyo extended his hand to her. "We dance then, for the pixies."

Leanna slid her hand into his hold. Between them, a blessing descended when one of the surviving pixies floated down and rested above their joined hands.

Countless tours across the rope later left Leanna feeling more prepared than ever. Whereas before she had danced for herself led by her spirit, this dance was about more than just her. Each plié dipped her into her soul where she asked for the pixies' forgiveness. Each arabesque sent her reaching higher for the heavens, to those that had passed. She closed her eyes and found no fear.

Reaching the other platform, Yelena's memory waited for her. She stopped and stared at the very place she once stood. One step brought her to that very spot, but surrounded by the smeared incandescent hues of pixie blood, Leanna faced the other platform and gave Kioyo a firm nod. Come opening night, she would be ready. She had to be. For the pixies.

A sky blanketed with thick gray clouds met Leanna as she walked out from the Big Top.

"Fitting for it to be such a dreary day," she murmured, turning her attention from the roiling clouds to the surrounding fog. "Does the fog ever go away?"

"It will, after the bonfire tonight," Kioyo replied as he slid on his coat and fell into step beside her. "Once the fire dispels the fog, we'll appear to the world as if out of thin air. It's quite magical."

"But what of the crystals? They may be magical, but they hardly look frightening enough to keep anyone away."

Kioyo chuckled and offered her his arm. "To us they may look like crystals. The outside world will see wrought iron gates—quite formidable gates, I might add." He paused, his eyes focused straight ahead to where roustabouts and performers alike banded together, piling logs into a pyre.

"It's for the ceremony tonight," he said, apologetic. "At the bonfire, we will say our final goodbyes and light the pixies' passage to the Otherworld."

"Oh," was all Leanna could muster, her throat thick and dry.

They started to move away, but Finvarra appeared from behind the pyre, and Leanna stopped. Coatless and sleeves rolled up, he helped Bertrand fill the hollow spaces of the pyre with kindling. Stepping back, he dusted his hands and surveyed their work, his skin impossibly pale.

Unable to take her eyes away, she watched how with his hands at his hips, he tapped his long fingers as if keeping time of his thoughts. How even as unkempt as he was there in muddy breaches working alongside subordinates, he was more regal than ever.

The crystal hummed against her skin with coolness. Across the field, awareness rolled over Finvarra, who grew increasingly stiff. He lifted his head and turned, focused on her instantly. Despite the heat that bloomed at her cheeks, Leanna held his stare across the vast field and unwound her arm from Kioyo's. She'd missed him, and seeing him there magnified the horrible ache in her chest.

After their previous night, she shouldn't have neared him, but resisting him was a lost cause. She took a step, as did he; the intensity of their stare could've very well set the pile on fire.

The coolness of the crystal pulsed against her skin, sharper. Finvarra's brows knit and his approach stopped. She mirrored him and paused. Slowly his hand came up above his chest where he rubbed it in a small circle. Lowering his hand to his side, he turned back toward the pyre.

"Come," Kioyo said. "Let's get you to your tent. It looks like it's going to rain."

Leanna forced her eyes from a retreating Finvarra to the roiling clouds of the various shades of gray and black. Indeed, it was going to rain, but gazing back to see Finvarra gone, she frowned as the first raindrops fell. She lifted her hood against it, wishing it were snow.

# CHAPTER TWENTY-ONE
## FOG & METAL

THE BELL OUTSIDE TOLLED. Leanna released her hands that she gathered at her lap and rose. She caught sight of her reflection in the mirror and swallowed deeply. The dress she wore was breathtaking, as were the others that now hung in her wardrobe—gifts from Minerva.

In returning to her tent after rehearsals, she'd found the gold and silver muslins in her wardrobe, some embroidered with threads that sparkled in the light. There were gorgeous walking gowns—even her morning dresses were made of fine material. There were wide scoop necklines, low squared ones, modest and some that made Leanna blush. She'd never worn dresses so... revealing. Just the thought of Finvarra seeing her in one of them made her a little dizzy. All in all, it was a wardrobe fit for a queen.

But it was the black gown and glittering veil she now wore that had been set out on her bed, waiting for her, to bring her back to the painful reality that the bonfire that night was also a funeral. Leanna exhaled. The last time she had worn mourning attire had been after her mother's death. Clad in black, all the time since that horrible day evaporated, leaving a very present pain.

She lowered the sheer veil, walked to the curtains, and parted them.

"As beautiful as I imagined." Minerva's lips curled to a half smile, her red lipstick replaced by a coal tint. She, too, abandoned color and wore black, as did all those who walked past behind her toward the open field. With the light of the pixies gone, it seemed all color vanished from the circus.

Though gladdened to see Minerva, Leanna cursed her childish hope that led her to believe it would be Finvarra escorting her that night. Surely he wouldn't want to be near her after their previous night and afternoon. How could she expect it when she'd nearly taken his heart—twice?

Ashamed of her confession and its consequence, she slid her fingers into

Minerva's waiting hand. It had been a foolish thing to say. Perhaps too much, too soon. But melancholy hung thick in the air, and she frowned. Her declaration didn't matter. Her and Finvarra's problems and confusion would be waiting come morning light. This night was not about them.

"Finvarra asked if I would see you to the ceremony," Minerva said. She adjusted her black, lace scarf over her hair. "Luna is taking it particularly hard and he wished to escort her."

At this, she felt even worse. Not about them, indeed. "Of course, as he should." She twined her arm around Minerva's and they joined the quiet procession.

Night was fully settled now and torches flared between the tents, all the way to the open field. The pyre stood in the distance, in the middle of the meadow. Slow steps drew the crowd forward and they gathered around the pyre, encircling it.

All murmurs ceased at once and the crowd parted. Under the light of the ever circling fire dragon, Tomas and Kioyo approached, led by Kia. They entered the mourning circle, carrying a wooden gurney between them. Upon it were countless small casings made of leaves laid upon a bed of moss. The small sleeves were bound closed with rings of daisies and a sprig of vanilla. Leanna's heart panged. Minerva squeezed her hand as the gurney passed by them.

Finvarra walked in behind them, his gloveless hand cupped before him. A small pinkish light pulsed at his palm, the faint light seeping between his fingers—a little pixie too heartbroken to fly. The remaining pixies floated in behind him. Performers and helpers held out their hands, giving each grieving orb of light a place to rest their weary wings and hearts. Some settled on shoulders, others on the bells of skirts. Bertrand was the last to enter, a bright flame cupped in his hand.

As Kioyo and Tomas set the gurney on the pyre, Finvarra approached Leanna. Her eyes fixed on his and pain roused in her chest. Noting him swallow, she knew he felt the same. But their hearts knew better that night, and she held herself very still. This wasn't about them.

Finvarra stopped before her and held out his hand, where Luna barely glowed. Numbing and terrible cold rushed through Leanna. How could she hold Luna when she was responsible for the death of her people? No, she couldn't do this.

"She doesn't blame you," he said. "None of us do."

Doubt warred, and Leanna cast a tentative glance along the crowd.

Sadness clouded every stare, but not one was of anger. Perhaps later they would hate her, but there was no room for anything else that night, only woe.

Leanna met the tip of his fingers, holding her breath to keep her hands steady. Though lighter than a feather, when Luna stepped onto her hand, the weight of guilt pressed on Leanna's chest and the first tear fell. How much more would she bring upon this circus? She cupped Luna close to her heart, just as her mother had done so many times for her. The little pixie nestled close against her, blanketing her small body with paper thin wings that quivered like the last leaf on a vine.

The gurney lay upon the pyre now. Finvarra stepped forward and slid his gaze along the crowd in silence, making contact with every eye as if to bolster them in this hard time.

"We know that death is but a door to everlasting life. While we will mourn that the pixies are no longer with us, we must never mourn their lives. May our tears carry them gently from us, but may our cries never drown the light they bestowed upon us in our darkest of times." Finvarra nodded to Bertrand. "We light this fire in their honor. May it illuminate their path to the arms of our ancestors, to their rest in the Otherworld. We pray our Father, we pray our Mother, bless thy spirit and thy journey home."

"Bless thy spirit and thy journey home," the crowd replied in a low chorus. Leanna whispered the same.

Bertrand held up the cupped flame. The fire illuminated his sadness in hues of crimson and blue. He trickled his fingers, and the orb of fire floated from his hand and into a small opening in the logs. With each wriggle of his fingers, the flames intensified until eclipsing the light of the dragon above.

Fire clawed at the logs and sparked a swirl of light with each pixie it devoured. Luna burst from Leanna's fingers with a pitched cry. Leanna moved to go after her, but cool fingers twined with hers, halting her steps.

"Let her grieve," Finvarra said. It hurt to think of Luna crying alone, but Leanna pressed her lips together and nodded. She stepped back beside him and trained her gaze on the flames. They stood like this, facing the fire together, until lights no longer sparked from the flame, all the pixies having found their way home.

Finvarra said to the assembly, "Though with heavy hearts, we must all perform tomorrow. Do so keeping in mind those we have lost and those on the other side of the crystals." He paused and glanced down at Leanna, before turning back to his troupe. "Perform knowing that freedom will soon be yours, not at the claws of Machina, but at the hands of forgiveness and snow."

Leanna clutched her dress as the horrid shakes of truth seized her body. Indeed, their forgiveness would come at the hands of forgiveness and snow... and death. His death. She squeezed his hand tighter. This was bigger than the both of them.

Finvarra concluded the assembly with a nod. The multitude broke away, but their eyes lingered. Not on the pyre, but rather on her and Finvarra's entwined hands. The bonfire chased out the darkness, but it was their joined hands that seemed to spark hope and lift every spirit. All now stood a little taller, glowing a little brighter as if magic were infused back through their veins.

And so Leanna and Finvarra stood like this until the last member of the troupe walked away, him a pale angel and she his Black Death.

The fire burned steady and the fairgrounds were quiet. Leanna curled up at Finvarra's side, watching the mist slowly thin and fade, revealing their circus to the world. Finvarra also looked toward the white vapors, his face clouded by thought.

"You worry for Krinard and his men," she spoke against his coat, smoothing a hand over his heart.

"Amongst other things." His cool hand covered hers, stopping her affection.

"You're not still worried about me, are you? I'm fine."

"For now you are, but what of when..." He trailed off. The last of his words remained unsaid, yet hung thick in the air. *Once I die...*

"Don't think of that. We haven't lost yet," she rallied. "You still have life and we can't give up hope."

He shook his head slowly and looked away, back toward the pyre. "Hope is a dangerous thing, especially after last night."

"Yes, but we are standing here now and have controlled our hearts. As long as they remain within our chests, there is hope." Finvarra said nothing, and a sinking awareness settled in Leanna's stomach. "Unless there is something you're not telling me. Did something happen last night?"

"I'm just making provisions," he replied, too quickly for her liking. "Whether we accept it or not, the end is coming and there will be death."

She knew he lied, and she could've demanded the truth, but what for? Deny and argue as she liked, they couldn't escape this.

"This is supposed to be your punishment," she said softly. "Yet, it appears I've offended the Elders as well. I have dreamt of you for so long, yet now you're here and I can't have you."

He turned a solemn gaze to her and gathered her into an embrace. "Indeed."

"What are we going to do?" she asked, trying to think around this. "If I were to decide to help you, which I'm not saying I will, will it hurt you?"

His hands tensed at her waist. "No more than what I deserve."

"But how will it work? What exactly am I supposed to do?" The word lover stood out in her mind, and she blushed at the thought. "I know the Leanan Sidhe inspires her lovers, but it appears our hearts need little to abandon us."

His hands took off on a journey of her back, an affection that came so easily. "There are no conventions. We let things develop as they will, as they have been since you arrived." A chuckle rumbled in his chest, the vibrations sending a warm shiver down her spine. "I daresay you started driving me mad the moment you snuck into my circus. I threatened to feed you to Kia just to get you to stay, remember?"

She lifted her eyes to find a small smile tugged at his lips. "You also said you would take my heart if I didn't return."

He grinned. "I did say that, didn't I?"

"You said a lot. You called me a witch, a troll, a banshee, a spy..."

Finvarra laughed, a rich sound, warm and free, and equally contagious. Leanna's giggles soon underscored his, and together they shared this mirth.

For the slightest moment, his eyes glittered with the after-happiness of laughter. Leanna's own smile lingered. How long had it been since he'd laughed that way? A part of her knew not for a long, long time.

"You also called me a liar." She lifted a hand to his cheek, wishing to hold onto this reprieve of happiness, even for just a moment longer.

He leaned his face into her hand. "Leanna, we can't," he breathed as she trailed her hand along the line of his jaw. But the words were weak and he lowered his lips to hers, hands winding around her waist.

The winds gust as if the hands of consequence pulling them apart. There were ramifications in a kiss. Leanna knew this, as did he. But gifting caution to the wind, she met his lips and arched her body into his. His hand at her lower back brought her closer. The other skimmed upward and cupped the back of her neck. She sank onto him, feeling her skin tingle and blood hum with the need for their love to burn right through the thick fabrics. With the need to feel skin against skin. To be one. To be whole.

Finvarra stiffened. At once, Leanna broke their kiss and shifted back. His heart didn't glow, neither did the crystals grow cold. Yet something was wrong.

The answer came from the trees.

In a contagious wave, they shivered and the ground trembled. A shriek resounded, one of rage and pain, of blood and murder. Leanna flinched and gathered against Finvarra.

The tangles of fog curled back, and a bloodied Krinard stumbled through the crystals alone. Large gashes were raked across his chest, and his skin folded outward. He trod forward a step before his legs gave way beneath him and he fell, a dagger stabbed into his back.

Finvarra was in her arms and then he wasn't. He took off toward Krinard in a blur of black to the sound of crunching ice. Leanna darted after him, as fast as her humanity allowed. She meant to help, but closer to the crystals, she stopped.

Under the light of the fire dragon, a woman stood embraced by the thinned mist, her red hair billowing around her like a halo. The fog parted for a moment, and the torn white blood-stained dress she wore came into view. One of her sleeves was ripped, and the metallic patches stitched onto her arms glinted in the hue of the flames. She was a horrible beauty, a fascinating nightmare. A paradox Leanna's human mind couldn't comprehend.

Her coal brown eyes fixed on Finvarra. In childlike fascination, Machina tilted her head. Her brows gathered with centuries old yearning as she watched him attempt to form ice webs along Krinard's injury to freeze it shut. As quickly as the webs formed, they melted over and over again. It was Finvarra who grew rigid, lifting his bloody hands before him.

"No," Leanna whispered. His magic was fading.

Finvarra slid his arms under Krinard's body and dragged him away. As if tied to him, Machina stepped out of the mist and neared the crystals. She lifted metallic fingers and reached out for him, but a white wave rippled between them when her iron fingers touched the invisible boundary formed by the crystals.

Finvarra spun to Leanna and his mouth moved. She heard his scream far away in her mind, ordering her to go back to his tent. But in her soul, she heard the cry of all the girls who lost their lives to this mechanical monster.

Tomas and Kioyo brushed past. Kioyo gestured for Leanna to go, but numb, she clenched fists tightly at her sides and stared at this nightmare that plagued her dreams all of her life. This demon that stalked, destroyed, and killed. That threatened her home and her love, and it now had a face.

Machina's brows dipped. In her obsession with Finvarra, she hadn't noticed Leanna standing there. But as if feeling the hate of Leanna's stare, she turned her head. Black eyes fixed on her in an instant. She retracted her iron fingers slowly, parceling Leanna body part by body part. When her gaze fell upon the crystal dangling from Leanna's neck, her scrutiny stopped. Her blue lips quavered and tears of blood fell from her eyes. She lifted trembling fingers to her face and trailed the tears with her metal nails that clawed her skin open. It was a terrible sight, but Leanna remained still, letting her image torture Machina the way she'd tortured so many others.

Gathering iron fists against her temples, Machina screamed, a feral cry that shook the trees. Tomas lifted a hand toward the crystals. The stones grew a slight brighter, their wintry hue streaming out toward Machina.

Machina's eyes widened and, fisting her hair, she skittered back into the mist like a cornered animal, screeching in pain. A black cloud curled around her, folded and unfolded, and with an echoing hiss, she was gone.

Frozen, Leanna watched the fog, aware that she was wrong. Death would not come dressed in black, but in white fog and metal.

# CHAPTER TWENTY-TWO
## FOR HIS BEST

"FAERIES NEVER FALL ILL," Leanna read to herself to keep from sleep. Long hours had passed since Finvarra had gone, having instructed Minerva to guard her. It had taken some persuasion to convince Minerva to leave, but she had much sewing to finish before the coming evening and ultimately conceded.

Leanna curled into her chair, having denied Minerva's invitation to join her. She felt safer here, surrounded by the canvas where Finvarra had kissed her.

"Nor do they sleep," she murmured, blinking rapidly to focus her eyes on the blurred words. "Only when reaching their time to... to pass into the Otherworld will their magic fa... fa—fade, leaving them to suffer from the... plaguing human conditions..."

Her lids heavy, Leanna trailed off, unable to keep from sleep.

She fell...

Fell...

Nightmares hounded her instantly. Trapped in a vortex of smog, Krinard's bloodied body lay motionless on the grass. The image was chased by that of Machina's coal black eyes. It was here that Machina clawed continuously at her face, until a metallic skeleton with sharpened fangs remained. She bit into Leanna's arms, neck, and legs. Leanna kicked and scratched, but Machina was a ghost and slipped through her fingers.

Feeling her skin ripped from her bones, Leanna screamed for release from this prison of her mind. But poisonous tendrils separated from the storm, wrapped around her throat, and squeezed tighter. The mouths of the other dead girls screamed for her, and with each wail, the living darkness stole at her breath. Her lungs constricted, and under the strain of this horror, her heart stopped.

Outside the winds wailed and Leanna woke with a gasp. Panting, she clutched at her chest, at the crystal that was cold against her clammy skin. The strong breeze whisked into her tent, wrapped around her gently, and cooled the sweat on her brow. By and by, her quickened pulse found its normal rhythm. With one final moan, the winds died down and the curtains snapped with their departure.

Growing up, she'd never known what it was that pulled her from her vicious dreams, but like those times, the scent of vanilla lingered stronger now, and Leanna had no doubt.

"Finvarra?" She glanced around the room. "Are you here?"

She toured her gaze around the room slowly, searching out the protector of her dreams. Surely it had been him now, and her heart yearned for him more than ever.

"Finvarra?"

There was no answer and the wind no longer cried. Leanna curled into her shawl, her heart dampened. She sat back slowly, her ear still attuned to the spaces around her. A moment passed. There was still no sound. She shook her head and turned her attention back to the book.

"Faeries never fall ill, nor do they sleep—"

She shut the book with a snap. It was useless. How could she possibly read not knowing how badly Krinard was hurt or if he still lived? She set the book aside and rose to her feet. Finvarra would never endure losing his best friend. He'd never forgive himself and she wouldn't leave him alone in his pain. He needed her.

She gathered her cloak, slipped into her boots, and abandoned the comforts of her tent for the cold night. The cloak was a barrier against the frigid air, but the cold seeped underneath, and in just a nightdress, the chill was terrible. Still, determined steps carried her through the maze of pavilions, and to Finvarra's tent that was illuminated inside. Leanna's pulse quickened and her steps doubled. Days or minutes, weeks or hours, she'd missed him so very much.

Breathless, she stopped before Tomas.

Arms folded over his chest, he stared down at her, unmoving. Leanna's brows gathered. She'd never had to *ask* to see Finvarra before.

She stepped closer to Tomas. "I'm here to see Finvarra."

Tomas slid his gaze out to the darkness behind her. His jaw tightened. "He doesn't wish to see anyone."

Leanna blinked. "But surely he doesn't mean me—"

"He doesn't want to see *anyone.*"

"Oh," she breathed, nodding through the hollowing disappointment. "Of course, but is he all right?"

Tomas made to answer, but paused, his eyes flicking over her shoulder again. His mouth bowed and helplessness brimmed in his stare. Stuck. He looked positively stuck. "Please, Miss Weston, you should go. It's cold and you should be resting for tomorrow."

Leanna peered over her shoulder to see Bertrand come up alongside her.

"Is the Ringmaster not in?" Bertrand asked. "If not, I should get back to Krinard." He transferred a large leather bag from one hand to another. A bag much like the dreaded Gladstone bag Dr. Luther carried to his appointments for so many years.

Tomas's immense shoulders lowered. He stepped aside and parted the curtain for Bertrand to pass.

Bertrand entered but stopped at the threshold. "Won't you be coming in?"

Cold and hollow, Leanna shook her head, understanding. "No," she whispered. "The Ringmaster doesn't want to see me—"

Heaving coughs resounded from within and silenced her. Bertrand ran into the tent just as a sharp gasp set off another round of coughs.

Leanna froze.

*Faeries never fall ill...*

"Oh, God."

"Go," Tomas said. "There's nothing you can do here."

"No, I need to be with him." She moved forward, but Tomas was large and blocked the door. Inside, Finvarra choked on his violent coughs.

"Please, Tomas. I can help," she begged. "I can do anything that is asked of me. Please."

Tomas turned back to the night, mulish, and said nothing.

Leanna pressed her lips together, her mind working out this horror. Finvarra had been fine earlier that night, but now she was being kept away from him. Only her, the one who could take his heart.

"When did it start?" she asked, knowing the answer yet denying it fully.

"Last night, after he left you. It happened again this evening before the bonfire, but last night was worst." He lowered his eyes. "He retched twice, and there was a lot of blood."

Both times his heart had tried to abandon him. Both times he had forbidden it. Leanna shivered at the truth of it all. "I did this."

Inside, the coughs lessened.

"If you care for him, you will leave," Tomas whispered. "Your presence will only make things worse. Go, and don't mention this to anyone."

She hesitated. He was right through the curtains, in pain. She could comfort him, hold him…

"Please," Tomas said. "I wish to be forgiven, but not in this way. Not with his death. Please, go."

Numb, Leanna forced herself away from the halo of lamplight. In the darkness, in her new living nightmare, she didn't need images of Machina nor Krinard to haunt her. The echoes of Finvarra's cough were enough, as was the memory of Kioyo's warning that a broken heart could still be broken.

Indeed.

Opening afternoon found Leanna sitting before her vanity, watching the reflection of the open curtains wave in a cool breeze. She lowered her lashes down to the stack of books before her and stifled a yawn. Morning practice hadn't been vexing, but the lack of sleep and emotions from the previous night was taking its toll. To keep from the horrid dreams and from Finvarra, she stifled her fear within the many books inside of her tent. The knowledge of Finvarra's life and his rise to power had been thrilling, but troublesome was the text that replayed over and over in her mind.

*Faeries never fall ill, nor do they sleep. Only when reaching their time to pass into the Otherworld will their magic fade, leaving them to suffer from the plaguing human conditions.*

Leanna closed her eyes. Finvarra's magic had waned. Perhaps it was the proximity of Machina's iron that caused his magic to dwindle. But, he'd coughed and heaved blood. Leanna sighed. It was useless to deny it. He was dying, and she was the cause.

She opened her eyes.

"Oh!" She startled at the reflection in the vanity mirror. "Krinard?"

He stood before her closed tent door, a door that was open moments before. A bandage was wrapped around his chest, tightly wound over one shoulder. The remaining bare skin glistened in the lamp light, each fiber of him exuding male and power. His lower half was no longer that of a horse, but human legs, breeches and all.

Leanna closed her robe tightly over her chemise and turned to him.

"What are you doing here?" She stood slowly. "I'm glad you're well and healed so quickly, but if you're looking for Finvarra, he's not here."

"I know," he said, his dark stare trained on her. "I've come to see you."

"Oh." Leanna wished for more words, but they wouldn't come. She slid her gaze around the tent. It wasn't shrinking, but the walls felt to close in around her, each breath a little harder to come by. Upbringings told her he should not be there, that she should leave, but he blocked the only door.

She cut a look back to him. "I'm glad I can be of help to you in some way, but I'm certain whatever you need from me can wait. I hardly find this appropriate." She tugged her robe closed even tighter, hating the look in his black stare.

"You seem nervous." A slow smile curled the corner of his mouth. "Do I frighten you, Miss Weston?"

On his tone, the shadows grew a little darker. Leanna blinked. Surely it was just a figment of her mind, of this fear she wished didn't exist.

"Of course you don't frighten me." She moved toward the fire and away from him. "But if you must know, yes, I am nervous. It would be a lie to say that last month I imagined this would be my life. Yet, here I am ready to perform." She glanced at him. "But I doubt you came here to speak of me."

Krinard abandoned the threshold, but just barely. Not enough where she could flee. Leanna frowned. Distance, she decided. She had to keep her distance.

He hummed. "You're right in being nervous. Machina got through before. Who's to say she won't again?" He trod a few steps forward, closer. "She can be sitting in any one of those seats, ready to destroy us all."

"I am certain the crystals will keep us safe."

"Unless Inara dies."

"Why are you telling me this?"

"Because Machina would do anything for Finvarra, just as I would do anything for Inara. I don't think you realize this. Every second longer Inara spends out there brings her closer to her death, a death I will do anything to prevent."

Leanna clenched her hands into small fists and met the unspoken threat in his stare. "Then let us hope she comes back or is found soon. If there was anything I could do to help, I would, but—"

"But there is…"

In her anger, Leanna hadn't noticed how much closer he was now. One step and he eclipsed the light of the flames, swathing her with his shadow. "If you are indeed the Leanan Sidhe, then take Finvarra's life or his heart and end this all."

Leanna managed a step back, only to find the wall. "I am doing what I can, but if he refuses to give me his heart, then I can't save him. I'm searching for a way around this."

The black of Krinard's irises devoured the white of his eyes and when he bore that inhuman gaze into hers, all of her words faded... so did her reason. Leanna exhaled slowly as if releasing steam, a release he called from her lungs the closer he drew.

"I don't care about your pathetic human sentiments," he murmured. The fire at the hearth dimmed. Caught in this shadowy abyss, Leanna was frozen. *Glamour,* her mind warned weakly, but his allure was strong, and this black magic she could not fight.

Krinard's lips twisted, knowingly. His hand slipped onto her waist, curving there. Leanna fought to keep her eyes open, fought to keep from shivering under his touch with want, but lust rushed through her veins and her breaths grew shallow. Like a poison, his glamour kept her body fixed and needing. She hated these panting breaths, but it was breathe under his hands or die.

"You are a woman, and one thing Finvarra can't resist is..." He dipped his head, drawing close to her ear. "A human woman."

He dragged in a slow breath and lingered there, a throaty moan vibrating in his chest. "We've waited for far too long, lost far too much to wait while you attempt to save him." He surfaced and trailed his nose along the path of her jaw. Now face to face, his devastating words fanned her lips. "Luna lost half of her people. I have lost my brothers and my mate."

His other hand smoothed up her arm in cruel calm, and he wrapped warm fingers around her neck. "You will do what you must to free us. Take his life or I swear it, I will take yours. That would surely kill him." His fingers abandoned her neck and moved lower, to the dip of her collarbone, to her chest that heaved as if calling his hands to explore. "Or I'm sure it will kill him to know that being the Leanan Sidhe you are, you inspired me to madness and seduced me when I was at my weakest."

Colors exploded behind her eyes as if staring directly at the sun. But Krinard wasn't the sun. A fire that hot and wrong could only be those of hell. Yet, as her mind begged her to move away and her heart mourned this carnal betrayal, her body arched toward him wanting to burn.

He responded and untied the knot of her robe. The silk shields parted, and he slid his hands within. Leanna sucked in a gasp, the heat of his touch feeling to scorch through the thin fabric. A smile at his lips, Krinard lowered his eyes to watch the journey of his hands as she writhed beneath them, as he lifted her nightgown higher.

Freed from those jailing eyes, a moment of clarity broke through the haze of her mind. She turned her head away from him, toward the open space of her room, toward the bed… toward the vase of vanilla flowers at her bedside.

She heaved as deep a breath as she could and shut her eyes tightly, seeking out the faint traces of vanilla in the air, the last shred of reality left in Krinard's invading world of glamour.

*Finvarra…*

The thought of him, of his pain, of his kiss, of his love for his people broke Krinard's lustful shackles on her reason. She pressed her palms flush against his bandaged chest and dug her fingers there. Krinard flinched and his eyes flashed back to normal, his flow of magic disrupted.

In this momentary distraction, Leanna shoved him back and brushed out of reach. "Get away from me!"

Knees weak and breathless, she clutched the vanity table as air found its way back into her lungs. Instincts flared, and she seized a four finger hair comb and spun. The damage would be minimal, but it would have to be enough.

Krinard's eyes washed over black once more, but cognizant of his power, Leanna gripped the comb tighter in her hand and conjured Finvarra's image in her mind. "Curse you and your glamour. Get out of my tent!"

He glanced down at the comb she held between them and chuckled. "What are you going to do, stab me? Tell Finvarra?" He cocked his head to the door. "Go on, then. He already blames you for the pixies, for Inara, for my men. He will only think you mean to destroy this circus from within. That you, the famed Leanan Sidhe inspired me, an injured man, to madness, and then he'll blame you for this too…" He smoothed a hand over the bandage she'd clawed. Blood curled outward and stained the white fabric.

As he spoke, Leanna flinched at the dark shadows that tugged at her gown, at the demonic fingers that brushed past her hands, taunting her. She stabbed at them, but they vanished into the surrounding black.

Krinard laughed. "No, human. You won't say a word. You will take his heart or his life, or I will take yours." One of the shadowy vines gripped Leanna's wrist tightly, holding her in place. Krinard reached for the comb.

A rumbling growl resounded.

Krinard whirled to the doorway where a snow leopard crouched low, its frame pulsating with each purr.

The dark vine slipped from around Leanna. She rushed out from Krinard's shadow, the comb held up against Krinard and the ferocious leopard bearing pointed fangs.

Krinard hummed. "Couldn't have the King's sister and now you want his mate? Very ambitious." He took a step forward. "Don't worry, clown. I've primed her for you. I'm sure she'll be willing."

A white blur whisked across the room. Leanna yelped. The snow leopard now pinned Krinard against the wall. Its white and black spotted coat radiated heat that curled from its body as luminous white vapor.

"Say that again," it rumbled lowly, "and I will tear out your throat." Its paws pressed down on Krinard's bandaged chest and sharpened claws slid out.

Leanna's eyes widened. Though the leopard's mouth didn't move, she heard the gruff voice in her mind—Kioyo's voice.

For a moment, neither of them moved. The fire at the grate then ignited back to life and the shadows in the room curled to their belonging corners. With their departure, Krinard blinked and his eyes returned to their humanlike black pits.

He raised his hands at surrender. "No need for such theatrics, clown. I was just leaving." Krinard hissed and his face tightened in pain as one of Kioyo's claws curved into his skin.

With a deep growl, Kioyo pressed down on Krinard's bandaged wounds before pushing off of him. His long tail swayed slowly as he dipped low before Leanna, alert and ready.

Krinard took a step back, and then another until he reached the curtained door. His smug grin never faded. "Best of luck, little sidhe, and be careful. You never know who is sitting in those seats, watching." With a final glare at Kioyo, he turned and walked out.

A gust of wind whipped around the room and on the rush of air, Kioyo's feline appearance brushed from his body in a cloud of icy and snowflakes. Droplets of water beaded from his hair, and his damp white shirt clung to his body, outlining the taut muscles of his back. He rose to his feet and turned slowly. Worried golden eyes were the last to change back to their comforting brown.

He stared at Leanna and she at him, both shivering for their own respective reasons.

"I'm sorry if I frightened you," he said, his voice deeper but gentle.

Leanna bit her lip. Unable to say any words, she shook her head.

Kioyo took a hesitant step toward her and stopped as if testing this. When Leanna didn't refuse, he took another until standing before her, the teeth of the comb flush against his stomach. With eyes fixed on hers, his hand came around her fingers to where she held the comb tightly.

At his touch, Leanna crumbled and released the comb into his hand. "Kioyo," she moaned.

Kioyo dropped the comb beside them and took her into his arms. His skin was still a furnace and seared hers, but feeling dirty and exposed, Leanna closed her eyes against him and let his warmth burn away the memory of Krinard's touch.

"Are you okay?" He spoke into her hair. "What was he doing here? Why did you stay? Damn it, Leanna. You should have left. You can't trust him. He could have…" He swallowed, but said no more. He didn't have to.

Leanna shuddered knowing all too well that not only her life had been in danger, but also her virtue. "I tried to leave, but when his eyes changed, I couldn't will my body to move, or my mind to think. And when he touched me…" She gripped Kioyo's damp shirt and turned her head onto his chest, ashamed. She'd hated it and wanted more of it. The memory of it thrilled her blood and disgusted her soul.

"Glamour," he said, voicing her suspicion. "Come, we need to tell the Ringmaster."

Leanna tore away from him. "No, we can't."

Kioyo blinked. "How can you pretend to keep quiet about this? He cornered and threatened you. The Ringmaster deserves to know." His jaw tightened. "If you don't tell him, I will."

"No!" Leanna clutched at his arm. "Promise me you won't. I won't ruin this circus from within. Krinard is Finvarra's closest friend, one who I begged him to reconcile with."

Kioyo said nothing.

"Please, Kioyo. Finvarra doesn't need this. I went to his tent last night and he was… he was coughing and Tomas says he's been ill, vomiting blood. I meddled, and now I must deal with the consequence. But I can't put this stress upon Finvarra, and you mustn't either. Especially not now."

Kioyo's mouth flattened, and for a moment he stared at her. "Fine," he grumbled. "But you're not leaving my side. I don't trust him, Leanna. Something isn't right."

Leanna relaxed. "Thank you."

"Don't thank me for this. Never for this. I could've killed him for what he did."

This reminded Leanna of the beautiful beast that had protected her and her virtue. A sad half smile tipped her lips. "You're a leopard. Why didn't you tell me?"

Kioyo lowered thick lashes. He bent and picked up the comb. Straightening, he held it up for her to see. "Brave. My kind are supposed to be brave and fearless." He chuckled bitterly and walked the comb to her vanity. He set it down, but never turned to her. "After what I did, after how I let my people down, I had no right to consider myself a part of them anymore."

"That right is yours now. You more than proved yourself. You stood up to Krinard..." She wrapped her arms around her body and turned away, ashamed of her own inability. "Meanwhile, I could barely move."

Warm fingers curled at the back of her neck, Kioyo suddenly before her. "You did well, Leanna. But the next time, even if it's just a whisper, you call to me." He grazed a thumb along her jaw. "I will always hear you."

She lifted her gaze, and a gentle brown stare met hers. And over Kioyo's shoulder, an icy blue one. Leanna swept away from Kioyo, but it was too late.

Finvarra toured his gaze along her, along her open robe, her flushed skin, her shambled state and ravished hair. "I see little has changed. It will always be a mortal woman to fool a king."

Kioyo stepped forward. "Ringmaster, it isn't what you think—"

"No, Kioyo. Don't," Leanna warned.

A smirk tugged at the corners of Finvarra's lips. Stepping back, he slid on his top hat and without another word walked from the tent, his cape billowing behind him.

Kioyo weaved his hands into his hair and let out a heavy breath. "We should have told him."

Leanna shook her head, staring at the curtains Finvarra had vanished through. "For once, the truth will only make things worse. This is for the best. For his best."

A faraway gong tolled and Kioyo sighed.

"It better be, but we'll talk about this later," he mumbled. "It's time for the show."

# Chapter Twenty-Three
## Swan Song

"AND REMEMBER, WHEN you get to the platform, lift your arm into the air just like we rehearsed." Kioyo demonstrated the regal pose one last time. He lowered his arm and blew out a breath. "You'll do wonderful. We've done this countless times. Besides, you're the Leanan Sidhe, beautiful, radiant, and magnificent. All will adore you."

Though heat bloomed in her cheeks at Kioyo's compliment, worry over the coming night and over Finvarra's illness stole at Leanna's joy. Before her, performers were lined up in glittering skirts and vests, balloon pants and ridiculous hats, all waiting for the opening introduction in the order they were to perform. She was at the very end of the convoy, sitting upon a Kia, who Minerva had doused with glitter. Above them, Bertrand suspended a fiery dragon that ran the length of the line, like a link of magic holding everyone together.

Kioyo squeezed her hand. "We've worked hard for this night. Do not let fear—"

"Rob me of my magic, I know," she said, attempting a smile. It was painful, just like the leather reins that cut into her fingers as she wound them tighter around her trembling hands. Kioyo nodded and walked back to his place in line, and never saw her sad attempts at a smile wither.

"You look marvelous." Minerva came up beside her, adjusting one of the pins in Leanna's hair. Leanna blushed, pleased to agree. She had not recognized herself immediately once Minerva was done transforming her. With her hair up in a rigid bun studded with diamonds and her face powdered pale, she looked like an angel. Feathers adorned the sides of her head in waved formation, matching her feathery skirt.

Minerva stepped back and gave her a once over. Her red lips twisted and she nodded approvingly. "Ellie was a dove. But you, my dear, are a swan." She cupped Leanna's cheek, black eyes keen with support. "Best of luck. You will make us all proud."

A hollow dong swallowed the rest of Minerva's words. Performers straightened, smoothing out their dresses and vests, adjusting hats and props.

The gong tolled six times and on the seventh, a glacial breeze devoured the light of the lamps. The audience inside the Big Top gasped as all went black. Their fears were tamed when the curtains before the performers opened and a gentle fairy song began.

The pixies rushed out first, and cut the darkness with their shimmery light.

"Be enchanted," Finvarra said.

The line of performers filed into the Big Top under the crimson light of the dragon. Ooo's and aah's underscored the sleigh-bell melody of the pixies and Vicente's song. Kioyo disappeared into the tent, and Leanna sighed. She'd done this with him at her side, but now she was alone.

"Be mystified, be seduced. For this evening I dare you to unhinge your mind from reality..."

Kia trod forth. Leanna closed her eyes and lost herself in the rocking motion beneath her, in the magic of the circus and Finvarra's voice echoing around her. She opened them just as Bertrand reached the threshold. He whirled his hands and upon clapping, the fire dragon abandoned the remaining performers and whisked on a tour around the Big Top. A collective gasp washed over the music as the dragon circled the tent. Under its light, all got their first glimpse at the infamous Ringmaster Finvarra.

At the threshold, so did Leanna. He stood at a small platform beside the rings, his attention focused on the audience. In a red riding coat, white and black striped breeches, and black top hat, he looked majestic, his glow in no way dimmed by the flames. Leanna blinked back her tears, immense pride and longing warring for the top place in her heart.

"I dare you to let your spirits soar and your hearts yearn, for only then will you laugh, will you cry as our performers bare their souls to you. Only then will you experience true, spectacular magic."

At this, Leanna and Kia reached the middle of the ring where Kia bounded up the ramp to a smaller platform. All the performers stood side by side in a half ring, and at their center was Leanna.

"Ladies and Gentlemen," Finvarra announced. "Welcome to Finvarra's Circus!"

On cue, Leanna threw her head back and spread her arms into the air.

Kia roared, and around them, Bertrand's fire dragon exploded into streamers and confetti.

The audience bolted to their feet. Their boisterous cheers were a deafening magic that blighted out Leanna's fears. She smiled as she lowered her arms to take in their applause. Fear meant nothing in that instant. That second was hers and nothing would steal its magic.

Under the rain of streamers, the performers waved to the crowd as Vicente played a livelier tune. Awaiting her turn, Leanna gazed out to the multitude and relished the palpable excitement. Children jumped up to catch the small flecks of glittery paper, others watched the performers exit with gaped mouths, or up to the pixies lighting up the tent sky. Her smile widened. Never could she have dreamt such a thing for herself. It was true, spectacular—

Leanna's breath caught. In the dark she hadn't seen her sisters sitting in the front row. They leaned into one another, both focused on Finvarra. Lydia was as radiant as ever, the pixie light accentuating her fair skin. She batted blue eyes, each lash a hook seeking Finvarra's attention. Beside her, Sarah offered the same. Dr. Luther sat next to Lydia. A rather unimpressed expression marked his face. His frame deflated with a sigh and he lowered his hands from a bored applause. He reached beside him then, and Kia's reins slipped from Leanna's fingers.

In a pale pink dress—surely of Lydia's choosing—and her hair pinned back, identical to Sarah's, was her doppelganger sitting in Dr. Luther's dreaded metal chair. Shadowed brown eyes stared up at Finvarra with a vacant expression, soulless. A cool chill curled down Leanna's spine. Though she saw herself, it was not her at all.

She took up the reins as Kia began their exit. She would have to walk past her family. But the closer she drew to them, the more her panic bowed to heartbreak. Would that have been her fate? A mannequin of her sisters, rolled around like a porcelain doll by her betrothed, a man she didn't love and could never love? She shivered. It was worse than death.

Kioyo burst out from in between the rows, tumbling and flipping toward the center ring. The audience roared with cheers and laughter. Lydia and Sarah looked away from Finvarra, and followed Kioyo's antics. Dr. Luther couldn't be bothered to look away. But back behind the curtains, Leanna knew he didn't see her, neither did her doppelganger. She gazed back one last time to the poor shadow of a girl and let the curtain close between her and the shell of who she once was.

Surrounded by the other performers who had waited calmly for their turn, Leanna too had felt some semblance of peace, as much as could be found over the hammering of her heart and knocking of her knees. During the acts, she remained hidden behind one of the curtain folds and watched many in the audience cry along with Kioyo's performance, stop breathing at Tomas's strength, marvel at the pixies' display of lights. It was Bertrand who now ignited the tent with his dragons and the other animals he fashioned of flames.

Her performance next, Leanna stood alone on the platform. She peered down at the bewitched audience who were but faceless outlines from up so high. Her knees bumped together as her meddlesome conscience found fuel in this last minute fear. Would she make across the rope without falling? Would she fall? Leanna trailed the light of the pixies and gulped. If she did fall, would the remaining pixies be enough to catch her?

Anxiety had little time to settle when Bertrand's last dragon roared upward to the peak of the tent. It curled into itself and exploded into an array of fireworks, all different colors illuminating the tent like northern lights. The drumming song came to a thunderous end and the crowd roiled back to life with applause.

Streams of red, blue, and green rained down, and as they faded, the tent lights dimmed.

Leanna gripped the railing tightly and closed her eyes.

It was time.

"And now, from her slumber in the depths of the fairy world, awakens the one yearning for a soul to inspire, a body to love, and sanity to steal. Gentlemen, I suggest that for our next and final act, you clasp a hand over your hearts for you will surely lose it. I present to you the radiant, the otherworldly beauty, the magnificent Leanan Sidhe!"

The lights shone up toward her. She lifted her arm toward the heaven above her. As if already enslaved to her magic, the applause and cheers intensified.

Vicente's gentle tune began. Leanna lowered her hand and the cheers quieted, leaving her to the plucks of the harp and cascading keys of the piano. To the rope and her dance to be performed.

The pixies were in position. The ones along the rope were not ignited, but present. The others floated in the dark, streaking the air with wisps of color. Though there were much less than before, they would have to be enough.

On the edge of the stand, Leanna pinned her gaze on the light at the opposite platform, her North Star in the darkness, just as the Big Top had been during her trek through the forest that first day.

She dragged in a deep breath. Back straight and chin up, she eased forward onto the rope. She had danced the routine many times before, but this night each movement took on a new meaning. Pirouettes sprouted the nightmarish vortex of Machina's eyes, but tricking sways forward chased them away. She pressed her feathered arms out, pushing away the memories of Machina's claws. She was free from her fear of this metallic demon. Threat and hurt as she wished, Machina had no power over her. Not anymore.

Mid-step, Leanna paused, her concentration jolted. The crystal flashed at her chest and grew bitingly cold. She cringed, the rims of her sight hazy and her knees weak.

The rope wobbled.

The crowd gasped.

Frantic, she shot her hands out into the open air. Soft whirrs and gentle pressure along her arms replied, the pixies there with their support. Stabilized but pained, Leanna closed her eyes tightly, wishing to ignore the iciness that hitched her movements. It felt as if it might carve out her very heart.

The crystal hummed against her skin, and once again she felt her spirit split in two. In the black of her closed eyes, she heard Finvarra's violent coughs. A vision came upon her then of smeared blood—of his blood, spilled because of her. It stained his hands and the handkerchief he pressed against his mouth to stifle the sound. He pressed another hand against his chest, where his heart glowed.

The vision vanished, but the truth remained. His heart threatened to abandon him again and there could only be one reason. Whereas before it had been her kiss to spark the beginning to the end of his life, it was now her dance that would lure him to his demise.

The music withered into discord that soon faded to the steady hum of the audience's murmurs. Luna buzzed a squeaking question, but Leanna looked past her, to the light at the opposite platform. A mix of blame and anger filled her. Clearly she saw the agony in Finvarra's eyes as his hands pressed down on Krinard's wound, his magic fading. And the coughing. That terrible, terrible sound.

Vicente queued the band once more and the beginning chords of Leanna's song played. She stood still, unable to move. Another step could mean the end of Finvarra's life. Not moving could cost the circus's.

It was her duty to cross the rope, to end his life.

It was her choice not to.

Could she, should she meddle with fate?

"I'm sorry," she whispered into the open air, to the canvas and the rings. To the circus. To Finvarra. "I'm so very sorry."

Her words fire, the ghostly remnants of her dance curled and frayed at the edges until dissolving into nothing. Leanna moved back steadily toward the platform to the tune of the audience's mumbles.

The crystal's coolness lessened with each step, Finvarra's anger no doubt superseding his love. She risked the life of his circus to save him, and he would never forgive her.

In reaching solid ground, Leanna accepted this. Her knees weak, she lowered to the cool wood, not yet ready to awaken, not yet ready to be free of him. Numb, she clasped her hands at her lap, her white dress red under the light of Bertrand's fireworks used to cover up her blunder. But it was no mistake, and alone, she embraced herself, holding tightly to Finvarra's rage rather than his death.

# CHAPTER TWENTY-FOUR
## AWAKENED & ASLEEP

LEANNA PACED IN AN AIMLESS CIRCLE. The flames at the hearth flickered, and her body shook as if following its tune. She plucked at the seam of her satin robe, an ever-changing song of rattled nerves and regret; their lyrics one question: *What on earth have I done?*

Whatever she'd done, it was too late to undo it. The circus was closed for the night, the show long over. All that remained were the rumors, that the magnificent Leanan Sidhe was far from magnificent. When Minerva had ushered her through the dressing tent and past the cookhouse, the eyes of the performers branded her skin, their stares saying just that.

Not even Kioyo had come to see her. He didn't even look at her when she had passed him. Through the pain, she saw his disillusion, all of their disillusionment. More, she knew of their disappointment in their king. Finvarra had brought her there. He'd promised them freedom. And like before, he'd been blinded. How could she think she would change anything with her meddling? She'd been a fool to believe it, a true jester in King Finvarra's court.

Sighing, she paced around the tent she'd slipped into—Finvarra's tent. He wouldn't want to see her, and would probably have Tomas carry her out and through the crystals for being a fraud. Oh, but she just had to explain.

At Finvarra's desk, she trailed a hand along a yellowed world map, marked with intricate symbols. Her heart panged. The circus may never see those places again.

A candelabra at the corner of the table gave her pause. Her fingers trembled as she lit the three wicks and forced herself to consider their meaning, something else she was guilty of.

"Bless thy spirit and thy journey home," she murmured to the memory of the three fallen centaurs.

A gentle breeze whispered past, carrying a familiar scent. She spun to the door. Like a moth to a flame, Finvarra appeared. Dark shadows cradled his eyes, his glow non-existent. He looked so terribly human, it hurt.

He slid off his coat and hung it at the coat tree. Abandoning the door, he walked to the bar while undoing his cravat. Each step buried his agony deeper behind a mask of cool indifference. At the bar, he reached for the bottle of brandy. The sloshing of dark liquor filled the silence, followed by a slight tap as he set the bottle back on the bar. He paused. Deathly still, he stared at his hand upon the glass bottle.

Leanna curled her fingers on the edge of the desk. She'd expected yelling; perhaps he'd clear the table in one furious swipe. But this dead calm was far worse.

*Leave,* her mind begged. But led by his unspoken grief and by her guilt, she dared a step toward him and another, until standing at his side. Taking in a breath, she moistened her lips to speak.

"Poison would be too quick for you, wouldn't it?" he said first. His gaze snapped to hers: dark, icy and lost. Black cores radiated violence, that of a man capable of violence.

"I beg your pardon?"

"No, were you able, poison would be entirely too quick, too kind." He set aside the untouched drink and paced to his desk. "I always told Ellie that the Elders conspired against me; digging trenches for the purpose of watching me fall. They knew I expected an otherworldly being, yet they sent you, a fragile creature whose strength is not in her beauty, but in the lies she spews from her lips, lies of love and freedom. And once again, I played their fool. I fell for your supposed need for me, for your supposed desire for freedom. I fell for you, the greatest deception of all."

Leanna swallowed, earnestly wishing to retaliate against this hysteria. Nothing would come from her mouth. His poisonous words swelled her throat and burned her eyes.

"But I know the truth now," he murmured, approaching her. "Before you grant me death, you wish to destroy me, to make me pay for all those girls who lost their lives. Lives that haunt my every breath; vacant eyes that are burned to the back of my lids, that persecute me with each blink every day of my cursed existence."

Before her, he lifted a hand to her hair, stroking it gently, too gently. "You seek to torture me first, to make me watch my people die, all the while you laugh alongside the Elders." He fisted the ends of her hair. "Shall I laugh too?"

He released the strands into the air in disgust. "Shall I laugh at this sham, at this ruse we are? Shall we laugh at my foolish desire to be different for you, to be something other than the heartless bastard this life has made of me? I lay down my pride for you and you trampled it. I bore my soul to you and you scorned it. You were within me but didn't care to see anything about my life. I tried, God, I tried to be something better for you."

He gripped his hair as if to keep from touching her. "I welcomed you into my circus, used black magic for you, and yet, knowing that you are my main act, that my death and my troupe's forgiveness is close, you ruin your performance!" He snatched her into his hands. "What more can I give you? How much more do you want from me?"

A frigid gust trailed his words and lashed Leanna's hair over her shoulders. Stunned, she stood still as his outburst echoed around her.

He released her as if touching her burned. "And you claim to care for me?" He took a step away from her, finished. "I may be heartless, but your kind are soulless. You know nothing of love."

"My kind?" She fisted her robe in her hands, hands that wished to slap him for saying those terrible words. Hands that wished to drag him into an embrace and away from the darkness of his thoughts.

"My kind? And what kind is that? For if I was a siren, I could sing and lure you from this darkness. If a banshee, I could scream and numb away this deafening ache within you. But I am just human. I breathe. I bleed. I love! That is why I did what I did. Fear of losing you robbed me of my magic and I faltered. I meddled. I didn't cross that rope because of this love you claim I don't feel for you, for this circus. Everything I have done, all my meddling was intended for the best. For your best!"

She remembered Krinard, and her anger flared. "I have endured attacks for you; scorn and hate for you. You gave me a chance to leave. But I stayed. For you. And now that I have found a place to belong, it will be torn from me too, regardless of what happens. My only guarantees are death or loneliness, but I stay. What more can *I* give you? What more do you want from *me*?"

She shook her head and it was she who backed away, finished. "I won't argue with you on this anymore. Perhaps in the morning we can talk about it with clear minds. But if my presence is such an abomination to you, and if all you wish to do is offend me, then I will leave."

She turned away.

In a blink, Finvarra stood before her. He took her shoulders in his hands roughly, but there was defeat in those eyes. They glittered in the firelight with the unshed tears of a desperate man. Outside the winds wailed, as if crying the laments he did not.

"You will leave me, then. To rot in the misery I deserve?" The fire in the grate extinguished with a hiss. "Do you finally see me for the heartless beast I am? Have you finally lost hope in me, too?"

His fingers upon her tightened. He brought her closer, his tone shifting from anger to strangled sorrow. "You will leave me and I will be left here to watch my people die one by one. As they die, I will wither away in hate because instead of mourning them, I will be mourning you, hating myself because I hurt you."

Leanna shook her head. It was a painful sight, that of a man lost with but an inch of candlewick left in the middle of nowhere, in the dead of night. Stranded, Leanna realized. They were stranded in darkness together. How could she possibly save him from this?

She gripped his vest with equal vigor. "Finvarra, please don't speak this way. I am here."

His hands came around her and he brought her closer, until his forehead rested against hers. "My sister was forgiven, taken from me to where I will never see her again," he spoke desperately against her lips. "If Inara dies, my soul will never recover. But losing you..."

He shook his head against hers, and held her tighter, possessive, mad. "I will never bear it. Death will not be enough to free me from the agony of knowing I ruined this too." He dug his fingers into her body like an anchor to his sanity. "Don't leave me. I will haunt this earth and drink from the memories of everyone that has known you if you do."

Hands trembling, she cupped his face, finally understanding Ellie's desperate words to him. She too had been losing him to this grief, and she was helpless against it. He was mad, irrefutably mad. Grief, anger and pain clipped his wings, and he fell burning.

Yet cognizant of his madness, Leanna held him. Before the circus, she too had been going mad in her illness, losing herself to her grief, and she was helpless against it. In this mirroring despair, she had run away from her home and found him—they found each other, and promised to free one another.

It was there in little light and little hope that she saw clearer than ever. She was going to lose him. Either to madness and death, or he gave her his heart and Machina killed her, they would never be together. Their fate had been irrefutable from the start, and denial would only embitter the short time they had left.

Her knees threatened to buckle beneath her, but she made her choice. Above broken hearts and proprieties, things that were and things that could have been, she said, "I will stay with you." She would, to grieve with him, to fall and hurt with him, to burn with him.

Yes, she would do all of these things. But of all, to keep him from madness, to gift him the freedom he'd gifted her, she said, "I will dance for you. Would you like that?"

The black cores of his eyes widened, the shock of her offer devouring the wintry blue. He swallowed and nodded slowly.

It was unwise and she thought to take it back, but with his hands in hers, Leanna led him toward the sitting area. She stood before him, put a hand on his shoulder, and encouraged him down into a chair. She caressed the blond strands away from his face and took a step back. Undoing the knot to her robe, she let the satin slip down her arms just as his gaze slid down her body. With her feathers gone, only a thin dance dress shielded her body from his eyes.

She slid one foot back and then another until finding center in the room. With the memory of Vicente's song in her head, all the fragments of her unfinished dance fused. Every caress and turn at adagio, she took Finvarra on an intimate journey of her soul, of her life up until that very moment. Only this time, she moved through each chapter of the routine without stopping. The crystal hummed at her skin, but she embraced it and let its coolness fuel her dance.

She opened her eyes. Meeting his stare, she felt as if she really saw him for the first time, the man that had been what she needed, that had given her the freedom he'd promised.

She had promised him something, too.

Arabesque and she reached for the heavens. If he wanted stars, she would give it to him. She reached to the floor, would give him the earth if he chose. Or—she retracted her hands to her chest—if he wanted her heart, he could have it too. It was already his. But her hands withered at her sides in slow flutters. He didn't want these things. She folded into herself and focused on the crystal, on the freedom that only she could bring him.

Spreading her arms outward, she bloomed, her crystal growing blindingly white. It chased away all darkness and illuminated the tent with its ethereal glow as it grew whiter and brighter, until all else vanished around them. Abandoned in this white heaven where tears glittered in the eyes of the

Faerie king, the Leanan Sidhe awakened.

A promise fulfilled.

In this frosted universe, she reached for him and drew back her hand like waves pulling him from the shores of this existence. Hands gathered at her core, she swayed like the ocean carrying him away from his nightmare, from his life. Tears spilled from her eyes when in finally finding this new piece of her dance, the end of her dance, she opened her arms and let him go. She then closed her arms around her body in a weak embrace and held herself, having reached the last of her journey.

Gradually the crystal stopped humming. Its glow dimmed, and left them in their world of shadows.

"Thank you," Finvarra said, his voice a hoarse whisper. With his head leaned onto the wing of the chair, he held one pale hand out to her, the other pressed at his heart. Beneath his fingers, a bright light glowed dimmer with each of his shallow breaths. Leanna moved to him and knelt down before his chair. She put her hand above his. When the light no longer glowed, he lowered their hands. Through the parting in his shirt, a bruise marked his skin. Tentatively she reached up and parted the fabric.

"Oh, God," she moaned. Bruises covered his torso, from just below his collarbone, over his ribs and down to where her eyes couldn't see. Her fingers neared his skin and she touched it gently. She winced though Finvarra did not, feeling this pain as if her own. "Keeping your heart from me is destroying you from within."

She rose in haste. "I will get help."

He didn't release her hand. Instead, he shook his head and drew her back toward him. He made to usher her down onto his lap, but she bristled.

"I just want to hold you." A sad smile twitched the corner of his mouth. "Will you deny a dying man a wish?"

Leanna swallowed deeply. How could she possibly deny him this? Surrendering, she sat. He leaned them back with a minor hiss of discomfort, and they settled together, fitting perfectly. She welcomed him into her arms and he rested his head on her chest as if seeking out her heartbeat for a lullaby. She let him, steadying her breaths to soothe him.

"There is so much I wish I could promise you," he murmured. "So very much."

She stroked his hair. "Perhaps in another time and another place, but this is the time we have. We won't think of such things now."

Perhaps another time and another place, but not now.

Finvarra pressed a kiss against the skin beside her crystal and said no more. Neither did Leanna. She smoothed his hair over and over, until darkness devoured the room.

Until his breath fanned her neck at regular intervals.

Until his hold around her waist loosened and he went limp in her arms, asleep.

Leanna caressed his hair away from his face. She didn't dare wake him, not when he looked so devastatingly peaceful there.

"Sweet dreams, my love," she whispered, and brought him back against her heart, hoping her heartbeats would somehow make up for his fading life.

As her tears dampened his hair, Leanna closed her eyes, realizing Minerva was wrong. Unrequited love wasn't the greatest madness. It was theirs.

When her tears ran dry, Leanna slipped her arms from around him and rose from his lap. Putting on her robe, she padded across the room, parted the curtains, and stepped uneasily into the open where Tomas stood watch.

He turned. "Miss Weston—"

"He fell asleep," she said.

Tomas stiffened, eyes frozen on hers. After a minute, he said, "And you accept this?"

"What else can I do but accept it? I have meddled and only made things worse. He refuses to give me his heart for fear of what Machina will do. If there was another way, I would do anything, but there isn't."

Tomas held her gaze, then lowered his lashes, but not before Leanna saw the truth there.

"Tomas..."

He said nothing.

She moved before him. "What is it you're not telling me?"

He shook his head. "The Ringmaster will never allow it."

"He is dying, Tomas! If there's a way I can free him from this curse so that he can go back home, I will do it. He may not have been the best king, but he is a good man. In spite of all he says, he just wants to go home. You all deserve to go home." Her voice broke, but no tears fell. She had none left. "Please, tell me what to do."

He smoothed one hand over his bald head and motioned to the wicker bench that she'd sat at the first night with the other. Leanna walked to the bench and sat quickly, before he changed his mind.

On the opposite side of the canopy, Tomas opened a trunk, set aside a book, a gourd of water, and pulled out a quilted blanket. Leanna's heart stirred. How much cold had he weathered in protecting Finvarra? How much snow, rain, ice, wind... and loneliness? He draped the quilt over her shoulder, pulling her from thought. The blanket was soft and smelled of honey.

He brought up a small wooden stool beside her and lowered onto the seat with a sigh. "I am of the woodland people, from the same realm as those who made Machina's heart. Only I'm an ogre, banished by my people because I refused to eat..."

He dropped his gaze, troubled. Plucking a tall weed, he twisted it in his thick fingers with palpable shame. "I refused to eat..."

"Humans," Leanna injected softly, knowing the gruesome tales behind the monstrous creatures. She encouraged him with a nod.

Tomas exhaled, his features relaxing. "Though banished, I still got word from back home and heard rumors of the heart that was made. The Ringmaster offered the trolls many riches in exchange for this heart. It was a mistake; the trolls could not be trusted. They have always been jealous of Forever, but the Ringmaster was desperate."

He shook his head and bent the weed in half. "They powered this heart with an ancient evil that has plagued our realms for ages. Its wish is to destroy white magic, and all that is good and bright. Everything that Forever stands for. Aithne was dead, her body but an empty vessel. By putting this black heart within her, they gave this evil a home." He met her gaze levelly. "Thus, the only way to defeat Machina is to destroy her heart."

He plucked a piece of the weed away. "Sadly, the Ringmaster can't get close enough to try. No one has been able to do so. Inara's white magic can stop her heart for few seconds, enough time for us to move the circus, but never enough to kill her. Something stronger is needed."

"But if Inara can't do it or Finvarra, it's..."

"Impossible?" Tomas held up the reed that was now fashioned into the shape of a heart. "So was the idea of the Ringmaster falling in love."

Leanna's brow dipped, a solemn smile tugging at the corner of her mouth. She took the offered gift, and with it found new tears. They splashed against the dry stem as if wishing to water it back to life.

"I know you're the only one that can do this," Tomas said. "It was always meant to be you."

"What more can I do?"

"The Elders punished the Ringmaster for what he did, and said he must give his heart away. When he did, he would be forgiven. But what would that solve with Machina still haunting him and shedding innocent blood in Forever? No, though the curse they gave him was extreme, the Elders are wise and just."

He met her eyes, conviction making them darker and intense. "The Faerie's are said to have descended from the Otherworld after a great war with the Old Evil. When they arrived, it is said their king wore one of their treasures around his neck."

Leanna touched her pendant, and he nodded.

"Those crystals defeated the Old Evil once before when the king's love for his people, his land, and his queen was magnified through it. Much like the way you just illuminated his tent. That magic is what can defeat Machina and free us all, your magic. Your love is enough to eradicate the dark magic within Machina and stop her heart. I know this is the way."

Leanna held the crystal tightly. "The only times I've ignited it, I had no control over it. How could I ever get close enough to try? And what if it doesn't work?"

"That doubt will kill your magic, as will your fear. That is why the Ringmaster has been unable to do it, why he has refused to. But you are brave. I believe in you, Miss Weston."

She smiled sadly. "I wish I had your conviction. After all I have brought upon this circus, I don't know why you even believe I can do this."

Tomas was quiet for a thoughtful moment, where his gaze focused on some faraway place. "We had a performer once named Gahn," he began slowly. "He had a bird, Silver. Silver read minds, and told Gahn their secrets. The audience adored it. But like many here, after years of performing, he lost hope in the Ringmaster. At some point—perhaps in a moment of drunkenness, of weakness," he waved a hand feebly, "the Ringmaster let down his guard and Gahn saw where he kept your necklace. He tried to steal it."

"Why would he do such a thing?" Leanna asked, half intrigued, half puzzled by Tomas's desire to tell her this tale.

"The crystals were forged so that when Finvarra found a woman to give his heart to, she could look into his soul and see all the things he was guilty of. With the crystal, Machina would have access to his soul and can poison him from within. She convinced Gahn that in this way she could get the Ringmaster to give her his heart and we would all be free." Tomas gritted his teeth, sitting back. "He was a fool."

Though under the blanket, Leanna shivered. To think of Finvarra caught in Machina's web of evil was an aching thought. She remembered how beautiful his soul had been, so many stars. She could've fallen forever.

"It was the Ringmaster who caught Gahn in his tent attempting to steal it. A scuffle ensued, and Gahn stabbed him with an iron blade. I arrived in time to stop Gahn, but Silver flew off with the box. All the other performers were at the Big Top, preparing for the show. Help wouldn't have arrived on time. Little did I know that a wild-haired girl had stolen away from her parents to catch a glimpse of the performers in the backyard, much like her daughter did so many years later."

"My mother..."

He nodded. "She saw everything transpire from her hiding place just outside of the gates. Thankfully burdened by the box, Silver was flying low. She took a stone and tossed it straight into the air, hitting the silver thief squarely and out from the sky." A small grin tugged at the corner of his mouth. "Meddlesome."

Leanna smiled, fresh tears glittering in her eyes.

"Ellie arrived then and brought her through the crystals while Inara and I combined our magic to destroy any of the goons that may have seen what happened. We were fortunate. Our magic was much stronger then, before this world diminished it."

Tomas looked to his hands, helpless. He closed them into loose fists and went on. "When the Ringmaster saw your mother standing there with the box, something within him changed. He knew the crystal was no longer safe with him."

"Why didn't you take care of it for him?"

"Desperation can lead anyone to madness. I didn't dare. We thought it best to send it far from here. Inara agreed, thinking no one could be trusted. And so Ellie, Inara and I vowed to keep the events a secret. The Ringmaster sent your mother away and told her only to return once she'd found his Leanan Sidhe." He shrugged. "I don't think he ever expected her to find it, thus he would never see the crystal again, never be tempted to give his heart away."

He stood up and smoothed down his pants. "So why do I believe in you? Because of the magic I just saw now illuminating the Ringmaster's tent. Because your mother gave you the crystal—not your sisters, but you. Because in the midst of his darkness, you arrived. And now you're here to bring us snow." He tipped her chin and encouraged her face up. "You're the Leanan Sidhe, and if you're to inspire death, then let it be Machina's."

Leanna was quiet for a long time. She stared down at the heart shaped reed in her hand. For her to kill Machina was as difficult a thought as losing Finvarra.

"Go now and rest," Tomas said, squeezing her shoulder reassuringly. "It's a lot to take in and a lot to ask of you, which is why the Ringmaster refused the idea."

"You mean he knew there was another way?"

"Of course. The story of the First King is one we are all told as children, but he will not risk losing you to Machina over a story. Machina's sole purpose for life is the Ringmaster. If he dies, grief will consume her and she will die too. He feels he can finally end this for certain. But, in the morning, if you wish, I will teach you to hone your magic and focus it on the crystals the way Inara taught me."

Leanna squeezed the reed. "You will go against Finvarra's wishes?"

"If you want to be the one to end this, then I will help you, but it is something you must believe in wholeheartedly. If you are to stand before Machina, you can't doubt. You can't fear, or you will truly lose it all—Finvarra, the circus, and your life."

Leanna rose, a bit lightheaded at all she'd been told, at all the decisions to be made. Finally, there was a way for them both to live, even if not together.

"Thank you for this, and for being a true friend to Finvarra," she said. On tipped toes, she kissed his cheek and made her choice. "I will see you in the morning."

Tomas lowered his head, a hint of a blush spreading beneath his dark skin. He nodded once to her and then faced the open field.

Leanna walked back through the maze of tents with one thought driving her steps forward: anyone could be anybody's Leanan Sidhe. Just as she was Finvarra's, he was hers. The desire to save him would inspire her to the madness of trying to destroy Machina's heart and could possibly lead to her own death.

But, she set her jaw. She would succeed. She couldn't doubt or they could lose it all. They already were.

The fluttery feeling of hope in her chest sent her walking faster, muscles tight with readiness. She thrust her curtains aside and stepped into her dark tent. She would rest, and come morning, she would learn to use her—

A hand came upon her mouth while arms closed around her waist firmly, trapping her. Leanna clawed at the hands, kicked and struggled, but her captor pinned her arms to her sides. Shadows enveloped them, and within moments, she fell limp in her captor's arms.

A slow blink, and a steady gallop carried her toward the crystals and then across them.

And as all went black, Leanna realized that before saving Finvarra, she would have to save herself.

# Chapter Twenty-Five
## Black Heart

SHE WOKE TO TIGHTNESS at her shoulders and her waist. A rough, gritted surface spread behind her, digging through the thin fabric of her dress and into her back. She made to move away when a sharp tug at her ankles sent awareness hot and burning through her thoughts. She'd been kidnapped, and now—she peered down with a groan—she was being tied to a tree.

Sobered by panic, Leanna darted her gaze along this foreign land. Forest stretched in every direction, as far as she could see in the pale light that seeped through bare branches. Creatures of the night were dead silent. The only sound was that of snapping twigs behind her.

"Krinard?" she asked, anxious. "Why are you doing this?"

Krinard appeared from behind the tree. He passed her in silence, and lifted a hand at his side. When he clenched it to a tight fist, the rope squeezed in reply. Leanna cried out; bile burned her throat and her ribs cracked under the strain of the rope.

He chuckled. Stopping by his satchel that lay on a log few feet away, he crossed it over his shoulder as one about to leave.

"Krinard." She moistened her lips; the dread at him tightening the rope further dried her mouth. "Please let me go."

He spun to her and Leanna gasped. From the scar on his chest, black webs marked his veins. Poison slithered up toward his shoulders and neck, mapping out their course along his sculpted torso.

"You've been poisoned. We must get back to the fairgrounds. Minerva healed me. Surely she can heal you too!" She wiggled, but the rope chafed her arms. Her skin was sensitive in the cold and that magnified the pain of the rope. "I know Finvarra will forgive you once he knows that your injury is the cause of this madness."

Krinard tilted his head in question. "You mean this?" He brushed a finger along the scars. "Indeed, I have been poisoned. How else was Machina to be sure I wouldn't fail?"

Memories of that dreadful night flooded Leanna's mind. "She stabbed you in the back yet left you alive. That was all planned..."

"So it was." He brought a shaky hand to his forehead and wiped the thick beads of sweat at his brow. "But do not fear for me. She'll drain the poison once I deliver this."

He trod closer and drew Leanna's crystal necklace from inside his satchel. He dangled it before her eyes and Leanna felt a part of her die. In her panic, she hadn't realized it no longer hung at her neck. Her only weapon against Machina, her only way to save Finvarra and his circus was gone. Though in open lands, the forest suddenly felt airless.

She dug her nails into the tree at her back. "How could you possibly make a deal with Machina after all she's done? She killed your men."

"It was a small sacrifice, like Yelena."

Leanna's fight stopped as he reached into his satchel and retrieved an amber feathery cap.

"Did you know that whoever owns a merrow's cap, controls them?" He admired the feathers along the top. "That is why they are warned not to lose it when they visit the surface."

Leanna's heart twisted, remembering Yelena's words. *I have no choice...* "You stole her cap, you bastard. You kept her from her home!"

"She was beautiful, and I wanted to keep her, but when we were cursed, I imagined Finvarra could give her his heart and we could be done with this all, but he refused her. With Ellie forgiven, however, I was sure we could have convinced him in the midst of his grief, but then you came and ruined everything. Suddenly she began to reject me. I'd broken her long before and rarely had to use the cap for her to obey me, but with your arrival, she began to hope."

He threw the cap at Leanna's feet. "Hope is a dangerous thing, and so she had to take a fall."

Leanna pressed her lips together, fighting against the tears in her eyes.

"No need to cry for her. She's in a better place now, as we all will be when I deliver your precious crystal."

"Listen to what you're saying. You think Machina will let you go?" Leanna groaned, the bewitched rope tightening gradually the more she fought against it. "She just wants to see the circus burn. Don't do this. I mean to break the curse!"

In a black blur, Krinard appeared before her and punched the tree above her head. The bark exploded with a deafening snap that rang in her ears. Leanna screamed and ducked her head to shield her face from the wood chunks and slivers that fell down onto her.

He snatched her chin into his hands. "I heard you talking with that repulsive ogre. You think a pathetic human can kill Machina?" He neared her face. "You think I'm going to rest my fate on you?"

He trailed a hand along her jaw, and lower, until he reached her neck. Clutching her throat, he pushed her head back against the tree. She winced at the jagged edges of bark that dug into her scalp.

"It never had to be like this. All you had to do was finish your performance. If you had only convinced him to give you his heart and accepted your death at Machina's hands, we would all be free." He tightened his grip. "If you refuse to take his life and won't convince him to give you his heart, I will give Machina everything she needs to make it happen."

He lifted the necklace at eye level between them, his black eyes following the glinting crystal like a pendulum. "With this, your likeness, and Machina's tenacity, we'll have our freedom."

He released her throat and stepped back. Securing the necklace back inside of his sack, he chuckled. "Foolish of Finvarra to leave an empty vessel walking this earth."

Leanna blinked, Krinard's terrible plot now clear in her mind. Machina's evil within her doppelganger...

"He won't fall for it. Finvarra knows me. It won't be long before he knows it isn't me!"

A wicked smirk twisted Krinard's lips. "A few seconds is all we need. Once Finvarra sees her alone in the woods, he will cross the crystals to get her. Then it will all be over."

Leanna growled and cursed and writhed to break free from those damned binds. "I swear to you, you will pay for this," she cried to his retreating figure.

Her words akin to a spell, he hissed and curled inward with a groan. He turned and pressed his palms flush against the nearest tree, twisting his torso as if wishing to evade the pain within. His body grew taut and long fingers clenched into the tree.

"I told you I would do anything for her. We will get our freedom, while Finvarra will get the punishment he deserves." He gazed at her over his shoulder. Black vines now framed his face. "As will you. A slow and lonely death for all the days my Inara has been missing."

Finished, he took a step back, his hoof beats crunching dead leaves. Their eyes locked, and for a moment, he tilted his head in a twisted fascination. "I suppose the tales about you were true. You truly did inspire him to madness and to his death."

Numb, Leanna watched him, not knowing how much of his hate was his own, and how much of it was Machina's dark magic.

It mattered little when he turned.

"May the winter cold and beasts of the forest be unforgiving," he said over his shoulder and galloped off. He vanished through the webbed tunnel of trees, and left Leanna tied, without direction, without a coat, without her necklace, and without hope.

Leanna struggled. She twisted and fidgeted, screamed and prayed, but the rope and tree bark were merciless to her pleas. They seared and dug into her skin the further she worked at freedom, bringing death closer the more she tried for life.

A breeze blew through the forest, soft as the imminent daylight. She hauled in a deep breath, hoping to find something in the fleeting gust other than the cold void of death. Perhaps Kioyo's soothing scent of pine. Perhaps Finvarra's welcomed trace of vanilla as he approached, coming to save her.

The winds passed.

No one came.

A sinking feeling settled in her stomach. With her doppelganger filled with Machina's essence, they would all be fooled. The circus—her home would be no more. They would all die, and no one would ever come.

Leanna lowered her head and wept tears of complete and utter helplessness, of being much too small in a big world of magic. Of being only human in a world of faeries and mechanical monsters.

She gasped. Currents of pain shot through her veins and her head slammed back against the tree. Her heart wrenched like it did for so many years when it felt like phantom knives sought to carve it out, its rhythm erratic.

But there was no doctor here, only a savage ache that had disappeared since she entered the protection of the circus and its crystals. Not in their midst anymore, her head lolled forward. Lids heavy, Leanna surrendered and closed her eyes to the sweet, inviting end.

Pale red overcame the darkness of her closed eyes. It drew closer and grew brighter, and in its warmth, the stronghold on Leanna's heart eased. Air burned as it rushed back into her lungs and her heart sought its rhythm. In the discord, she opened her eyes. Soft light filtered through her lashes. Amidst the trees in the distance, a silver cloud loomed. Its light stretched toward Leanna's muddied feet and moonflowers sprouted from the earth, curling at her toes.

Leanna's head snapped up. The frosted cloud blew past her as dissolved icicles. In its wake, only a white unicorn remained.

"Inara?"

The mare nodded and lowered her head. She brought the tip of her new, twisted horn up along the rope. The binds snapped with a hiss. Leanna's knees buckled beneath her and she fell forward, but Inara ducked her head and caught her before she met the earth. Folding her front legs, Inara ushered Leanna down to the ground and back against the tree.

"How did you find me?" Leanna asked, her throat raw. "Where were you?"

Inara turned pale eyes to her, but said nothing. After a moment, she whiffled, but no words left her still. Her stare, however, was keen with emotion and Leanna knew that though she didn't hear her, Inara spoke.

Leanna shook her head, wiping at her tears roughly. "I don't have the necklace. I can't hear you."

Big, gray eyes widened. Inara neared Leanna and pressed the tip of her glowing horn to the center of her forehead. A cold current cut through Leanna's head, a welcome relief from the headache that had settled over her eyes.

Inara shifted back. *"Is that better?"*

Leanna nodded. "Where were you?"

*"I was on my way back to the fairgrounds when the trees told me you needed help,"* she explained. *"What's happened?"*

"I will tell you on the way." She gripped the tree and attempted to stand, but weak knees gave way beneath her. She fell back to the damp ground. "Damn it!"

*"I know you are angry,"* Inara coaxed her quietly, *"but give your heart a moment. Without the crystal, it will weaken faster. Tell me what has happened."*

"Krinard went mad because of you. He kidnapped me, bound me to this tree, and took the crystal." New tears fell. "Why did you leave?"

*"I was riding for my life."*

"Then you should've returned so the crystals could protect you," Leanna said.

*"No, I was riding to find a reason to live. I was dying, Leanna. My magic was fading."* The moonflowers around her withered and her glow dimmed. *"I needed to get away from the anger and the pain and find myself again. Riding for my life lest I die. Wise words from the Leanan Sidhe."*

Around Leanna, white vanilla flowers bloomed. Her lips quavered at the welcomed and painful sight. "I didn't think saying that would have cause you to leave. We needed you."

*"It wouldn't have mattered."* Inara bowed her head away. *"Krinard's darkness has always been there. I love him, but he is not perfect. Had I stayed, he would've found another outlet for his anger, and I would have fallen deeper into despair."* The star shaped flowers grew black and limp. *"I needed to leave. Forgiveness would have meant little if I didn't find myself first."*

Leanna wrapped fatigued arms around the mare's neck and held her, understanding. "But now you have your magic and we must get back. Krinard means to give Machina the crystal, and I fear Machina may already be there."

Inara aided Leanna to her feet. She trod back few steps and her horn kindled. A bright glow centered at her back. It diminished then, an intricate gold and silver saddle now at her back.

Leanna lifted a foot to the stirrups. She paused. "But I don't have the crystal. How can I possibly defeat Machina now?"

Inara's swung her head to Leanna. Though Inara said nothing, Leanna heard the words in her soul. *Doubt and we will lose it all.*

She mounted Inara in an instant, winding the reins tightly around sore and bloodied knuckles. Inara stomped in a circle and stopped when facing the path Krinard had vanished through. With a piercing neigh that sent the creatures of the forest scurrying to safety, she bolted forward, her horn a beacon of hope.

They rode hard, Inara's furious gallop a metronome to Leanna's heartbeat. Branches scratched her bruised skin like nailed fingers trying to keep her from the fairgrounds. The winds conspired with the trees, and whipped her hair over her eyes as if wishing to blind her. Leanna held the reins tighter and welcomed this war against her. She would weather any discomfort for the circus and for Finvarra.

Inara's gallop slowed to a stop.

"What's wrong?" Leanna asked, brushing her tangled mess of hair away from her eyes. "Why are we—?"

*"Shh! The trees are speaking."*

Inara spun in a tight circle as if chasing their phantom words. Leanna turned her ear to the air, hoping to hear even a whisper of this secret language.

A breeze gust. The branches shivered, and their gnarled fingers tapped against one another.

*"No,"* Inara breathed. Her horn dimmed and the muscles at her back tightened beneath Leanna. She galloped to a dense brush where there was a clearing on the other side.

Leanna's hand flinched to her neck, to where her necklace would have offered her its quiet support. There was nothing there and she fisted the hand at her chest. "What are they saying? Is Machina near?"

They reached the edge of a cliff, where the terrible answer spread out before them. The entire forest was visible, from Winter Abbey's bell tower in the far North, to the bridge that led to neighboring lands in the South.

And at its heart was the circus, burning.

# CHAPTER TWENTY-SIX
## BURNING HEART

SHE DIDN'T BREATHE.

As Inara galloped furiously toward the burning fairgrounds, Leanna held her breath. Maybe in refusing the world her air, it would stop turning; and in stilled time, keep the circus from burning.

It didn't.

In the distance, orange and red flames continued to devour the Big Top. The crackling fingers of the fire clawed toward the sky as if the canvas's cry for release. Caught in the smoke that cloaked the field, Inara's horn ignited. The frosted hue cut through the blackness and Leanna sucked in a choking breath at the sight.

The protective stakes around the fairgrounds were now sharpened spikes. The crystals that once crowned them had been crushed and scattered like rubble on the ground. Their glow pulsed slowly as if the heart of the circus, dying. And behind the fallen crystals, a slaughter.

Inara neighed and half reared to a halt. *"All in Forever..."*

Massive machines the size of men sliced the air with scythe-like arms. Ruby eyes gleamed in the black fog as they brought jagged blades down, destroying the tents and the outnumbered performers that fought to protect their circus. Steam hissed from their seams, underscored by gurgling screams and the slosh of innocent blood splattering against their breastplates.

"Why are we stopping?" Leanna cried. The large machines had not seen them yet, but Machina had eyes everywhere. Metallic crab-like creatures skittered along the ground, shooting venomous daggers at those who fought back—at Kia, who lunged onto the backs of these monsters, at Bertrand who sought to control the flames. "Inara, we need to help them!"

Inara snapped from her agony. *"The shattered crystals will only magnify my power so far. We must draw them close. Hold on tight."*

Obediently, Leanna twisted the reins tighter. Inara reared with a piercing neigh once and again, each whine louder than the last. Her cry was a kaleidoscope of sound that echoed over the roar of the flames and scrapes of metal.

The large beasts paused in their carnage and cut red eyes to Inara. They turned, head first, bulky bodies following. The ground rumbled, their approach fast and steady.

Inara bowed her head. A funnel of white fire kindled at her horn. On the ground, the crystal remnants glowed brighter. A blast of white fire burst from Inara's horn and the stones at once. The violent gust of power snapped Leanna back, nearly thrusting her off. She bit her nails into the reins, groaning in pain at this icy wind that clawed at her skin.

Digging their clamped feet into the earth, the mechanical ogres powered through the frigid fire. It corroded their armor and froze their feet to the earth, but within seconds they crushed through it.

"They're getting closer!" Leanna cried.

The ground began to ripple as if pooling all of its energy to a point beneath them. The temperatures plummeted and the gathered power pressed down on Leanna's chest.

"*Whatever you do, do not let me go,*" Inara said through their connection. Her horn's glow intensified. Leanna struggled against the countering wind and ducked into Inara's mane, clutching her as tightly as weary arms would allow.

With a strained cry, Inara touched her horn to the ground. On contact, a shaft of white light rushed from her and the crystals with a whoosh. A thunderous crackle shoved them back, and Leanna screamed.

The winds died in an instant. All was quiet, save for the distant snaps of the burning Big Top and the ringing in Leanna's ears. She unearthed her head from Inara's neck, and her eyes widened. The beasts glinted in Inara's light, frozen with their blades in the air and eyes still red.

Inara rose onto her hind legs and stomped her hooves down on the earth. The ground jerked beneath them on contact and the metallic ogres exploded into shards of icy springs, coils, and metal.

The path now clear, Inara rode past the fallen crystals, trampling the rubble underfoot.

Bertrand ran toward them, eyes wide and red like the fire behind him. Only from this close, Leanna noticed that amidst the fire consuming the Big Top, black fire also burned.

"The Ringmaster is in the Big Top," Bertrand gasped. "I've tried taming the flames, but they're too powerful." He keeled over, clutching his side. "Tomas and Kioyo went inside, but more of those monsters are in there, and Machina. The Ringmaster let her in thinking it was you," he told Leanna. "She's wearing the crystal."

*"Keep trying to control the fires. I must save what magic I have for Machina,"* Inara ordered Bertrand. *"And Leanna, keep your head low. It isn't' safe in there. Once we're before her, you must get Finvarra to use his crystal against her. It's now you must inspire him more than ever!"*

How she was supposed to do this, Leanna didn't know, but Inara left no room for argument when she bolted forward. Enveloped in her speed, Leanna held on tightly. The world faded to smears of flame when they hurtled through a flaming loop in the canvas.

Thick, black smoke shrouded them immediately. Disoriented, Leanna leaned into Inara. This inferno was not her Big Top. She didn't know this maze of tumbled wood and fire. She sought to get her bearings, but there were only downed planks of wood and patches of burning canvas. And darkness. A thick black wall of fog shielded the center of the circus, the rings no longer visible.

Moans, howls, and screams emanated from the black fog. Leanna stifled a gag at its offensive scent, that of decay and burning skin, and of all that was wrong and foul in the world. The smoke unfolded and it its midst was Vicente, surrounded in a halo of white. He played a song that though barely audible, created wisps of white that countered the evil.

A growl tore at Leanna and Inara's attention and they spun. In a halo of his own, Tomas ripped into a metal monster, piercing its breastplate with bare hands. Behind him a white leopard marked with blood and soot tore ferociously at another one's chest. Sparks set off into the dark as sharpened claws tore through the metal armor. The machine jerked and trembled underneath Kioyo's powerful frame, until with a deafening growl, Kioyo bit into its neck. One furious jerk and he tore off its head. Golden eyes followed the detached head as it rolled to Inara's hoof.

Kioyo's feline appearance brushed from his body as snowflakes. A gash over his brow bled into his eyes, and his ribs were bruised. Tomas limped beside him, holding onto his side. Blood stained his yellow vest and seeped from in between his fingers.

Leanna dismounted Inara quickly and rushed into Kioyo's arms while Inara trot beside Tomas. The iciness from Kioyo's transformation clung to his

213

skin and was a slight reprieve from the stuffy heat of the flames.

"Are you alright?" Leanna asked desperately, pulling their bodies away. She scanned him, skimming her hands along the cuts on his arms. Hot tears washed over the smoke in her eyes.

"I'm fine, but the Ringmaster—we're losing him, Leanna. Machina wears the crystal now. With the iron and her magic, he is weak and at her mercy."

*"Where is he?"* Inara asked, touching her horn to the wound at Tomas's side. The blood leached back into his body while black ooze dripped out and onto the ground with a hiss.

Kioyo motioned past the black abyss that curled outward and devoured the real flames.

"We've been unable to reach him. With them bound, she borrows from his magic," Tomas replied. "She holds him at center ring, but the fog keeps us out."

*"It's Machina's evil, magnified,"* Inara said. The seemingly impenetrable cloud obliterated the surrounding canvas and red fire. All view of the belonging circus slowly vanished. Bertrand's fire was still visible as dragons of white fire twisted about the dark flames, but it was futile. There was too much evil. *"Soon, there will only be darkness. Once her evil reaches the outer crystals, all is lost."*

"Tell us what to do." Kioyo flexed his fists. "She cannot win."

*"You two clear out the perimeter of those beasts. Leanna and I will get the Ringmaster. Leanna, now that they are bound, she has access to his powers. She is much stronger. You must tell Finvarra to use the crystal. He must center himself in it, lose himself in it. Tell him to cast aside his guilt, his hate, his anger. It will only dampen his magic and add to this darkness. His love must be pure if we are to cast her out and defeat her."*

A thunderclap resounded and the ground shifted beneath them as the blackness swallowed up more of the flames. Kioyo grabbed Leanna by the waist and lifted her back onto Inara. He bore a worried golden gaze into hers, and squeezed her hand. Releasing her fingers, he shifted back beside Tomas.

*"Be safe,"* Inara told them. With agreeing nods, they met one another's eyes quickly, their stares saying it all. Kioyo tore away first and transformed with a growl. Leanna's heart hitched in watching him turn away and lunge fearlessly into the black. Tomas followed. The darkness pulsed and the hollow imprints left upon the black cloud disappeared.

Inara turned to the black void that skirted closer. With her horn kindled,

Inara galloped into the fog. A ray of light illuminated the way before them to the other side. Hands detached from the shadows, desperately reaching for Inara's light. In touching the white hue, they hissed and curled back into the black.

Inara entered the clearing on the other side and stopped. Spread before them was the circus, only this wasn't their circus. In this desolate tent, the world was gray. Large gashes in the canvas above revealed a funnel of black that howled with feminine cries and moans of agony. Where snow once fell telling of forgiveness, only ash floated down now. Rings of wood were now rings of iron. And at center ring, the Ringmaster to this circus.

But not their Ringmaster.

Leanna's doppelganger stood there, radiant and regal, her form fitting white gown billowing in a non-existent wind. Black light hummed from the crystal at her neck, matching the black top hat angled slightly on her head. One human hand was closed around the handle of an iron whip. At its end was Finvarra on his knees, the iron links wrapped tightly at his neck. His head was bowed forward and blond strands draped over his face. He trembled though the heat was stifling and stagnant.

Leanna made to dismount.

*"Don't leave my light!"* Inara warned her. *"I won't be able to save you if you step into that void."*

Leanna bit her fingers into the reins to keep from running to him. She tried at a breath, but couldn't, feeling as if the leash were wrapped tightly at her neck and not his.

Machina tilted her head. A slow smile twisted her lips and black tears spilled from her eyes. "The famed Leanan Sidhe has decided to grace us with her presence."

Hearing her own voice coming from Machina sent shivers down Leanna's spine. Though it was a replica of her body, it was awkward on Machina, like the vessel was too small for so much evil.

Machina wiped a black tear away with the tip of a metallic finger. She reached down beside her and caressed Finvarra's hair. "Now I have everything I've always wanted. Well, almost everything..." She lowered her gaze from Leanna's eyes down to Leanna's chest.

Beside her, Finvarra struggled to lift his head. "Leanna?" Terrible shivers seized him and his voice trembled.

"Hear my voice, Finvarra, please. You are not without power here. You must fight her darkness. God," she sobbed, "You will not surrender to this!"

215

Machina bore her teeth with a hiss and yanked Finvarra's leash. "He belongs to me! He isn't bound to you anymore." She lifted a metallic hand to her chest and stroked the crystal. "I bear your semblance and your name now. You don't exist anymore. There is only me. He loves only me," she said, over and over in an eerie sing-song. "Only me."

Her sweet lullaby leashed itself onto the air and echoed around them. The cries and moans in the fog intensified, as if her voice ripped the skin from their phantom bodies.

*"Leanna, tell him what you must!"* Inara screamed through the cries.

"Finvarra..."

"Shut up!" Machina thrust a hand up. Metallic snakes shot out from her upturned hand toward Leanna. Leanna jerked back. She slipped from the saddle and slammed against the ground. She groaned, but scrambled close to Inara's legs as the serpents turned to a cloud of ash upon entering Inara's light.

Machina gritted her teeth. "Oh, Inara, you defend her after all the agony she has brought you and this circus? Spare yourself the trouble. Deny her your light and you too can have everything you've always wanted."

A spotlight of gray light shone into the ring beside theirs. Another mechanical ogre stood there. One hand was a serrated ax and the other was a clamp, where he dragged a bloodied centaur by the neck. Krinard's golden skin was now charred and black poison seeped through gashes across his body.

Inara's light slightly waned.

Machina smiled. "That's it. Deny her your light."

Finvarra's head snapped up and his hands came onto the iron binds. His skin sizzled against the whip, yet through the vapors he bore a feral stare into Inara. "Don't you dare!" Blood seeped through his fingers as he tugged at the leash. Machina yanked it, and Finvarra grunted, falling forward onto his hands. He twisted and clawed at the poison that coursed within him. Leanna dug her fingers into the earth and shook her head frantically, watching black vines curl under his pale skin through his torn shirt.

Machina released Finvarra's leash and strut to Krinard. She ran an iron finger along his jaw. "What do you say, Inara?" She leaned into Krinard and trailed her nose along his neck, and her tongue along the blood dripping from his jaw.

"Mmm, so sweet. Give her to me and you too can have a taste. Come now, just give her a little nudge. I will take care of the rest."

With his face caged in Machina's hands, Krinard turned bloodshot eyes to Inara. "Please," he begged over Finvarra's grunts. "Save me."

Inara turned to Leanna and an icy tear streamed from her eyes. *"Krinard made his choice and I have made mine. As I have followed the King, I will follow his Queen."*

Machina smirked. "Smart steed."

*"You cannot have the girl!"*

Machina's eyes narrowed. Her smile fell slowly. Too slowly. "How noble." She moved her head away from Krinard. "What a pity."

With eyes pinned on Inara, Machina snapped metal fingers. In the spark, the beast tightened his grip on Krinard's torso and Krinard arched back with a pitched cry. The beast ran his blade straight across his neck, and Krinard's scream gurgled. The ogre released Krinard's body into the pool of his blood and poison.

A weakened Finvarra turned his head away.

Wide-eyed, Inara whimpered Krinard's name. He didn't respond. A moment later he had yet to move. Inara screamed, her shriek tearing through Leanna's mind. Leanna clutched her head and fell to her knees with a like cry as wild fire exploded from Inara's horn, speared in every direction. The white bolts dissolved Machina's ogre to ash in an instant.

Machina's crystal kindled black. Its hue enveloped her, a barrier to Inara's attack. She thrust up a hand and black magic shot out from her palm. Her fire clashed with Inara's in a thunderclap that flared the surrounding flames. The two beams of light warred for control, a give and take of love and hate.

Clutching Inara's leg tightly, Leanna anchored herself against the winds that threatened to topple her over and into the darkness. The terrible pain within her head made her shiver, but she lifted her gaze to Finvarra. His face was framed in black and his lips blue, but at his chest, the crystal pulsed white, though faintly.

"Finvarra, think of the crystal," Leanna yelled out to him over the winds. "Focus on its light!"

Finvarra lifted his face. Tears of ash seeped from his eyes. His gaze was distant as if he no longer knew where he was, who he was... who she was. At his chest, the crystal pulsed white one moment and black the next.

*"She is drawing from his guilt and anger, Leanna,"* Inara groaned. *"My magic can't hold both of their powers off for much longer. Speak to him!"*

"What you did in the past doesn't matter anymore," Leanna called above the moans and cries of the darkness. "Don't think of the pain, of the deaths.

Think of Ellie. She needs her brother. Think of your people, of your land. Fight for them. They need you. Forever needs her king!"

In the shadow of Machina's magic, Finvarra shut his eyes tightly. At his chest, the crystal hummed white for a slight longer than it did black. He weaved his hands into his hair and curled into himself as if wishing to tear Machina from his mind and thoughts.

The light of the crystal grew steady as his magic warred against Machina's poison. He pushed back onto his knees and pinned his gaze on Leanna. His body quavered as shafts of whiteness spread from his crystal like rays of moonlight. The poison that spread across his face and chest curled away. So did the black mist around him.

As Finvarra claimed the rights to his magic, Machina's fight weakened and Inara's light pushed closer. Machina speared an orb of black fire toward Inara. It stalled Inara's beam of magic for a second, enough time for Machina to whirl away behind Finvarra.

Finvarra's body grew rigid, his eyes wide.

Inara gasped and her magic shot back into her horn. The moans and cries of the fog too hushed. In this unnatural stillness, Finvarra met Leanna's stare. Pale blue eyes glimmered with tears before he blinked and blackness washed over them.

Leanna opened her mouth to scream, but found no voice when Finvarra's crystal turned black at his chest, and beside it, a metal blade stabbed him straight through the heart.

# CHAPTER TWENTY-SEVEN
## DEAD HEART

"WHAT IS THERE TO FIGHT FOR NOW?" Machina rested her head on his shoulder and stroked the bloodied blade. "He can't give you his heart and the curse can't be broken. His beloved circus can't ever go home."

Time and space vanished around Leanna and her legs gave way beneath her. Beside her, Inara touched her flaming horn to the ground repeatedly, desperately. Through their connection, Leanna felt Inara trying to struggle against her agony at losing Krinard, at never being able to go home. The sadness and doubt clouded her magic, and her circle of light grew smaller.

"And without this heart and crystal," Machina said, "you, too, will die."

"*Don't listen to her, Leanna,*" Inara begged in her continued plight to dispel the surrounding blackness. "*Climb on. Do not suffer our fate!*"

Frozen at Machina's words, at the blade through Finvarra's heart, at all the magic she ever believed in burning, Leanna lifted a hand to her chest, to where the crystal had been for most of her life but was no longer. Her fingers brushed the bruised skin and her broken world came back together in a new way.

The only way.

To free Finvarra from the clutches of Machina's darkness, they needed the strongest of magic. But something strong was needed to spark it within Finvarra.

Leanna gazed around at the black fog obliterating the Big Top—something worse than losing his circus.

She glanced at a lifeless Krinard—something worse than losing his friends.

She looked back to Finvarra, the faerie king brought to his knees—something worse than losing his life.

"*Please, Leanna,*" Inara pled. "*Once her evil overtakes him, I won't be able to defeat them. I won't be able to get you out of this. You must come now!"*

Darkness edged at her toes, but Leanna rose and met Machina's eyes through the falling ashes. As if linked by a common thread of being, awareness swelled in Machina's stare. Her blade slowly withdrew from Finvarra's back, and snakelike, she rose.

"Go with Inara," Finvarra said weakly. He fought to keep himself upright, but his arms trembled. "I will keep my magic from her for as long as I can."

Straining, he blinked and the black of his eyes faded to a murky blue. "Go!"

A sad smile arched her lips as she remembered those eyes, remembered every kiss and caress, every word. "Remember when you said death would not be enough to free you from the agony of losing me?"

Finvarra's eyes widened. "No, Leanna, don't!"

She thrust herself into the darkness. Streams of Inara's magic reached for her, but Leanna came face to face with herself, and it was too late.

Before a scream, Machina's metal hand clutched her neck.

Before her heart beat again, a loud crushing conquered the sound.

And before a breath left her lips, a shock of pain stole it away when metal hands tore her heart from her chest.

Leanna thought everything would fade to black when she died.

Yet as Machina's eyes brimmed with victory, beams of white stretched outward from behind her. With her hand still around Leanna's neck and the other holding Leanna's beating heart, Machina turned to Finvarra. His blond hair whipped in the icy winds that sent the fog whirling around them and aided him to his feet. His moonlit glow expanded and joined with that of the crystal. A tired smile spread on Leanna's lips. He was like the dual rising of the sun and moon, the most beautiful thing she had ever seen.

Awed at the sight of him, Machina's grip around Leanna loosened and she dropped her to the ground. Machina's stronghold on the darkness weakened, Inara was able to cut a path of light to Leanna.

She touched her horn to Leanna's hand. "I will keep you alive for as long as I can. Hold on to my horn!"

Leanna curled weak fingers around the flaming horn that didn't burn her skin. Prickles of coolness coursed down her body as Inara's magic pulsed within her like a heartbeat.

Rapt by her obsession, Machina failed to see Inara keeping Leanna alive, just as she failed to notice the crystal at her chest growing brighter. Spellbound, she lifted Leanna's heart to Finvarra. It beat once and again, and then beat no more.

"It is complete. I have everything of her, don't you see? I am her. You can love me." She sobbed and tears spilled from her eyes—human tears. "Finally, you can love me."

Finvarra lifted his face and raised a hand to Machina. Tendrils of white snapped from his fingers. They whipped around Machina's neck, and her head snapped back. She shrieked as vapors hissed from where Finvarra's magic shackled her arms and feet.

He wrenched the whips and yanked her before him. Machina gasped and her body grew rigid as Finvarra's bare hand pierced her chest. Leanna's dead heart fell from her fingers.

A shaft of blinding fire burst from Finvarra's crystal. He arched back with a cry—a chorus of agony, of lament, of pure love for his circus, for his troupe, for Forever, for Leanna. His magic enclosed them in a cloud of white fire that curled outward. The ground jerked violently and the fog exploded with frantic shrieks as darkness and light burned together.

Machina screamed, and the surrounding black whirled to a funnel that twisted back into her mouth. Ghostly hands clawed not to return to the evil abyss within her, but Finvarra's light chased them back to their hell.

Clawing wildly for release, Machina dug human fingers and metal nails into Finvarra's arm, but he withstood the ache of her iron and shared in her pain. He held her as her body convulsed and head whipped side to side. As dirt seeped from her pores and the metal fragments stitched onto the body rusted and her skin charred. As her body dissolved around his hand, blowing away as curls of ash, springs, screws and dust.

A mechanical heart remained in Finvarra's palm. The metal sizzled and burned his skin, but in spite of the pain, he opened his eyes. Looking to the culmination of his nightmare, he closed his fingers to a fist and crushed the heart.

Light shot back into him. The raging winds tamed, dragging away the remaining smoke until only his circus remained.

It was over.

And as each breath grew harder to take, Leanna knew other things were close to being over, too. "Finvarra…" She closed eyes for a moment to gather strength. A familiar scent filled her lungs and she blinked open to Finvarra above her.

"Oh, you foolish, meddling girl," he whispered, his tears wetting her cheek. His wound healed, he took her into his arms. He pressed a hand against the opening at her chest and a white hue illuminated his face. "I will fix this. I promise you, I will fix this. Just please, don't leave me."

Coldness pricked the skin around her injury, but her strength still faded. *"Her heart is dead, Finvarra. It is too late to heal her. She needs a heart!"*

Frantic, he took Leanna's hand and pressed it against his chest. His heart beat beneath her fingertips, but the melody was slow and erratic.

"Take my heart. It's damaged, but it's a heart. Take it, please," he moaned desperately against her lips. "I need you to live."

"Wait, the crystal!" Kioyo's voice came in from behind them. In a brush of white and snow he appeared beside them, crystal necklace in hand. He looped it around Leanna's neck. At Tomas's urging, he moved back beside the remaining troupe that gathered around them.

Finvarra cupped a trembling hand over her crystal. "I give you my heart, Leanna. It is yours. Do you accept it?"

Hearing the words of a dream come true, Leanna nodded weakly. "Yes."

Finvarra bent his head and neared her lips to seal their vow with a kiss.

"Finvarra, no!" The ground trembled under the thunderous voice. All eyes snapped to the voice—to the most unlikely of people standing in their midst. Finvarra pressed Leanna against him, his body tense and alert.

"You can't give her your heart. Not yet," Minerva said, moving forward to the jingle of bells. Her vibrant colors were replaced now by a white chiton, a coined silver belt at her waist. Flowing black hair streamed down her shoulders and back, no longer hidden under a bandana. Her red lips were the only traits to remain of the Minerva that Leanna remembered.

Leanna made to speak, but her chest locked and trapped her words under wracking coughs that sprinkled blood onto Finvarra's skin. Losing feeling in her limbs, her fingers loosened around Inara's horn.

*"He must do it now, Minerva,"* Inara said, her voice weak. *"I can't keep her alive much longer."*

Ignoring Minerva's warning, Finvarra turned back to Leanna intent on a kiss. Before a blink, Minerva was beside him, a glowing hand alit on his shoulder. Eyes of white fire stared down at him and she shook her head. She kneeled down beside Leanna and placed a hand where Leanna's heart once was. Warmth spread through Leanna's body and she coughed repeatedly, assimilating this heat that intensified all color, scent, and sound.

Minerva smiled. "That should help keep you alive until we've had a chance to talk," she said and nodded to Leanna's hand upon Inara's horn. Leanna dithered, but Minerva had always been there for her. She wouldn't doubt her now. She loosened her fingers around Inara's horn and let her hand fall away. She still lived.

"Who are you?" Finvarra asked her, shielding Leanna away from Minerva. "You're not—"

"A vampire?" Minerva shook her head. "I pretended to be whatever I needed to be to stay within your circus. I am a Guardian. You don't think the Elders would have sent you to this realm without some guidance, do you?"

A cool breeze whisked past. Leanna shivered at the iciness that nipped her skin through the rips in her nightgown. Still unconvinced, Finvarra brought her closer to his being as if scared the breeze or Minerva would take her away. He cradled her in his arms and in a cloud of ice, the Big Top faded and Ellie's butterflies appeared overhead. They no longer draped the ceiling, but hung down in tangled messes of wings, cloth, and strings. The canvas too had been slashed, but thankfully the tent still stood.

Finvarra turned in place and slowly webs of ice formed over the rips, thin threads of spider silk weaving the fabric closed. He stalked to the bed, moved aside the blankets, and laid Leanna down.

"If this is a ploy from the Elders, they can't have you," he said. "I won't let you die."

Leanna lifted a hand to his face at once. Though Machina's darkness had been dispelled, Finvarra's look then was equally dangerous. "Don't speak this way. I want nothing more than to be with you, but if I should have to go..."

The curtain flaps snapped. "Let us hope that is not the case," Minerva said, appearing at the bedside. "If you will only let me explain why I'm here."

Finvarra didn't look at her. He only stroked a hand gently along Leanna's cheek, his jaw taut. "You can't have her."

Minerva pursed her lips. "I am not here to take her from you. The Elders have never been against you, Finvarra. Had they been, I would not be here. I wouldn't have been here all of these years."

"I welcomed you into my circus, thinking you needed refuge yet it was all a lie. Now you are asking me to believe that the Elders sent you here to help?" Finvarra scoffed. "Where were you when Machina destroyed this circus? When she tore out Leanna's heart? If the Elders are so concerned, then why are you here now telling me that I can't give her my heart?"

Leanna put a hand on his arm, and with her look asked for him to stop. In spite of it all, Minerva had been a friend. She didn't deserve this.

Finvarra skimmed her jaw and his brows gathered as if in one more second nothing would keep him from her lips. "Speak quickly, Minerva, or I swear to you..."

Minerva sat opposite him at Leanna's side. "Machina was for you to defeat, Finvarra. I could never interfere, only guide you just as I am trying to do now. Giving Leanna your heart will not save her life. Your heart only beats now because of your magic, because of the curse. Once it is within her body and the curse is broken, the heart will stop and she will die. But Machina was right. You two are bound through these crystals, you've always been."

Minerva offered Leanna her hands and nodded encouragingly. Leanna slipped her hands into Minerva's and accepted her help in sitting up. Finvarra remained close. He slid behind Leanna and supported her against his chest, smoothing his hands down her arms in slow strokes.

"Just as Finvarra's agony seeped into you and your hope bled into him through the crystals, his life can sustain you both," Minerva said.

Finvarra's hands stilled upon her arms and Leanna too froze. Sustain them both?

"With these crystals between you, you will forever reflect into one another. That was why you felt him in your dreams, and that is why she came to you in your despair," she said to Finvarra. "When either of you was in need, you filled the other with what they needed most, whether love, comfort or hope. You are bound."

A fury of emotions trailed Finvarra's eyes. "Then I can sustain her and keep her alive, even when I give her my heart?"

"Yes." She regarded Leanna then. "Just as you were going to accept his heart, you must accept his life. When his broken heart fails within you, you will die out of this human existence but be born again, faerie life flowing through your veins. That is the gift from the Elders, the only way you can ever live in Forever. However," Minerva said instantly, cutting them both off before they had a chance to speak. "You can't ever enter this realm again. The places you wished to go, the normal life denied you will be no more. Your family... You will never see them again."

The luster of Minerva's previous words dimmed. Though Finvarra had told her she would never see her family again, she did hope to one day return, at least to tell her father a proper farewell. To tell him that in spite of it all, he'd been a good father. Finvarra kissed the top of her head, his affection telling of his understanding.

"But this is for you to decide. You have found favor in the eyes of the

Elders, Leanna. They have allowed me to meddle this once," she said with a smile. "Should you wish to remain in this realm, I can heal Finvarra's heart. With it, you will be free to live the life denied you by your illness. You can dance again, travel the world. You can live."

Leanna leaned back against an equally speechless Finvarra. The choice was appealing, and there were so many places she had read in books that she had only dreamt of visiting. No longer would she be bound to a bed, watching life happen around her instead of to her. She would be free. It all sounded so right, yet, Leanna turned her head toward Finvarra and filled her lungs with his scent. "But what of us?"

Minerva's lips pressed to a thin line. "Once you accept this heart and the curse is broken, the doorways between our worlds will close forever."

The world stilled around Leanna. Behind her, Finvarra kept to his silence. Were it not for him holding her, for the steadiness of his breathing, she would have thought him a figment of her dreams.

"I truly wish there was another way, but it is the only way." Minerva stood up. "I will give you time to think over your choices."

"There is no need." Leanna sat up, decided. "I know what I want. I choose to remain at his side."

Minerva arched a brow. "And you will forfeit this life and every adventure you've always wanted? You can see the world, fall in love with another should you wish. Choice is what you are being given, Leanna."

"And a choice is what I am making. I wish to remain by his…"

Leanna cut off when Finvarra rose from the bed and walked to the unlit fireplace. Arms crossed over his chest, he didn't say a word though his frame was tense. Leanna's brows furrowed. Wasn't he happy she was choosing him?

"Like I said, I will give you time to think over your choices." Minerva pressed a kiss at Leanna's forehead and swept through the curtains, leaving them to quiet and the fading melody of her bells.

Minutes after Minerva had gone, Finvarra had yet to speak. His hands were at his waist now, and he stared down to the shadows at the fireplace.

Leanna sat on the edge of the bed and gripped the cool necklace. "Is it that…" she started, but fear swelled in her throat and cut off her words. Asking would bring about the truth, perhaps a truth that would hurt her more than anything. She'd faced Machina and death, yet the chance of his rejection was most frightening of all. Still, she swallowed. "Is it that you don't want to share your life with me?"

Finvarra's hands slipped from his waist. *"My life?"* He turned to her, eyes narrowed. "My grief and agony haunted you for years and you call it *my life?*"

He strode to her and crouched down at her feet, taking her hands in his. "This is not my life, Leanna. However many years I have belong to you. They have been yours since I gave your mother the necklace." He lowered his eyes to their entwined hands, ashamed. "I didn't know my misery would haunt you, that my sadness would hurt you. I never would have given it to her had I known. That is why I can't take this from you."

Threading his fingers into her hair, he grazed her cheek with his thumb, soft caresses that knotted her stomach. "I want nothing more than to take you into Forever this instant, to share my life with you, to make life with you, but I don't deserve it. I don't deserve you."

He rose and stepped away from her. "All I deserve is to watch you live the life I stole from you. You can have your adventures and see the world you only found in your books."

Leanna stared at him. Attempting to speak a few times, she closed her mouth, speechless.

*"Adventure?"* she said finally. "I sit here without the heart that was torn from my chest by a mechanical demon, after I rode here on the back of the unicorn to save the faerie king and his court. And you speak to me of *adventure?* I daresay I've lived my fill of adventures that can rival any found within any book."

She walked to him and stroked his cheek, hoping the gentle touch would quiet his thoughts. "I have spent a lifetime alone, never belonging anywhere. Always being told what was good for me and what I should want. But I have found my place here." She lowered her hands from his face and boldly slipped it into his shirt, coming to rest on the cool skin above his heart. "I know what I want, should you wish to share in it with me."

"This is your choice?" His voice broke upon the last word. "After everything, you still wish to share in this circus that is my life?"

She nodded and a tear spilled. "Always."

Finvarra weaved a hand behind her neck, an arm at her waist, and crashed onto her lips. Leanna fisted his shirt, meeting him with equal vigor, no longer needing air to survive. He was enough.

Tasting blood and ash in his kiss, she sighed. Never had she tasted anything sweeter. Finvarra drank in her breath and obliged her unspoken desires. Caging her in his arms, he lifted her against him and deepened their kiss. Their bodies shifted and aligned until flush against one another. For

Leanna, it was still too far. A hunger kindled in her womb and she arched into him, aching for more, for things she didn't know yet wanted from him, to give him, to make with him.

Finvarra's fingers tightened upon her and he broke their kiss slowly. "Will you accept my heart, Leanna Weston?" he asked against her mouth, "Will you accept my life as yours?"

At her chest, the crystal grew so cold it burned. But gazing at this man—at the faerie king asking her to share in his life, she embraced the ache. In that instant, living a life without him and death were one and the same.

"I do." She brought him back onto her lips and sealed their vow.

The moment their lips touched, the crystals ignited. Finvarra clutched her tightly and stiffened in her arms with a sharp groan. Leanna bit her nails into his shoulders, the heaviness of a dead heart settling slowly within her chest. Her knees buckled under the agonizing pain that seized her lungs.

Together they crumbled to the floor where Leanna clawed at the open air for a breath that would not come. Finvarra held her to him, coaxing her while her body writhed and fought with the instinct to live.

But this heart within her did not beat, and her fight dwindled quickly. Her arms fell lifeless to her sides and all feeling seeped from her limbs. With Finvarra's face above her and his heart failing within her, Leanna closed her eyes. Her chest lowered with a breath—her last.

A tinkling shatter exploded through the darkness of her closed eyes. Her body rounded up and a rush of ice coursed through her veins. She hauled in a wild breath, feeling her spirit burst like the crystals. It shattered into countless slivers, each containing pieces of her life. These fragments of her existence soared upwards through a sky of endless falling stars. Each of these stars that cascaded around her were memories—Finvarra's memories. They fell into her freely, just as the shards of her life soared into him.

Lost in this blissful exchange, the lines of reality and magic blurred and she no longer knew the difference between rising and falling, between the end of her life and the beginning of his.

By and by, Leanna found the rhythm of her new breath. Now at the bed, she nestled at Finvarra's side. Lingering shivers still afflicted her, but Finvarra turned her into him and held her tightly against his body as if to will them away. Smoothing his hand along her back, he eased her from her tremors with kisses on her eyes, her cheeks, her nose...

And they lay like this, with no enemies in wait and no broken hearts, joined by life, bound by love, and blessed by the snows that fell above them.

227

# Chapter Twenty-Eight
## The Grand Finale

SNOWFLAKES GLITTERED LIKE FROZEN STARS under the white light of Bertrand's dragons. The gentle song of the harp and slow whines of the violin gave the pixies a melody for their dance through the snow. The chattering audience sat mesmerized by the display, unknowing of all that had happened earlier in the day.

Closing the curtain, Leanna turned back to the gathered troupe that lined up as if a curse still bound them to the canvas. Forgiveness had come. The proof of it dusted the ground and fell continuously over the circus. Yet they all remained willingly for one last show.

Gleeful chatter of returning to Forever had dominated all talk from the moment she had stepped from her tent to see the field covered in white and the performers spinning like children in the falling snow. The talk was no different now as she made her way down the line. Many spoke wistfully of their mother's cooking, or their spouse's smiles, of the many places they would go, and of how they would never forget one another.

While Leanna understood their joy, a slight of sadness found a home in her soul when she reached her spot at the end of the line. She wanted more than anything to go to Forever. That had been her choice, but she would never see her family again, not even to say goodbye. A flush warmed her face.

"Your cheeks match your dress," Kioyo whispered in her ear, coming up alongside her while ruffling the red feathers of her dance dress. The snow dampened his hair and black strands clung to his forehead. "Nervous?"

Leanna shrugged, giving him her most stable smile.

"You will do fine." He gripped her shoulders and shook her gently with each word. "You accomplished what you set out to do for our best. We have been forgiven. Now it's time for you to dance for you."

"And for you," she admitted. "I owe you this dance."

Kioyo's brows knitted. "For me?"

"I ruined my performance after we worked so hard. You were angry and didn't even look at me afterwards. And don't tell me you weren't angry. I saw it on your face."

Kioyo took in a breath to speak, but in the end said nothing.

"See, and I never got to apologize."

Kioyo shook his head. "You don't owe me this, Leanna. I admit, at first I was angry that you didn't cross the rope and finish your dance. But then…" He paused and tilted her head up to his. "But then I realized that I always pushed you to do things for yourself, regardless of what your duty was. By not crossing the rope, you did."

Leanna made to speak, but his hands came upon her forearms gently. "You stuck by what you believed in. You risked the wrath of the Ringmaster, the wrath of this troupe because you believed you could free us all. That is bravery, and I couldn't be more proud of you. I'm just sorry I was too foolish to realize it before."

She knew he would say something as such, but tears still filled her eyes.

"What's this now? Sadness, when snow falls upon our heads?" Kioyo cupped her chin. "No, no, we can't have that, your highness. I told you I wasn't angry, silly girl." A small smile crept onto his face. While beautiful, sadly it was not contagious.

"That isn't it, and please, don't call me that. I'm not your queen."

He chuckled. "Even I know it's only a matter of time before everyone calls you such."

"But never you. Promise me you never will. They can," she gestured out to the troupe lined before them, "but not you."

Kioyo's hand fell away from her slowly. "What's going on, Leanna?" He slid a careful, scrutinizing gaze along her, and by and by all color drained from his face. "Do you… do you regret your decision to come to Forever?"

"No, never that," she assured him. "I wanted a new life. I wanted things to change, but the more I think about leaving this world, the more I'm scared everything *will* change."

She watched Kioyo try to understand this. Sighing, she shook her head and waved a hand airily. "Forget it. Don't mind me. It seems I not only lost my heart, but all sense as well. Forget I said anything at all."

When she made to move away, warm hands came upon her shoulders. "Tell me what's wrong, Leanna. We're friends, are we not?"

"We are, and that is what frightens me most of all," she admitted, no longer able to deny it. "You have proven yourself and have been forgiven and redeemed. And I am so very happy for you. You're free to go home, and probably wish to forget all that's happened, but…"

"But," he encouraged her.

Snow fell freely over his head, a much deserved coldness that warmed her heart. She couldn't lie to him. Not there, with truth and forgiveness dusting their feet in white, and the crossbars of the dressing tent freezing in the cooler temperatures of a waiting world.

"But if I could ask for one thing to be frozen in this cold and snow, can it be us? Regardless of what has changed and will change, let us remain the same. Can I ask this of you, not as the order of a queen or a muse, but the request of a friend?"

Kioyo massaged the back of his neck. "I'm not sure if I should be angry or offended that you would ask that of me."

"I know. You probably want to forget this circus ever happened—"

"That you feel the *need* to ask this of me," he said over her. "I am here and will always be here for you, Leanna. When you need me and when you don't, whether you ask it of me or not. My promise to you will always remain. If you ever need me, you just whisper my name and I will be there. And I pledge this to you, not as a subordinate, but as your friend."

Emotion swelled her throat and she hugged him tightly, but in breaking away, she slapped his arm. "You scared me!"

"Well, I *am* a clown." A wide smile underscored his painted one. "Though I hope this is not enough to subject me to this horrible punishment you have yet to think of."

Boisterous voices came through the curtain and silenced them. Vicente's music withered into a discord of plucked strings. The troupe shifted forward and peeked through the curtains at the voice now saying,

"Pardon the interruption, ladies and gentlemen, but we are here on official business so if you would please remain seated."

Leanna gasped. "The Constable. He's here for me!"

"You stay here while I talk to them. Bertrand," Kioyo called over his shoulder. "Get the Ringmaster!"

Bertrand nodded and dashed past them. In a blink, Kioyo brushed through the crowd in a cloud of white. He materialized before the curtains, parted them, and strode through, sure to close the curtains behind him. Leanna followed Kioyo's fading trail of ice through the troupe. She reached the curtains and peeked through in time to see the Constable step forward from beside two officers.

"I am here to speak with your Ringmaster," said the small man. "I have reason to believe that a girl is being kept here against her will."

Kioyo hummed noncommittally. With one hand at his hip, he pointed to the Constable as a mother would when scolding a child with the other. "Now, now, Constable, that is a grave accusation. I think you are mistaken. There is no one here who doesn't want to be. Not anymore. It's snowing, don't you see? Now if you would please allow us to continue on with our show. It is our last one, and we would very much like to go home."

Word of it being the last show raged through the crowd like fire. Murmurs sparked to life again, much louder than before.

The Constable's seedy brown eyes narrowed. "I've no time for your cryptic talk. The girl is ill and we must find her immediately."

"As I have said, there is no one here who does not wish to be."

"You lie, sir!" another voice came from out of sight that made Leanna freeze. Had she a heart, it would have pounded to a stop that second in hearing her father's voice.

She angled her head to see her father, Lydia and Sarah beside him. Though Sarah fought to seem indifferent, her eyes were wide and afraid. Lydia's face was reddened and her hair unkempt.

"I have a letter in my possession stating that my daughter is here. I demand she be returned to me." He held up a white envelope.

"Read it if you wish, just please return our sister to us, before it's too late," Lydia begged of him. Mr. Weston held out the letter to Kioyo. Seeing his hands tremble and genuine worry mark his eyes, Leanna clutched the curtains tighter. If she ever had a doubt her father and sisters loved her, their concern then obliterated the uncertainty.

A hand came onto Leanna's shoulder and she spun. Finvarra stood close behind her, Bertrand at his side.

"My father is out there, and the Constable," she told him, as if he hadn't been told such by Bertrand, as if he couldn't hear Kioyo and the Constable having words on the other side of the curtain.

He grazed a finger gently along her cheek. A small smile touched the side of his mouth, a smile that lit his eyes and drew Leanna into his thoughts.

She gasped. "The letter, you sent it. You ordered one last performance so that he would come and I could say goodbye."

"Did I do wrong?"

She shook her head unable to find any words. How could he possibly think that when he continuously made her every wish come true?

He held a hand to her. "Shall we?"

Leanna slid her hand into his and with a mutual nod, they turned out to the striped curtains. Hand in hand, they walked through.

Mr. Weston was the first to see them. He studied Leanna slowly, her pinned up hair, her feathery gown, her hand entwined with Finvarra's, and a furious flush colored his face. "Leanna Weston! What on earth is the meaning of this?"

Lydia pressed a hand to her lips, a sob escaping. She gripped her skirts and dashed across the rings to meet her. Throwing her arms around Leanna, she dragged her into an embrace. "We were so worried. We thought you had run off and died somewhere in the forest. I thought I had driven you to your death for forcing you to marry, and I never would have forgiven myself." Lydia broke away a slight. "Are you all right? Did they hurt you? Come, Dr. Luther must take a look at you. You're freezing and pale."

"I am well," Leanna assured her. "For the first time, I am perfectly fine."

As though finally seeing her, Lydia's eyes widened. She stumbled back, taking in Leanna's dress, her hair, the makeup, and Finvarra behind her. "You're…He's…You're a part of his circus?"

Mr. Weston scoffed. "Preposterous! No daughter of mine will be a part of this sham. Whatever you are playing at stops now, Leanna. We are leaving this instant."

Leanna released Lydia's hand and took a step toward her father. "Father, I can explain."

"Explain how you've disgraced your family's name? You will explain nothing here before these people." He held a firm hand to her. "Come now, we're leaving."

"Listen to Papa," Sarah said from beside him, trembling. "If anything happens to you…"

Leanna went to her older sister and touched her cheek. For years they had quarreled, and it was Sarah's toxic words that had always hurt her the most. Yet there, no rancor found Leanna and she hugged her sister.

"Do not fear for me, dear sister. And do not blame yourself. This is the way things were always meant to be." Leanna snapped a feather from her feathery tutu. She took Sarah's hand in hers and pressed the feather against it. "No fear."

"What have you to say for yourself now, Finvarra?" The Constable smirked. At his side, a pale Dr. Luther simply stared. The murmurs swelled.

Many in the audience shared glances as if wondering if it were all part of the show. Leanna exhaled, wishing it was.

"Go with your father, child," the Constable said. "You are safe now. This monster will not terrorize another town ever again."

"He is not a monster, and I am not leaving. I have my own feet to guide me, and my own mind. I have made my choice. I have a life now, and I will not leave it behind."

Stunned, Mr. Weston sputtered the beginnings of few unintelligible words. Beside him, Dr. Luther broke from his mental pause.

"If you refuse to listen to your father, then listen to me. Not as the man you are to marry," he said pointedly, "but as your doctor. If not for decency and proprieties, think of your health. You do not belong here with these... *people*. You are a young and inexperienced girl with a weak heart. You can be easily manipulated. Your being here tells me you already have been. Come." He reached for her.

Finvarra's hand wrapped tightly around his wrist and he never touched her.

The Constable whirled a hand, motioning for the officers to intervene. A rumbling growl resounded from Leanna's side, underscored by Lydia and Sarah's screams. The two officers stumbled back, their shocked gazes pinned on Kioyo, now in leopard form.

"Good heavens," Mr. Weston breathed. He reached out to Leanna, frantic. "Let us go home, Leanna, before someone gets hurt!"

With Dr. Luther frozen by fear of Finvarra, and the Constable and his men being kept at bay by Kioyo, Leanna walked to her father and placed a palm at his cheek.

"There is nothing in this world for me. Not after all I have witnessed, after all the magic I've lived." Behind her, the troupe exited the tent to stand by their king and now by her. "This is where I belong and this is where I will stay, but if I could have your blessing then I will truly be happy. I've had a lifetime of broken hearts and it would pain me to know my goodbye has broken yours. Be happy for me, please."

His chin quivered. "You look just like her. Your mother's eyes gleamed with the same deluded hope that all of this nonsense was real. What have they done to you? I told you, there is no such thing as magic. Please, heed my words. This is all an illusion. None of it is real and I can't accept this, Leanna, forgive me. The letter says you mean to leave, but... but what you are asking of me is impossible. I can't be happy for this, and I can't let you leave."

"Then you will deny me this to have me waste away in a metal chair, married to a man who thinks I'm easily manipulated? Forget your fear and what this world thinks is wrong or right. Look me in the eyes and tell me that you want that miserable existence for me."

They stared at one another in silence for long moments, moments where Leanna watched her father struggle with the impossibilities presented him.

"I am trying to understand, but...but I'm scared for you."

"There's no reason to be frightened. Not anymore." She could have explained to him how she no longer had a heart and perhaps ease his fears that her heart would fail, but instinct told her that would do more harm than good.

Instead, she put a hand on his heart with all the love she felt and focused on what her life had been like before the circus—a never ending torrent of bad dreams, aching loneliness, and the denied desire to belong, to simply live. Coolness rushed through her veins, flowing to her hand against his chest. Her father's look changed as she shared her memories through the currents of her magic.

"All of these years I've tried keeping you safe and alive, and you were dying of misery," he said, his voice weak. "I didn't know you were so unhappy."

Leanna walked into his chest and hugged her father. However many times she felt betrayed, angered, sad, and alone, it didn't matter now. His arms came around her, and she understood that no love could ever be perfect.

She spoke to him then, words for his ears only, words of forgiveness, appreciation for having been a good father, the best he knew to be. Words to soothe his heart and assure him she'd found all the love she could ever dream of. She kissed her father's cheek and stepped back.

Perhaps it was shock or the effects of her faerie magic, or perhaps it was simply the link between a father and a daughter, but though he was still unconvinced, a sad acceptance settled in his eyes and he nodded.

"You're letting her leave with them?" Dr. Luther sputtered.

"My daughter wishes to leave and your services are no longer needed," Mr. Weston said. Lydia and Sarah looked to one another, speechless.

"But surely you can't allow it. This is madness!"

"Yes, well, she's been known to inspire such," Finvarra said. "Now if you would allow us to begin our show. I reserved some seating for the Westons up front. You are welcomed to join them."

"This is absurd!" The Constable made to step forward, but when Kioyo

235

growled, he jumped back, shuffling quickly behind his men who scrambled to get behind him. Many in the audience laughed, finding it as comical as Leanna did.

"Enough of this," the Constable clipped and pushed his fumbling officers away. "When I return, it will be with all of my men. This treachery will not go unpunished." He spun on his heels, puffed up his chest, and strode through the curtain, his men and Dr. Luther close behind him.

An awkward and slow clap waved through the tent, many unsure whether it had been a part of the show or not.

Mr. Weston watched them go, worry still in his eyes. Leanna put a hand on his shoulder wishing there was something she could do that would assure him all would be well, that there was magic in the world. Perhaps then he wouldn't worry.

Vicente queued the band and Leanna smiled, knowing the perfect thing.

"And for our final act, I bring to you the one who freed us from our nightmares and iron chains. May the memory of her dance soothe you in your darkest of times. May her light give you a glimpse into Forever where she will be adored and loved," Finvarra said, nodding once to Mr. Weston. He motioned to the platform above him. "Ladies and gentlemen, I present to you the magnificent, Leanna."

The beginning chords of Leanna's minuet resounded. Trusting in the music and in herself, Leanna steeled her spine, tipped her chin, and stepped onto the rope. Sway and reach, she danced unafraid. As she spun freely, unencumbered by curses, mechanical monsters and broken hearts, the coloring of her gown curled away from her as tresses of crimson smoke until only she remained at center rope in a glittering white dress.

Her body hummed, yearning to share with the world her joy of dying into a new life. But they couldn't see the tears that spilled from her eyes, tears of childhood fairy tales coming true, of sickness and loneliness forgotten. No, there was only one thing that could be seen from great distances, in the thickest of darkness.

Leanna brought her hands to her stomach and curled into herself. When she exhaled and arched back, love poured from her body in frosted streams of light. The audience gasped, bathed in her blinding hue of life, of love, of magic.

Straightening, she swayed naturally like the ocean that once pulled Finvarra from the shores of his madness. Only now, with each wave of her arms she hoped to have pulled her father and sisters from the shores of disbelief, proving to them that her mother was right. Finvarra's Circus was truly magical.

When she reached the platform, applause roared from below. On their feet, the audience cheered wildly and the air vibrated with their praise. With a hand over the memory of her heart, Leanna bowed.

Applause followed her down the ladder where the troupe lined up outside of the rings. Finvarra stood at their heart, the pixies glittering above him. He held a hand to her. Entwining her hand with his, Leanna let him draw her beside him and turned to face the crowd alongside her new family. Hand in hand, they stood a moment, taking in the applause. Then slowly, they either bowed or curtsied, marking the end of Finvarra's Circus.

The audience howled and cheered, while others clapped heartily. Mr. Weston was amongst those. Pride beamed in his stare and in the tears that spilled from his eyes, like her sisters beside him. Leanna curtsied one more time, a special appreciation for their applause.

A gust of icy wind whisked through the tent that sent the snowflakes into twirls of frost. The curtains billowed and silver light streamed through the ever-changing seams.

Minerva smiled from beside the curtains. "Forever waits."

Inara was the first to move, leading the line with a kindled horn. The troupe followed, and one by one vanished through the curtains until only Leanna remained at Finvarra's side.

Leanna released Finvarra's hand and walked to her family. With each of her steps, the clapping faded and the audience took their seats again as if truly believing this was all part of the show. She stood before them and gazed back to where Finvarra now stood beside Tomas on one side of the curtain, Minerva and Kioyo on the other. Frosted light streamed out to her, the hands of Forever beckoning her home.

"We have to go now," she said.

Her father swallowed deeply. "You don't have to go. I know you were unhappy, but I can change that now."

"We all can. We promise you, we will. And what if your illness should return? What if you're unhappy?" Lydia fretted, wiping her tears. "We can be the family we should have been, the family you needed."

Lydia trailed off, her hand taken from her by Sarah. "This is her family now," she said. With the feather still tight in her hands, Sarah smiled. "You have my blessing."

Leanna swept into her sister's arms, finally feeling the affection she'd wished for so long.

"Goodbye, sister," Sarah said, bolstering a grieving Lydia who held on a moment longer before letting go. They moved back together, leaving Leanna to her last farewell.

"Papa?" she whispered. "Please. There is no way I will be truly happy if I know you're not happy for me."

His plump cheeks reddened. "I don't know what awaits you on the other side of that curtain, but is it truly what you want?"

She nodded. "It's all I've ever wanted."

Her father cupped her cheek. "Then you have my blessing, dear girl."

The image of him smeared behind her tears and a sob broke free as she hugged him. Though she had no heart, in that instant, Leanna felt something inside of her break.

A cool breeze whispered past again. Leanna and her father peeled away. Knowingly, he offered her his arm. She slipped her arm into his and curled up at his side, and he escorted her to the curtains.

Finvarra slid off his hat and extended his hand. Mr. Weston met it firmly. No words were spoken between them, but the intensity of their handshake and secret conversation of their eyes pressed down on Leanna's chest. She knew then that no two men could ever love her more.

Mr. Weston kissed Leanna's hand and guided it into Finvarra's. Releasing it into his hold, he moved back one step and another. "Goodbye, Leanna."

Tears streamed from her eyes, the last of her mortal wishes come true. "Goodbye, Papa."

Farewells said, Kioyo whirled Minerva under his arm in an impromptu dance, and they vanished together through the curtains. Chuckling, Tomas shook his head and followed. When he reached the threshold, he stepped aside and held the curtain open. A shuddering breath curled from Leanna's lips. The sight spread before her was a dream.

An icy forest waited where frozen crystals glinted on skeletal branches. The winds sent frost swirls pirouetting from in between the trees, toward Leanna and Finvarra. The icy tresses twined about their bodies, encouraging them forward.

Leanna turned a teary gaze to Finvarra whose eyes followed the quiet journey of the snow across his lands to the icy towers in the distance. He closed his hand over hers, and together they stepped forward.

The light of the palace kindled as if knowing their king had returned. Wintry light spilled from within and streamed across the land. The silvery hue made diamonds of the snowflakes and marked a glittering path through the forest and to the palace gates.

Finvarra leaned into Leanna and placed a kiss at her temple. And as the curtains closed behind them, he whispered, "Welcome home."

# THE END

Monica Sanz

# ABOUT THE AUTHOR

Ever since reading Wuthering Heights as a child, Monica has been obsessed with dark and heartbreaking romances (and brooding fictional men!) Now she spends her days writing all about cursed ringmasters, tortured soul collectors, grumpy magicians, and the girls who fall in love with them.

When not lost in one of her many made-up worlds, she can be found on the sunny beaches of South Florida where she resides with her husband and their three kiddos, or scouring YouTube for new bands to feed her music addiction.

**To learn more about Monica and her books:**

www.monicasanzbooks.com

facebook.com/monicasanzauthor

twitter.com/monicabsanz

wattpad.com/distantdreamer

Made in the USA
Lexington, KY
11 May 2017